POWER AND CONTROL

To Ken,

Happy Reading

Ralph

POWER AND CONTROL

RALPH WHITE

LIBRARY OF CONGRESS CONTROL NUMBER:		2011906458	
ISBN:	HARDCOVER	978-1-4628-6218-4	
	SOFTCOVER	978-1-4628-6217-7	
	EBOOK	978-1-4628-6219-1	

This book was printed in the United States of America.

To order additional copies of this book, contact:
Xlibris Corporation
1-888-795-4274
www.Xlibris.com
Orders@Xlibris.com
85687

Acknowledgements

I owe much to my wife, Virgie, who challenged me and presented the ideal place and opportunity to write.

Deep appreciation is due to our sons, Sean and George, who provided encouragement and critical reading with suggestions that helped greatly. I am also thankful to all others who offered comments.

The Xlibris staff has been outstanding in all stages of production and has quickly responded to my many minor changes and questions. It has been a very good experience.

This book is dedicated to the memory of George Leaton White Sr., father and friend, avid reader and wonderful man.

CONTENTS

****

THE LEADERS' PLANS

****

THE ENTANGLED WEB

****

A THIRD CAMP EMERGES

****

Chapter 1

THE REALIZATION

Dieter Brunehoff was sharply awakened and instantly alert as the Lufthansa 767 landed and bounced on the icy runway. He had been dreaming, finally able to dose off after eight of the ten-hour overnight flight from Los Angeles to Frankfurt. Sleep for this fit, tall, blue-eyed agent of forty had been by limited measure since the Christmas Day devastation that changed the world forever. Perplexed by his dream, he acknowledged the brief rest that he knew would be in even shorter supply in the days and weeks to come. He brushed his golden hair, straightened his necktie, and exited the plane.

After fetching his one silver suitcase, Brunehoff cleared customs and then proceeded outside the main terminal. A polished black four-door Mercedes sedan idling in the no-stopping zone awaited his arrival. Inside the car bearing official government plates, he handed the silver case to his backseat companion, who hurriedly unlatched the straps and delved directly into the contents of the case. It was as Brunehoff had stated over their secure connection of twenty-four hours ago. It was all there. The map, the encoded instructions, the hidden compartment, and the vials—the two stainless steel containers—sealed secretively and ingeniously inside the carrying handle of the silver case.

Brunehoff patiently awaited the response of his superior. As a young boy with exceptional athletic and intellectual abilities, he had been noticed, recruited, and then forced and trained. Finally, like a great wild stallion, he was "broken" into the ways of his masters and rulers. He knew how to wait. He also knew how to strike quickly with deadly conviction in all the ways of all the great combative techniques. Three years ago he had mercilessly destroyed four martial arts masters, each a world champion in their particular specialty. This he had achieved by crushing his opponents one by one in a matter of seconds and not minutes. Two were maimed forever and one was dead. A fifth and supposed grand master fled the unsanctioned Manila massacre before Brunehoff's piercing look could beckon him forth. Truly, he was the world's greatest fighting human.

Waiting was easy for such a man. His mind would usually click directly to mathematical problems as a form of mental exercise. Yet this time, in the confines of the leather-seated car, speeding north through the morning traffic of the rising masses, he found his thoughts returning to his dream and the confusion that he experienced therein. Confusion was neither an acceptable nor normal response for this disciplined warrior. To be certain, these were anything but normal times.

The scrunched-up, balding older man could only stare at the instructions through his thick rimmed glasses and confirm the contents after translating the encoded page. Again it was as Brunehoff had stated and was also the worse possible message that he could have received. It was now a death race against time and at least seven other competing nations. He and his inner circle would have to muster all the resources of the best of the best of his country in order to save his people from the impending epidemic that would be unleashed to shock and annihilate the majority of the peoples of the planet Earth!

Within hours of the Germans' arrival in Frankfurt, seven other special emissaries landed in their home countries, each with a silver suitcase identical in style to Brunehoff's and with each suitcase containing the exact same contents. Official sedans and limos, also very similar in nature and all bearing official plates, whisked their agents to secret meetings in the great cities of Moscow, Beijing, Washington, Jerusalem, Tokyo, Paris, and London. The game had begun and the stakes were higher than even the most pessimistic of governments could imagine—life on earth was to be severely and abruptly interfered with in the most horrific of ways. Most inhabitants of most countries have no idea what would happen next or who was the cause of the mass genocide display or even why. They could merely shudder with disbelief and a gut-wrenching fear of such a magnitude they could not have previously even imagined.

Chapter 2

THE WHITE HOUSE

James W. Rush, president of the United States of America, presided over the urgent meeting of his country's joint chiefs of staff. They had just finished reading the silver case's decoded letter, and a deadly silence had befallen the group. Rush, a man of many words, who usually spurted them out in rapid succession, could only hold his head low and could not utter a sound. Others, commanders of millions of solders and leaders of complex large departments, also were stifled participants in the deathly silence.

Finally, General H. T. Roth, the Marines supreme commander, stated, "Gentlemen, we are at war, a war greater that we have ever known and against an enemy that is nameless, faceless, and whose whereabouts are unknown to us. What is known to us is that this group calling themselves the earth cleansers will strike again and again and again unless we can determine a way to ID and destroy them."

"Brilliant, just f'in' brilliant, H. T. Restating the obvious for those of us idiots who may not have gotten it the first time. Don't you ever remove that stupid f'in' hat and tie of yours and let your tiny little brain get some freakin' air?" It was Secretary of State Wilson Gilburger that blasted his verbal venom at the five-star general. Tempers were short fused, and discord was breaking out since no one had any concrete answers or even prospective solutions or . . . anything.

"Up yours, Gil, and your wife's too, you lousy loser," Roth struck back.

"Gentlemen, gentlemen, ladies, quiet please, let's think. We need to work together if we are to solve this riddle." It was the president that spoke.

"Some f'in' riddle," murmured Gilburger just low enough so that the president, seated at the far end of the table couldn't understand, yet his military adjuncts to his left and right clearly heard. They returned his fiery glance with slight but discernable nods of agreement.

"What's that, Wilson?" inquired the unsettled president, further exposing his lack of ability to lead and total failure to discipline the house staff.

"I just remarked, Mr. President, that it is ah, er, a challenging riddle." The secretary felt confident that he could "manage" this president. Even at times as dire as these, this city-slicker lawyer from the finest of pedigrees and best of schools could easily manipulate the puppet president and most of his advisors. Gilburger felt particular pleasure in dominating this group of less-gifted associates. He would be the next president, he felt, and he was pissed that this little world crisis came along and screwed up his well-planned procedures for power. He was really pissed and he wanted everyone to know it.

"Fine. OK then, let's—"

"Mr. President, if I may. I suggest that we project the translation onto the GFC screen and reread these statements collectively." It was Vice President William T. Walker that spoke with a strong and clear pronouncement. Previously ignored by the press and White House staff, Christmas Day and the around-the-world deaths had changed everything. He had become the chief spokesman for the USA government regarding the current world crisis. As another possible candidate to replace the aging and weak Rush, he relished in the attention he was receiving and the speed at which he had supplanted the president as the go-to guy for the American public. This too really angered Gilburger; and as the flamboyant VP rambled on, Gilburger could only think of ways to destroy Walker, his closest contender.

"My thoughts precisely, Bill. It's as if you read my mind," lied the inept Rush.

More bullshit, thought Gilberger, Roth, and most of the other twenty-three assembled leaders of America the Great. This president is not *full of it* because judging by the way he continued to push it out, there couldn't possibly be much of anything left.

"GFC mode, Rebecca," requested the president to his personal assistant.

Although as competent as she was strikingly beautiful, Rebecca Sarquas was somewhat of an oddity as was her recently created position of "special advisor to the president." She made most men stare with wonder and lust, and no one was very sure of where they stood with her as she openly flirted with them all—including Treasury Chief Annaliza Barbera. With a magnificent mix of aboriginal and European blood, she was one beautiful woman, and her brain was superbly stacked as well.

The translated code appeared on the giant electronic screen, and again the harshness of the situation and the words quieted the room. The screen displayed the translated message in giant red lettering.

You have witnessed our power and might. You and seven others will compete to save your nations from total death as we cleanse the earth.

We have aligned our Bh297 virus delivery systems to totally annihilate all the men, women, and children of all nations of earth. Come second in this competition and you and all your people and animals and crops will all cease to exist. Win and you shall repopulate the globe with your peoples and we shall provide you with all that you will need to regenerate Mother Earth. If you win and are permitted to survive, all of you will submit to our rule without question or challenge. Anything less than total obedience will result in death—painful, agonizing, and excruciating slow death.

There was a second silence, and repeated looks of stunned disbelief throughout the room as Walker paused to compose himself and his now-trembling voice. Lucky for him the media was not present, for they would surely also portray him as being weak and lacking leadership. This they had done to the current president and the one who preceded him. Like hungry dogs, they gathered daily at the White House "butcher store," awaiting any scraps that the spokespersons would throw their way while continuously stuffing their faces with designer donuts washed down their gullets by endless containers of Starbucks coffee. Oh, the good life of America's media—say anything you want about anybody you choose and then drape yourself in the American flag and apple pie and strut the newspaper columns with lies of indignation and self-righteousness. Not bad at $110,000 a year plus incentives for uncovering anything of significant controversial content. Another double latte, sir? *Poke your stir stick up your donut where the sun doesn't shine*, thought Walker, and then he continued on.

> *Each of the eight nations will select two members—a man and a woman. The men may be as old as forty, but the women must be thirty or younger. Together they will be the hope of their nation and may be the only means to regenerate a lost race of people if they fail in their quest. The vials you have are symbolic only. They do not contain the actual virus.*
>
> *The rules of the competition are simple—there are none. Follow the clues on the map to arrive at your destination. The first team to arrive will be the victors.*
>
> *A warning: all is not as it seems, and there will be surprises awaiting all of you. Be prepared with your minds and bodies for a most challenging chase. You must reach the terminus or you will surely be terminated. You have until the fifteenth of March to succeed, or bear the consequences of a barren land and a country devoid of life.*

Chapter 3

THE CHINESE REACT

Beijing had read their own red lettering on their own giant GFC screen, and they were not amused. Through the squabble of shouts and screams in the inner chambers of the ruling party, one clear message emerged: whoever destroyed all life in portions of the towns of Pingwu and Songpan would be found and executed—publicly. Killing simple, hardworking peasants was not acceptable and no one but the *zhuxi* ("chairman," "president" to the outside world) and his executive council could order and would carry out such an abomination. How dare they, whoever they were, meddle with China! Were they not aware that the giant had awakened and that his shadow was cast long and deep to the very recesses of life on Earth? Did they not know that China's infiltrators had nestled themselves snugly into the economies and governments and bedrooms of the capitalist world? They would be found and they would pay. Not for the death they had brought to all life in these two adjacent rural villages, but rather for the arrogance and foolish decision to tangle with China.

It would have been wise for these "earth cleansers" to have avoided China, they collectively thought. This was not America, which searched fruitlessly for Arab terrorists that had no might or power or weapons compared to China. What fools these American leaders were, forsaking their power and crippled by the acts and implanted fear of a few fanatic extremists. China would have found the heart of this Muslim menace swiftly and exterminated them and all their children.

Chairman Li Wi Yung, an overpowering, stern, and disciplined hulk of a man, slightly raised the index finger of his right hand; and the room became void of sound. All eyes turned to the undisputed chieftain who has orchestrated the latest installment of the meteoric rise to power and rags-to-riches unfolding of the People's Republic. The very name *People's Republic* was an anomaly, for surely there were people, over 1.3 billion of them; but the wealth and power and all else was concentrated into the hands and foreign bank accounts of a few. So very few that by themselves would need only a city state the size of Singapore or Hong Kong in order to spaciously relish in their personal grandeur and opulence.

"Find them, cut their balls off, and bring them to me on a golden platter. Take the offenders bleeding to the palace dungeon. No food or water or heat or light. Chain them to the walls and let them wallow in their own stench and festering wounds. Make these bastards suffer for what they have unleashed. Do this and do it now!"

A fury of footsteps fleetingly escaped the room and carried bodies directly to each of the chairman's realigned domains to advise and then let loose China's elite warriors. In the palace square, as they boarded their limos in the quickly fading afternoon sun, there were no media dogs or java light or sneaker swooshes looking for gossip or even news. There were only these intent men fearing not so much the virus of the unknown aggressor as the vengeance of their own supreme commander. Chairman Yung was not a man to cross or disappoint, not if you wished for your life to continue and for your sons to father heirs.

Chapter 4

Moscow Mobilizes

"Now we have heard it all," grumbled one of many white-haired, dark-suited, and severely outdated relics of an age and alliance that once was and was never to be again. "First, our conquered states break away and then they rise up and attack us their very rulers. Now this. Why didn't these bastards cleanse Georgia, Chechnya, or one of the '-stans'? Why the Russian people and why the ancient town of Belozersk? We have grown too soft by allowing this continued freedom of speech and assembly and expansion of human rights. We need to use this, shall we say, 'opportunity' to bring back the old Russia, tighten our borders, spend much more on our military, and crush without mercy those that oppose us."

"Go back to your dreams, old man. Or wake up and realize that the way we manage the affairs of state have changed forever. You are dated, and dust gathers on your shoulders. Shoulders that once bore the might of our armies are now frail and of use to no one. Polish your medals and drink your tea and leave the fate of our peoples and the value of our ruble to a younger, wiser, and more capable generation. Go home and take that ratty crew of wrinkled old faces with you. Your time has passed."

The new president, Boris Pretnekof, vented his angered response at the old guard; and no other spoke. This was the new Russia and this was its new leader and he was very much a member of the Newly Ordered World, or NOW, as it had become to be known. Educated at the Oxford school of economics and boasting an exceptional Harvard law degree, few knew that he was also *el supremeo* of the Russian mafia! His connections went deep into the governments of all the most powerful nations. No "riddle" was too tough or unsolvable for this cold, calculating criminal. He would find the little pricks; and like his old friend from London, Li Wi Yung, he would make them suffer greatly.

"Ruszinksy, brief the Krems. Have them ready for Rome by noon tomorrow. Code 3, mode 4, level 7. The rest of you, except Markov, Flaski, and Harlemnov, stand by your posts and be prepared to enact 7-7-7 upon my command. It may be the Yanks, or Sheik Cheeks, or some other lunatic breakaway. We shall find these 'cleansers' and scrub them with their own poison until their skins fall off. Russia shall rule! Russia shall rule!"

"Russia shall rule!" This they chanted in unison as Pretnekof left the room. A few of the white-haired and weak old men had heard a similar chant before, so very long ago. It had brought with it unheralded death and destruction and ethnic cleansing. The very vibrancy in this new Russian chant sent shivers up their spines. The world did not need another Adolf Hitler, and they would continue to plot against this new fiend—the very man they had selected as their leader. Oh, how the world had changed!

Chapter 5

ISRAELI MOURNS

Israel is known to be a very tiny nation of well-educated and progressive people. The trouble is that when you are completely surrounded by enemies that would do anything to destroy you, your quality of life is not all that it could be. Exploding Arab teenagers in coffee shops and city buses and the constant threat of invading forces by air, land, and sea had made the citizens and leadership seek a peace settlement while continuing to amass greater and greater weapons from their friend and ally—the United States of America.

The progressive young rabbis and businessmen and lawyers knew that a strong military that was superbly trained and had a zealot's zeal and determination was something required in order to deter the adjacent extremists. A reactionary tank trampling display of force into some poor Palestinian town encapsulated with razor-wired fences and shrouded with poverty was frequently used to show the world that Israel was not to be tormented—not by any size force of rock-tossing teens or an adjacent nation just now learning to accurately fire the weapons and guided bombs it had been able to procure with the billions of barrels of oil that it sold to the energy-addicted world.

These government men and women were hard-liners and would not sit around and wait for another attack from an unknown assailant. This was Israel, the nation of God, the begotten of the prophets, and the home of the chosen people. Moses, Abraham, and David had found a way to counter aggressors. The rightful heir to the Earth, the nation Israel of the twenty-first century, was not about to see any backward movement toward their desire to lead this earth. They already controlled much of America the Great through well-placed "-bergs" and "-steins" and hardworking and cunning Jews in every conceivable business. Now their tentacles were extending further and into new markets and businesses ever seeking the sweetest of nectars—power and control.

They, like other ambitious nations, had become completely disrupted on Christmas Day. This ethnic or earth cleansing was not expected. Here was an unknown, extremely skilled and superbly equipped, totally heartless new terrorist group. Not on anyone's radar and unleashing death everywhere at once!

The little coastal town of Shave Ziyyon had been used to awaking to the putt-putt-putt of its fishermen heading out to the sea and workers leaving for lush farms as the sun rose each clear morning over the *chosen people*. On December 25, the sun had risen as usual, but there was no putt-putt-putt or sounds of vendors preparing the morning food for sale. There were no dogs barking or sounds of babies crying for nurturing. There was only a deathly silence.

By 7:00 a.m., the first travelers from the neighboring village of Evron had reached the crest of the windy road that separated the two towns. They had stopped and exited their vehicles and looked around and below with aghast at what they saw and at what they didn't see. Crops withered and brown, bodies dropped where they had been sitting or standing, and no horns blaring or carts rolling.

No living thing had survived, yet where they stood, all was as it had been yesterday and the day before and the day before that. They were shocked, and as they sent text messages and scampered back to their own town of safety, they wondered what had happened and how it had happened and why oh why this great atrocity had occurred.

"I'll tell you why and I'll tell you who," shouted the enraged national hero, known in English as the slippery one. This general had survived many gun battles and had used the military and his department's investigative powers and ever-open ears to plan and conduct such memorable raids as the assault on Entebbe and the freeing of the American airport captives. Clean, fast, and precise. This was the trademark of the Israel military.

"It is Iran to be sure and the chemical weapons that we have allowed them to amass. They want our heads on sticks and they are responsible for this plague. We must strike back and do so quickly. We cannot allow the world powers to see us as weak and disjointed," he continued but was cut short.

"It was not Iran, and it is not a plague. If it were Iran, do you think that they have the delivery systems to hit nineteen unsuspecting nations, all in one twenty-four-hour period? Do you think that if they wielded that much might, they would have allowed any of us, their hated infidel enemies, to live and breathe another day? No, it was not Iran nor any Arab nation. They don't have the wherewithal . . . none of them. Besides, we would have known about it before it could happen," Rabbi Raheim Berhinstein spoke clearly and without apparent emotion but with a particular authority.

For such a young rabbi his power base was very strong and growing daily. Especially with the much more liberal younger crowd. It was these young voters that had accelerated him to power and groupied up to make his name and face appear as the symbol of the new Israel: a modern and advanced and friendly Israel, with open-minded and well-educated clerics.

He was handsome and eligible and, like many politicians, said all the right things to all the right people at all the right times. He had mastered his crafts in London and America by studying political science and debating and drinking with elitist new friends late into the weekend nights. He had purpose and ambition and solid international connections with others like him whom he has met first at Oxford. They had through drunken stupor and extravagant living been able to forge an alliance of influence that allowed them privileges not afforded others of even lordship status. They were the new thinkers and self-appointed doers.

They could have whatever they wanted. An alliance such as this did not falter. After London and America, these well-educated members returned to their home countries to start the process to ascend to power. They had a plan, a very carefully developed plan, and they would share world power together and align nations like never before. This they would do to prove their abilities and to parade their brilliance, but mostly they would do it to further their own power and fortunes and to control the unfolding of the Newly Ordered World, a team of like-minded, rich, and mostly pompous, power-hungry thugs. They were not despicable, Berhinstein mused, just better than the others, a cut above and clearly the rightful heirs for control of the planet Earth.

His ambition would have to wait. Now he must uncover who was behind the cleansing of Shave Ziyyon, a peaceful fishing hamlet, a town where all had perished. A town where his merchant father had procured them a home, high on the cliffs to the north. A town that he had run to six days ago to find his mother, father, two sisters and only brother, and all his siblings' children gone forever. Snatched without mercy. He would find these terrorists. His team was assembled. *Now I shall tighten my hold*, he thought. *These earth cleansers have presented me with a very fortunate opportunity. None will dare oppose me once I have found them.* For mama and papa, his big brother and little sisters, for all of them, he would find them!

Chapter 6

LONDON LISTENS

White wigs and long black robes seemed very out of place in this discussion for life on earth and the future of all mankind. The British were famous for their pomp and ceremony and also clever deductive reasoning but found themselves sadly lacking at this time of turmoil. They had no clues, no evidence, not even a serious hunch as to who has delivered death to the southern sector of the city of Plymouth. Tens of thousands dead in the streets, at their breakfast tables, and curled breathlessly in their beds. Everyone and every living thing. Gone. Finished. Over. Not to return.

Sorrow and emptiness. Loss and fear. Gripping the nation and the world. Fear of *the Phantom*. Fear of the unknown.

The Conservative Party leader, Anthony Burgess, would continue in the role of prime minister. He had been born to rule, he felt. But he needed answers—now! It was January 2, one full week since DD (death in Devon) Day. No other country had loss near as many people as England had. The press was furious, and the tempers of everyday citizens were boiling over. Like soccer hooligans they had taken to the streets of cities throughout the now-not-so-Great Britain. Innocent people caught in the jaws of the terror and rage, helpless fathers and sons demanding actions and answers.

The desired accelerating, chaotic effects of the virus had firmly set root. If this continued then *the Phantom* may not be required to expend much effort in the revisit to merry ol' England. The growing rage and fear of the masses could make it self-destruct. The military would be overcommitted to control civil disobedience; Parliament would be in hiding, each member fearing the bloodlust of the enraged mobs. It would be easy to finish the job; ever so easy.

"We will avenge this diabolical and cowardly act of human carnage. We will take a calm and carefully measured response. But we must also take immediate and direct action and suppress the uprisings in the streets and quiet the media rags who are cashing in during our hour of despair. Scotland Yard, MI5, and the Queen's special forces are all on full mobile alert. They will be dispatched to the ends of the earth if necessary to find these cowardly swine and bring them lamenting to their judges. We will rid ourselves of the perpetrators of this nonprovoked massacre," firmly stated Burgess to a house that had learned to listen to his reasoning, to an opposition that did not oppose. This was his big meeting. This was his spotlight. He knew it and he would use it to solidify his position.

"Willingdon, give us your update. What do we have?" inquired the PM, knowing already every last detail of the investigation and progress to date.

"Not a great deal, I'm afraid, my lord." It was the Yard's top investigator that responded. "We have found evidence of bacterial residue, but there is no crashed plane or bomb or . . . well, there is one thing," stammered the chief inspector. "It is most peculiar."

"Out with it, man! Tell us what you have found! This is not the time for dibble-dabbling around."

"In southern Plymouth, my lord, we have found a shattered steel container, approximately the size of a common oil barrel. It has virus-linking readings that are truly beyond the scale of anything our labs have ever encountered. Or any other labs of the world that we have shared samples with—America, Canada, Australia, Germany. We suspect that this 'barrel' was dropped from high above and shattered upon impact and thus released its poison to the citizens of Plymouth, Prime Minister."

"Yes, but who could fly at *any* level and remain undetected? A drone plane or stealth bomber? And how could they be so precise? A beacon from below and a high-quality guidance system? What countries process such technology?" exclaimed the PM.

"Only the USA, that we know of, Prime Minister. The Yanks still control the drone technology and most-sophisticated guidance systems. They are not anxious to share their secrets with even us, their closest ally."

"But surely they couldn't be behind this. Their own little wine haven in California has been decimated. They would not have done this to their own people," shouted the enraged PM.

"Maybe and maybe not," coldly stated the red-faced chief inspector. A permanent red that came from daily drinking of considerable amounts of single malt scotch whiskey. "History has proven repeatedly that the best cover is to cause a little damage to yourself so as to deflect attention and scrutiny."

"Eleven thousand men, women, and children—a little damage? I think not! Not even Washington with all of its slippery and corrupt lawyers would have killed so many of its own. No. It has to be someone else . . . perhaps Russia or China. I don't think that there could be anyone else that could possibly be advanced enough to deliver this payload and to do so undetected. Contact Pretnikof and get Yung on my direct feed to Beijing. Let me speak with these two first, and then we shall reconvene and fully formulate a plan. One which will succeed and restore Britain to its lead role of criminal research and swift, accurate action. Meanwhile, contact Rush, no, Walker, and see if he has any updates or can possibly know who we are dealing with here."

"As of this moment, I will personally lead the investigation. Ensure all correspondence and tactical response is coordinated through my office. Get me pieces of the barrel and a contained sample of the bacterial remnant. These will need to be thoroughly analyzed to extract further clues."

This was a new breed of PM, a decisive one, an intolerant one, and one who had many friends throughout the world, friendships that had been forged in the pubs of London and the bars of Boston. If anyone could locate and dismantle the perps, they would need outside help and who had been better at assembling outside alliances than Burgess, a product of the rich and mighty, Burgess, who was ever so friendly with the power leaders of the northern world.

There was something strangely peculiar if not familiar with the words of the "cleansers." It ate at his insides. He had heard talk somewhat like this before, years ago at Oxford and then in the States, but could this diabolic display possibly have be formulated by the brazen outcasts of his college years? Maybe and maybe not, but Berhinstein, Yung, Boris, and the others would have to meet—and soon. This Phantom's havoc had derailed their plans, plans that had been flowing perfectly along, plans that would have to wait or be greatly accelerated.

Burgess smiled knowing that if he was right about the identities of the cleansers, he would be rewarded with great wealth and considerable power.

Chapter 7

JAPAN'S RISING SON

"We must quiet the people, Mr. Prime Minister. We have to give the media something to feed to the people. Even if we fabricate a response laced with lies, it will be better than sitting here idly and without apparent action. Our country looks to us for leadership and decisiveness. Give them something to quiet the rage. Restore the confidence that we have lost as never before. Make them listen and go home and wait for us to unlock this mystery. Tell them we are very close to solving the mystery. Keep our power intact," alerted Masatsu Karakanni, leader of Japan's curtailed military. A large and obese man by Asian standards, he wiped his sweating brow as he finished his thunderous plea to his country's leader.

"Japan cannot strike back at an unknown phantom, but I agree with you, Most Honorable General, that we have to keep our people from rioting. We have gone from centuries of orderly behavior to chaos in one week. The English have their hands full, and trouble and dissension are breaking out in what had been stable countries. Our people have endured atomic bombs, numerous earthquakes, and incredibly destructive tsunamis and have remained orderly and respectful to authority. This time it is very different. Fewer people have died, but our people do not know why or how or anything else.

That it has happened in eighteen other countries has heightened the alarm. I fear that the worse is yet to come. We are all scared by these acts of unprovoked terror. It has shaken the world. I can fabricate a statement for the media that should stifle them for today. By tomorrow I will have to appear live for the evening news. Unless something miraculous happens, the fury will increase. Then what actions do you suggest we take?" inquired Japan's newest leader, Ikaro Sasami, a tall, gaunt, and frail man of sixty-eight.

"We start with curfews from dusk to dawn, and we patrol the streets with double or even triple the regular forces. We push the troublemakers back inside or completely out of the cities. Then if necessary, we eliminate them permanently!" exclaimed the general.

"Treat our people like cattle and exterminate the noncompliant ones? Is that what you are suggesting, Masatsu? I could never give such an order!"

"Don't trouble yourself with our civil problems, honorable Sasami. This is the work for the military and the police. Use your wisdom and talent to solve the problems we face from abroad. Find the killers and bring them to justice . . . imperial-style justice—swift and complete. Then we will not worry about trouble in the streets of Tokyo or elsewhere. Then we will have order restored to our nation and homeland." The general was emphatic and rose in his chair to make himself appear even larger and more insistent.

"Yes, I suppose you are right. We must get control of our people . . . at whatever cost. Make the necessary arrangements, but I don't want to know any of the gory details. This is your war and I am removing myself."

"Yes, honorable leader," half smirked Karakanni, knowing he had cornered his PM exactly as he had planned. Now there would be more guns and more police and more power for him and his aids.

Japan's military would show itself again, not just to the confused young men and women in the streets of the Japanese cities, but to the entire world. It was time to rise again from a tedious and uneasy sleep. It was time for Japan to once again be a force to be feared. Soon his power and might would be escalated and the threat of riots firmly crushed. Then he could fix his ambition on what he truly wanted: control of Japan! The leadership. The opportunity to rise up as before. The opportunity to rule again with imperial power. To be one of the elite nations again, not just economically but with might, military might.

He had waited a long time; and like his collegiate friends Burgess, Yung, Rabbi B., Pretnekof, and the others, he also felt that the earth cleansers had greatly helped accelerate his grasp for power, his reach for control, and their plans for the Newly Ordered World. After the people had been quieted and the cleansers destroyed, he and his secret team of wealthy international elitists would have greater power, complete and unchallenged power. It was merely a matter of time.

The death and stench of the three erased towns in the Kanagawa Prefecture has served the ambitious general well. Now he could wield a greater sword and a stronger army and now he could march his presence directly to the imperial throne that he so long coveted. Japan would be his, and soon the entire world would be theirs. Oh, how he had awaited this day.

Chapter 8

FRANCE'S FOLLY

It was entirely new to France: a woman president. A female ruler. The end of an age.

Many a sad male dinosaur in Paris and throughout the country had participated in the election, had planned on their candidate, their president, their winning. Only the elegant but too liberal Jean Charach to smear and defeat. But then *she* entered the campaign and everything changed . . . for a while.

They knew that they could smear and defeat her also. They had access to enough media poison and ample flash and splash and more. It was working, and Michelle duEsi was cornered. Another victim falling prey to the perfect model, the strong masculine man of training and grooming and bloodline, made for the new France to be!

Pierre Langois had that bloodline and been expected to win. All the right preparations and schools. All the right connections around the globe. A plan to deal with immigrants, definitely. Eight weeks before the vote, Charach and DuEsi were limping a distant second and third with a combined percentage of 47. "You will win, nineteen times out twenty," the pollster guaranteed. Langois appeared to be headed to a slim majority throughout France.

Then the unthinkable. On the last possible day, a fourth candidate entered the race—Claude Cambert, the cell phone billionaire. Millions hooked on his systems. A very wealthy and squeaky-clean political unknown. A man of culture and refinement. The candidate rising from years and years of Parisian Pride Parades and so much more. A gay candidate. Secure. Open. Tough.

Day by day, Langois's lead eroded away; and when a hopelessly fourth-place Charach threw his support to Cambert, the gay candidate charged atop the country's polls and Langois and DuEsi both began to fade. Two weeks to go. It started to seem certain that Charach would be rewarded by a gay French president. Langois and DuEsi would lose.

Then came the call from Boris. Langois listened. The next day, his *new friend* Michelle duEsi and he were united, in public, a new team for the new France. He would be the king maker, or queen maker; but it would not be Cambert, but DuEsi. He would patiently wait. Like Brunehoff, he too had learned to wait.

Then the next unthinkable happened. Cambert, trailing duEsi by four percent with four days to go, decided to opt out. Said he just wanted to make a point. Just wanted to prove that his people could do what they wanted, if they wanted. Said he just needed to send a strong message.

Hated to lose at anything ever was more like it. Cunning, intact, glorified, Cambert withdrew and was free again. A national icon throughout the streets and nightspots of modern France.

Four days to go—no opposition, a giant majority in the making, and as Boris had said, "Just leave Ms. DuEsi to me. You shall have your throne, Pierre!"

President Michelle DuEsi was pleased, surprised, and felt capable. Smart, organized, not easily rattled, she would lead France, she believed. "My dear members, we have had no success in uncovering this Phantom, but we will or one of our close allies will or even the Americans will, considering the number of personnel they have assigned to the search."

Her engaging green eyes brought with them a feeling of conviction and confidence—she knew how to manage. How to work a room. How to lead. She knew how to win over others. She had that full appeal to most, and that alone had bought her time in light of the boggled election.

She was good, very, very good, thought Langois; but Boris had promised and Boris always kept his promises—always.

"We have lost forever 2,169 of our residents. Annihilated without cause or reason. A despicable action by a despicable enemy. We have a map and two vials with bogus contents and a decoded threat. Now here we are seven days later and no further ahead. No clue. No trace," stated the president. "Only we need to choose two very capable warriors, a man and a woman to save our country, our France. Can this be real?"

"Actually, we have learned something via our great trading partner and friend. From the Russians, Chairman Yung was able to determine that Israel had also recovered a splintered metal container, laced with deadly virus and dropped with precision from a very high elevation. Just like the English barrel. Now we must search more carefully in the Champagne region, starting at the extremities of the death virus and cross-referencing the meteorological data to determine the winds in that region at that time. Then we shall find our own barrel of death. And we will have material to analyze and lists to run and these nasty little pricks to catch," spoke a heated but prepared Langois.

"Well, it's news to me, but thank you for informing us and keeping the international connections working well, Mr. Vice

President. Will your informants be providing further updates?" inquired the president.

"I think, Madam President, that it would serve us well to expeditiously seek our own barrel of destruction and to do our own untampered and undisturbed examination of all the materials. Then we shall at least be on an equal footing with other world powers. We will not be in need of others' services and France will appear strong, especially if we can solve this mystery and find these earth cleansers before . . . before." His voice trailed off, not able to utter the words he and everyone else were thinking "before it was too late for all!"

"I bring also, Madam President, news of a summit. I received a phone call early this morning on my private cell phone. Few people know this number, and it is for emergency use only. The call came from Moscow, and it was from President Pretnekof himself. He provided instructions and stated that I should represent France this very weekend in a location yet to be announced. Security, as you can imagine, remains of the utmost importance for all of us."

"A phone call direct to your mobile from the Russian president? Am I missing something here? Shouldn't my office have received the call?"

"It's all quite simple, Madam President. President Pretnekof and I were schoolmates at Oxford and again at Harvard. In England we led our highly powerful rugby team to unheralded victories. We also debated and discussed world affairs long into the early morning hours. He knows me and he knows my thought process. Pardon me if I may, but you are a relative newcomer and have yet to meet Boris Pretnekof or, for that matter, Chairman Yung or many of the others. I have deep-rooted associations with many of them."

"Well, it still seems a little hasty and lacking in protocol."

"My dear president, these are strange times, and haste is what we will need if we are to catch this Phantom. You have to learn to trust me as your partner. Together we do what we do for the good and for the love of our nation. For France!"

"Yes, for France, but kindly ensure that you provide me with a *full* report immediately upon your return."

"I'll call you from my mobile as soon as I touch down," answered Langois.

Chapter 9

THE NOW ASSEMBLES

The Rabbi was the first to arrive in the great city of seven hills. It was as he had planned, easing through customs and immigration and met by a white bulletproof limo driven by a personally selected gun-toting Roman henchman. Entering the limo, he placed his briefcase upon the seat and stared directed across to the expressionless face of fifty-five-year-old Antonio Anatelli. This man with the unreadable eyes was the one person who was privy to all the illegal doings of him and Boris. This was their "bureau chief" who had been groomed for the job and then required to commit a horrific deed in order to rise to his position of prominence. A single slug to the temple of his sleeping brother who had committed no sin greater than being related to Antonio. When Boris demanded proof of conviction, it was carried out, or the one who refused surely was.

Anatelli briefed the Rabbi regarding security preparations as they sped away. Berheinstein was satisfied that all was as should be and that the special additional measures that he had ordered were indeed in place. With no more questions, the Rabbi reclined slightly and closed his eyes. At first he briefly thought he and Anatelli had one thing in common: they both had lost their only brother. He felt no guilt for Anatelli's circumstance. It was Boris who had ordered it, and Anatelli had carried it out. He shot his own brother. *Why should I care about a man such as that,* he thought, and then felt relieved that such a man was under their control and not someone else's.

His thoughts wandered away from the silent, statue like Anatelli and to his own level of power and respect he wielded in Rome of all places. He was a Jew, yet he was virtually untouchable in this heartland of Catholicism. Associates had been as brazen as to joke that he would be the first Jewish pope—if he so desired. That would shatter the Roman church! There was no need to shatter the church, he mused, just to control certain individuals that controlled it. Through this manner, he could avail of all the benefits without having to abide by any laws or attend any of the never-ending pompous functions intended to show the masses their man god and earthly source of forgiveness.

Rome, not Tel Aviv or Jerusalem, was the Rabbi's command post; and with his closest ally, the great Boris Pretnekof, and their combined influence and connections, they controlled much of their power base from here. Weapons, drugs, gambling, prostitution, money laundering, blackmail, influence peddling, murder, and more, all orchestrated and administered from the seat of Christendom. Today, these items would be all set aside as the two of them considered strategies while awaiting the others to descend throughout the day.

Brunehoff, Langois, Karakanni, Burgess, Yung, Gilberger, and Rebecca Sarquas, the chosen few members of the NOW, meeting at their special fortress that had been procured with blood money and set aside for their clandestine meetings. Meetings that to the outside world were apparently for the purpose of solving world problems, not fulfilling elitist personal agendas. They would all be there. All waiting to hear what Burgess had not dared speak aloud, had not dared to even mutter in his dreams as he lay in a restless sleep next to his Malaysian mistress.

Burgess was now convinced that he knew the identity of the Phantom, the Earth Cleansers, and he knew that his reward would be great. His smile grew wider as he reclined in his first-class seat and pondered how his associates would thank him in a first-class way.

Langois was on the same Airbus 360 from Paris and sat next to Burgess, who had avoided the media and paparazzi by fleeing England in the dark of night via the Chunnel that connected their nations. During the flight, they spoke only briefly, of the weather and how France had humiliated England at a recent rugby match. Rugby was what had initially brought them together at Oxford and had been the sport that attracted both their allies and foes back in the days of idealism and critical thought and pounding flesh. To the casual observer, it seemed that anything but the current world crisis was on their minds, yet inside they itched to reach their destination and put Boris's 7-7-7 plan into action.

After a while, Langois also reclined, closed his eyes, and recalled his conversation with Boris. He thought of his false allegiance to his French president and how it would abruptly end with her body parts scattered throughout the streets of Paris or found floating down the Seine. Then he, the president that should have been, would be; and no Frenchman would dare challenge their hero who would claim to have unraveled the death mystery and ended the terror of the Earth Cleansers.

Chapter 10

YANKEE-DOODLE DANDY

Meanwhile, Air Force One had left Andrews Air Force Base in a rainstorm during the dark of night and was streaking across the Atlantic, carrying Secretary of State Wilson Gilberger and the ever-dangerous Rebecca Sarquas as its only passengers.

It was the slick-tongued Gilberger who had recommended Sarquas to President Rush. He has convinced the president that she was the perfect person to silence the American aboriginal unrest since her people viewed her as their inspiration and pride in the white man's world. At the same time, because of her French father and European roots, Gilberger had argued that such a stunning and gracious lady could appease the EU nations who grew tired of the American-instigated battlegrounds of Iraq and now Iran. It wasn't just her mixed heritage and dazzling rhetoric that won the American administration over; to be certain, it was also her immensely good looks. Thirty-nine years old, single, and a smile and a strut that could melt a room. She appeared polished and competent, but for most men, just having her appear was enough. She was hot and she knew it and she used it to the fullest of her capacities.

Rebecca, or Trugol as her intimates called her, went way back with Gilberger, just like the others, to the Oxford days of the mid-'90s. Unlike Gilberger and the others, however, she made her mark not on the rugby fields or at the debating forums but between the sheets of the rich and influential. Her bedroom skills were legendary, yet none dared to call her a slut or a whore. All had been mesmerized by her intense dark eyes, enticing form, and shorter-than-short skirts that displayed covetous calves and titillating thighs that surely led to the most precious of delights. All had desired, but only a fortunate few had sampled, and it was those that had named her Trugol—true goddess of love.

Gilberger, on the other hand, was cold and calculating and from "old money," a "good ol' boy" who had parlayed his influence into politics because of his lust for power. Now with the dimmed cabin lights and with a cleared moonlit sky, he turned his attention to his other lust. He was all alone with Rebecca in the president's bed, streaking across the heavens, and her talents were primed like an animal in heat. *Much heat*, thought Gilberger as he happily succumbed to her charms and played bedroom gymnastics with her until he appeared dazed and his eyes were crossed and his tongue limply hung from the right side of his mouth. She is beyond belief, he thought as he fell helplessly exhausted into a deep sleep.

Rebecca was far from satisfied, and wearing only a seductive smile, she approached the cockpit and found the captain thumbing through a girlie magazine as the jet soared along on auto pilot. "Let me help you with that," she cooed to the awestruck captain, who became happy victim 2 on what had otherwise been a very boring trip.

Ninety minutes later, still unsatisfied, she uprighted the captain, poured coffee down his throat, and sauntered back to the presidential bed to find Gilberger curled up like a ball and sucking on his thumb. She had such effects on men, and she knew it and used it for all that it was worth. A half smile crossed her face. Another conquest, she thought, and this time at thirty thousand feet. Not bad for a poor aboriginal girl born on a tiny reservation in backwoods South Dakota to a carefree mother and a vagrant and soon-to-disappear Frenchman father. As she was a very bright and gifted girl, her opportunity had immensely improved when the USA reached an agreement of cash for land. Her people went from bikes to Benzes and moonshine to Merlot. Rebecca, for her part, had bought no such frills, instead turning her wealth and status into a world-class education and ascent to power and influence.

"I need a real man," she proclaimed aloud while slumping down next to the donuted secretary, and then she recalled that tomorrow she would see Brunehoff. "Then the real action would begin," she purred, as she closed her eyes, opened her imagination, and fell off to her sweet, sweet dreams.

Chapter 11

THE WARRIOR WONDERS

Brunehoff had chosen the high-speed rail rather than a flight. Too many questions and too much disturbance, he reasoned. On Germany's latest bullet-class train, he had his own private coach complete with one carefully screened attendant. At 450 kilometers per hour, he could read, sleep, exercise, and enjoy solitude. The cuisine was superb and as always was tasted first by his most loyal attendant, Henrik Ruetz. Brunehoff the warrior relished in the opulence of his position. Planes were for long trips over water and for people in a considerable hurry, and Brunehoff avoided them as much as possible. Even he, the earth's greatest fighting machine, could do little, he reasoned, if the aircraft were to fall from the sky or carelessly crashed due to some strung-out halfwit at air-traffic control.

After a salad of fresh Italian greens and Moroccan olives drizzled with a mango vingeratte, he thoroughly savored the pan-flamed oysters with ginger, green onion, and French cognac. It was a recipe that he had learned to crave, subscribing to the popular belief that these mollusks gave men a special sexual potency that pharmaceutical suppliers could only hope to someday replicate. Finishing the meal, he brushed the plates aside and for a brief moment thought of Sarquas and the hoped-for opportunity to be with her while the others slept.

He had already determined that upon his arrival in Rome and hopefully before the full camp officially met, he would seek out the Rabbi and relate his dream to him. If anyone could cast some light upon this tormenting mystery, it would be his coach and confidant, Berhinstein, the Rabbi who seldom was at a loss for words or carefully executed actions. Brunehoff respected Berhinstein for his insight and intellect and smooth, surgical precision. He felt assured that the Rabbi would be able to ease his torment. Yes, the Rabbi and, of course, Rebecca.

Years ago at Oxford when they were first introduced, their eyes instantly locked and they both knew that they would be lovers—wild, passionate, completely uninhibited lovers. She was nineteen and had just arrived from America, and he had just been "released" or rather "transplanted" to London from deep within the recesses of a country that no longer officially existed.

At twenty-one, he was a testosterone-infused creation, and she yearned to be free of the trappings that tied her to her old world and traditional ways. Together, that first year in college, they would satisfy the cravings and needs of each other.

She was attracted to something very special about him, something mysterious. He was intent upon being with her from the first time he sat next to her. He ached for her. He moaned when thinking about her; she filled his thoughts and fantasies, those wonderful fantasies with her, him, and nothing but complete abandon. That thick black shoulder-length hair, that perfect dark complexion, and her beautiful body. She could turn every head in a room full of celibates, he had once joked to himself. This from a man who rarely joked—about anything. She released him back to his stolen youth, back to the youth and freedom that he has missed, a youth replaced with electronic shock and white milky injections.

He remembered her diary entry, "First it was the power of his eyes. Those eyes that enchanted her and brought her closer to those lips, oh-so-warm and tender lips, that parted and freed his strong, probing tongue that moved with a gentle but heated passion within her willing, tender mouth."

Also, he recalled the day that he had taken her hand. She had not known what to do initially. But he led her patiently and helped her to explore the depths of their sexuality. He freed her to share abundant pleasure together.

She loved it when they were together and they made love. Both of them giving and sharing and continuing, over and over again. She loved him and had given herself totally, completely and without reservation to him.

She had become a woman who needed a man to satisfy her and this was the man that she had longed for, dreamed of, and hoped for. This was her Dieter and she loved him without measure.

Brunehoff, for his part, had received back his boyhood and laughed aloud and frolicked like a newborn lamb. He was happy as never before with his darling Rebecca.

When he was recalled to the fatherland at the end of his first year, she was left alone in an empty dorm to idle away the summer. She soon became bored and found herself visiting the campus pub first once or twice a week and then it quickly became the meeting place for her and her new friends, summer students and local lads and other foreigners.

She reluctantly gave in to the array of suitors and compliments, which were made more attractive by the pints of Guinness that she had learned to enjoy. By the time Brunehoff returned four months later, she had bed-ridden half of the men on campus and had completely morphed into a full-blown nymphomaniac, never completely satisfied and always wanting more.

Brunehoff was enraged and busted more than a couple of horny young heads. Eventually, he realized that it was over, that Rebecca was hopelessly lost, and that no matter how she begged for his forgiveness, it would not be forthcoming.

A dejected Brunehoff turned to martial arts and rugby as a means of release, but no amount of running and judo chopping could make up for the loss of his dear, sweet Rebecca.

It would be four years later that they would finally reconcile their differences, although it could never be the same for Brunehoff. The warrior, who was forced to show no pain or emotion, had been hurt deeply by a soft and luscious woman; and that could never be undone.

They were in the same social-law class at Harvard, and their eyes were always stealing glances of each other. One day she cornered him outside the cafeteria and confessed to him that she had been with so very many men but none had moved her like he did. She said that maybe it was because she was anxious to explore and was totally inexperienced and that he was such a great lover or maybe it was because she truly loved him.

By now Brunehoff had become despondent, and love was no longer an agenda item. But sex, that was something different, and he knew he still longed to lie with her. And so it was that they developed an agreement whereby he would visit her two to three times per week and in the meantime she could do what or whomever she wished. Signed, sealed, and delivered—they were an item again. This time there was no laughter from Brunehoff, and try as she would, she could never fully help him return to that first year at Oxford when the world has stood still for their love.

After Harvard they returned to their homes and their countries and lost touch with each other, yet neither lost hope that one day they would be united again. That one day occurred twelve years later when they found themselves at a party in Rome, hosted by Rabbi Raheim Berhinstein, a friend to both of them and a confidant of Brunehoff. For three days the world stopped for both of them and they reached new levels for their voracity in lovemaking. Now here they were again, two years later, about to arrive in Rome and again by invitation of the dear rabbi—again craving for each other.

Then suddenly, it flashed into his mind: the dream, the confusing dream! Filled with phantoms that he could capture and unmask, only to see his own reflection staring back at him? What did it mean? How was it related to the Cleansers? He was certain that there was a connection, but he could not unravel the mystery, and this troubled the warrior greatly.

Chapter 12

THE UNEASY EASTERN ALLIANCE

Chairman Li Wi Yung and General Masatsu Karakanni had several things in common. They both came from very wealthy merchant backgrounds. They both thirsted for power and control and would do absolutely anything to achieve it. They were 6'2" tall and presented fearsome figures complete with an ever-present sneer of entitlement.

That is about where the similarities ceased. The most obvious difference was that Yung's mass was in upper-body muscle, while the general's girth was well established around the midsection.

Yung remembered his father's stories of the Japanese occupation and their cruelties, while Karakanni envied the now-powerful Yung and the new China of influence and economic might.

Currently, Karakanni was particularly perturbed by Yung's insistence of "I'll pick you up at Narida," another overt sign of Yung's personal power and China's view of Japan as something it could now take as it was attempting to do with Taiwan. It was Yung the conqueror. *I am royal Masatsu*, he thought, descendant from the Japanese imperial throne, with unbroken lineage. *One day this barbaric olf will kneel before me. One day all that is Yung's will be mine.*

"Welcome aboard, honorable Karakanni," smirked Yung without looking up from his papers or standing in his plush leather and gold surroundings. Power. Opulence. The things of man. The things of Yung. "Make yourself comfortable."

"Thank you for the ride, Chairman sir," slighted back the not-to-be impressed imperialist.

"You like my plane, Karakanni?"

"Well. I hadn't really noticed. Since you mention it, yes, it is quite nice. I'm not much of an aviator, but I believe that it is like the four which we recently decommissioned due to . . . age."

This snide comment really struck a nerve with Chairman Yung, and he felt that inner surge and the desire to let loose the volcano that was steaming up inside him. Anger like this is what crippled Singh in England and later sent unknown scores of "citizens" of the People's Republic to an early death. After an intense stare, Yung restrained himself, and his steaming fury subsided. He knew that Karakanni was correct. It was an old plane, and he had yet to receive delivery of his fabulously outfitted, latest-greatest Airbus.

"Dear Karakanni, an aviator you are not. Apparently a connoisseur of fine items is also something you are not. The 747 is the greatest plane ever built. Like a Rolls or a Bentley or a fine brandy, it can accelerate in value with time if carefully maintained. This plane is outfitted with everything you could possibly imagine, including beautiful ladies of my personal choosing, and it is all solely for my use. Its gold and artwork are worth tens of millions. It is the ultimate magic-carpet ride."

"Thank you, Chairman sir, for the history and safety lesson. I trust you will age graciously with your plane. I'll be sure not to worry about keeping my belt too tight since this is such a safe machine. Personally, for me, I am more of a Ferrari man and must confess I know little of old, pardon me, I believe the word is vintage, yes, vintage. I know little of vintage things, I prefer to be modern with modern everything for this modern world."

"Like your decrepit military arsenal, general? Is that your definition of modern, or would that be vintage, pardon me, aged? No, neither, I believe the word is relic," shot back Yung.

"Our weaponry is amongst the best on earth, Yung, and it is growing stronger each day now that the restraints have been lifted."

"Yes, restraints applied long ago by world leaders who saw your folly and punished you for it. Growing? Yes, I suppose so. What do you have now, Karakanni, about as much firepower as the Bahamas or maybe the Ivory Coast?" Yung laughed as he felt the control of insults swing his way.

The silenced general slid into his swiveled seat and rustled with a newspaper on the tabletop in front of him, seeking an answer to Yung's brazen assault. He had insulted the wrong man and now he was captive within the chairman's confines and about to soar to thirty-five thousand feet.

"Now that we have the pleasantries out of the way, dear general, may I offer you a snifter of forty-year-old Spanish brandy or perhaps something more modern, like a Coke light?" A now fully in control Chairman Yung dug deeper. "Sit back, Karakanni, and relax, if you wish, and enjoy the facilities of leadership. We have a long flight ahead of us, and I have much to prepare. Rest while you can and enjoy what you wish. When we land in Rome, there will be no time for sweets and no time for idle chatter. Boris is expecting us to be the last arrivals, and I'm sure he'll not want us to be haggard and ill prepared. No, Boris definitely would not want that."

Chapter 13

THE MASTER INSTRUCTS

Seventy minutes before the meeting commenced, an impeccably tailored Boris Alexi Pretnekof used his retina scan and voice print to enter the empty inner chambers. Others needed to additionally use daily-issued passwords and enter in twosomes, no earlier than ten minutes before the appointed hour. Not Boris, he issued the passwords. This maneuver guaranteed a quiet place for preparation for the masterful leader, a leader who manipulated all that felt his reach.

He was truly a leader among men, among nations, and especially among the know-no-country, greedy criminals of the world. He now believed that he had descended from above and not risen to power from below. This from the leader of earth's largest nation whose official state religion was atheism. He was indeed one of a kind. After him, the Maker broke the mold. That is, if there was a Maker, and in Russian politics, there was not. This left Pretnekof, who had turned around a turbulent and failing Russian economy and gave the average citizen a reason to believe again, a much-greater advantage that most of his international associates. Put simply, he didn't have to compete with God or Allah or Krishna or Buddha or any deity. There was only Mother Russia and its darling son, Boris the Magnificent.

As deluded as he was, he was also the smartest and the cagiest and the undisputed kingpin of the inner circle of criminal masterminds that influenced most economies of the world. Those that had followed his plans and strategies carefully had risen to power in their home countries. Those that had wandered or sought their own minstrel no longer danced or even walked. They were dead.

Power and control. Power and control. It was what wakened the disciplined Pretnekof, the Russian mafia *el supremeo*, each and every day, early, very early. It is what he focused his brilliant mind upon as he planned and schemed his way to the top. It was what sustained him as he amassed his political and economic might. It was what made others bow to his wisdom and also his whims.

In 1994, barely 5'8" and 150 pounds, a lean young Boris had strolled up to the sideline to try out for the Oxford rugby team. Just arrived from South Africa, he was an unknown to the stately institution and especially the arrogant young jocks whose daddies assured that they attended "only the best schools." They, of course, told their daddies that they would have a "jolly good time," study hard, and follow in their fathers' footsteps on the rugby field and bring the family increased prominence. Bashing brawn against brawn and brains against brains. Daddy, for his part, fed his son buckets of cash and fast cars and knew that before him he had played the same game with his father.

"So what do we have here, lads?" cried out Wellesley, a senior and the hooker on the team. "I think it's a bloomin' mascot. No, it's not big enough for that. It must be one of the children's toys. Wait, maybe it's a lass—with whiskers, no less."

The whole group of returnees laughed and continued to heckle as Boris stated that his name was Boris Pretnekof, that he came here from South Africa, and that he wished to contest for the position of fly half since that is where he had the most experience and felt that he could contribute the most.

"You want to *lead* this team, Boris from Africa? What will you use, smoke and mirrors? No, wait, he'll be the invisible man, lads. He's small enough. No one will see him as he sneaks down the field." The main English group roared with laughter as Wellesley insulted Boris further.

"I ask only an opportunity to display what skills I have," retorted a calm but insistent Boris.

"Skills? You? Some half-arsed albino jungle bunny not any bigger than a good-sized rabbit. Get lost, invisible man. Make yourself invisible, now! Or I'll flatten you right here," brashly bullied the supersized Wellesley for his adorning flock.

"As I have said, I wish to contest for the position." It was then that Wellesley had had enough and shoved hard against the chest of Boris. When Pretnekof didn't fall down or even move, all were startled.

"You are a friggin' magician, little bunny. I've heard of your kind, some kung fu crap. Well, it's not worth squat around here. Here is where the real men romp, and we have no place for half pints. For the last time, get lost or there won't be enough left of you to feed to a good-sized rabbit. You are really beginning to bore us. Get it lads, bore us, Boris?" As if on cue, all laughed loudly at Wellesley's play on words.

"Don't *ever* touch me again, Wellesley. If you do, I will bring you down. And if you decide to get up, I will crush you to the field again—but then even harder. Be careful who you tangle with. Consider yourself as having received your one and only warning."

Things grew strangely quiet, and everyone looked at each other. The other outsiders, Langois, Yung, Karakanni, and Brunehoff, eased closer to the tightening circle surrounding the two talkers.

After what seemed like minutes, a sweating and by now fuming Wellesley hunched and charged Boris, who deftly sidestepped the larger man and in a flash brought a piercing elbow directly down on Wellesley's neck. The larger man fell to the ground dazed; he stumbled to get up but was met with a knee to the face by Boris and then a defining foot to the throat. Pretnekof stood over his fallen and defeated foe and continued, "As I was saying, my name is." No further intros were necessary. Boris had arrived, and Oxford was about to experience a substantial change and witness how things were done in Boris's world.

It was now ten minutes before 2:00 p.m., and the leaders of the NOW started to assemble. Two by two, they entered the lavishly outfitted boardroom and slid into their seats. They all saw Boris's dark eyes focused upon his laptop screen, and all chose to quietly prepare themselves for what promised to be an especially important meeting.

At precisely 2:00 p.m., the doors autolocked and the great Russian leader looked up. He surveyed the group and ensured that all were present.

"Good afternoon," he commenced. "Welcome again to my Roman home. I trust that you all had uneventful journeys and are prepared to respond with discussion and intelligence to what you are about to hear."

"Let us be very clear about the facts," carefully emphasized Boris. "We have been assaulted by an up-to-now-unknown enemy. The world is in turmoil and is looking to us for answers. I believe the threat to be real but doubt that the contents of the silver cases you have all received are anything but an elaborate ploy to put our nations in competition with each other. We must not compete or follow a trail that will lead nowhere. Rather, we, the ascended leaders, need to catch this diabolical enemy and use that success to secure our positions and prominence for a very long time to come. We believe that we have found the enemy, a network of clever and detestable operatives posing as legitimate leaders and business magnets in their own countries. It is time to uncloak the Phantom! Burgess, you may proceed . . . but keep it brief."

Burgess was fuming but sought to gain his emotional control. "The enemy *we* have found" and *keep it brief* translated into "This is my team, Burgess, and don't fill this announcement with anything that will lift your position at the expense of mine. In other words, be careful to always credit your leader."

"Thank you, Master Boris, and yes, we do indeed have something of the utmost importance to discuss with our comrades. You instructed me to assemble a team of four top thinkers to do some further checking, and I had these Scotland Yard men dig deeper after mine, eh, our, early suspicions. We now have unequivocal proof that our college enemies of so long ago are indeed the Earth Cleansers."

Feeling particularly pleased with his breaking news, Anthony Burgess took time to view the expressions of the assembled powers. He loved drama and felt a surge knowing that he had such a captive audience and that they were waiting for him. *Power and control*, he thought and was then brought back to the moment by the sharply uttered words of Boris insisting that he continue without delay.

"At first," stated Burgess wanting to ensure that everyone could see his brilliance, "I was puzzled. Who could have dropped these barrels of death and why? Then it came to me in a flash. It had to be the Curtailment Club, as we referred to them at the time. The noisy little buggers that felt that they should make the decisions as to who should live and who should die in this exploding population we continue to experience. Balderous, Brown, Cloiters, Singh, Anhebo, and the lot. We see Balderous, but what has happened to the rest of them? Our hatred was deep, and after our idiot Jamieson and his little friends killed Brown's girlfriend, we all know what happened next."

"Not to mention how we busted Singh," laughed Karakanni.

"Silence," ruled Boris. "Continue, Burgess, and spare us your self-adoration. Stick to the facts."

"It's them and I am sure of it. I have done my homework. Oxford and Cambridge and as well as Harvard and MIT keep very good records. It wasn't difficult for our four agents to learn of the Curtailment Club members' current whereabouts. After that it was easy.

"I have here details of flights taken to Johannesburg by seven of the then-known club members. These records show each and every one of them traveling there at least four times in the past two years and always within a day or two of each other. Coincidence? I think not. Also, we know that Johannesburg is the home base of Cloiters and that he has returned there to take over his family's farms and diamond mines. Since only Balderous is in the public eye and subjected to daily scrutiny by the media, it is easy for the others to come and go without fanfare or announcement."

"Finally," boasted a very-pleased-with-himself Burgess, "we all know that Mexico signed a major trade agreement with South Africa twenty-eight months ago. It has been a good cover for Balderous to travel frequently and for Prime Minister Mabuto and his entourage to visit Mexico. And guess who has traveled on these trade missions with Mabuto: Andrek Cloiters. The perfect cover for clandestine meetings on both sides of the Pacific," ended a self-impressed Anthony Burgess.

Boris was deep in thought, processing the information that Burgess had presented, quickly formulating an intelligent response. Everyone silently waited the wisdom and instructions of the master, everyone in the room aware that Boris had spent his youth in South Africa, everyone knowing that his family and Cloiters's family had become entwined through the marriage of Cloiters to Pretnekof's sister.

"This is what we must do," commenced Boris. "We must set a trap, a very carefully planned and executed trap. One which will catch all of the club members at one time in one place."

"*Wait*," implored Boris. "Burgess, when were they all last together in Johannesburg?"

"Let me see here, it was early October last year," answered Burgess.

"And before that?"

"That would be six of them in the first week of July."

"And before that?"

"Five of the eight, April 2-6."

"You fool Burgess! Can't you or your famous Yard see the pattern?" fumed Boris.

"You are correct of course, Boris," interjected the Rabbi. "That would place them in South Africa right about now."

"Yes, and you, Burgess, should have informed me of these dates as soon as you had them. Now you have jeopardized our one chance to catch them before they strike again. They will surely strike again and soon. Idiot! Leave the Sherlock Holmes work to the Rabbi and me."

"But I just received—" He was cut short.

"In my country you would be a dead man, Burgess. And it would not be quick. You fool," growled Yung. "You fucking fool."

"Just hold on there, Chairman Arsehole, I uncovered the club. What did you do?"

"Shut up, the both of you," ordered Boris. "Burgess, you *are* lucky to be alive. For now we need fast action, and you will have a chance at partial redemption."

"Anything you ask, Master Boris. Just name it," uttered a clearly upset Burgess.

"Get your precious Yard on the phone immediately and have them give us a listing of travel by all the club members *this week*—not last year, but this week. Do you think you can do that without screwing up?"

"Consider it done." A spared Burgess beamed.

"I consider nothing done until it is accomplished—and inspected and confirmed. Get to it, now!"

"Yes, Boris, thank you, yes, immediately."

"The rest of you, leave. I will summon you here when Burgess is ready. The Rabbi and I will formulate our strategy. Be ready to move on a moment's notice, 8-9-9."

Chapter 14

A FAILED ENCOUNTER

It was much, much earlier than expected that Boris had brought the afternoon session to an abrupt close. Brunehoff knew that he had exactly two short hours before his scheduled thirty-minute audience with the Rabbi. After that it likely would be whatever Boris and the Rabbi determined was the best plan of attack. For certain, if Boris was going after the club members while they were still in South Africa, and 8-9-9 surely suggested that, then Brunehoff knew he would be on the next jet to Johannesburg with a squad of Krems and his meeting with the Rabbi would have to wait. Right now might be his only chance to be with Rebecca, and he was intent upon making the most of it. Over a hasty lunch, Brunehoff had arranged to visit the anxious Rebecca immediately after adjournment. Well, the meeting was adjourned, and he was headed directly to her chambers.

"Ppppssssstttt. Dieter, over here." It was Gilberger, and he was practically jumping up and down, desperate to talk.

"Do you know what this means?"

"What what means?" curtly answered a delayed Brunehoff.

"What the discovery of the Earth Cleansers means. What it means to us, you and me."

"I know what it means. It means I have even less time than I had anticipated. It means that I have to prepare sooner. It means that you are in my path, and you know that I don't like people in my path."

"Whoa, hold on there, little cowpoke. You need to hear this."

"OK, what is it that is so important that you are willing to risk me getting upset and tossing you down the shaft over there?"

"Strange you should mention shaft because that is exactly what is in store for you and I. I overheard Boris and the Rabbi talking just before I left the room. Luckily, they didn't see me, and because of the brevity of the meeting, the timed doors stayed open. I didn't stay long, but I don't think you will ever get out of Africa, my German friend, and I will be lucky to get out of here, unless—"

"Unless what?" wanted to know the now fully engaged warrior.

"Unless you align with me. We win the others over and then we do away with Boris and a new captain rises to lead our team."

"You, I suppose, Gilberger?"

"Yes. I would think that that would be the most appropriate action given that the USA is still the only superpower."

"Aren't you forgetting that your shot at the presidency is still almost two years away and until then you will be just plain, boring little Gilberger, with no power at all? And I don't believe a word you have said. You are trying to manipulate the situation, just like the sleazy lawyer that you are. Get out of my way now."

Gilberger knew that while it appeared he had failed with Brunehoff, he had planted a seed of uncertainty, and any Ivy League lawyer knew that uncertainty or doubt was often all that was needed to swing the process around.

"Heading for Rebecca, are we? I suppose that she will still be up for it . . . even after the serious banging I gave her on the flight over here." Gilberger smirked. "She's all woman, but she has had a real man, so I'm not so sure that you will be ample prey for the lioness."

It was then that Brunehoff had had enough. He took one look into Gilberger's laughing eyes and contorted face and then delivered a right-armed thrust to the throat that fell the American quickly and quietly.

Crawling over the unconscious mouthpiece of a jerk, Brunehoff shook his head as he continued down the hallway, now with an increased pace.

"Excuse me, Mr. Brunehoff, may we speak?"

What now, thought Brunehoff. *I am getting tired of this.* He wheeled about to see a droopy-eyed Langois peering from his barely opened door. He appeared to be in considerable distress.

Brunehoff entered Langois's room and saw that it was in disarray. The usually neat and very tidy Langois has clothes strewn about everywhere, and he looked a mess. Brunehoff could smell brandy on his breath. He knew that something was up.

"What seems to be the problem, Langois? Hurry up. I don't have much time."

"You'll have time for this. It seems that Boris is planning to cancel me rather than reward me as he had promised. He has always been so positive to me, regarding the elections, you know, and how he found a way for me to be VP and await the unfortunate demise of Ms. duEsi. Now I have heard that he plans to cancel me and that you will be cancelled also."

Brunehoff did not like the word *cancel*. It was like you were worth keeping up to now, but no longer. *So I'll just cancel or, rather, exterminate you. Arrogant*, thought Brunehoff; but this was a very arrogant, conceited, and devilish lot. And he was one of them. This he no longer enjoyed, but he knew that his real masters, not Boris or the German government, had the ultimate control over him. They still held his mother and father in exchange for his continued silence. He received pictures of them on their birthdays, but he didn't know where they were being held unless it was within the mountain fortress. Brunehoff didn't want them subjected to the same pain and torture that he had endured during his training and summer sessions, so his silence had been assured.

"Learn to wear the bridle, Dieter. It will be easier for you," the older boys had warned him. But he was stubborn and endured much more electric shock than his fellow selected children did.

"Do you really believe that crap, Langois? Who have you been speaking with? Wait, I know, Gilberger, right?"

"No."

"Not Gilberger, then who, Langois?"

"It was Karakanni, this morning before you arrived. He said some very strange and scary things. He said that he would survive because Boris and the Rabbi need Japan and its advanced workforce. He said that you and I and Gilberger, Sarquas, and even Burgess were all expendable. He said to be ready for trouble and that he would try to help us."

"Help us? Karakanni? I don't think so. He's a prick with a capital P. He doesn't do anything for anyone unless there is something greater in it for him. I think that he has probably got something cooked up with Gilberger, who just fed me a similar plate of lies. The best thing that you can do is to stay in your room until we are all summoned. Avoid Karakanni and Gilberger. They have their own agenda and ambitions, and they will never be powerful enough to overthrow Boris and the Rabbi and Yung. And clean up your room and get it together, or Boris *will* have reason to get rid of you."

Shaking his head in disbelief and anger, the usually calm and collected Brunehoff was running out of time for his soiree with

Sarquas, and he was not pleased. He turned the corner past Yung's suite and increased his stride down the hallway toward Rebecca's room. *No one else better bug me,* thought Brunehoff. *I am getting really tired of this.*

Just as he was about to tap on her door, the bell rang, summoning them all to the boardroom. It was time to hear what Boris and the Rabbi had decided, and he was out of luck with Rebecca—for now at least.

Chapter 15

THE FORCE LET LOOSE

The procedure was the same as before—enter two at a time. Only this time the Rabbi was already there, which meant that there would be a singleton left out. In this incident it was Gilberger, and he was left out cold.

When all were seated, Boris commenced. "It seems that Gilberger will not be joining us this afternoon. He had an unfortunate accident and his neck is busted up quite bad. He's still unconscious. Apparently, he slipped and hit the hallway floor. The odd thing is that the floor was dry, and how do you fall and hit your throat?" inquired Boris.

"He does have a small head," commented Sarquas and then smiled.

"Back to business," stated Boris. "We have all heard the good news regarding the identification of the Cleansers members. Unfortunately, our latest intelligence update suggests that they will be out of Africa before we can get to them. We could likely get Singh, Varez, and maybe Garcia. Cloiters I can get anytime. The suspected real leaders, however, are the first to leave, and we have no chance of capturing Balderous, Brown, or Anhebo within South Africa. If we take out their assistants, they will retreat deeper and we risk another attack. The strongest item in our favor is that we know who they are and we will be able to determine where each of them goes and whom they meet with. This we can do undetected. The very fact that they don't know that we are aware of them will work to our advantage."

"So what now?" asked a disappointed Yung. "We travel halfway around the world for an emergency meeting, receive the shocking news of who they are, locate them, and then just decide to what, wait for the right time? I say we take down as many of them as we can *now*—before they strike again. Capturing three or four of them will make the remainder think twice before striking again—especially when they know that we have their associates and that we have the means to *extract* information."

"My dear Li Wi. In case you hadn't noticed, this is not a democracy. We don't vote or solicit *opinions*. Rather, we follow the leadership and abide by its decision . . . or suffer the consequences. Not so different as to how things are done in your country, is it not?" slashed out Rabbi Berhinstein.

"You tell him, Rabbi. And while you're at it, ask him, why the name *Wi*? I'm sure it's a reference to his brain size and not his shoe size." A pleased-with-himself Karakanni laughed aloud.

"Speaking with some level of insider knowledge, I can assure the group that Wi does not refer to either brain or shoe size." An amused Sarquas chuckled.

Rebecca's comment started a chorus of laughter with all except Boris, Brunehoff, and Yung. Boris was displeased with how the seriousness of the meeting had deteriorated. Brunehoff didn't laugh without extremely good reason, and Yung practically had steam coming from his ears.

"Maybe you could use some of that pent-up energy to fly that 'magic carpet' of yours, Wi One. That way we wouldn't have to refuel the old girl every few hours." The Japanese rubbed a little harder.

"Silence—all of you. This is not the time for joking or bickering. We have serious business to attend to, and I need a room full of thinking members with serious, rational thoughts and not some circus sideshow. Address the matter at hand and keep your comments to the topic, or there will be ramifications, I assure you."

The room became completely quiet. Each member waiting to see if anyone challenged the world according to Boris or if the mighty Yung would pounce upon the mouthy Karakanni.

"As I was saying, it is too late to capture the leaders at this time, but we must now prepare for the next opportunity, and then we strike with force and speed. It may be that we will not be able to get them all together again for at least three months. That would be too long and maybe even too late. Therefore, we must study their daily routines and where they go and what they do. We must isolate each of them. When we are assured that we have locations and times where we can take them *all* quietly in a twenty-four-hour period, it is then that we shall strike . . . before they have a chance to warn each other and before there will be any suspicion due to their absence."

"Each of you shall be assigned ONE cleanser member to study, follow at a careful distance, and be prepared to eradicate or hold captive, depending upon the decision of Boris," stated the Rabbi. "The study and tail must be conducted by two of your elite agents who will report directly to you each day. Each of you, likewise, shall report to me each day. I will then apprise Boris of the daily activities. Each of you shall also be assigned a team of two Krems to work with your own agents. Your agents and the Krems should not be seen together in public. Rather, we shall create a protocol for meetings, secret meetings. The Krems all have special diplomatic passports and are very free to travel throughout the world without being detained or questioned. With Russia's raging economy, it will be easy to pass them off as exploring new business opportunities or simply as well-to-do Russian tourists looking for a little R & R. What better places for rest and fun than the Mayan peninsula of Mexico, the beaches of Brazil, and the ski slopes of Canada? Home to Balderous, Anhebo, and Brown. Once we are within each of the target countries, travel will be unchecked and with ease. You are to follow the instructions precisely and we will thereby gain success. If you deviate from the plan, then there will likely be fallout, and your agents will be subjected to torturous treatment. The Krems all have a level of immunity and should be able to escape back to Russia before they can be held."

"Are there any questions thus far?" continued the Rabbi.

"Yeah, who will be assigned to whom?" stated a stern-faced Yung. "I want Garcia. That little prick cheated me at poker at Yale and I have been waiting a long time to get back at him. Give him to me and he will cheat no more!"

"OK, Yung, we will keep that in mind, but the final decision as to assignments will be rendered shortly and will consider a number of factors. The final decision, as always, will rest with Boris. Meanwhile, each of you will have precisely one hour to prepare for your departure. Get packed now and return to the outer conference hall with your luggage. After receiving your target and the contact coordinates for your assigned Krems, our drivers will take you to the airport and train station. No further questions? Good. Boris?"

"One last thing. Return to your home countries and governments and convince them of the need for two agents and considerable resources to uncloak the Phantom. Under no circumstance reveal to your people the identity of the club members or their suspected whereabouts. Tell them that we suspect a mole and we need to set a trap, or fabricate your own storyline that best fits your needs. Deflect inquiry! No one outside of this room must know that we know the identities of the Cleansers. I will personally see to it that the four Scotland Yard members involved are rewarded for their service and silence and that absolutely no one else knows what we know. We must have this level of security in order to prevent any leaks. Be ready when I call. Dismissed."

As the boardroom emptied and each member headed to their suite to prepare for departure, Rebecca brushed past Brunehoff and whispered, "In my room, now."

Brunehoff's heart jumped with expectation. He was mostly packed and ready and needed only five minutes maximum to load his laptop, fold a shirt or two, and then leave. That left him with at least forty minutes for dear Rebecca.

Just then, the Rabbi called out, "Dieter, over here, please. I'm sorry for the delay and change of circumstances, but right now I have about thirty minutes to discuss this strange reoccurring dream of yours. Come in, my friend, and let us talk."

Torn between two desires, the obedient Brunehoff's choice was made for him. He and Rebecca would have to wait—again. Things were definitely not going according to plans, and the warrior did not like it, not one little bit.

Chapter 16

BROWN'S BURDEN

Coincidentally, over three thousand kilometers away in a fortified enclave, the Phantom members, *the earth cleansers*, the first-strike power-pushers were already assembled, ready to accelerate their agenda—an agenda filled with death, takeover, and revenge. Sweet, sweet revenge against the princely pack of pricks assembling in Rome.

The cleansers' leaders were from the rich elite of Mexico, Nigeria, South Africa, India, Chile, Canada, Brazil, and Cuba. They were the main brains. There were others also who felt they were equals but looked blindly to this group for leadership and instructions. They were the Cabinet, as Willie Brown, *the crazy canuck*, had labeled them.

During Oxford and early MIT days, Brown had been fun loving and almost too smart. A jock with brains. Capable of outthinking his professors. Not nerdish but cool. Like many Canadians, he would try anything on a dare. It came natural and set them apart from other peoples. Made them appear "weird" but captivating to outsiders, like Canada's great wild caribou, moose, and polar bears! No wonder they had thought at MIT that he was a freak among freaks. A brain from a wild northern tribe somewhere. He didn't mind the jokes; he was white, so he knew they would only go so far. The many exchanges, matches, and debates throughout six years at college in Britain and USA assured him of his place in the emerging pecking order; and he knew how to play the game ever so well.

Why worry about the man with the puck, he would say, when your team is ahead six to nothing and the game is late in the final period? A goal or two by the opposition would be too little and too late. "What's a puck?" his friends would apparently seriously inquire and then laugh aloud until Brown would join them. Invariably, over rounds of beers, it would end with something like "Puck you" or "Rugby is for wimps" or the classic Brownism, "Strap on your blades and let's rumble."

Ice hockey, a Canadian national pastime filled with even more great wild animals, but this viewpoint no one dared utter aloud.

In NCAA college football, most players feared the superbly conditioned 6'6" Brown, who at 260 pounds could still run the one hundred meters in sub-10 seconds. He could also carry half of the opponents tackles, clinging helplessly to him as he made cutting runs into the end zone to adorning American chants of "Willeeee Willeeee!" followed by a chorus of "Yes, he will!"

Brown's attitude and manner all changed forever one day when the "pricks" went *too far* and raped, bludgeoned, and left to die his girlfriend and her two roommates. Wanting to show their arrogance and might, they struck out in a rage at the vulnerable, exposed, and forever-gone friends of Willie Brown. Brown, who had shunned them and had aligned himself with the foe. As much of a genius as he was, he did not anticipate that the consequences would be so painful and so bloody. Now there was a score to settle and he knew how to settle it—once and for all.

Indeed it had all changed forever and he had changed and now he was numb to anything that these assholes controlled or had

domain over. His anger was restrained with time, but his desire for vengeance had grown. For fourteen long years he awaited this opportunity. There was no turning back. Not now, not ever.

The others were political and practical, he reasoned. He supported their foundations for *greatly curbing* the human population as well as lashing out at that pompous and arrogant gang that was trying to grab hold of the world. Those slimy little pricks that had killed Narissa. That had eluded the law and were unscathed and untouchable, they felt. "We are above all others," they boasted. No, he was not about to change his mind regarding extermination in exchange for new growth. *Pruning* was the term the cleansers used for their plans to control the runaway explosion of the human race. A very serious pruning was about to commence, and he was the chemist with the shears!

Chapter 17

A Heated Exchange

During college days at Oxford and Cambridge, the line had been drawn in the sand early for some of them. For others like Brown, it had taken longer to be moved to one side or the other. Gradually, this group of wealthy debaters and tagalongs separated themselves into two very distinct camps with very different viewpoints and objectives. One group focused upon domination and power and wealth. The other lusted for order and sustainability, which they believed could only come from curtailment of the human population. The one thing that they had in common was that each camp was prepared to do anything to achieve their objectives.

Both camps also had one other item they agreed upon—their hatred for each other. It grew and encased them all. Blinded them, fortified their conviction. When college ended, much was no longer visible. Invisible but not forgotten, as they scattered to the ends of the earth—to their homelands to grow their power and unfold their plans. These two forces would silently get stronger, undetected as alliances by the media and mainstream politicians. With them would grow their diabolical plans for power and control and the unquenchable thirst to rule. This would not be a battle of good versus evil, for indeed both sides were overflowing with evil; and "good," if it existed at all, was relegated to the lowest of seats.

Deep inside the mountainside, in an enclave undetectable to modern surveillance wizardry, the cleansers met. Enrique Balderous was about to speak, and all were poised to listen. He was a dominating, cultured personality with a bigger-than-life smile and a knack for convincing others that his way was the right way. Handsome and rich. Tall and lean. He was a Mexicans' Mexican. A leader of his people. All his people. Open to the cultural diversity of ethnic minorities. Open to giving land ownership to those who recognized only their own clan as their own nation. Open for business with those that he has chosen as his allies. Open to grasp power and to wield it with all its might.

"We have much to discuss. You have all borne witness to the disarray that is rampant throughout the world. You see how these northern nations of power have been crippled by our undetectable display of force. You see how their peoples have reacted like crazed animals. How they furiously search for answers and how hopelessly they blunder in their attempts to find us, to know us, and to unravel the death that has swept their nations. We will turn up the heat. Soon it will be time for us to strike again with a greater sting and to bring these countries to their knees."

"We have chosen you to lead us, Enrique, my friend, but is it wise to act again so quickly? Why not wait until Brown has prepared and deployed all of the virus necessary? Then we will be sure of victory, and Pretnekof, the Rabbi, Yung, and the others will be helpless to stop us or, better still, maybe even dead already," stated Ambewa, the Nigerian oil magnet. Coming from a hugely overpopulated nation with historically corrupt governments, he was one of the most vocal proponents of human-population control. He even wanted to destroy much of his own homeland.

Balderous glared at the Nigerian. He rose to his feet. His captivating smile turned to a frown. "You want me to proceed slower, Ambewa? Perhaps curb the population one-by-one? You challenge my authority and reasoning?"

A single shot resonated throughout the room, and Ambewa slumped forward with blood dripping from his forehead. "Anyone else want to slow the process?" inquired Balderous.

"For fuck's sake, why did you have to do that, Enrique? He was like your brother! Now I have to revamp my deployment systematic for Nigeria and much of Northern Africa. Ambewa was key to our distribution process. This really sucks!"

"Tough shit, as you Canadians say." Balderous smirked. "You will have to use your genius IQ to find another African with influence . . . perhaps Bhotto from Cameroon. I was tired of Ambewa. He was weak, and we have no place for weaklings in our camp."

"Well, just stop with the killings, OK, Enrique, or—"

"Or what, Willie? You will take your ball and go home? I'm afraid it's too late for that. You *will* find a replacement for Ambewa, or you will be the next to go!"

"Yeah right, Enrique, we both know that without me, you have absolutely no chance of accomplishing our goals. You need me and I know it, so don't threaten me. It won't work."

"And don't question me again, my brilliant friend, or you may find that I have other means to deliver the death virus," shouted an enraged Balderous.

"You're bluffing, Enrique," clamored back Brown.

"Don't try me, Willie!" exclaimed Balderous, still wielding his pistol.

Willie Brown assessed the situation for a moment, viewed the hostile Mexican and his still-smoking gun, and considered it wise to let it pass. After all, Balderous has just shot dead his college roommate and close friend. Perhaps he really was a madman, and a show of power and control was more important to him than the cause that he said he stood for.

"OK, Enrique you win, but no more shooting," answered the Canadian. He had made his point but didn't want to push it too far. Two things were certain: Balderous was unpredictable and Willie Brown wanted to live long enough to see the murderers of Narissa and her friends dead and gone forever.

"Let us continue," slowly stated a less-hostile Balderous as he snugly snapped his weapon back into its holster.

"As I was saying, we have much to discuss. There are the matters of transportation and security. Then mass deployment. Singh, first you and then Varez," curtly ordered Balderous as he sat deeply into his chair and then made authoritative eye contact with each of the cabinet members. *Balderous the Great*, he thought. It sounded good.

Chapter 18

THE SINGHER SINGS

Narinder Singh Singh was an odd fellow, tall and gaunt with glasses and a hobble of a gait. To the unsuspecting, he appeared as just another East Indian looking for an opportunity to escape to America and live the good life in the perceived land of plenty. That suited him just fine as he knew that a low profile was one's best cover during unlawful actions.

His was a crippling, painful walk that had been sustained when his leg had been mangled like hamburger during the annual Oxford versus Cambridge rugger match; broken and twisted by the crushing tackles of Yung and Karakanni, vicious oafs who lived to inflict pain—physical and otherwise.

Why hadn't he stuck with cricket? he often asked himself when the pain became almost unbearable, and he had to resort to his morphine injections that had him firmly hooked for life. But no, he was young, from the colony; and he had something he needed to prove. He had to show these drinking and scheming buddies of his that he was more than a precise, calculating brain. He had to show them that he was tough, and he knew that the rugby field was the one place where he could be noticed. So he had taken his gifts of blinding speed and agility, soft hands, and extra peripheral vision and had as fly half twisted and curled unscathed through opposing lineups, advancing the ball and advancing his position of respect and prominence. All was going so very well until that match, the match that had separated not only his leg but also the teams and the camps—forever.

When the ambulance's siren blared its way across the field and whisked Singh to emergency surgery, his teammates had huddled and agreed to "one for the Indian" and returned to play with a renewed vigor and intensity. They had battled hard through the first half and deep into the second; but Cambridge had no answer for the vision and ball distribution of Boris Pretnekof and the uncanny coaching of the young substitute, Berhinstein, and no man on earth it seemed could contain the straight-ahead power and thrust of the German, Brunehoff, who appeared impervious to pain. When it had finally ended, the scoreboard displayed Home 31 and Visitors 26. Yet instead of wild cheers by the thousands of loyal Oxford fans, there was a sullen remorse. All had witnessed the destruction of the fleet-footed and widely entertaining Singh followed by another hour of total human carnage. When the referee blew the final whistle, he hung his head and walked directly to the official's dressing room. He would not don his black strip ever again. What he had witnessed, failed to control, and had been a part of was not rugby or sport, but war, in the trenches by animals not men; and he, like the thousands of usually rowdy and carefree fans, felt so very ashamed. Downcast and ashamed.

Singh's leg was put back together as well as possible. He promised himself to become a perfectionist, vowing silently to never again allow himself to be open to danger or overcome by the rush or adrenaline or the roar of the adorning crowd. Sport was over for Singh forever, and now it was his mind that would lead him and not his athletic ambitions. He had developed new ways to claim respect and adoration, and although he would risk his life in the process, he still had one good leg and an otherwise mostly unscathed body to show for it.

A true perfectionist, he accepted nothing as truth without cold, hard, irrefutable evidence. He was the consummate doubting Thomas; and he would cast his hands into wounds, corpses, encrypted government files, or a garbage dump halfway around the world to find proof—if that's what it took to make him certain of the facts. On the negative side, he took longer than the rest to finish his assignments. Yet he always delivered a product or a conclusion that had never been challenged by any other member. His findings and actions were beyond superb, and that's why a special tolerance was afforded him by Balderous and the others. If Singh said this or that, you could take it to the bank and gain interest along the way. He knew that Balderous and the others needed him, relied upon him, and listened to him.

He was prepared. He turned the cover of a folder marked Transportation, adjusted his glasses, and commenced. "Since our last meeting, analysis has taken place regarding the movement and transportation of the 27,602 barrels of Bh297 to all of the locations throughout the seventy-nine countries we propose to strike during phase 2 of the project. Currently, all of the barrels are secured in our compounds throughout the countries to be hit. Each region has timing and protocol procedures prepared so as to have the maximum distribution achieved in the least possible time." After a pause and a smirk that filled his face, he added, "They will not know what hit them, and by the time they do, it will be too late—for most of them will be dead!"

"Yes, but what if we are discovered at even one location? Wouldn't that compromise our mission?" inquired Balderous.

"There is little chance of that, Enrique. The leaders of the world are busy searching airports and interviewing everyone, hoping to randomly catch some possible character related somehow to the cleansing of Christmas Day. We know they have remnants of one, maybe two barrels, but no clues. They are left believing that the barrels were deployed from very high above and shattered upon impact. They have no evidence that the destruction occurred otherwise. They are looking up when they should be looking down. Even more so, the clever plan of Varez and Garcia is solid, and the barrels are so evident that they are virtually invisible—unable to be found."

"Don't give me any *virtual* shit, Singher, and don't screw up! Give me only finality and . . . control!"

"I am convinced that Willie's protocols are without fault or reason for worry. Our chemist has laced the brown-painted outer shells of the barrels with his Canadian concoction of acids. These acid clusters will react electronically, blister, eat into the barrels, and explode. Explode and splinter as if dropped from space and without a trace of paint. A simple but unique cell phone tone will activate the acid. Little if any residue will remain, and the virus will be set free precisely ninety minutes after delivery. This will give our people plenty of time to follow the evacuation routes. Also, they will be equipped with breathing apparatus just in case of—"

"In case of what?" snapped Balderous.

"In case of traffic jams or flat tires or the unforeseen, Enrique."

"There will be no unforeseen! All must be according to the plan. No screwups, Singher," commanded Balderous.

"As you all know, each barrel will be bear a sticker identifying the contents as *wet and soiled clothing*. Meanwhile, our worldwide network of laundries will continue to be manufacturing plants and secure temporary homes to the virus until we load our transport vans each bearing our Bright White International logo, each loaded with our cargo of Bh297. The trucks will drop one, two, or three barrels at the designated GPS coordinates and set the cell phones to trigger the acid burst. We will, in fact, be airing our dirty laundry and cleaning up the human race all in one move." The proud Singh laughed.

"Save the laughter, until we have completed our mission," ordered the Mexican. "Then we shall all laugh at the imbeciles as they gasp for their last breath. Then we shall reorganize this earth and make the world work for us."

The handsome, confident, and ruling Balderous adjusted himself in his seat. He lived for power and control. Soon he would wield it with a might and speed that Alexander; his father, Philip; Napoleon; and even Hitler could only imagine in their most hopeful of thoughts. He, Enrique Balderous, would outclass them all, ten times over. He liked these thoughts very, very much. Then he shouted, "Varez! Security."

Chapter 19

CUBAN CHARISMA

Pedro Varez was ready for his turn. As a Cuban under the iron fist of Fidel Castro, he had learned to be prepared when the boss called upon him. He knew only too well what befell those who were not prepared. If they were lucky, they lived with hunger and grew tobacco forever, or they died quickly. If not, they became shark bait, set afloat shackled to a plank, with legs slashed and bloody, pointed toward a distant Miami. Either way, they never lived to make another mistake. He knew that an even worse fate usually awaited absolutely anyone who disappointed Balderous.

When Castro first learned of Varez's unique ability for quickly acquiring languages coupled with his flair for accents and performance, he knew that this was a man that he could use. When Varez was given the opportunity to follow Castro's plan or see his little brother set afloat, he succumbed without complaint but with resentment.

The plan was simple. A Cuban gunboat would chase a fleeing Varez into American waters and the coast guard would detain Varez's speedboat and escort it to Miami, where all fleeing Cubans were processed. During the interrogation, the Americans were led to believe that Varez had access to many high-level Cuban secrets, and he was passed on to the CIA for more in-depth processing. Varez lied to and charmed the American CIA officials to the point where they wanted him to sneak his way back into Cuba with false papers and to spy for the Americans. Citing the way he was mistreated by his military countrymen, he happily agreed with the Americans and vowed results. He was to be a spy for the CIA; but really he was Castro's man and he would load up on CIA operatives, missions, and tactics and bring it all back to Uncle Fidel while the Americans were fed a pack of mostly worthless, time-consuming lies. This earned him decorations in both America and Cuba and led to his placement by the Yanks at the prestigious Oxford University Languages Department. From here, they believed, Varez could penetrate international secrets while appearing to be a language student. They were right . . . except Varez's secrets were for Cuba and the Cleansers and not America. He fed a litany of lies laced with half-truths to the Americans that confused their tactics for years.

Pedro Varez was very bright, cultured, and uniquely trained. He was not about to feel the wrath of Balderous. He lightly twirled the left side of his moustache, showed his perfect teeth, and smiled knowingly as he began, "We control the largest laundry service in 164 countries and we have spent approximately twenty-five billion of our resources to attain the facilities that we need. We have spent approximately four billion more in obtaining the appropriate personnel and ensuring that they cooperate fully. The remaining oblivious workers will go about their everyday laundry activities, which, in fact, because of our dominance in the marketplace, is actually turning us a profit. How's that for taking the Yanks to the cleaners?"

"Shut up with the jokes and continue," insisted Balderous.

"Now we know that with one, possibly two barrels, found and no doubt more to come, we have had to determine ways for the barrels to be undetected. Here's where Brown's disappearing brown paint comes in, and may I say, the ingenious additions of Garcia. Our Chilean colleague has cleverly placed black rubber bumpers around brown soiled-clothing canisters. The pricks and everyone else are looking to the sky for falling aluminum-colored drums. Our laundry cans will go unnoticed, and with the material already existing in the seventy-nine phase-2-targeted countries and no borders to cross, all should be simple. Our trucks are known everywhere, and we service most of the major contracted hospitals, restaurants, and construction sites of the world. Nothing will look out of the ordinary. Nothing at all."

Pedro Perfecto, he thought, when no comments or inquiries barraged him. Astute, with a larger-than-life ego, he was known to be overtly conceited.

The smug Cuban angered Balderous, but he knew that el Perfecto would be necessary, at least for phase 2. After that he was expendable like most of the others. After all, it was he, Balderous, who would rule.

Chapter 20

HOT CHILE

Another egomaniac still in the pack, thought Garcia. *As if we didn't have enough already. Bullshit and stupid jokes when we should be putting forth clear facts. What was this veiled compliment of cleverly placed bumpers? I just put a little disguise. No big deal. Are all Cubans like the cigars they make? Enjoyable up to a point and then we tire of them and snuff them out and discard them to the sewers where they belong. I sure hope not.* Garcia silently laughed to himself, knowing he was bringing his wife and children to Cuba next year after The Newly Ordered World was defunct, and the cleansing was complete.

An arrogant nationalist bastard for sure was Antonio Garcia. He lauded the nonfact that the Nazis had landed everywhere in South America except Chile and was always praiseworthy of how Chile had advanced as an economic power in the Southern Hemisphere based upon work ethic and strict policy adherence. He was right; there were dark-suited, tight-tied, drone professionals everywhere. Chile had become the new economy, and its male prominents worked like the Japanese of the '60s—nose to the grindstone, with little time for play or family.

Garcia never mentioned the German hamlet of Valdivia or spoke of how Chile's 10 percent indigenous people were being systemically extracted from their lands in the name of manufactured wood products grown with seedlots from Monterey, California, and exported back to the USA. America was deeply rooted in Chile; and the power brokers, of Santiago of which he was one, knew how to make Yankee bucks—lots of them.

He was of wealthy European extraction, and his name had originally been Gareutz and not Garcia. His father had fled Germany with thousands of others and millions of marks, during the mid-1940s—this also he never mentioned and few knew, other than Balderous and a scattering of paid-off relatives back home. He planned to keep it that way, and thus he would do anything that Balderous asked.

Balderous did ask. He asked for Garcia's money, his laundry network that had grown into Bright White International, and he asked him to kill for him also. Kill anyone and everyone who created a roadblock here or an impasse there. As the head of one of the richest families in the world, Garcia had power, power which rested firmly in the hands of Enrique Balderous and not his family in Chile. So a fatal accident here, a noncorrupt politician with cement boots there, or a drive-by shooting gangster style were all within the repertoire of Garcia.

"The plan is solid. The particulars are correct. The teams are ready. It is as has been reported. We are prepared," clearly stated the monotone Garcia and sat down softly in his seat, being careful not to crease his $4,000 Italian suit.

Looks and dress were important to the elegant Garcia. He felt that the rich should look rich and act rich. It was the natural and correct order of things. That's why he threw money around in college years, and that's how he drew the attention of Balderous, who immediately used his family's own international crime connections to uncover the dirty little secret of Garcia. When Balderous made the German connection, Garcia belonged to him.

"Excellent, Antonio, excellent! Then we shall proceed. It shall be March 15th as planned, and we shall obliterate any that stand in our way. Our adversaries are busy preparing to follow a map and clues that leads nowhere, and they will not foil our agenda. It seems that our team has performed well and we have cause for celebration. Let us adjourn for now and take refreshments in the lounge."

Almost in unison, eyes rolled and members drew a breath. They knew what was coming next: a mescal-drinking contest where all would try to outduel the Mexican, but to date, none had succeeded. All had suffered the most horrendous of drunks and resultant loss of memory, shakes, and strung-out hangovers. Balderous had *ordered* participation and not requested it. This they all knew.

Chapter 21

ETHNIC CLEANSING

After the fourth round, they started to really feel it. That power surge of high-quality mescal that made one feel invincible. That brain hit that said to oneself, "There are no limits or borders." They were all becoming very high on the famed Mexican cactus drug and they loved it—for now.

"Cheers," toasted Brown as he held up the fifth shot.

"Cheers," echoed the group, who then thrust their shots down as quickly as possible, each expressing some sound of satisfaction at their achievement.

After a considerable pause, Balderous called out, "And now you, my South African Springbok, how do you toast?"

Andrek Cloiters looked at Balderous and the others. He had one eye squinted close, and the mescal had hit him hard. His was one of the early Belgium families that herded the unsuspecting black aboriginals into serfdom and segregation while they got rich from land and diamonds. He didn't like men of color, and now he was about to say so. Willie Brown quickly but quietly pinched Cloiters' elbow and applied considerable pressure to gain the South African's attention.

The message was received by the drunken Cloiters, but still he burst out, "With a partied."

"What's that?" snarled Balderous, approaching the partially bent over Cloiters.

"He said *with a party*, Enrique. He was talking about our party, now," interjected Willie Brown. "He's wasted, Enrique. Let's party! Round 6—at a party!"

"Don't defend him, Willie, he's a racist swine, and if we didn't need his network connections and this sanctuary, he would be gone, boom, right now," shouted an enraged Balderous.

"Just leave it, Enrique, for tonight, please. For your ol' buddy, me."

Balderous flared his nostrils and clenched his fists.

"OK, OK, it's because I think that I can finally drink you under the table, and I don't want that little racist twit to foul my fun. Let him be, Enrique."

O Canada—always on guard for others while exposing itself, thought Balderous. *That's why they are weak. Resources and educated people but weak in the ways of the world. They were so meekly conforming that even their criminal gangs were imported,* he mused. Bikers from USA HQ'd in Montreal, Nanaimo, and elsewhere. The early waves of Vietnamese "boat people," the few lucky true refugees blended in with the Asian gang element. Then the Russians arrived. Never mind the sheikhdom of Surrey and Little China in Richmond and suburban Toronto. Where easier to escape to than Canada. A Canada that hired locals at its embassies and contracted out services and somehow believed that no bad guys would show up for immigration processing.

Balderous looked at the stupefied Cloiters and then back at Willie Brown.

"Screw him. Screw them all, those white pigs. Not you, Willie. You I know to be different. You think you can take me down, Willie, with my own Mexican poison? I don't think so. Round 6—and the rest of you, get your asses up here to the bar. Let's see who will be the next to fall."

Chapter 22

BONGO BEHEMOTH

By round 9 they were down to Balderous, Brown, Varez, and Anhebo—the 6'9" Brazilian princess.

Up to her retirement, she had destroyed opponents in Greco-Roman wrestling and held the gold medal for four consecutive Olympic games. Now at forty-one, she was a brilliant business tycoon with extremely respectable credentials. The "some level of ancient goddess" and a cattle-rich lawyer daddy didn't hurt either. Feared by men and women alike, she was extremely powerful physically, a true Amazonian of legendary status: the stance, the build, the beauty. Most wisely steered clear of her because she was also known for her violent temper, and now that she was feeling the buzz of the mescal, she wanted to tango.

She flipped her brown ringlets over her bare shoulders and repositioned her flame-red ayeyon skirt while looking directly at Balderous. "OKKK, Enriiiqqquuuee, myyyy turnnn," slurred the Amazonian. "Leyt'sssss makkee it a douuuubbblleee. OKKK? Nyyeeennn anddd teennnn. OKKKK?"

"OK, Anhebo," said the 6'1" and much-slighter Balderous. "Remember you tried this before and you know what happened. You want to prance with the maestro? OK, let's go! Willie, your turn to pour, and you, Varez, keep your little commie mouth shut until I say drink up. Let's separate the boys from the bongos."

"Drink up!"

Balderous looked to Anhebo and then Brown and then to Varez. He looked and he waited. Soon Varez slid to his knees and then toppled, splitting his forehead open in the process.

"Leave him!" immediately commanded Balderous. "He knew the rules of the game. He could have faded early like the others, but he wanted to challenge me. Challenge me, Enrique Salvador Balderous. And now there is but you, my Canadian friend, and what is left of the behemoth."

"Careful, Enrique, she is not done yet. You don't want to have to shoot a woman, even if she is about to tear you apart limb by limb."

"Thhhhaaattt's s rriigghhttttt," mumbled the princess. "Annnnddd bbbyyy thhh waaayyy, ittt's ss rrrrooouuunnnddd eeeyyeevvvennn, Ennriqueeeee, and Iiii'mmm gonnna taaakkkkeee yyyyouuuu dowwnnnn.

"My turn to pour, Anhebo. Let's make it another double. Eleven and twelve. Let's see if you can take another round of this. You too, Willie, let's see what you are made of."

"Bring it on, Enrique," coolly stated Brown. "It's time for you to meet your match."

"Yeahhhh, wwhhaattevvverrr hee saaaiiidd, meee tooo," slurred the Brazilian.

"Drink up," announced Balderous and then thrust his double shot down without a sound.

Anhebo and Brown followed suit, and soon they were all at an even dozen shots of pure mescal, and each of them was feeling its rush and effects. The world began to wobble for all three of them, but none appeared ready to quit.

"Swaaattt nooowww, Enttttiiki?" teased Anhebo. "Thought you could bring down a princess?" inquired the now clearly spoken giant. "It will take more than you this time, my little Mexican friend. I can tolerate more of this desert drug than you or Willie. I have been practicing, and you are about to be defeated at your own game!"

For once in his life, Balderous was truly shocked. He had been surprised, caught totally off guard and fooled by a woman of considerable . . . everything. He glared at the Amazonian and her smile of confidence. He had been outwitted, yet the mescal lay between them. *One last chance*, he thought, *to restore my authority and dominance.*

"I knew you were faking my dear, sweet princess," lied Balderous. "I have seen you mescaled before, don't you remember? Perhaps not, you were too busy crawling on the floor. And it is to the floor that you will return now that you dare challenge your leader."

"Pour! Thirteen and fourteen, princess. Pour!"

"Yes, pour 13 and 14, dear princess, and remember, the puck stops here," joked a half-lucid Brown as he sauntered up to the bar and squeezed in tight next to Balderous. Now they were three with the much-smaller and apparently off-guard Balderous wedged between two hulking giants, both believing that tonight would be the night that Enrique would finally fall.

"Salut," sounded Balderous, and again the trio cast the spirits into their bloodstream.

"Cheers," called Brown as 15 and 16 were put down.

"Saúde," retorted Anhebo when 17 and 18 were set up and thrown back.

It was 6:00 a.m. when security processed the kitchen staff from their enclosure and into the guarded zone. As they were passing by the lounge en route to their stations, they glanced in to see three bodies tripoded together at the bar and a bloodstained man sprawled on the ceramic floor. There were four other bodies strewn about. Enrique Balderous had survived, but his power had been challenged as never before.

Chapter 23

FAR EASTERN PLANS

Returning to their home turf, each of the NOW leaders were preparing to go after the cleanser member assigned to them by Boris and the Rabbi. There were no longer lab tests to conduct or barrel pieces to hunt down or mystery maps to decipher. Even the securely sealed and guarded vials and threat of mass death by virus had become less of a concern than the concentrated efforts to get to those that controlled the death bug. They had found the villain, and now it was time for action—action that should lead to death and ultimately the total eradication of the brazen phantom.

Chairman Li Wi Yung had been assigned the Chilean Antonio Garcia as he had requested. *Pretnekof and Berhinstein have taken my request seriously*, thought Yung. *They know I control the largest army, and everyone knows that inevitably, the reach for world domination would come down to hand-to-hand combat—as it always did.* No amount of nuclear devices or heat-seeking missiles would fully do the job; and in the end, like in all wars, the victor would be the one with the most troops on the ground and the one who controlled the supply lines. If nothing else, Afghanistan and Iraq had proven that. First the Russians and then the Americans with their "aligned willing" had tried to control and defeat the local combatants without success and with substantial losses—young men and women, some barely more than children, sent home in body bags to grieving parents and smartly dressed honor guards assembled to pay tribute to their cold corpses. Confused young people who had no real idea why they were in Baghdad or elsewhere other than to follow orders and to rid the earth of the enemy—whoever that may be.

Yung was pleased and carefully selected two trusted and skilled agents to dispatch to Santiago to meet the two Krems who awaited their arrival. Chung Lee and Wah Yip had been chosen because they were unknowns outside of China and could easily pass as buyers for the energy-starved Chinese who were taking over mines and oil companies around the globe. It would be easy for them to enter Chile under the guise of mining and mineral-acquisition investigations and to be hosted by the emerging open-for-business South American economy. No one would be the wiser. Inside Chile, they could use their connections and techniques to study the movements of Garcia, and when the word came down to strike—it would be sudden and without ragged edges. China was prepared, and Yung was anxious.

"One more thing before you leave," said the chairman. "When you have Garcia and you are about to put a bullet in his miserable head, tell him that the chairman never forgets—never! Tell him that he is fortunate that I am not there to kill him myself, for in such a circumstance, he would die a slow, painful death. Tell him that it is his lucky day. Now go. Your plane awaits you. And oh, yes, one final thing: fail and you will not find a mine shaft deep enough in Chile or elsewhere to hide you. Succeed and you shall be honored and richly rewarded. Now go!"

The chairman did not mince words, only body parts, as he ground his way to the top, not the top of China, but the ultimate top, the world! Like the others, he had grand thoughts of a smaller, cleaner, more organized world; but what really motivated him was the power that he could and would control. Power to take down Boris, Balderous, or anyone he chose. This was his thirst, and he believed reachable delight.

The monstrous Yung's evil plans were evolving even as he dispatched the two agents. What if he were to take down Garcia quickly? A mistake by one of the Krems, he would say. The Krem he would have one of his henchmen shoot dead, and the other Krem could be left unconscious and unaware of the happenings. That would royally screw up the plans of Boris for an all-at-once roundup of the Cleansers.

Then the chairman, with eyes and ears in mah-jongg rooms and opium parlors throughout the world, would mobilize his implanted force to wipe out all the Cleansers who were still under surveillance by Boris and company. The news of the shooting death of Chile's richest man by a Russian agent who in turn was shot by some unknown killer would alert the Cleansers and set them fleeing their watchers while Boris still waited for "the perfect time." Indecision against assault, preparedness against reasoning, reasoned the mighty Yung.

Yung would be ready by having his thugs watch the watchers and then destroy the cleansers before Boris could. Yung could prove the strength of his network by capturing and torturing them all, by getting their confessions and locations of the virus stockpiles and then *humanely* turning them over to the World Court to pass judgment. This he could accomplish without any foreign agents or Krem secret service. Total victory could be his once it was revealed that the murdered and captured leaders were all part of the same evil team intent upon population control. He could state his insightfulness and the need to move swiftly. Within the NOW,

Boris would be disgraced for his lack of action and Yung would be praised as the savior of the human race. His ascent would be clean and complete. Then he could get back to some very serious cleansing of his own.

Karakanni was delighted to have been assigned Singh. He had longed to mangle the remaining one good leg of the Singher, and after many years, this would be his chance. *Show your power and crushing might*, thought Karakanni. Let the fear fill his face and then piece by piece take him apart. Never mind the clean assassination methods of Boris. Masatsu would have his pound of flesh, and it would be prepared to his particular preference. This was befitting his imperial lineage and would show the others his power to do things his way. Boris and the Rabbi would not dare challenge him, he felt, for they knew that Karakanni had no limits concerning the disregard for human life and also could prove to be a worthy adversary. This unquenchable thirst for power and control was what had led him to pressure Langois and to secretly align himself with Gilberger. If he could win over Langois, Burgess, and Brunehoff, then he would control the most members and then Boris, the Rabbi, and the hated Yung would be displaced as the power leaders. Then the world would witness his coming to power and the rise of the Japanese military once again—imperial Japan!

He had another more immediate concern to deal with: how to convince Prime Minister Ikaro Sasami to assign two top agents to India. For what reason? If only he had the throne already. This would be superficial dribble. He would just do it! For now, at least, he would have to find some clever reason to have Sasami assign the agents; and he had only a Boris-ordered, seventy-two-hour window to complete the organization and dispatch. How he envied Yung and Boris and even Burgess, as their country's leaders they had considerable more direct decision-making power.

Two hours to touchdown and he needed a plan that would be unquestioned. But wait, maybe there was no need for major deception. The PM knew that he was returning from secret-strategy sessions at some undisclosed location in Italy, talks aimed at finding the cleansers and disarming their biological brutality before more terror and death could be unleashed. It was the PM himself that received the phone call direct from the Russian president requesting that his top military man attend the secret meeting of twenty-five selected military generals. He recalled that Sasami had viewed it as an honor for Japan to crack the list. He recalled an excited Sasami telling the cabinet that Japan had been selected to participate in a world "think tank" to solve the riddle of the group calling themselves the Earth Cleansers. The fool! It was he, Masatsu Karakanni, that been selected long ago, both by the now international incumbents and much longer ago by the imperial masters.

"What news do you bring us?" blurted out an anxious Sasami as Karakanni entered his office.

"Honorable Sasami, it is with great pride that I can report to you that we have successfully identified the leaders of the cleansers. We also believe that we have located their main manufacturing plant and distribution center deep within India. The generals, upon witnessing my computer methodologies and deductive reasoning that led to this information, have agreed to bestow an unheralded honor upon Japan's loyal servant and have selected me to lead the infiltration and direct the overthrow of the cleansers headquarters. Let the glory and honor be to our great nation, and let us prepare to be the pride of the world."

"Most Honorable Masatsu, today you bring great pride to our nation. You bring tears to my face, and I promise you all of the resources that you may need. Kindly state your requirements and

I will personally facilitate your requests. Well done, my loyal and faithful son."

"It is I that feel privilege, Ikaro, for although I may face hardships and even torture and death, I do this most willingly for the honor of our country and for the freedom of our planet. I have been gifted and must use my abilities for the good of mankind. I have been enlightened to a new reality, and I freely put forth my life to rid the planet of this pestilence and its evil developers."

"Dear Masatsu, you bring me great pride."

"We will need to move quickly. I have less than seventy-two hours to be en route to Delhi. There will be no time to call an assembly or to discuss and consider other options. The military might of the planet has put its combined faith in me to orchestrate this mission and I must not fail. I will need your jet and money—lots of it, in USA currency, 20 million dollars in unmarked, untraceable bills. I also need two top agents, Yokahama and Isito, and two very competent clerks. The best are with your personal staff. I will take two of the young, bright, and obedient ladies from the receiving section. That is all for now."

"Masatsu, it will take time to arrange such a large sum of money, and I will have the entire assembly to answer to for the money as well as the decisions. Couldn't we call an emergency meeting and inform the others? I would feel better about that process."

"My prime minister, the world leaders have spoken, and Japan and you as its leader have been greatly honored. You have the skills and diplomacy to make placid any internal outrage. Once they all realize that Japan has been favored above all others, their pride will do their thinking for them and all shall be in full agreement. Tell no one until we have departed and immediately make open and without restriction all departments of government to me during the next three days."

"All shall be as you request, General Karakanni. I want to thank you on behalf of Japan and most especially on behalf of me personally."

"Save your accolades, dear prime minister, until your faithful servant has delivered the phantom to its judges and restored order to our earth. Then we shall both feel the outflowing of generosity from the entire world, and Japan shall once again be elevated to its rightful position of power."

What an idiot, thought Karakanni as he left the office of Sasami. *I ask him for his plane, $20 million in unmarked bills, and the two sweetest young ladies from his personal staff. He will go back to both houses of the Diet and say what a great hero I am and that Japan is fortunate to have such a great general. Meanwhile, I get the jet, the money, and the babes, and all I have to do is locate one gimped-up Narinder Singh—and let the agents or the Krems extinguish him. Why, I might even do it myself. More glory and power*. The general chuckled.

He had three days to plan his methods, to initiate the hunt for Singh, and to ensure that no one anywhere would tip off Singh of the plan or, worse still, would inform Boris of his total disregard for his explicit instructions. Oh well, if he could win over his PM in a matter of minutes and bilk him to the hilt, then he could get away with these other shenanigans also. After all, he was imperial and would rule. But first he was going to enjoy himself and $20 million would go a long way in India.

Chapter 24

THE AMERICANS

Onboard Air Force One headed for Washington were a still-groggy Gilberger and a very upset Sarquas. After learning from Langois how Gilberger had been knocked out by Dieter, she was livid. She ragged on about how idiotic Gilberger was and how he had brought the USA from the only two-player participant at the summit to an almost nonentity. She went on and on about how the two-member USA had only been assigned one lower-level Cleanser between them. One who hailed from the Fideldom of Cuba and was somewhere within the CIA's own network.

Even if he was in Cuba, both Sarquas and Gilberger knew that Guantánamo Bay was an easy way in to an island where the USA had a permanent presence with a not-yet-empty terriorists' compound. A little payola here and there and Varez would be found and put down, in and out before anyone knew anything. How hard could it be? They hadn't even been assigned the token two Krems. Their stock had fallen within their camp, and Rebecca feared that Boris and the Rabbi may know more about the foolish talk of Gilberger to Brunehoff and his pact with his buddy, Karakanni.

"What the hell is wrong with you?" finally questioned the fiery temptress. "Don't you know what you have done? What if

Brunehoff mentioned your feeble little scheme to the Rabbi? Do you think that you will live long enough to even get started? What if he includes me with you? I would get cancelled also. You have really outdone yourself this time. Asshole!"

Instantly, Gilberger was alert. She had pressed the right button. The one marked opportunity—for him, not for her. She would merely become the contestant as he pranced his abilities and cunning with refinement and grace.

"Calm down, my dear Rebecca, and remember who elevated you to the position that you now hold. One which combined with your considerable charm and feminine prowess could let you rise enough to be my running mate and even VP when I am elected president. Now shut up with the nagging or I will have you tossed out at six miles high. That would give you a minute or two to consider your allegiance and foolhardiness."

Gilberger continued, "Don't ever again question my reasoning or the seeds of uncertainty or doubt that I sow. All is for a well-conceived reason. Brunehoff wants out and he knows that currently that is impossible. I plan to convince him that there is a way, a way which he will freely accept. After that I will even my score with him. Karakanni is a decoy, a pawn, and when the time is right I shall dispose of 'His Imperial Majesty' in a most fitting manner. As for Brunehoff, he will also suffer a crushing demise at the hands of the president of the United States of America—and the new unchallenged leader of the Newly Ordered World."

Sarquas appeared stunned, and for a moment or two she was silent.

"Me? Your running mate? Me, the vice president? Vice President Rebecca Sarquas. I like the sound of that. With the proper planning, we could eliminate Boris, the Rabbi, and Yung. We could gain total control. First the Cleansers, then the American opposition, and finally our own camp leaders. That would please me greatly, Gil. You know how I love to be pleased and how responsive I can be to those that aid my quests. Come closer, big boy, and let's talk some more. I am becoming attracted to this plan of yours," cooed a smiling Rebecca.

Gilberger raised his handsome face, lifted his square and dimpled chin, and pursed his lips in triumphant style. He brushed back his rich deep-black hair, exposing his slightly graying temples. He had sprung another trap, and he relished in his beauty and his brilliance, never once considering them to be conceit and arrogance. He was pleased with his reasoning, with his conniving, and especially with his newly found power over Sarquas. Now she was his and he would use her as he had others in his vault to the top. He would have them all, and the world would know who called the shots.

"So how do we go about this, Gil? We will be landing in a few hours. What do we tell Rush, Walker, that jerk Roth, and the others? What do we have to say regarding what was discussed? We can't tell them that we came back with our own CIA agent at the heart of the problem."

"Can't we, Rebecca? Leave the thinking to me, and meanwhile, make yourself useful. Get me some tea and maybe a danish. Then pretty yourself up. I want my staff to look good. If you are to sit next to me, you will have to appear stunning—always."

As she left the settee and moved aft to the kitchen area, she thought how things had changed dramatically in the past few minutes. Gilberger was still an arrogant asshole, but now she knew that he was one with a plan. A plan that could work. A plan that would work. "Announcing Vice President Rebecca Sarquas." It had a nice ring to it. She would play Gilberger's game—as long as necessary. Then things would unfold differently. She and Dieter would be together again. There would be no Gilberger. Only her and Dieter. This she knew.

Inside the White House boardroom, the inner circle had assembled. All were anxious to hear from Secretary of State Gilberger as to what had transpired at the meeting of the task force to uncover the Cleansers. All hoped that the mystery had been solved or at least there were positive and concrete leads as to their organization and leaders. None were prepared for the words of Wilson Gilberger.

"My dear friends, it is with a high level of urgency that I address you today. As you know, we have just turned from Rome and a summit with many of our allies. All of whom are intent upon determining the identity of the Phantom and then taking appropriate corrective action to rid our world of these barbaric creatures. Most fortunately, for our country and the summit, I was able to determine that this group were directly linked to a *club* from my Oxford days and an entity that has remained intact up to this very day, a group of like-minded thinkers that felt the earth was overpopulated and could only be saved by a serious purge, or pruning, as it later became to be known as. These Earth Cleansers have been identified, and even as we speak, the summit leaders are preparing elite teams to wipe out the invisible force that has inflicted so much pain on our world."

"You mean you have found the little pricks?" interjected General Roth. "Give them to me, and I will make them talk."

"This is not the time for such actions as you soon will hear, H. T. When I am able to relate the summit happenings . . . without further interruptions, you will know more."

"Yes, continue please," urged President Rush. "We really need to learn more. And General Roth, please contain yourself."

"The summit was attended by many of the world leaders that we have come to know as our allies in this time of crisis. In particular, I was able to work closely with Chairman Yung and President Pretnekof. Even though our college days seem so long ago, it was thrilling to have these old friends look to me again as the source of a solution to their problem, this time, a far-greater problem for all of us—the threat from the Cleansers. I feel confident in saying that they were truly impressed by my thought process. This combined with the charm and grace of Ms. Sarquas made the USA the darling of the meeting . . . until the riddle unraveled a little further. In fact, I would think it fair to say that the respect that we have seen slide in recent years was initially returned and the USA was more respected and appreciated than ever before within the domain of the northern leaders."

Gilberger smiled and paused for a while to scan the faces of the assembled group and to relish in his own lies as a form of self-gratification. Vice President Walker would not be able to contest him at the primaries or in the debates leading up to the next presidential election. Once the press knew that it was Gilberger who had solved the riddle of the Phantom, it would be so very easy. He would point to uncloaking the Phantom as the single most-defining reason to choose Wilson Gilberger as the Republican candidate and the next president of the USA. Few would argue that in spite of his planned deception. As for the press, well, Rebecca had already tipped off the scavengers. He knew that soon the airways and newsprint would be full of the heroics of the American *dynamic duo*. Everyday citizens would sleep well tonight knowing that America had once again come to the rescue of the world.

What they wouldn't know were any names or countries or very little else—only that Gilberger aided by Sarquas had developed some very strong evidence and that the unnamed cleansers were about to be rounded up. *That should put some heat under the burner*, thought Gilberger. And when Boris calls, he would blame it all on the tabloid press fishing for anything that would bite.

"So what happened next?" asked a clearly saddened Walker, knowing that his position of prominence had been compromised, maybe even shattered. He silently cursed himself for not attending the summit. He had speeches to make and interviews to give, and the luncheon of the Women of Washington was an important place to garner support. All of it now seemed petty and even worthless in light of Gilberger's statements.

"Next, my dear vice president, was the most revealing aspect of all. We used the best technology available to determine the last known locations and travel history of the known cleanser members. Then we deduced where the most likely depots are and where we need to concentrate our efforts to unearth these stockpiles of destruction. What we discovered was a shocking surprise to us. I must ask you all to vow that what I am about to tell you does not leave this room. Any leak to the press or casual comment to a staff member could impact adversely upon our capture plan by a combined strike force. We will get every last barrel of death, and we will be certain that we have captured all of the Phantom members.

"I ask you all for a show of hands to confirm that you will keep these secrets secret. All those in agreement, raise your hands."

Without hesitation from Roth, Walker, or any of the others, right hands were all thrust upward. All were in agreement.

"Good," continued Gilberger, his pleasure with his command and control of the proceedings showing on his face. "This is what I can tell you as of now. We know that the death virus stockpiles must be sizable considering the threat issued. We have thus surmised that there is at least one central dispatch POC in or near to each of the countries that were hit on Christmas Day. The fact that all eight of us who were *awarded* our silver briefcases by couriers at LAX points to the unfortunate fact that movement within our homeland borders has been open and undetected. That means that there is a depot close by us, or—"

"Or what?" shouted a frenzied swarm of anxious Americans.

"Or that the depot is right here under our noses. Probably on a military base where high-flying, long-range aircraft are kept. Even worse, also likely on bases throughout the world where our aircraft are deployed, aircraft that fly routine surveillance missions throughout the globe. Several such American aircraft were indeed in the air during a thirty-six-hour period encompassing Christmas Day. Here," said Gilberger, tossing a folder of loose papers onto the polished mahogany table. "It's not all there, but there is enough to substantiate my premise!"

"Planes that originated within the U.S. would be approved by base commanders and their bosses but, at really high elevation, would be undetected by even our own monitoring agents outside of the base of origin," continued Gilberger. "It is yet another example of how disjointed and relaxed our military has become."

"This is outrageous and preposterous!" shrieked General Roth. "No American pilot or crew would knowingly drop barrels of death anywhere, regardless of the reason. We as Americans just don't do that!"

"No?" inquired Gilberger. "Perhaps you have forgotten about Hiroshima and Nagasaki and even the Agent Orange days of Vietnam?"

"That was totally different, Gil, and you know it. We were under attack and times of war require special measures."

"Under attack by who exactly? The Vietcong or the Japanese? Let's be certain that other than Pearl Harbor, we haven't been attacked by anyone for a very long time. Even the Pearl bombings could have been prevented with an astute military leadership, something that we continue to lack even up until today. Sophistication, speeding technology, the world's most-advanced guidance systems, and delivery protocols—all run by a bunch of fat-assed military dolts at the top!"

"I resent that, Gilberger," shouted Roth.

"I also," seconded Colonel Clayton Cranmore, head of America's massive air force.

"Resent and object all that you want, but can any one of you provide a more plausible answer? Can any of you point to another country that has the wherewithal needed to drop the death virus and remain undetected on anyone's radar? Hhhmmm. I thought not."

"So are you saying that we have one or more American air force bases with a staff of infiltrators that have control of aircraft movement and can drop death barrels at will? That is a stretch for even you, Mr. Secretary," sneered a not-yet-destroyed Walker.

"No! That is not what I am saying. What I am telling you is that there need only be two or three personnel involved at each location. Someone in the hangar. Someone with access to the planes. Someone aware of the flight plans. Someone with clearance for software uploads. Uploads encasing hidden instructions to open a cargo door and let loose a barrel of death. That's what I am saying, and you better damn well get your act together before the Russians and Chinese figure this out, for then we will be really facing an uprising as well as an invasion!"

"OK, supposing that you are right. What should we do? ID all possible bases and do a thorough search and interrogation of all of the assigned personnel?" asked Cranmore.

"That would be the way an inept air force would likely tackle the problem. Warn everyone, interview everyone, and by the time your interviews are concluded, the infiltrators will be long gone. Relocated or replaced by others. This is too open of a country still and too large of a one to track disappearing small fry players. We need to catch the biggies."

"And exactly how do we do that, Wilson?" inquired the president.

"Monitor them, all of the bases where the stealths and drones and high-flying bombers are kept, and we do it without showing our hand."

"Now that would be near if not totally impossible," coldly stated Roth. "All abnormal monitoring has strict methods, and scores of civilian as well as military personnel would be involved. It would be impossible to keep the lid on that one, and your so-called infiltrators would be tipped off under this scenario as well."

"Now here is the magic, H. T. We don't monitor them at all. We get someone else to do it for us, someone who is forever watching our takeoffs and landing and flight paths. Someone with most adequate technology."

"Who, who?" rang out a chorus of totally confused listeners.

"Why our old enemy, Cuba, of course. We know that they have the Russian monitoring equipment and that they are very proficient at using it. They are close enough to be able to follow all takeoffs and landings and only lose track of us when we venture beyond six thousand miles or so or above fifty-five thousand feet. They could provide us with all that we need."

"But what makes you so sure that the Cubans will cooperate?" asked Walker.

"Oh, they'll cooperate, all right. Correct me if I am wrong, Weinrich, but don't we have a very clever and highly decorated

Cuban double agent within our CIA ranks? Varez, I believe, is the name. Send him by to see me tomorrow morning, and I will brief him on the information that we will need. Remember, not a word to anyone. Our national security and indeed that of the entire world may depend upon it. There are eyes and ears everywhere."

"OK, Gilberger, we'll play it your way for now, but release to us the names of the known cleansers and their countries of origin," demanded a thoroughly put-off Walker.

"I would be very pleased to do just that, Mr. Vice President, but the summit members all swore an oath. We are not to inform anyone outside of the task force until such time as we are ready to take down the entire group at once. Only then shall you have all of the names."

"You answer to this government first and foremost, Gilberger. You have no right to withhold information that could be detrimental to the security of the United States," challenged Walker.

"Exactly, Walker. Sharing this information with you and the others could be detrimental to our security. If we can drop barrels on the world and devastate nations with our own planes and not even know about it, I consider it most safe to tell no one in this room any more than is absolutely necessary. Our national security comes first . . . with some of us, at least."

"Well, if there is nothing else, I believe we are adjourned until we hear back from Wilson. I must commend you, Mr. Secretary, on how well you and Ms. Sarquas have represented us at the summit. Your efforts will be duly noted," stated the president.

"At your service, my captain," mocked Gilberger to a president who responded only with a polite "thank you."

Chapter 25

LUCKY LANGOIS

On the short flight back to Paris, Pierre Langois sat alone, the adjacent first-class seat having been purchased and paid for by a concocted alias of Langois's. He needed to be alone, alone to sort out this mess he found himself in. One minute he was the golden boy of Boris, then Karakanni changed all that with his lies—if they were lies. Then Brunehoff had set him straight—maybe.

Then Boris assigned him Ambewa as his Cleanser to find and wipe clean. Why? Boris knew that he detested anything or anybody that was black. Black and African—surely Boris must know that he was approached by Karakanni, and that he listened. Maybe it was Brunehoff that tipped off the Rabbi or Boris. He remembered the Rabbi calling Brunehoff to an audience. To top it all off, he had to appear in front of duEsi and the country's inner cabinet and report on the progress of the summit. What would he say? That Burgess had connected the dots and correctly ID'd the Phantom as the Curtailment Club from Oxford? Why hadn't he figured it out first? they would ask. "You are the intellectual Oxford whiz, Pierre, why couldn't you be the one?"

Coming second in the election had not occurred to him as his juggernaut gained momentum early on. Being second to a woman was below his status, he felt. But it was only for a short while since Boris promised. There he was again filling his mind with the fear of Boris and not allowing his calculating self to deal with the situation.

He knew now that he should have gone directly to Boris and told all about Karakanni. But it had happened so fast and he had been taken by surprise. Now it was too late—or was it? What if he called Boris now and told all? Maybe that would remedy the situation. But Boris did not like to receive unexpected calls, and he had the entire camp to consider. Maybe it was best if he just left it alone. If Karakanni continued to shoot off his big mouth, then this information would find its way to Boris, better to let someone else be the bearer of bad news. Yes, that was it; let someone else be the one to approach Boris. If anyone questioned him, he would say that Karakanni appeared to be joking and that he didn't take him serious and he didn't want to disturb the delicate and important proceedings by crying wolf where there wasn't one.

If Karakanni had been telling the truth and Boris found out that Langois knew, then surely there would be no President Pierre or Pierre anything. Why had he listened to the Japanese general? All this to consider while fabricating an update for an anxious duEsi as well as a creative plan to take down the Nigerian, Ambewa. Just when he thought that his position and status would bring him power and control, he found himself having to answer two masters and at the same time not knowing whom to trust.

Langois twirled his curly brown hair with his thumb and forefinger, just as he always done when he was troubled and nervous. There must be a solution that could save him face and at the same time elevate his position. He was sweating inside the very cool cabin, another sure sign of his lack of answers and uncertainty.

"Are you all right, sir? Is there something that I may bring you?" asked the Air France hostess. "Perhaps a beverage or a mineral water?"

"No, nothing. I just need to be left alone to think."

"Yes, sir, I will go. Please just ring if I may be of service."

"Just ring if I may be of service." If only it were that simple. Just call up, "Hello, this is me and I need the following services carried out *tout suite*. Good-bye."

Then it came to him. Maybe it was that simple. The hard part was knowing whom to ring and when to do it. His mind was racing as he plotted a trail that the mice would follow. A trail carefully crafted by the great Pierre Langois, an aristocrat with great social standing and impeccable bloodline.

A broad smile returned to his somewhat wrinkled and strained face. He used his right hand to press the call button on his console.

When the attendant quickly emerged, he looked up and said, "I'll have that drink now. French champagne—and leave the bottle."

A somewhat tipsy and certainly bubbly Langois disembarked the plane and was ushered through customs without need for processing. As he walked to the exit area of Charles de Gaulle International Airport, he reached into the left-side pocket of his suit jacket, removed his cell phone, and turned it on. There were two text messages. Both from the same number. Both were noted as coming from RB—from the Rabbi. What could this mean? Maybe Brunehoff did talk.

The texts were short. They simply said, "Call this number as soon as you land." A look of seriousness came over Langois's face. Just when he had thought that he had connived the perfect decoy and plan. Now this. What could it mean?

A trembling left hand held the phone as a right thumb carefully pressed the digits of the keypad.

One ring, two rings while Langois sweated. Was this to be his cancellation?

"Identify yourself," calmly stated a voice after the third ring.

"It is Agent 5," answered Langois.

"State the code word," came the clear response.

"Victory," replied Langois.

"Agent 5, we have a cancellation for you."

"But, but, I didn't do anything, I swear," pleaded a visibly shaken Langois.

"I repeat. We have a cancellation. We have just learned that your assignment has already been terminated. There is no need for your agents to travel to Africa. The problem has been eliminated. Stay close to your phone and be prepared for a new assignment. That is all."

A click and then silence. The Rabbi had concluded his business. Langois had just been informed that Ambewa was already dead. There was no mention of Karakanni, Gilberger, or Brunehoff. Maybe he was in the clear after all and now he had the added good fortune of not having to organize a team to work with the Krems to go to the wretched African continent. *I should order champagne more often*, thought Langois as he placed the phone back into his pocket, picked up his pace, and whistled a sweet French love song as he left the terminal building and approached the waiting limo.

With Ambewa out of the way, he would be able to concentrate on his deception intended for duEsi. "Too easy duEsi." He laughed aloud at his pun. Then he entered the left-side rear seat of the limo, whose door was held fully open by a smartly dressed chauffeur.

Inside he found himself sitting next to President duEsi herself. Anxious to hear the latest news as soon as possible, she had rescheduled an audience with the head of the large Credit Suisse bank in order to meet Langois. She was desperate for any news of the Phantom, knowing that all other matters paled in comparison. She was also intent upon getting advance updates from Langois before he shared his ego-laced dialogue with the members of her cabinet. She knew that theirs was an uneasy alliance, and she wanted to prevent any further erosion of her power to a not-to-be-fully-trusted Langois.

"So, Pierre, what do you have to report? The short version, please. Save the verbal dance for the others. I need the facts—now."

"You seem to be distraught, Michelle. Perhaps you need a drink or a body massage or—"

"I don't need anything. Just the facts. What went on. While you were away at your enclave, all hell has broke loose here. The people have followed the Brits and the Japanese, and now it looks as if the Americans are having trouble also. For the last time, exactly what do you have to report?" asked the obviously anxious French president.

"Well, I must say that things went better than even I had hoped for. There were twenty-eight nations represented, and the leaders of fourteen governments were present. After the general assembly over which President Pretnekof presided, we broke into strategic teams for roundtable discussions aimed at unearthing the identity and whereabouts of the Phantom. During the morning session, it suddenly occurred to me that some of the diction I was hearing repeated seems vaguely familiar. It really bothered me, and then when I heard the word *curtailment*, it all came flooding back to me.

"What came flooding back?"

"The Curtailment Club from Oxford. It was a group of wantabees that thought they could capture more attention by making us all aware of the pending world-population explosion. They were forever talking about how to control the exponential rise and considered many options including education and the like, but they usually came back to war and forced birth control as the fastest ways to lessen the accelerating population increase. Some of the group were all right, but we thought most of them to be a little bit off the deep end. That was more than fifteen years ago, and most of us had completely forgotten about them. When I estimated that our runaway population has increased by more than 20 percent in those fifteen years, I knew that these insistent believers must be still around and intact. Most came from extremely rich backgrounds, and with their family wealth and prestigious education, they could be poised for a move, one even more severe and thorough than we would have imagined back in the '90s."

"So what happened next?"

"Well, I approached Boris, eh, President Pretnekof, and shared my information directly with him as the chairman of the summit. He also had a feeling that the Phantom must be a group that had existed for some time and with considerable resources. When I mentioned the Curtailment Club, his eyes immediately lit up and he quickly called the assembly together and announced that I had in all likelihood cracked the case. Then his exceptional perceptive and organizational skills kicked in, and before we knew it, he had a short list of the names and whereabouts of nine Club members—all prominent figures in their respective countries."

"So who are these club members, Pierre, and how do we capture them?"

"Unfortunately, that information I am unable to share with you or anyone just yet. Security must remain tight, and any leak to the press would be an early warning signal to the Cleansers and we may lose valuable time in the process—time which we do not have."

"You are telling me that you go to a secret summit, solve the mystery, return to France, and cannot inform your president of who you have unearthed?" pressed the outraged duEsi.

"Precisely," uttered a smug Langois, fully enjoying having control over duEsi.

An unhappy duEsi fiddled with her watch strap and then with her string of pearls. She was the president, but Langois was the king, and everyone knew that the king ruled and that the president enacted his wishes. There was a marked difference, and for now she felt more like a joker than a queen.

"I can tell you this, my dear Michelle," sweetly chirped a triumphant Langois. "Nine of us more prominent leaders have been assigned one Cleanser each to study and to take down when all have been found and the time is right. I will need two of our very best agents to accompany me in my search for my assigned Cleanser. We shall be going to the most dreadful of places—the African continent—and although I detest the place, I go most willingly for the future of the earth and for the glory of France," concluded Langois.

And for the glory of Pierre Langois, thought duEsi to herself. *This chauvinist has outdueled me again, and I am beginning to get the feeling that he and his Russian master are the ones running the country and not me. That will have to change and soon, very soon.*

Langois smiled and stretched his legs and arms wide. He reclined his head and closed his eyes. Without opening them or turning toward her, he said, "All of this nonstop brain burning has tired me, Michelle. Be a dear and let me rest awhile before I am called upon again to rise to the occasion and represent our great republic."

You arrogant bastard, she thought, but it was a thought only and remained unuttered.

Chapter 26

THE ENGLISH CHANNEL

On the surface, Prime Minister Anthony Burgess had more to be proud of than any of the members of the NOW. It was he that had cracked the case, he that had figured out the connection between the Curtailment Club and the Earth Cleansers. He that had gotten his country's finest to do the sleuth work necessary to present the connections between the Club's member's flight itineraries.

Yet Burgess was dismayed and felt downtrodden. Mostly, he was genuinely afraid for the first time since college. Boris had called him an idiot, had said he was lucky to be alive after his colossal screw up of not looking at the current month's travel. Worse still, he had chastised him in front of his peers. Then Burgess had caved in and groveled with a "yes, Boris, this and an immediate, Boris, that." He had been ridiculed in a manner that he had succeeded in applying to most others—all his life. Now the shoe was on the other foot and the fit was awkward and tight.

As if this wasn't enough, Boris really put fear into Burgess by assigning him Anhebo and insisting that he personally join the team to find her. Just the mention of her name brought back nightmarish memories of the beating he had taken at the hands of the giant Brazilian so very long ago.

In college days, Burgess, the suave and debonair gentleman, was infamous for his favor with the ladies. He was tall, athletic, and ruggedly good-looking; and he knew London like the back of his hand. The latter factor played prominently when the beer parties turned into city tours with Burgess as the scholarly historian. This always impressed the foreign students, and most of them were ladies: young, delicate, innocent ladies awaiting just the right gentleman to expose them to the pleasures of the world.

One night he had hit upon a nineteen-year-old Brazilian who was so beautiful that Burgess knew that he must have her, another triumph for his trophy case. He had fed her full of booze and isolated her like a wolf does to a wounded prey. Then, when he was certain that he was alone with her in her dorm, he struck with a vengeance—practically shredding her clothes as he clawed them from her. Her screams were met with fowl and disgusting retorts and Burgess was well on his way to his first south-of-the-equator conquest. Then Anhebo appeared, having been awakened by the bashing around and muffled cries coming from the adjacent room.

When she saw the state of her abused young fellow Brazilian, she went ballistic, grabbing and throwing furniture out of her path until she reached the bedroom. Then with one thrust of her right arm, she clutched a drunken Burgess and tossed him across the room, bashing his shoulder into the chest of drawers.

Grimacing in pain from an obvious dislocation, Burgess attempted to get up but was struck again and again and again by the huge fists of Anhebo until he was rendered unconscious and near dead with blood flowing from his many open facial wounds.

It had taken five security guards and half of the floors' residents to restrain a totally out-of-control Anhebo. Few had ever witnessed such rage, and all were forever in fear of the behemoth from Brazil.

Burgess recovered and after three weeks of hospitalization was sent home to rehabilitate. Then there was the matter of legal action. Burgess was from a prominent London family and his father was a judge. The family tried to convince young Anthony to file charges that should lead to Anhebo being removed from Oxford and put in jail or at the very least dismissed with shame and sent home to the jungle from whence she came.

Burgess knew that no one but Anhebo and the young Malana were aware of the circumstances and that his family crew could easily explain away the torn clothes and claw marks. Malana was just like the giant, they wanted to say, vicious and full of rough and consensual play. Poor Burgess was an unwilling victim, seduced by the charm of a beautiful young lady and then pounced upon by her extraordinary, violent, and crazed friend. His father felt that it was an open-and-shut case. The bruising and swelling and discoloration of his son's face and his mangled torso made Burgess Senior want to punish the colossus.

Daddy did try, but without success. Anthony just wanted to recover and stay as far away as possible from Anhebo and anything Brazilian. The security guards were fearful to say anything that might anger again the giant, and the dorm mates all said they saw nothing, other than the ambulance attendants wheeling away the unconscious youth. As for the school and the hierarchical council, they were disappointed with the unfortunate misunderstanding that had taken place and felt that the matter was best left alone and forgotten about. In some small way, the rather-large donation to the athletic department by Anhebo's rich father didn't hurt matters for the Brazilians. In the end, it was Anhebo who continued to destroy opponents in the Greco-Roman ring while Burgess was left to nurse his wounds and forever avoid the behemoth.

Now this. He was assigned to take down the giant. In her own domain no less. With what, a couple of Krems and two MI5 agents? She would eat them for snack food and spit out the bones. He had seen recent pictures. Even though it hurt so much, he had viewed these photos of Anhebo. At forty-one, she looked strong and dominating and was, no doubt, to be as feared as ever. *Why me?*

It is your punishment, Tony, he convinced himself. His punishment for failing the NOW by not being absolutely perfect and 100 percent prepared. He had left it with Scotland Yard, and the fools had not thought to look ahead rather than back. Now it was he that must pay the price. He that must outwit the princess and he that must eliminate her once and for all.

These were not the things that made for a very happy return to merry old England.

A few hours later, inside the House, it was a new, less-commanding Burgess that addressed his team. He was so very preoccupied with his fear of Anhebo learning of the plan and getting to him first. It would be like getting taken by Yung except that it would be the princess personally that would administer the beating. He couldn't take another such beating, not even fifteen years later, or ever again for that matter. He feared her more than he feared Boris and Yung combined. This was not healthy, and he knew what he must do, with whom he must consult. He couldn't take this pressure for long, not long at all. He would surely crack.

"Ladies and gentlemen," began the prime minister, "I must first tell you that if I appear less than my cheerful, upbeat self, it is because I am totally and utterly exhausted. For the past three and one-half days, I have been almost without sleep, all the while having to engage my brain fully. Suffice it to say that the summit was a success, that my suspicions were correct, and that the Phantom team has been identified and will soon be cancelled, eh, pardon me, will soon be caught. As you can see, I am direly in need of rest and at this time will turn the assembly over to Chief Inspector Willingdon, whose team has attended to the assemblage and transmittal of material that I requested for and during the summit. The chief inspector can provide you with more details of a general nature, but under no circumstances can we, as of yet, reveal to anyone the identities of the Cleansers. This will have to wait until such time as we have completely baited the developing trap. Security comes first. This is the future of the human race that we are dealing with, and I for one will do my utmost to stand on guard for the protection of all of mankind. Thank you. That is all."

Immediately, the applause broke out and members of all persuasions leapt to their feet to congratulate their leader, their hero, their human hope. They clapped hardily until Burgess had descended the chambers and left the room. They continued to applaud him even after he entered the hallway and made his way toward his waiting limo. He was their prime minister, their England, and they felt so very proud.

After a minute or two, the members settled down and all eyes turned to the chief inspector. As always he stood erect and sported his flushed red cheeks. This time, however, to the very careful observer, there was something very, very different about the short balding chief inspector. Behind the red cheeks was a face of pale gray, a face of fear. A face that had reacted with outrage at first, just six hours ago, when he was contacted on his mobile. A man that at fifty-two had thought that he had seen it all. But he hadn't.

Now he appeared more like seventy-two, and he was sure that there was more to come.

The caller never left a name. Only the two words, UNKNOWN CALLER, appeared on his mobile. No number showed or was traceable he was sure, even with the Yard's sophistication. That is, if he had tried to trace the call. He hadn't and he wouldn't. He would do exactly as the caller had instructed during the second call, and he would be very careful about ensuring that there was no evidence of any kind left anywhere that would link anyone on the Club's list to the summit team.

The first call came while Burgess was about to board his aircraft in Rome. It was brief and said only, "Listen. Do not speak. Go directly to building C3 and witness that I am very, very serious." And then the line went dead.

Poppycock, thought Willingdon and then for some unknown reason decided that he should have a look anyway. There was something very strange yet familiar about the voice, but mostly it was the authority with which the message was delivered that made the chief inspector feel uneasy. This was no ordinary crank call, he concluded. Building C3 was the secretly assigned area of the four investigators that communicated directly with Burgess during the summit.

As he approached the Yard's smaller modular buildings, he continued to feel uneasy and hastened his step. The hair on the back of his neck was rising, and he felt cold shivers down his back. Something was definitely afoul. Then it happened. *Ka-boom!* Building C3 and all its human and electronic inhabitants disappeared forever.

Shocked in his steps, the chief inspector held to the railing of the garden post as he looked in astonishment at the devastation and viewed people running and scurrying from all the other buildings in every which direction.

Within a minute, the second call came. His trembling hand pressed the Yes button, and immediately the same authoritative voice said, "That was necessary. The four inspectors were dead already by lethal injection. Two of them had to be found and brought there. It was a propane explosion, a gas leak. There will be no autopsies or findings. This will be forever known as a tragic accident. You will ensure that any would-be connection between this team and their assignment will be downplayed and considered coincidental. Any and all remaining material associated with this investigation is to be gathered by you personally and purged or destroyed. This was an accident. Got it?"

"Yes, you bastard, I've got it and I will get you also, you slimy little rat!"

"Careful what you say, my dear chief inspector, and be especially careful whom you say it to. I'm finished with you for now, but call your wife, why don't you, and ask her why your thirteen-year-old daughter, Melissa, hasn't returned home from school yet. Then when I call back, you will address me as master, and if ever again you utter threats at me, more than Melissa will go missing and more than C3 will disappear. Got it?"

The phone clicked dead and Willingdon fumbled with the mobile, dialing directly to his wife. When Gertrude Willingdon answered the phone, she confirmed that Melissa had not arrived home yet and she was starting to worry. The chief inspector tried to calm his racing heart and also tried to calm his increasingly frantic wife, who demanded to know how he had known that Melissa was late.

"Here she comes now!" exclaimed the worried wife to a very relieved father. They soon learned that a man claiming to be a new substitute teacher and requesting directions to the headmaster's house had approached Melissa and offered her a ride home in exchange for her pointing out the suburban home of Headmaster Thatcher. It was a cold January day, and Melissa accepted the ride in the shiny black car. The teacher/driver claimed to be James Roberts from Brighton and he was thankful for her help. He even stopped at an ice-cream vendor to reward Melissa for her help. *He asked a lot of questions about Daddy*, she thought, *but otherwise he seemed very normal.*

"He was so polite and interesting and so very good-looking, Mama," she had said. "He even told me I was pretty." *Just what I need*, thought the chief inspector. *My daughter with a crush on some unknown fiend with the capacity to destroy and kill at will.*

"I have very little to add to what the prime minister has already made known to you all," stated the chief inspector. "He indeed did unravel the mystery of the identity of the Phantom and was aided by four of our most experienced staff. Unfortunately, as some of you may already have heard, there was an explosion at the Yard earlier today, caused by a gas leak, and all four of these dedicated inspectors were fatally wounded just hours ago by this tragic accident. Our sympathy and prayers go out to their families.

"As you have heard, for security reasons, I am not permitted to share details of the investigation with you yet. I can say that the PM anticipates that soon the time will be right to capture these unsavory characters. He is developing a grand plan with a group of like-minded northern leaders, and they are all very optimistic, I have been informed. It seems that it may be only a matter of time before the net closes tight and the flagrant murderers are caught and brought to trial. Since I have little else I can share with you and since I have the responsibility to visit the grieving widows and children, I ask you to please excuse me at this time. I promise to inform you of any new developments that I am permitted to share with you. Thank you."

The PM's limo raced north to the French sector, where black magic and sorcery were ever present à la Haitian immigrants. As on many previous occasions over the past several years, John, his driver, had stopped at number 13 Doncaster Lane. As always, Burgess instructed, "Wait outside, I shall be not be long." *If only the country knew*, always pondered John, but he would not be the one to jeopardize his cushy job.

Inside the home of Eluija the White Witch, he arrived to find the sixtyish woman sitting cross-legged on the wooden floor and in a trancelike state. For a child born to black Haitian mystics, this albino woman was exceedingly strange to behold. A frail-looking bleached body no more than eighty pounds was not common anywhere—strange, perhaps, but not too scary. However, once one made contact with her red eyes and their deep, penetrating stare, it was different. It made even the strongest of people and total disbelievers of voodoo startled and most uncomfortable.

The room was filled with burning candles, and some sort of foul-smelling concoction was bubbling within a clay pot atop of the gas burning stove in the adjacent small kitchen. Paintings and objects of creatures of all sorts filled the walls of the large open room. These included half man and half snake, twisted and contorted faces, and bright-red horned goblins.

"I have been expecting you, my child," came the high-pitched, hollow-sounding voice of the witch. "You have much turmoil in your being and are in need of counseling and a potion that only I can provide. Come, sit here next to me and I will give you release from your troubled mind. Drink this potion I have poured for you and the demons shall be released from your inner self."

Burgess downed the terrible-tasting elixir all in one deep gulp and then shook his head and cleared his throat. Almost immediately the effects of the mix of unknown ingredients made his head swirl, and the walls and the witch appeared to wobble as if driven by a warm breeze. He was hallucinating and his blood pressure lowered, his beating heart slowed, and his eyes appeared to be looking beyond the room in which he was contained. A feeling of euphoria took him far away from his troubles and deep into the world of the unknown dark side. He floated and soared and perched and expanded. He was free.

"You have had much to consider as of late, my child, and Eluija is here to aid you in your quest for the demise of the Amazonian princess that is known as Anhebo."

Startled back to pseudoreality, Burgess asked how she could possibly know that he was to find Anhebo and deal with her.

"Eluija sees deeply inside your mind and spirit and finds your fears running from your human self. I know where you have been and what you must do and where your menservants will go. Focus on this candle now," she said as she placed it directly in front of him.

Obedient to the witch, he cast his eyes upon the candle, whose flame flickered upward; and he started to see images shoot forth from the bright light. There was Boris and Yung and the Rabbi and the chief inspector and Brown and Balderous and Anhebo. When Anhebo's image emerged, it floated upward, was surrounded by a ring of fire, and burst into flames with a loud, agonizing scream. Then there was quiet and stillness as the flame extinguished itself.

Burgess appeared to return to normal and glanced around the room, which now seemed quite ordinary. He felt rested and relieved and rose to his feet to leave.

"Remember the needs of Eluija," cautioned the thin-lipped witch. Burgess quickly withdrew his wallet from inside his breast pocket and placed five new 100-pound notes within her cold and outstretched hand.

"Go now and return to your world. Your trouble and fear of the princess has been removed. Return to what you call reality and go about your business and leave the Amazonian's spirit to me. I will aid your men so that she will be relocated—permanently."

Without question, Burgess left the house and entered his limo. "Ten Downing," he instructed John and then settled comfortably into his seat as the limo sped along the back roads en route to the prime minister's official residence. He was no longer troubled and wished only for a warm bath and a nice cup of hot tea and, oh yes, maybe a bicky. Yes, by George, a bicky, or even two, it shall be.

As the White Witch placed the crisp bills inside of her earthen pot and closed it tight, she thought of how she had influence over the prime minister of England, a nation approaching seventy million people and a power to be reckoned with. She thought also of how her potion worked its powerful magic. Conjured up with just the right mix of not snake blood or toad innards but LSD and sodium pentothal.

She smiled an evil grin when she considered that what the PM had experienced was not what had really happened. What had felt like ten minutes to him was actually more than an hour. An hour during which she had questioned him and learned his most recent secrets. Secrets that she would use to expand her own power and control and to increase her riches and her influence. Perhaps she would even move to a palace where she felt that she rightfully belonged.

All this from an abandoned outcast from Port-au-Prince.

Chapter 27

INDECISION

Dieter Brunehoff was not at peace with the arrogant and self-loving NOW, or with the evil monsters that held his parents captive, and especially not with his assignment of the club member. Of all the names that he knew or at least recognized from college in London and the States, this was the one Phantom member for which he held respect and something akin to friendship.

This was the singular player that competed as he did—with all that he had and without fear. This was the one member that he had felt sorry for that day long ago when Jamieson and his lot had conducted the massacre at MIT. This was the once-jovial and very likeable Willie Brown, a man whom Brunehoff had always admired and one whom he also envied. When Brunehoff returned home for "summer holidays," it was to be with his masters and rulers and evil doctors. When the fun-loving Brown returned to Canada, his summers were filled with beer and weed and all-night beach parties.

Why couldn't he have been born in Canada? he thought. *I could have spent my summers with Rebecca, and our love would have lasted forever. Instead I had to return to those bastards that still existed so long after the fall of the Berlin Wall and long after things were supposed to be uniform throughout the united Germany.* Brown was indeed very lucky, and so were all of Brunehoff's free countrymen. He was not. He was being groomed by his liberal Western government while the old fort still remained: smaller, less visible, but nonetheless still existing. How he hated those old men that had tortured him and other "elite" children, young women and young men like him. Now the evildoers were suppressed and forced underground. Yet they still held his parents and they still trained and produced *juiced* athletes.

He was living proof that success came from discipline, rigorous training, and that milky white substance that the IOC had banned so very long ago. Now there were new drugs and new techniques designed to beat the urine tests and mask the illegal ingredients, drugs designed to produce a winner—at whatever consequence to the user. He remembered the awesome and muscular American sprinter, Flo Jo, and how she became the darling of the Los Angeles Olympics with gold medals galore. He also remembered how a few years later she was found dead amid rumors and reports concerning her steroid substance abuse. Abuse administered to the unknowing or misguided or captive competitor, representing their nations and the cruel coaches and doctors that emptied their syringes into the bodies of these young athletes.

Maybe he would find a way out of this colossal mess, or maybe he was meant to be tortured forever. He was the warrior, the strong and unbeatable, the mathematical genius, the fiercest man alive, but he was deeply troubled.

His heart longed for love and tender care. His mind ached trying to determine the best course of action, the right decision, the correct choice. His psyche flared when thoughts of his reoccurring dream crept into his subconscious. The Rabbi, with all his talents, had provided no insights.

Outwardly, he was a well-dressed, handsome, and obviously successful and fit picture of perfection. Inward, he was a total mess. He even thought about ending it all, but he couldn't and wouldn't because there was Francesca. His darling. His princess. His child. A product of mating the best with the best. Of taking the strongest desirable features from the best males and mating them with the equally most desirable features in strong, young, blossoming females. Like plant breeding for resistance or early maturity or fuller flowers or less seeds, but with human beings. All this twenty years ago when Dieter was about to leave for Oxford and Hannah, at seventeen, still faced at least two more years of incarceration before she would be sent to America to study science and to compete for the fatherland.

"We must ensure that we create the child before we send him away to display our superior logic and power," stated Dr. X. "It would be a step backward to miss this opportunity after we have come so far. The subject female is now at the height of her receptivity, and we must complete the fertilization within the next three days."

"Correct as always, Herr Doctor," replied the lab leader and elder of the two. "We shall proceed immediately. Have the matron prepare the chamber suite and bring them both there tonight at eight p.m. We shall commence with the breeding component of the experiment."

"Yes, master" came the immediate reply.

When young Dieter entered the unknown room, he had no idea of what would happen next. At nineteen, and after eleven years with these monsters, he thought that he had been exposed to and tortured by all the evils kept secret deep within this mountain fortress. But what he saw startled and confused him as never before. There was a table and two chairs, and there were flowers on the table, beautiful

135

red and orange and violet flowers that he now remembered from his boyhood years before he that been brought there. There was also a decanter of what looked like red wine and two long-stemmed glasses and some cheese and fresh bread. Beyond the entrance room was another room with a bed with sheets and a mattress. There were even chocolates laid neatly against each of the two pillows. He approached the bed and lightly touched the smooth silk sheets. So clean, so soft, so beautiful. He could see that there was also a bath and a basin and a flush toilet. Just then he heard the outer door open and turned to see Hannah enter the room. She hadn't seen him as she was busy scanning the entrance room in disbelief much as Dieter had. Then she looked beyond the table to the bedroom and saw him standing there looking directly at her.

For an instant, they both froze, bewildered, not knowing what to do or why they had been sent there, ordered to this strange, wonderful place with brightly painted walls and soft, gentle lighting. Dieter walked toward her and said, "Hello, Hannah, my name is Dieter, and I have no idea why we have been brought here, but it appears to be a re-creation of something wonderful from outside of these cold, cruel confines. Perhaps they are preparing us for the outside world?"

"Hello, Dieter, and I knew your name also. I have seen you in the gymnasium and sometimes around the track and on the field. I know that they have had you here for a very long time and that they have been frustrated by your persistent resistance to their commands. You have become somewhat of a hero and a champion to those of us that need strength to get through each pain-filled day. I am pleased to finally meet you and see our symbol of courage and hope."

"I have seen you also, Hannah, even when they first brought you here. You were a screaming, kicking, defiant teenager with

136

fire and spirit. It made me hope that someday we could meet and share our hopes and dreams with each other and then . . .”

"And then what, Dieter?"

Brunehoff surveyed the room and noted the lamp shade, the flower vase, and the air-conditioning duct—all places where listening devices and microcameras could be and surely were planted. He looked back into the deep blue eyes of a fragile and anxious young Hannah. He understood the reason for their being together now. The wine, the soft linens, all of it. He took her by the hand and led her to the bathroom.

When Hannah started to inquire as to why, he lifted his left index finger perpendicular to his lips and lightly sounded a "sshhhhh" and Hannah became acutely aware that they were continued to being studied. Inside the small room, Brunehoff shut the door and turned the basin faucets on full and then the bath handles also. When the door was closed and Hannah was seated on the edge of the bath, he turned off the light and took her hands into his in the darkness and safety of the room.

"Well, I always believed that someday we could escape this wretched place, and then once free and armed, I would return to burn it to ashes and completely destroy all of the evil that it contains. Get to the outside world and be free of these evil doctors but return to release the captives. I never stopped believing or planning. It is what has sustained me throughout all of these years."

"So you have a plan, a means of escape?" she urgently inquired. "Tell me. Please tell me. I don't believe that I can withstand another day of this torture and pain. Just yesterday, they took my cellmate, and well, she didn't return. Some of the girls saw the delivery van being loaded, and we do not believe that we will ever see Maria again. Maybe she is the lucky one, no longer chained and forced to submit. A new girl, Katrina, just ten years old, was assigned to my cell this morning. She is in an awful state of shock and despair. She sobs constantly and has no idea of what is in store for her . . . and I couldn't tell her. I just couldn't tell her. Now tell me about your plan, please, please tell me."

"Hannah, it will not be easy and the timing must be perfect and you must follow my instructions exactly as I will relay them to you."

"But, but aren't you coming with me, Dieter? This is your plan, and you must lead us."

"No, Hannah, you must do this alone and bring no one with you. I will be released from here within the week and will be sent to college in England. Oxford, of all places. The seat of higher learning and the country of justice. There is no justice here, Hannah, only cruelty and sick, twisted old men that take delight in inflicting pain upon others. You will have to bear two or three more years of this or follow my instructions carefully and get out of here."

"Two or three more years? I don't think that I can tolerate two or three more days! I will follow your plan, Dieter, and I will someday find a way to bring back someone good from somewhere to rid this mountain of its diabolical doctors."

"What is happening? I see nothing and hear only the roar of rushing water," inquired a confused Dr. X.

"It appears as if they have entered the bath, Herr Doctor. Perhaps our young male is more aggressive and anxious than we have thought. Soon he shall mate with her and then we will have our future within the womb of the young female. All is going according to our plans."

Back in the chamber apartment, Brunehoff had relayed the escape plan to Hannah and told her to follow his lead when they left the room and returned to the outer quarters. He instructed her to keep the conversation candid and to make no mention of the escape plan. He then instructed her to undress, quickly shower, and drape herself in the large white towel that he handed her from the shelf. When she had entered the bath he joined her, and they touched as goose bumps tingled her entire being. They embraced finally and kissed and then they washed each other clean, trying to somehow rid themselves of the stench and the thought of the awful prison that had become home.

Even in the darkened quarters they could make out the outline of each other and see the shining white light from within the eyes of each other. Hannah did as she was requested and soon found herself draped only in the soft, clean material of the towel. Emerging from the room, hand in hand they appeared as lovers, and this brought smiles to the faces of the monitors.

They went directly to the table and sat closely together as Dieter poured a glass of wine for each of them. Nibbling on cheese and fresh bread and enjoying the slow, creeping sensation of the wine, they spoke softly with each other, and within an hour or two or three, they had emptied the contents of the decanter and were both feeling the warm effects of the wine. Floating and free, he motioned to the bedroom, and a willing Hannah took his hand and followed him. He was so wonderful and gentle, she thought.

A bump and then a grinding halt brought Brunehoff back to his current reality. The train had arrived in Frankfurt, and he needed to prepare for his audience with the chancellor and the executive committee. All of whom were doubtlessly hopeful that Brunehoff was returning with news of the Cleansers and with an action design to eradicate their poison and plans.

He would go to Canada and find Brown and either reason with him or destroy him. He was unsure. The warrior unsure. The martial arts expert without peace. This was not good and he knew it. He needed his mind to control his body and his emotions. Emotions that, left to run rampant, would surely be his undoing as had been the case with so many great warriors before him. He would regain his composure and then he would visit Canada, not only to find Brown, but to see once again his dear, sweet Francesca. The product and wonder child of him and Hannah. Poor, dear Hannah who had managed to escape to freedom and give birth to Francesca, only to die herself in the hospital delivery room.

Unknown cerebral hemorrhaging causing violent and uncontrollable convulsions, the Austrian doctors would say. Brunehoff knew otherwise; it was the "juice" that she had been injected with, the very same juice that they had forced into him. The poison that continued to eat away at his nervous system and cause him to have early symptoms of twitching and shaking. He could still control it—for now, but this was all the more reason to see his darling before his body refused to function as it should and he could not be the "noble knight" that he had discreetly been for her for so long.

Back on German soil, he felt some level of relief. This was his country on the surface at least, but just a few hundred kilometers to the southeast, a mountain continued to house the true villains of his life. He knew that he must find a way to release the captives held therein, a way that would destroy the terrible lab and torture center forever. A way to free his mama and papa that had been taken from him so very long ago. A fail-safe way to protect the victims and expose the evil doctors to his furor and revenge.

As his awaiting Mercedes sped to Berlin to meet the chancellor and representatives from the legislature, he hatched a plan, one that should accomplish his goals and allow him to escape to some faraway place of peace and quiet with his dear Francesca.

"Please report your findings and needs to the legislative committee," requested the chancellor. "From what you have told me so far, I am sure that we all need to know what you have learned and to then, after discussion, take swift and forceful action. We must not allow for any more virus to be released, and we must forever put to an end the threat that this Phantom brings to the free world."

Brunehoff was not an experienced liar. Instead, unlike most of his NOW associates, he had used his muscle and his iron will to overcome obstacles. When that hadn't been appropriate, he reverted to his carefully calculating brain to find solutions to problems. Either way, Brunehoff always succeeded, and this time he would again. The life of his family and the still-tortured children depended upon it.

"I am not permitted at this time to release all of our findings and particulars to you. It is for reasons of security, and any loss of secrecy could compromise our plans to capture and destroy this group known as the Earth Cleansers. Please understand that, first and foremost.

"Secondly, I have some very distressing news to report to you, news that will be shocking and will make you most unhappy. The summit team has determined that one source of the manufacture and stockpiling of the death virus is within the confines of our own German borders, far away from the cities and nestled in the mountains in what appears to be a quaint alpine village. But of course, it is no such thing. Instead it is the epicenter for all of Europe. We must carefully plan to capture this fortress and all of its residents and the virus which exists therein. Anything but an extremely well-planned and conducted mission will result in failure and will make the Cleansers aware of our knowledge of their European operations. This could spell death to more than the core of the town of Hemer as we have witnessed thus far. Failure could bring doom to our entire country and those all around us. It is for this reason that I request the chancellor to deploy up to five hundred of our most skilled combatants to storm the fortress and rid our nation of this evil threat to world peace and human life. Our nation must survive, and we must purge the villains from their perch.

"Finally, you must manage this assault with quiet and cunning, and you must assign a warrior capable of leading the mission and accomplishing the task."

"What of you, Brunehoff, you are our greatest warrior? Won't you be leading the charge to rid us of this terror? What could be more important than that?" inquired army general Werkowitz.

"I was getting to that general. My mission will be different and even more critical. I am to travel to Canada and find and destroy the chemist that is behind the production and recipe of this unknown and deadly virus. We know his name and his last known whereabouts, but for the past six months he has been unaccounted for. A sabbatical away from work in some idyllic place where he could rest and rejuvenate was the official line. His exit point was Toronto on July 15th of last year, and he flew alone, nonstop, to Amsterdam. Once he landed, he was free and could have gone anywhere. His pension administration files indicate that he will return to fulltime work on January 15th, five days from now!"

"Although Canada is one of the easiest countries to gain unrestricted access to, we are dealing with a most delicate situation here. We can't just send in a SWAT team to take out one of Canada's finest. This is a squeaky-clean and highly decorated scientist who on the surface is a brilliant contributor to disease control and viral containment. The Canadians will assign tight security to him and are ever conscious of what can happen when your top scientists are whisked away and forced to work for the enemy. I'm sure that none of you have forgotten how our own great scientists were captured and brought back to the USA so many years ago and how their knowledge and skills were used to develop bombs that ultimately ended World War II. Canada, for all of its open society and freedoms, has at least the wisdom to carefully guard its most accomplished of scientists. You can be sure that he is being watched by agents now—even though he may be unaware of it. He's too valuable to leave unattended. Once he resurfaces in Canada, he will be under twenty-four-hour protection. Therefore, I must go alone and find this man and destroy him. I may not return to greet you ever again, but you can be assured that the chemist will not create anymore of the deadly virus. This I promise you."

"Ladies and gentlemen, you have heard our emissary speak, words that are both disturbing and shocking. We have to develop an assault plan, and we have to start preparations immediately. Mr. Brunehoff, as always, we thank you for your immense contribution to the fatherland and your dedication to the safety of our world. Kindly provide my adjutant with all of your needs and I will personally ensure that every last requirement is promptly addressed. When shall you be leaving for Canada?"

"In three days and there is much to do. I will fly to New York as Dieter Brunehoff. Once there I will rent a car and drive north to Niagara Falls and return the vehicle. Then I will walk across the bridge into Canada at its busiest entry point, using fake credentials identifying me as a Swiss national. This way there will be no flight lists or paper trail indicating me as a German official entering Canada. The Swiss passport and visa will allow me easy access as a tourist to view Canada's Horseshoe Falls and see an igloo or two. I will be just another European tourist anxious to spend some of our highly valued euros and to tour the Great White

North. The Canadian officials at the busy border should be most accommodating, and once inside the country, I will directly rent another car with Canadian plates and head north to Ottawa, where I will surely find a means to locate and isolate the chemist that I seek. When my mission is complete and the chemist has been terminated, I will ditch the car anywhere in Canada and make my way back to New York via whatever means. Once there I shall be back into my diplomatic role and no one will know that I have ever been to Canada."

"Brilliant as always, Dieter. You are indeed the one man that can pull it all off, as the Canadians say. You know who to see in printing. Make sure they drop everything and attend to your ID needs."

Outside, Brunehoff actually smiled. He had realized that he could play this game also and with considerable skill. He thought about how he had made a joke about Canadians and igloos and how he had convinced all present that the fortress was something other than a human lab. The children would be freed with his parents and all others. The cruel master Dr. X and their team would be incarcerated, placed in solitary confinement, and eventually driven mad by their own diabolical selves. Solitary confinement, a just reward for evil men. The death penalty would be too humane. They deserved no consideration whatsoever. He hoped that they would live for a very long time and suffer each and every day as he and so many others had.

Now there was just the matter of what to do about Brown and plans to get to see his daughter, who was thousands of kilometers away from Ottawa at a very special international school. He would see her first, he reasoned. Brown could wait since he would just be arriving from wherever it was that he had been. Dieter still wasn't sure of how Brown had managed to make three trips to South

Africa in the past six months, continue to meet with the Cleansers, and not raise the suspicion of his own CSIS security agents. Then again, not so many years ago, the Canadian prime minister had found himself in his bedchamber with his wife and an intruder while the on-duty RCMP officer was asleep at his post. If some unknown and unskilled psycho could get to the country's leader so very easy, it was quite plausible that a skilled tactician like Brown could confuse and shake loose from the agents that were assigned to follow him.

Anyway, the few days on Canada's beautiful and rugged west coast would give Brunehoff time to decide the fate of Brown and to formulate his plans to escape it all with his darling daughter. He would contact the Rabbi as required, and he would advise him that he would go to Canada via the USA and be waiting for Brown in Ottawa when he arrived. He would tell him to keep the two Krems and that this mission was best conducted alone by Brunehoff himself. He would cite the security surrounding Brown and ensure that Boris and he knew that the less visible the presence is, the better. If he needed help, he would ask and Krems could promptly be dispatched.

He chuckled again when he thought of how the five-hundred-strong strike force would storm the fortress and, instead of a virus stockpile, find the evil doctors and their awful labs. The chancellor and his team would be surprised that Brunehoff's intelligence had been wrong. Yet at the same time, they would be immensely pleased that they had finally located and captured the bastion of bastards that they had known still existed somewhere within their boundaries. No virus would be found, but the prize would be still worth the effort.

Chapter 28

CONNECTIONS COUNT

He was the true master of reasoning and intellectual insight. The incredible crafty and debonair diplomat. The talk of the town. The man that everyone wanted to have present at their most important social functions. The one they were all excited to tell their friends that *he* was a personal friend of *their* family. Everyone wanted his attention constantly and this caused some level of difficulty for him in his maneuvering and working of his own special brand of magic. Magic not created with smoke and mirrors and distractions but with speech and presence and deep, deep thought.

It was very deep thought that Rabbi Raheim Berhinstein was currently administering to himself, the type of head-wrenching concentration that left one totally exhausted when it finally ended. He needed a solution, and he needed it fast.

When Boris had assigned him Balderous, the Rabbi was surprised. On the one hand, it was a compliment and a vote of confidence. Who better than he to penetrate the security surrounding the president of the Republic of Mexico and a definite kingpin of the club? On the other hand, he knew that Balderous was tough, cunning, without any measure of human compassion, and certainly never left unguarded by his legion of secret service operatives. Yet

Balderous had managed to extract himself from them long enough to attend the Cleansers' South African meetings. How did he do it? the Rabbi wondered. How could he get free long enough to attend unsanctioned meetings, perhaps even lengthy ones, and not raise at least a few eyebrows?

Raheim personally possessed all the necessary connections within Mexico to get fairly close to the president but decided that the takedown couldn't be accomplished by two top-notch Israeli agents and a couple of Krems. Not to bring down the mighty Enrique Balderous. He would have to journey to Mexico himself, he decided, and use his personal network to get close enough to the president to administer a lethal dosage of his deadly powder, released from the holy ring that he bore as a sign of his dedication to Judaism and his people. This was dedication of the finest kind, he told himself, to put himself in the direct path of the adversary, a very worthy opponent and one who held home-court advantage.

He could fly to Mexico City direct from Madrid. Getting there would be no problem. Explaining his mission to the 120-member Knesset should be easy enough. Advising Boris of altered plans would be no problem to justify to even the master of the NOW. But getting close enough to Balderous to ensure the death dose, well, that would be much more difficult. How would he do it?

The phone rang and broke his concentration. "Agent 6 reporting in. All is well on the eastern front. Our team leaves tomorrow. No problems anticipated."

"Good," said the Rabbi as he abruptly ended the call from Karakanni. Now he must get back to determining a means to get to Balderous. There were more calls soon to come, and then he would have to give the daily update to Boris before he could finally get out of Rome and return to Tel Aviv, where he must provide a very effective explanation to a roomful of intelligent Jewish leaders early the next morning.

Back in the land of his people, the Rabbi prepared to meet his peers. They had all agreed to send him as their representative to the summit. It was not because he had coached the great Boris Pretnekof in rugby on the Oxford playing fields. It was because of the 120-member Knesset, Berhinstein alone had lost his entire family to the Phantom's poison.

The Russians were still not to be trusted, it was widely felt, and allowing Berhinstein to go forth to avenge his family losses was something that they could all go along with. It would be a great chance also to learn more of the Russian plans perhaps if the young rabbi was as friendly with the Russian leader as it appeared.

Ensuring that he had been briefed with what he could and couldn't officially say and that he would observe the assembled emissaries and listen to their rhetoric was their job. There was the matter of official policy answers and so on and so forth. The Rabbi recalled all this while laughing aloud once he was alone and outside. They had no idea that it was he that would dictate to them what was and was not to be.

He was not laughing now. He was thinking, still deeply thinking.

"Revered ones, ladies and gentlemen, I return to bring you news of the summit's successful findings and the resultant action plan developed to unmask and capture *all* of the Earth Cleansers members. Many nations provided insightful information during the open discussions, and gradually the group representing twenty-five nations found its way back to one common thread weaved throughout. This thread or link, if you will, proved to be the key in identifying all sixteen of the Phantom members."

"Once identified, the electronic wizardry and the brainpower behind it provided flight itineraries, and we were even able to view three members of the group at a minisummit of their own. In short, we know who they are, where they have been, and for most of them, exactly where they are right now."

"So tell us, we are all itching to know, who are these Earth Cleansers?" demanded Prime Minister Karitsibon.

"Sadly, that is not something that I have the privilege, at this time, to share with even you, my fellow brothers and sisters of Israel. I promise that I will be able to tell all very soon. Meanwhile, all summit participants have taken an oath of secrecy since we fear the possibility of a mole. If there is one, secrecy will be the only way to expose the traitor. If all twenty-five of us were to share with our respective governments what we have learned thus far, we would in all likelihood be exposing ourselves to several other possible traitors and informants. Worse still, we fear that any knowledge of our findings by the Phantom may trigger another virus release, likely a much bigger one with enormous death tolls throughout the earth."

"Then what of the action plan you referred to?" inquired the PM.

"We have to be very, very careful about the handling of this most delicate situation. Sixteen of the summits twenty-five members have been assigned one Cleanser each to monitor and to be ready to seize at a moment's notice. The nine remaining participants, of which I am one, have been assigned administrative and coordination roles. My job will be to coordinate Central and South American member activities, and I am to leave for New York in the morning, en route to Belize. It is from there that I will assemble updates and dispatch information to the agents in the field.

"I can tell you no more at this time, and I sincerely regret having to be silent. I know you all want answers. Please trust me, my esteemed friends, and know that what we are dealing with here is the immediate threat to most of the human race. Please don't pressure me for answers that I cannot give," pleaded Berhinstein.

"Only one question," inquired the battle-scarred "slippery one," who at seventy-five years old remained an influential force in Israeli's powerful military and was still in charge of DIG (the Department of Intelligence Gathering). "Why is it that the nations of the summit are undertaking this plan without the direct aid of our mighty military and our very proficient undercover agents? Answer me that, Raheim," demanded the very-angry tactician.

The Rabbi looked directly to face the general whom he had totally embarrassed at their earlier encounter immediately after the virus had struck their nation. For a brief instant he toyed with the idea of bringing more insults and verbal abuse to the old soldier but quickly reconsidered. It would gain nothing and just further alienate him from what could become a valuable source of aid and intelligence.

"My apologies for not completing my statements, General. They had been reserved for a one-on-one meeting with you directly, but since you have asked the question, I shall respond. Our military and your department will indeed play an important role in the uncloaking and capture of the Phantom members and the destruction of their facilities. Two of your finest DIG agents will join me in Belize once I have established my command post there. They will be extremely valuable in day-to-day surveillance as we prepare to strike quickly and with a vengeance. Once we are ready for the assault at least one hundred of Israel's finest combat troops will be called upon to respond. No other nation of the twenty-five were asked for as many soldiers, a sign of the high respect, which you and others have helped garner for our nation. We must ensure that the assault force is selected now, are at full alert, and are ready to be airborne at a moment's notice. Without our specialty people, this mission would not go as smoothly as hoped. It is for that reason that I convinced President Pretnekof that success would only be guaranteed with the inclusion of Israel's great warriors."

A very pleased and smiling general spoke the two words that were seldom heard coming from his usually abrupt and foul mouth. "Thank you," he replied.

Then the PM excused Berhinstein to prepare for his challenging task with the words, "Yes, thank you, my son. You have represented our people extremely well. May Yahweh be with you as you venture into the jaws of fear and the mouth of evil. Go now and make ready for your journey of hope. All of Israel goes with you in spirit and prayers."

Back in his apartment, the Rabbi did not rest or eat or even take time to relish in the clever way that he had handled the Knesset. There was no time for that. He must formulate his plan to strike Balderous, and he had little time before his report was due to Boris. Belize would provide easy entry into the Yucatán of Mexico, and he would arm himself with an array of passports to deal with any potential problems. His biggest problem remained, however, how to get close, very close to Balderous.

Then it came to him. The memories of so long ago. Balderous was a sporting fan although his favored items were ones that brought pain and death. Bullfighting, big-game hunting in the wild north of Canada, and the brutal, fight-filled games of Canadian ice hockey. Ones he watched with Brown, no doubt. He never participated in the direct action; he just watched, enjoying seeing the great stag fall to the ground, a bloodied hockey player, and the occasional loss of an all-too-cocky and gored bullfighter.

Balderous had been there at that fateful game when Singh had been crippled for life. He had cheered loudly at the no-holds-barred play. Even though everyone else left in distain, he alone had stood to applaud and to seek out young Berhinstein and congratulate him on a thoroughly enjoyable and extremely well-coached victory. The Rabbi was a natural master of maneuvers, and after Oxford, his tactical fame and his by-now-close friend Boris had gifted him with an opportunity to coach at the professional level in the South African league. He did just that for one season, and together with his on-field commander, Boris, they had achieved a never-before-imagined perfect record of 16 and 0 in an extremely competitive league. When play-off time came, both he and Boris abandoned their team and left for Harvard. They cited family demands and the need to obey their fathers as the reason for leaving. In truth, they were both somewhat bored and anxious to advance their plans for victory beyond the playing field, and they wished to elevate their "game" to the world stage.

The Rabbi could use this knowledge of Balderous, use this opportunity and weakness to get close to the Mexican president. The wheels were turning within his scheming mind. There was a way, after all. But it would take some organization and cooperation from others. Yet there was indeed a way. For the first time in what seemed like months, a slow, widening smile spread across the Rabbi's face. He had found the Achilles heel, the weakest point of Balderous—the thirst for bloodletting and the enjoyment of the kill. Now he must put the pieces together and the president would come running to him. Perhaps in Belize and not Mexico, after all. Yes, that was it. Now finally, he could rest for a while before he connected the dots and brought forth the plan to take down the mighty Balderous.

After an hour of shut-eye that felt like a week, a fully refreshed Berhinstein returned to the matter at hand: get Balderous.

He would have to set the stage with great care. His Mexican network informed him of Balderous's schedule for the next thirty days. Enrique would be in the Yucatán in just one week to view the progress with the cleanup of the latest of seemingly nonstop class 4 and 5 hurricanes to hit the peninsula and tourist mecca of Cancún. A gathering place that was almost no more. One where the cabdrivers, bartenders, and entire hospitality industry that had arrived as poor peasants to transform to patron pleasers were being cast back to their outlying pueblos. Not by the dramatic fall of the U.S. dollar or by greater, more fantastic resorts elsewhere, but by the forces of nature that ruled out Cancún as America's favorite playground.

It seemed the perfect opportunity if he could move quickly enough to assemble the pieces of his emerging plan. Balderous would surely come. Belize was a favorite retreat of his and Cancún was practically next door. It was time to bait the trap and to have the mouse come running for the cheese.

The Rabbi decided upon a grudge match, to be played on neutral turf, in Belize. It would be rugby, pitting the Springbok B team against England's B team. Bitter rivals who had clashed many times in recent years. Unlike their famous A-status teams, they still had something to accomplish and improve upon to gain notice and elevation to the top squad. They would play hard, and the Rabbi would ensure it by generously greasing all the palms on both sides of the ball. There would be incentives also for best kick, most-entertaining try, and of course, for the hardest tackle. All these monies would come via an anonymous donor, and all would be very hush-hush. Really big money had a way of keeping things quiet, the Rabbi reasoned, while petty thank-yous only encouraged the recipients to talk. There would be no talking about these rewards; that was for sure. The Aussie referee would be bought and paid for also. He would be instructed to "let the boys play" and "Don't be too quick with your whistle."

Finally, the pièce de résistance, Rabbi B. himself, would be the bench boss for the South Africans. Away from the game for almost fifteen years, he still had the skill to manage a mob of oversized brutes, he felt; and with Boris's say so, the current coach would gladly step aside to see the previously unbeaten mastermind parade his magic. This single factor would be enough to ensure that Balderous attended. Balderous, who had long since lost track of the Rabbi and would be thrilled to see the maestro out of retirement and at the helm. Balderous would even be invited by the Belize government to line out the ceremonial first ball. Best of all for Enrique, he could see some good old blood and carnage, human blood, and perhaps even a broken leg or two. Such were the wicked wishes of the great Balderous.

If all went well, Balderous would want to greet the magician before the game. When all did go well on the field of play, Balderous would surely insist that the Rabbi would be his special guest for dinner that very evening. During the meal or over after-dinner drinks, Raheim would find a way to empty his ring's contents into the glass of Balderous. Then an hour or so after they had parted company, the president would fall violently ill and start to convulse; and then within minutes, he would be dead. The Rabbi would have already fled by road to Mexico under one of his many aliases. The Mexican government would be in complete disarray as they searched the airport and international airlines' passenger lists for the Rabbi. Raheim would be safely on his way back to New York via Miami. Then it would be Madrid and home to Israel and a hero's welcome. Once on Jewish soil, he knew that no Mexican government could extradite him or even be permitted to question as to how he had left Belize. *Just another trick from the master magician to an unsuspecting and completely dumbfounded audience,* he mused.

He would contact Boris to confirm the game plan, and then Boris and Burgess could attend to the official details with the respective national governments regarding the match. Cooperation should be without hesitation. All was shaping up well and the Rabbi was most pleased with his plan.

Chapter 29

Easy Pickin'

The Rabbi had reported in, and the president was back safely inside his home country's secure Moscow perimeter. Things had gone exceedingly well overall at the summit and for Boris in particular. He has shown his brilliance and superior organizational skills and had allowed for each member to voice their opinion. Some opinions that he gladly received and others that he immediately rejected—in silence. Such were the methods of a leader who knew the value of every participant, both large and small.

While preparing himself to address the Politburo, he kept returning to the matter of Cloiters and how his soon-to-be widowed sister and her three young children would react to the news of her husband and their father's demise. It should be clean and swift and avoid any additional pain and anguish to the family, he reasoned. An accident perhaps, one that was freak and unavoidable and one that would make Andrek appear the hero and not a slaughtered villain. This he would gladly ensure for his sister, his only sister that meant so much to him. That had cared for him when they had been left by their father, so very long ago in a strange country with strange people and a color clash such as Boris could not have imagined in his most disturbing of dreams.

Thinking back to all his years in South Africa, Boris reviewed the good and the bad memories that he still held close to him. There was the wonderful opportunity to attend a high-quality private school, but it was full of racist asses who felt that blacks were less than slave material and that they should be ruled and restrained like domesticated beasts.

Then there were his real friends, the black servants and street vendors who called him Sir Boris and answered his every wish. It had not always been that way. At first, he was considered just like all of the other "whities," a wealthy jerk and a racist who had little or no regard for the black indigenous people. That all changed one day when Boris happened upon two whites who were kicking a prone black man over and over again until he moved no more. A fuming Boris, much younger than the two whities, succeeded in thwarting an obvious death by boots but was to suffer a great bashing and bruising for daring to challenge these landholders and their right to discipline their servants.

A white youth standing up against other older whites to protect a helpless black man? The word spread fast, and soon Boris found that he went from being ignored to chants of "Sir Boris" throughout the black majority of all Johannesburg and the surrounding townships. These blacks would become his allies and later his eyes and ears, and he would forge friendships that would not be broken.

His iron will made him strong, and the martial arts and magnificent moves that he learned from his poor black brothers prepared him well for the rematch that was sure to come.

One day about three years after his terrible beating by the two whities, Boris encountered them again. This time they were at a local market and were toying with a pretty young servant girl, and he knew what was upon their minds.

"Leave her alone," he had pronounced to the two merciless men, but they just sneered and returned to their play.

"I said, leave her alone, assholes."

The *asshole* part really struck a nerve; and the two rich, racist, elitist pigs left the young woman and approached Boris.

"Aren't you the little nigger lover that we beat the livin' shit out of a few years ago, lad?" the older of the two inquired.

Not waiting for an answer, they charged Boris, intent upon teaching him another lesson. But Boris was prepared. He thrust a straight arm to the face of the larger man and then a knee to the groin of the second. As they lay on the cement floor of the market, he cursed them in the local dialect and told them to get up and get out and never ever to trouble this girl again. They saw the flame in his eyes, his rage and his fury and his at-the-ready stance as he stood over them. They wisely determined that the next fisticuffs would have to wait until they came back with additional like-minded landholders to squelch this all-too-fierce foreigner. Yes, they would return with rich and nasty friends who had grown accustomed to terrorizing the local population as a form of sick entertainment. Now they would have a new prey to stalk.

Once on their feet and at a safe distance, the older one had called back to Boris, "You will get what is coming to you, you little licorice lover. You can be sure of that!"

Boris made a quick move toward them, and they scurried to their pickup truck and sped away. The girl, Helena, was very thankful and had never met such a man before. A white man who stood up to other whities for the protection of a black girl. Truly this was a special young man who had lightning-fast reflexes and an outrage that her people had longed for. Perhaps now things were starting to change and this cruel system of segregation and wealth separation would finally come to an end. This young man brought her hope that even the impossible could come true.

"Let me know if they ever trouble you again," he instructed her. "Swine like that have no place in a civilized society. It makes me ashamed of my color and my family's position and power."

"You have no need for shame. You are my hero," softly spoke the round-faced young woman with teeth so white that they lit her dark face. "You alone have saved me from those bad boys that have tortured my older sisters and made them submit to distasteful desires. No one has ever come forth to protect us but you. I have heard your name in the streets and hoped that someday I would meet you. You are the one they call Mahuloo or 'chosen one.' I am so very honored to meet you, and I thank you again for saving me from the cruelty of those bad boys."

Looking back at that helpless young girl, Boris recalled exactly what he had said and precisely what happened next.

"It is I who should thank you, miss. For you have allowed me to release my inner rage that I have kept locked deep within and to direct it toward the evil that has tormented you and your people for so very long."

"Not only my people but *your* people also," spoke a gleaming Helena as she motioned to a quickly gathering mass of black bodies and white teeth. "They have never imagined that such a man would come to exist in their lifetimes. Surely you are the promised one of our ancestors. The appointed one, come to set our people free."

Boris recalled also how at first that he was totally embarrassed by the girl's flowery talk. Then somehow with his continued exploits, it had grown on him until he succumbed to the realization that he was indeed the God-sent one, come to incarcerate the villains and bring his people home.

He fondly remembered how he and Helena had spent that spring and summer together. Frolicking like carefree children in the fields of cotton that his family still owned. How she had . . .

Footsteps nearby brought Boris back from his youth and to the reality of the moment. It was time to address the Politburo, and he would be prepared as always. He checked his watch. One minute before the doors opened and the room flooded with followers and foes alike. Unknown to those that plotted against him, he knew about it, every last detail; and he would use their aspirations and desire to destroy then forever. He would clean house, or as the Phantom had said, "cleanse it."

"Comrades, I have great news to share that will bring smiles to all of your faces. We have located and isolated the Earth Cleansers and have them within our sights. We have a plan to capture them all, but there are still a few items to be finished before we set them running and into our waiting arms. These urgent matters I shall immediately attend to at the end of this announcement.

"All of you shall be able to witness their capture, not on some foreign television broadcast, but live and in person. How, you ask? Well, we now know that the entire Cleanser club will meet early next week in Kazakhstan under the guise of the Energy Conference. Markov and his aides will be representing Russia, and Markov is also to act as conference chairman. He has left already to make all of the necessary preparations. When the time is just right, I will signal him to contact their leader and indicate that the NOW is on to them and, even as they speak, are closing in, with the airport and two major land arteries already secured. He will cite a mole, one who is strangely absent from the assembly. He will convince him that their only guaranteed escape will be by back roads initially and then via a Red Cross convoy through Afghanistan and into Turkey. He will insist that they must move without a moment's delay.

"When Markov is questioned as to his loyalties, he will cite his thirst for power and knowledge that he will never achieve it while I rule Russia. He will tell their leader that the escape of the entire Phantom membership will be at the cost of my presidency since I was the one that developed the foiled plan to catch them. He will promise to support their principles and plans. Membership for power. This, so I am told, is the methodology of men and women, such as these. Markov, being the pompous ass that he is, should have little difficulty convincing an exposed and by now frantic leader of his desire to dethrone me and to rule Russia.

"Meanwhile, we have the agreement of the summit members from China and USA and all of the others with regard to the capture of the entire bunch of brazen bastards. Russia will be the lead, and I have been asked to be commander general—another step forward for our great nation."

"And before you ask," continued Pretnekof the Great, "I will explain to you what will happen according to the real plans and not the fake ones of Markov. The Red Cross trucks carrying the Cleansers will travel through the night, but not towards Turkey, rather, directly to our own Russian border town of Soci. It is there that we will deliver the Cleansers to you as the sun rises. All of them together and helpless and their tyranny clearly obvious to the press and the world in the documents and video, which I shall release.

"If we are to make this work, I shall need 100 percent cooperation and sworn secrecy from each and every one of you. You will all leave Moscow in the morning by military transport trucks, posing as a food-supply caravan, three trucks in a group, so approximately nine groups, assuming you all want to be there for the grand capture and spotlight of all of the world. Each group will depart twenty minutes after the other so as to not draw attention or suspicion within our own boarders. You will be assigned your vehicle number in the morning when we reconvene here at 0800. Unfortunately, your ride shall be long and not of the comfort level that you have grown accustomed to, but crews are making alterations right now to make your moving quarters more habitable. I know that the reward will be well worth the journey. Go now and prepare for your departure. Russia shall rule!"

"Russia shall rule! Russia shall rule," they exclaimed as they rose to witness the exit of their president, a president who had once again shown his cunning and flair for the dramatic.

Back in his villa, Boris was very pleased with himself, as always. He had totally fed a pack of lies to the hungry hounds, and they had gobbled them up without taking time to digest. *Such was the nature of dogs*, thought Boris, and smiled.

The trip to Soci would be to get the Politburo out of the way while he continued with his real plans. First, he would inform Markov that Langois was the Cleanser leader. Of course, he would apprise Langois of the decoy and ask him to show his loyalty to the commander, who would soon offer up France to him. Langois would meet Markov as Markov proposed, but he would be alone as would be Markov. A single shot to the temple was all that would be needed, and Langois would surely deliver it for his commander and the hope of his own chance to rule. The meeting place that Boris suggested would be secure, and Langois could ditch the gun and return to his hotel. The next day, the Energy Conference would be shocked at the cold-blooded murder of the meeting's chairman but would continue anyway.

Next he would contact first Burgess and then Gilberger and have him release to the American president news he had just received from their ally and friend, Prime Minister Anthony Burgess. Gilberger would inform Rush that there was a convoy in Russia headed for the Afghani border via Iran and that three of the trucks were carrying nuclear components, components capable of aiding the Taliban in their desire to launch a nuclear device from within Pakistan aimed directly at Israel. Boris would have Gilberger argue that only the USA had the power to fly undetected, take out the appropriate trucks using their stolen Chinese missiles fitted with American precision guided systems, and escape away to friendly skies. The convoy would be hit in a very out-of-the-way place, and the Americans would be able to blame it upon the Chinese. Yung would be outraged and Russia poised to react, but when Boris informed the remaining members that Markov had failed to contact the Cleanser's leader and that this attack was a nonrelated incident, they would be less hostile and trigger-happy. They would, in fact, be most embarrassed at the failure of Markov. It would be then that Boris would inform them of the lucky situation that they now found themselves in. The failure of Markov would never be uncovered. The world would be questioning China and fearing a Russian retaliation. Best of all, by some apparent strange fluke, the three destroyed trucks would all contain the dead bodies of seats 57 through 98—the very seats that were occupied by the foes that had united against the rule of Boris.

No Markov. No Cleansers alerted. No opposition on the home front. A world sympathetic to Russia's losses. America and China left to fight it out in the press. Yung embarrassed and having to answer to the NOW. Gilberger shrugging his shoulders in disbelief at the faulty information of Burgess and the ever-conciliatory Burgess expressing regret to America and condolences to Russia. The perfect plan. Now he must return only to the takedown of Cloiters, and that should be the easiest picking of all.

Chapter 30

THE PLAYERS

The stage had been set. All the actors had their roles. The rehearsals were complete. Only the very serious and power hungry were still standing as leaders and club members. All this while the peoples of the earth grieved and wondered at what would befall them next. The general public's knowledge of the evildoers was limited to the unknown Phantom. They had no notion that their very leaders could also be villains and distasteful, corrupted officials.

On the one side were aligned the Earth Cleansers, with their well-thought-out agenda and preparation and their mass network of business and influence. There was Balderous, its leader and the only politician in the group. He ruled the diverse alliance with an iron fist and swiftly dealt death to anyone that opposed him. Ambewa was the most recent proof of Enrique's intolerance and bloodlust. Oppose or even irritate Balderous and most likely you would be dead. Cloiters had been spared by an enraged Enrique only by the quick response and distractions of Brown.

Balderous came across to the public and the press as a warm and compassionate president who cared for his people and offered them understanding and land, in exchange for love and worship.

The billions that Pemex, the Mexican nationalized oil company, brought to the country were largely appropriated for the projects of the president, projects aimed at tightening his control of the people and suppressing any would-be opposition. He would easily be reelected to a second term if not for the plans of his secret club. Widespread death and destruction during phase 2, which was fast approaching, would send the governments of the world into a tailspin. It was likely that elections would be suspended everywhere and martial law declared by most of the countries destined to inhale the odorous contents of the barrels of destruction.

In all, approximately 30 percent of the earth's population would be "cleansed" during phase 2; and although he would enjoy the massacre of the masses, Balderous was not pleased that there would be less Mexicans and less people almost everywhere to bow down to his every whim. He would ensure that the other Cleansers would fall in line with his grandiose plans or that they would just fall permanently. He was a very evil and self-adoring man who had little time for the concerns of anything that didn't directly benefit Enrique.

Then there was Brown, the chemist, the virus mastermind, the one cleanser who seemed to have a soft spot for human life. As a Canadian, he originally had had little concern about the exploding world population. He lived very comfortably in the second-largest geographic nation on earth. With a population of only thirty-five million and a slow birth rate attributed mostly to a society where both Mom and Dad went to work and had scarce time for excess baby making in their pursuit of suburban happiness. In Canada, most couples would have one or two children that they could adequately care for and provide opportunities to. Their government would leave the doors wide-open to immigration to fill the necessary jobs required to support the country's large middle class. Canada was an oddity as much as was its representative, Brown.

It is unlikely that Brown would even be associated with this lot of God-acting bastards if not for the convincing debates that occurred at Oxford and Cambridge. Then the murder of his dear Narissa by Jamieson and other thugs acting on behalf of the opposing club that was led by Pretnekof and the others sealed the deal for Brown. That was, indeed, the turning point for Brown; and he vowed revenge upon the entire group of wealthy and apparently untouchable monsters that had taken away the love of his life forever. Gradually, he had been won over by the statistics, statistics that never lied. To the numbers that showed that by the year 2030 without some great war or huge natural calamity or human intervention, the earth would be unable to produce the foodstuffs and supplies necessary to feed and care for its overflowing population. A peaceful, immediate, painless death versus starvation, disease, and conflict everywhere. His virus was the most compassionate solution to the fastly approaching problem, and he was now convinced that it was not only a reasonable solution but also that it was becoming the only apparent option.

He was not cold-hearted or power hungry like the rest, just practical and hopeful of a new and better world. One in which the ruling ruthless would be removed and good government could share the resources of this beautiful but currently overcrowded planet. He knew, however, that the new world should not be led by the likes of the cold-hearted and cruel Balderous; and the last drinking match of mescal with Enrique was meant to make Balderous aware that he would not proceed with all his personal agenda without challenge.

The defiant Canuck to the end, this was Willie Brown: athletic, loving, and a brilliant mathematician and chemist, who held the future of the world in his formula. At times this pleased him greatly, while other days he was deeply troubled by his actions and the club's plans. Brown remained uncertain but, for the present at least, committed to phase 2; and then he would see how the new earth unfolded before he would mix any more of his death drug to be administered to the unsuspecting general population.

Next came Anhebo, the great, beautiful Brazilian princess and larger-than-life warrior who remained a powerful physical force with a network of businesses that stretched around the world. She was committed to a less-populated world and one in which the male of the race didn't make most of the important decisions. She had seen the poverty and overcrowding in her own country as a young girl and had wondered and wished for an answer. The debates and gradual convincing that went on in England during college days seemed very much like the solution that she was seeking. Yet it was not until Brown had developed the virus and she had witnessed the controlled demonstration with the lab mice in their carefully sealed enclosed room of plants and insects that were swiftly and painlessly annihilated that she had become a true believer. The dastardly deeds could indeed be conducted in a manner that brought little suffering and much hope.

Anhebo reserved her desire for suffering for Burgess and Langois and others like them. Arrogant male chauvinists who felt that women were put on the earth to serve man and not to be mothers of cared-for children or equals in the workplace. She recalled with delight the beating she had delivered to Burgess so very along ago and knew that that fury still lived within her being. She was in for the long run. There was no turning back. But after phase 2, things would surely be different and they would start by her crushing the great Enrique, whom she hated to the core. They could agree upon the numbers and the need for a "pruning" and even where it needed to take place, but she would never be like Balderous; and at the first opportunity, she planned to crush him—with her bare hands. After that she would rule and bring forth great women from throughout the world to work with her. This would not be at the expense of good men like Willie Brown and selected others but would include them also, even if they were a minority. Such were the inner thoughts of the mighty Anhebo, who would reforest the lands that her rich father had denuded for cattle and greed, and would be an inspiration to all who survived the approaching holocaust.

Deep inside, Anhebo knew that the only things that stood in her way were her intolerance and vicious temper that flared at the drop of a pin. She knew that she must somehow control this demon within and almost daily attended Mass to pray to her god to give her strength to overcome her uncontrollable temper, a temper that remained the one flaw that could foil her plans for a better world led by the females of the human race. Not the male assholes who had made such a mess of everything to date.

Also, there was Singh, who hailed from the second most-populated nation on earth, India, which already had one billion people and was rife with disease and poverty. It, like China, had enjoyed great economic growth in the early years of the twenty-first century, but now the economy had started to slow and the population continued to increase. There was no need to convince Narinder Singh of the need for population control; he witnessed it firsthand each and every day: the crowding in the streets, the pollution, the lack of family planning, and the old ways of the old people. This was his country, but he did not love it or care for it. He longed for a new world where there was food for all and clean air to breathe and tolerance for peoples of diverse origins. He also was not convinced that the cleansers had all the answers, but he saw no other possible solutions.

Mostly, like Brown and Anhebo, he was driven by the desire for revenge. It was not Boris or Burgess that he wanted but Yung and Karakanni that had disfigured him for life and forced him to resort to daily morphine fixes to overcome or at least lessen the pain that still persisted. He was the tactician, the brain that could implement such a feat as phase 2. He knew that he was very important to the club. Without his tactical awareness and strategic planning and concern for every last detail, he knew that the Cleansers would be without the ability to realize their ambitious plans. Without him they would fail, he truly believed.

Next came Antonio Garcia, the Chilean billionaire whose worldwide laundry empire was the cooking pot and distribution centers for the Bh297 virus. He was a proud and arrogant egotist that favored only the rich and had little need of the poor other than to carry out the menial tasks of his laundries that now approached nearly one thousand facilities worldwide. He had been convinced many years ago that Mother Earth was overrun with vermin of all colors and race and that there was a great need to severely curtail their numbers. A 30 percent pruning would mean a great reduction to his laundry empire, but he didn't care. He had more money than he could ever spend and would probably enjoy then for the rest of his life in Patagonia or some other sparsely populated place where he could live out his years in splendor. He would leave the ruling of his great nation of Chile to others, subservient businessmen and politicians that he firmly controlled. He had no need to appear larger than life on the world stage. Others in the group could be afforded that opportunity.

But it wouldn't be Balderous, maybe Brown or Anhebo, both of whom he had come to tolerate, but certainly not Balderous—the one who had learned of his father's background and had used this against him to gain control and power over him. He had a plan for post-phase 2, and it called for the elimination of Enrique Balderous—the one man alive that could manipulate him, bilk him of millions, and still treat him with disgust and make him murder when and as required. The day of reckoning would come, and he would be the one to take down the great Enrique, and it would be ever so sweet. This he promised himself. There would be no Balderous to rule in post-phase 2. He had developed a plan and one that he would share with no one. Indeed, no one would know of it, not now, not ever. They would merely see the crushed body of the dead Balderous, and then Garcia would have his peace.

In many ways, Pedro Varez was a different manner of man altogether. He excelled in languages and acted as a secret agent for not only his home, Cuba, but also for the USA, which he had infiltrated to the point that he was one of its most trusted spies. He constantly cursed the Castro legacy and their families within the confines of the USA's CIA when it was to his advantage to do so.

Back in Cuba, supposedly spying for the Americans, he delivered up to the now-near-dead Uncle Fidel and his rising star brother all the intelligence he was able to accrue while playing the part of the American spy. The Cubans gobbled it up and used it to develop surveillance techniques to monitor their enemy and giant to the north of their island nation. The leadership detested the powerful Americans and at the same time laughed at their naïveté and stupidity. When Castro had wanted to rid his prisons of the burgeoning buildup of thieves and crooks and political adversaries, he opened wide the gates. He then provided an armada of vessels to take the flotilla of undesirables to the open and waiting arms of a friendly and welcoming President Jimmy Carter.

That had been many years ago, and today, Miami was more Cuban than it was American. A stopover at the international airport was enough to inform most travelers of how this southern beachfront had changed, for almost all announcements were in Spanish and very few broadcasts used English at all. Little Havana? No, this was Big Havana, and Miami had come to be run by the sewer rats that Castro had so wisely flushed from his holding tanks. Rats that would change the face and inner workings of the city forever.

Much of this was of little or no concern to Varez. He was tired of working for two governments; both of whom did not offer him the pay or respect that he felt he deserved. With the Cleansers, he had more power and access to more wealth even if he had to endure the ridicule of Balderous. Even that could change in time. After phase 2 and when they all assembled in Cuba to witness the royal treatment and extravagant food and entertainment that he would convince the Castro clan to present to the "new leaders," he would gain prominence. There would be no more answering to America the Great; there would only be America the Late. For indeed a disproportionate number of the barrels of death were to be released into all the urban centers of the United States. This would bring the nation to their knees and would crush Washington and all the politicians assembled there. Left without functioning cities or power supplies or transportation means, the remaining population would flock to smaller centers in hope of food and work. Chaos would break out everywhere and America would be without government or authority or rule. It would be then that the mostly untouched of the world—Mexico, Cuba, Canada and, others—would come forth with humanitarian aid and assistance. Meanwhile, Varez would get what he deserved and longed for—wealth, which brought with it increased power and respect. He would await his fortune, which he knew would be coming, and then he would answer to no one but Pedro Perfecto—the Cuban farm boy who had risen to rule his island and those others within the Caribbean archipelago. It was enough for him, and he would enjoy it and all its benefits to the fullest.

Finally there was Cloiters—the last of the cleanser cabinet. The brother-in-law of the Russian president, Boris Pretnekof. He was an extremely wealthy landowner from South Africa who was of Belgium extraction, a landowner who lived in opulence while planning ways to rid the earth of the undesirables and people of color that he openly detested. It was he that had found and developed the secret enclave deep within his adopted country and far away from the press and national government. He was cruel and heartless, and in spite of visits and warnings from Boris, he continued to raise his children as racists and bigots, believing that theirs was a superior race and that all others should be subservient.

He had never been popular within the cabinet, which had only him and Willie Brown as white members. But he had not shown his "true color" during college days and had instead exerted his considerable oratory skill and interest in the cleansing talk to secure a place of early prominence within the group. By the time the club put the racist telltale signs together, Cloiters had already become firmly entrenched as one of the leaders. With the safe haven that he had built up complete with escape routes and hidden approaches and outfitted with all the latest technology and comforts befitting royalty and heads of state, there remained a place for Andrek Cloiters. To be sure, he was not popular even with Brown, and it was inevitable that sooner or later he would be removed permanently. Balderous had been tempted to do so at the last drinking party but had been thwarted by Brown. He would get his just reward after phase 2 was complete, and it could be at the hands of almost any one of the cleansers—unless Boris eliminated him first as he planned. For sure, the days of Cloiters were numbered, but he was too aloof and self-centered to see it coming.

Opposing and searching for the Phantom were the members of NOW, the powerful princes that controlled most of the Northern Hemisphere and had their roots deep into the soil of all nations worthy of exploitation or filled with oil and precious metals—the commodities of commerce and control. They were a charming but ruthless lot, consumed by their desire for increased power. They were very displeased that the brazen Phantom had chosen each of their nations to make its inaugural statement on Christmas Day. How dare they tinker with the Newly Ordered World and its powerful leaders. This despicable lot would be found now that their identities were known, and a plan had been hatched to destroy them all.

First and foremost there was the great Russian president, Boris Pretnekof. Brilliant and firmly in control, he garnered more respect from the members of NOW than Balderous did as the leader of the Cleansers. He was tough and could be ruthless but didn't take life lightly and usually found ways to solve problems with his mind and not his emotions. He was careful and calculating and had seen it all, the proverbial "been there, done that" character that had learned from every move by all who crossed his path.

During his youth in South Africa and his experiences with the wealthy white farmers who mistreated their black servants, he found himself aligned with the poor blacks and turned away from the white landowners. Over time and through experiences, he came to believe that he was very special indeed and that he had been gifted with God-like qualities that were needed to make the world a fair and equitable place—for those that controlled it.

By the time that he arrived at Oxford, he was already dealing in drugs while hostage taking and blackmail were also part of his repertoire. In England, he met other like-minded individuals from many different countries, and he forged friendships and alliances that were all part of his master plan to return to Russia and one day claim the seat of power that had eluded his father and sent him and his family into exile.

His willpower and determination were rivaled only by his physical prowess and mental alertness. It had been said that if you left Boris alone long enough with *any* problem, he would find a way to solve it; and if you were idiotic enough to challenge him to a fight, you would be up against a pit bull that never quit and never let go. Not until his opponent was clearly dispatched or torn to shreds. The whities in Johannesburg, the players on the rugby field, and the sinister characters that made up his Russian mafia knew this only too well.

He was Boris the Great; and after Harvard law school, he had returned to his native Russia, to expand his criminal powerbase. He became elected to the governing party and carefully and skillfully, using all manner and means, climbed and clawed his way to the presidency that he so long had thirsted for. He had made Russia a world power again and turned the economy around by enticing all comrades to contribute to and work for a stronger Mother Russia. His enlightened thinking and creative economic principles together with allegiances with Western powers had vaulted him to world prominence. Television sets throughout the globe were forever reporting on the great deeds and marvelous character of the little man who had challenged the unfair rulers of South Africa. He had superbly educated himself and had returned to his beloved Russia to lead his people and to make level a playing field for all the peoples of the world—peoples that would be led by the rising Russia and its all-star president.

Never before had a Russian captivated the world audience as this Boris Pretnekof had. Even that was not enough for this man who felt that he alone had or could extract all the answers. On the surface, he was the darling of the new world; with great oratory and kisses to babies and smiles to schoolchildren, he endeared himself to the world. Beneath it all were a paid-off press and extortion and even elimination when required. Nothing would, or seemingly could, stand in the way of the great Russian mastermind.

He had in a few short hours developed the plan to take down the Phantom and at the same time eliminate those that dare oppose him in his native Russia. All that remained for the time being was to put an abrupt end to Cloiters and to ensure that each NOW member attended to their assigned cleanser. Then he would rise even higher and become even more powerful, uniting the world as never before and having men and women of all nations look to him alone as the supreme leader and one to be followed. Then he would ascend to his throne and dispatch logic and rule of order to the world. He would enact laws that were binding and that provided for food for the hungry and medicine for the sick. Deep inside, he knew already that the cleansers made a valid point about the runaway population and the need to curb its growth. For this reason alone, he desired the formula and the virus so that when the time was right, he could discriminately unleash its deadly mix to the overpopulated regions of the earth. This secret was his alone, and he never shared it with even his closest friend and fellow mafioso, Rabbi Raheim.

The Rabbi was the most charismatic of the lot, even outdistancing the great Boris. He had an exceptional mind and was gifted with talents of speech and showmanship and was considered by many to soon find his way to the top of the Israeli government. He knew how to stay close to Pretnekof without ever falling into his disfavor and he used his position of religious leader to learn

175

secrets that would not be easily attained by others with even more visible power. He was cunning and always one step ahead of any adversary, be it during open debates, on the playing field, or at the chess table. His mind was open to all sorts of influences and opinions that he would carefully sift through in his search for more power and more control.

He had developed a very clever plan to get close enough to Balderous to deal the deathblow and had moved quickly to put the pieces together. His mind raced with thought and precision planning. It was said that he could concurrently attend to many diverse matters while never losing track of any of them. This he proved over and over again in all his dealings with all his friends and adversaries alike. Playing chess against the five top players in his nation all at once and soundly trouncing them all had lit up the airwaves and morning papers. But this was not the game that the Rabbi wished to play but rather one that he used to keep his mind sharp and to build his fame within his nation.

For the Rabbi, all was proceeding as planned until the Phantom struck on Christmas Day and dealt death to all his dear family. This had given him even greater resolve and made him even more attentive, for he knew that rage and uncontrollable anger were for the weak and not the truly strong. He would avenge the loss of his loved ones and he would do it by taking down the leader of the sinister foe that had dealt death to him and his people. He was ready, and soon he would leave for Belize to carry out his carefully constructed plan.

The game was set, and he would don his coaching suit and put aside his cleric cloak for the opportunity to get Balderous. His ego was at stake also, and he would ensure that his Springboks would use every tactic in his playbook to excite and exhilarate the fans. He was a coach, with a remarkable record, after all; and he didn't want to resume match play and have even a slight blemish added to his perfect record of wins and no losses. Men like him were few, and all of them sported not only the finest of clothes but also the largest measure of self-love. They basked in the limelight and praise that successes brought along with the rich rewards that they created. This would not be just any game. It would be his stage to parade his masterful strategy and make known to all that even with many, many years away from the game, he was still the best of the best and the master of deception.

Li Wi Yung was not a happy man, not now, not ever. Only one thing could bring ultimate delight to his life, and that would be total and unchallenged leadership of the NOW and ultimately control of the planet Earth. He knew that this would take time but that his plan to kill Garcia and point the finger at the Russians would be most helpful. He knew that his great network of spies and infiltrators would move quickly once Garcia was down and that he could round up the entire Phantom team before Boris would have a chance to make his next move. Then he would be master of all, and he would wield his own brand of cruel punishment to all those that opposed him or had even slighted him in the past. The Rabbi would be the next to go after Pretnekof and then that irritating asshole Karakanni, whose tongue was even larger than his hulking frame. The rest, he felt, were weak or controllable; and he would use them to further his ambitions and ultimate quest for total control.

The oldest of lot at forty-seven years, he was a mean, cruel son of a bitch who had suffered torturous treatment as a youth. His leathery hands and scarred torso attested to that. He had stolen and cheated and killed to get the power and foreign currency he needed to escape his masters and exact his revenge and eventually make his way to the west. Oxford and then America had been the perfect places for this physically powerful and totally ruthless devil of a man to advance his ambitions. At first, he had been refused entry to the prestigious Oxford because of his lack of adequate educational attainment. He changed his name, took the chancellor's daughter hostage during her tour of China, and threatened to throw her from the Great Wall unless Oxford immediately approved entry of fifty Chinese students. Then doors had opened in a hurry.

As for emigration from China, this had also been easily arranged by the powerful and cunning Yung. He had insiders within the chairman's walls—loyal infiltrators who feared for their children's lives. Yung had orchestrated the drunken party and had ensured that the required entrances were open and unattended. Then his cutthroat *shadows* swiftly let blood until all guards were dead.

The next morning, the then chairman returned home a trade mission to Vietnam to find a crowd gathered at his entrance gates. Inside, all his palace guards were slaughtered, his wife was missing, and his only son was hanging from a noose in the dining room. Attached to the lifeless body was a note, which read, "I will always be able to get to you my dear chairman and to all of those that surround you. Of that you can be certain. You must immediately free my people held captive within your confines and allow safe passage to all of them as students to the western world. Then you must deliver 100 million yuan and 10 million American dollars to my northern encampment in Harbin. Mark the cargo boxes as educational material courtesy of the United States of America and fly them here today. Send one panel truck with one unarmed driver to quietly leave the boxes outside my residence at precisely midnight. Tie green ribbons on the boxes containing used dollars of various denominations from 10 to one thousand. Hurry! If all is completed as ordered, you will have your precious Lei Lin again." It was signed *Choi Lu Chen.*

A shocked and shaken chairman hurriedly complied and quickly released over 360 political prisoners, ordered passports and papers, and set the "students" free on jet planes to receptive England, France, the United States, and Australia. Then he delivered a king's ransom to the gate of the leader of the dissident, Western-leaning faction of China's desire for freedom.

When Lei Lin had been released to safety missing only the little finger of her right hand, the chairman had angrily and without haste amassed his fiercest fighters. He had stormed the bastion of the bewildered and unsuspecting Lu, still found counting the mysterious money that had been delivered during the dark of night to his front gate. The chairman's forces had killed the modern thinker and voice of freedom and publicly displayed his head on a stick in the city square for all to see.

The chairman mourned his losses, licked his wounds, and left the students to the countries to where they had fled. He felt confident that the beheading of their leader was enough to quiet them forever. They would never dare to return to China.

During the entire ordeal, the fearless and brazen Yung had managed to bribe his way into incarceration within the dissident's prison. Money was no object, and he had already been informed that the green-ribboned boxes had been safely fetched within seconds of the delivery. Imprisonment brought him a passport and papers of the cellmate that he had disposed of and sent to the furnace to burn. Cruel, careful, and complete—this was the trademark of Yung, and he would continue with his evil ways until the time came to grasp the ultimate control that he craved.

Masatsu Karakanni was a power-hungry brute of a man who, like Pretnekof and so many others in both camps, felt that he had been born to rule. Like Boris he also believed that he was from a special lineage and that royal or godly blood flowed through his veins.

He hated having to answer to anyone, especially his idiot prime minister and the ignoramus Yung. Boris and the Rabbi and the others he could tolerate, until such time as he could seize control. Then his own brand of justice would be swift and without any jagged edges, like that of a master sushi chef who wielded sharp blades with flare and perfection. Rough cuts and mercy were for uncultured barbarians and fools like Yung and the Yankee twits that occupied Washington and the White House. This was not the culture or ways of his dear imperial Japan, the nation that he alone would bring to rise from the ashes of the war of so long ago and he alone would restore to its former and even greater prominence.

His now-devised plan to eliminate Singh was nothing short of brilliant, he felt. Get the Indians angered and outraged by smearing the industrialist Singh with carefully placed pictures in all the leading papers and video clips catching him in compromising positions. That should be able to be accomplished with a paltry million or two. When Singh was embarrassed, disgraced, and exposed, he would be vulnerable and easily reached and brought down. He would be ridiculed and mocked in his own country, and the deep bruises and gashes left on the face of his mistress would ensure that Singh would be jailed for a few days at least.

Inside police HQ and in the lockup cell for sexual offenders and common criminals; another million or two or even less would ensure that the Singher had voiced his last note. After seeing the pictures and news clips and learning what had happened inside the holding cell, the Phantom members would have no link to connect Singh's beating death as a strike against their club. He had just done the wrong thing and had got caught doing it. *No problem at all*, thought Karakanni. With sixteen million or more still to spend, he could arrange for a large explosion at a pharmaceutical factory and claim to his prime minister to have taken down the master milling plant of the cleansers. Pharmaceutical plants were always being blamed as the central hiding points for weapons of mass destruction. This would be no different from Iraq or Iran. He would return home to a hero's welcome, with a suitcase full of cash and after a few fun-filled nights with the girls from the receiving section. No one would be any the wiser. Congratulations would be forthcoming from Boris and the Rabbi, and he would have taken another giant step on his climb to power.

Wilson Gilberger was a horse of a somewhat different color. He used his cheating, sniveling, and cocky mind to get what he wanted. He never got his hands dirty and would ensure that he had weekly manicures and pedicures to keep his lovely self looking polished and appearing ultrarefined. Grooming came with the family pedigree he felt. His ancestors had been plantation owners in Georgia during the "good old days" when whites could buy the slaves they wanted and use them for their every desire. Gilberger believed that those who had power should show their beautiful presence to all the lowly people that they governed. He was quick-witted and perhaps the most narcissist and biggest liar of the lot. He toyed with people's emotions and was never happier than when he had managed to deceive others.

He knew what lies to feed to what people and when to do it, which was always at the most opportune time. He had Brunehoff confused and enraged; that had cost him a badly bruised throat, but it would heal. He had succeeded in sowing doubt and anger, and the pain he endured was worth it. Also, in a matter of minutes, he had turned an out-of-control Rebecca Sarquas into a maid fetching him muffins and listening intently to his lying plans to make her vice president of the United States.

Then, he had totally disarmed and surprised the American president and all the joint chiefs of staff by convincing them that the barrels of death were stockpiled on United States military bases and being dropped from planes stationed there. All this facade to get close to his cleanser target, the Cuban Varez, and to do so without having to even leave Washington or his own office for that matter. Such were the mendacious means of a man without scruples, morals, or regard for his fellow man.

Rebecca Sarquas was an opportunist who would go to bed with anybody and everybody to further her own rise to power. She used her beauty and charm to seduce the rich and powerful of the world; and few, if any, could resist her words of passion or her flirtatious ways. Her eyes carried a power of irresistibility, and her short skirts and curvaceous long legs made men hoot and holler as she passed their way.

Gifted with such beauty and a meticulous mind, she worked hard and long to achieve her current prominence. "I am more than just another pretty face," she often told herself, trying somehow to balance her desires of the flesh against her well-tuned mind and to justify her success as coming from her brain and not her body. When she admired herself in front of the mirror, she would smile at her form and then slowly let her lips turn downward, knowing full well that without her beauty, her mind was equal only to the other bright lights that filled the offices of the White House. She knew that she needed both beauty and brains intact if she were to be the running mate of the ambitious Gilberger. Whatever she had to do to achieve this rise to prominence, she would do without a second thought. Such was the hold that the thirst for power brought to yet another member of the NOW.

Anthony Burgess was one of the most outrageous of the lot. He schemed and lied and played one opponent against the other while he stood back and waited for one or both of them to destruct. Then he would race in with a quick fix and do whatever was required to bring more attention and adoration to himself. He used his silvery tongue and intellect to save him in times of trouble, and when all else failed, he turned to the White Witch to ease his troubled mind. He had fallen victim to her and was not aware that she had a hold of him and knew or could bring forth all his inner secrets.

His immediate concern was not with his country or his cabinet but with the dreaded Anhebo. The witch had instructed him not to worry, but the farther he was away from her, the closer that the princess seemed to be. He thought of the images of fire and Anhebo exploding into flames and the feeling of relief and satisfaction he felt knowing that she would never hurt him again. On the other hand, these were just dreamlike images, and he knew that it would take more than voodoo and pins stuck into a doll to bring down the Amazonian. He must find a way to silence her, and he knew that it would have to be soon and on her own turf. This would make it all the more difficult, but he felt that the witch had seen beyond into the dark side and that somewhere and somehow, fire would be the agent to consume the mighty Brazilian. Then he could face Boris and his club members and then he could return not only to the leading of his nation, but indeed he would also gain a higher position of prominence within the NOW. Then he would deal with the nasty Yung and others that annoyed him. Perhaps being assigned the princess was the best thing after all, for if he could take care of her, then all else would seem fairly easy by comparison.

Pierre Langois was a racist, lying, chauvinist, elitist, detestable lowlife who wanted nothing more than to rule France with his like-minded and supercilious male friends. He cowered when danger approached and was considered by the other NOW members to be the weakest player in the band. Why Boris kept him around was unknown to the others. They felt that he must have some redeeming qualities or was to fulfill a particular function, because like Balderous, Pretnekof had no time for racist swine.

Langois took great joy in duping duEsi and felt that France was for him to rule and to hell with the rest of the world. He especially cared nothing of the immigrants who flooded into his nation and declared that he would rid the country of them when the time was right. He knew that duEsi felt differently and that he would have to await the promise of Boris to have her removed, or rather cancelled, in order for him to ascend to power and introduce new laws forbidding all sorts of things, laws and protocols that would send the immigrants back to where they belonged, back to anywhere as long as they left France to the French, the nobility, the rightful class of men who could bask in their arrogance and self-important ways. Refined and rightful, he thought, that was his people and the ones who should lead France, not some woman wearing britches and acting like a man, but a true, red-blooded Frenchman.

It was thoughts and actions like these that made Karakanni outsmart and put fear into the cowardly Langois that he despised so much. The general had tricked him, sowed seeds of alarm and doubt, and then laughed at the weak and shaken Langois. It had been a game for Karakanni, and he played it well, so well that poor Pierre was an utter mess when Brunehoff saw him last and was sniveling again when he received the call from the Rabbi.

If only the populace knew what terrible thoughts and proposed actions occupied the mind of their vice president, they would surely find a way to oust him for good. That was not soon to happen, for one thing that Langois commanded was a clever and crafty mind, and he could see trouble brewing and avert it before it could claim him as a victim or prey.

Finally, the last member of the NOW was one of the very strongest of all. Dieter Brunehoff had been through so much and had answered to so many masters of various persuasions that he finally had had enough of it all. His plans to change the order of things were unfolding with rapid fire, and he had come to loath not only the mountain laboratory and all its evil contained therein but also his NOW members and what they stood for and how they acted. He had even started to question his own chancellor and what might be his true intentions and motivations. He also hated the Earth Cleaners for the indiscriminate damage they had done to helpless families and how they felt that they were invincible and could play with human life as if it were some child's toy. He had been used and abused by so many people, and he had had his fill of the whole damned mess. Soon he would change everything, and if all went well, he would escape to some faraway place with his darling Francesca and never look back.

He knew that the "juice" that had been pumped into his veins would eventually catch up with him and he would soon no longer be the world's greatest warrior. This never bothered him in the least since he had known for some time that no one could stay on top forever and that twelve years of complete domination of all challengers was longer than any before him had ever lasted. Finally, he reasoned, even if he shook and convulsed, peace would be his.

Chapter 31

BRUNEHOFF'S JOY

A windy road dissecting a lush forest and snaking through beautifully-cared-for gardens and occasional pastoral settings was navigated by Brunehoff. From the airport at Victoria, British Columbia, where he had rented the no-descript car, he had headed southwest along the scenic secondary roads and toward his destination.

It was approximately forty kilometers to the quiet and peaceful oceanside hamlet known as the Lester B. Pearson College of the Pacific. One of only thirteen United World Colleges, this thirty-nine-year-old school had a very special purpose. Named for the 1960's Canadian prime minister, known for his foresight and regard for humanity, it attracted two hundred students from all over the world. Each year, two from each participating country were "selected" and brought together to complete high school and to dedicate two years of their lives to the building of peaceful and caring relationships with other youth from throughout the world. Many were from influential families and many had witnessed the tyranny of their fathers, either through business dealings or on the political stage. Here, things would be grossly different, and who your daddy was had no place in how one was treated. To be sure, all were treated equally and with understanding and compassion by the highly regarded international instructional staff.

The college's concept was that communal dormitory quarters would allow for sharing and exchange of ideas. Four or five boys or girls shared sleeping quarters. The curriculum was nontraditional also. There were many outdoor activities such as ocean kayaking and hiking and mountaineering—all aimed at challenging the stamina and mental fortitude of the students while exposing them to the splendor of the natural world that surrounded them. Classes dealt with social parity, solutions for racial and economic problems, and there was also ample time dedicated to theater and dance and writing as means of expression and ultimately comradery and worldwide awareness.

For some of the bright youth that arrived each September, the school was at first strange and uncomfortable. Gradually, most came to embrace its methods and principles and were soon firm believers that they could return to their respective societies and make a difference—even if they had to convince their power-hungry and control-minded fathers of the need for change. Who better than Daddy's little girl or favorite son to exert the influence needed for a change, or renaissance of thinking, as the faculty preferred to refer to it as. These were indeed special and generally gifted students who became acutely aware of the chaos that greed brought to their peoples and who were still young enough to not have been firmly grasped by its pointed talons.

The new writing and literature teacher had caught the attention of many of the students and of Dieter's Francesca in particular. The young man's name was Eli Bayanni, and he was the son of Ethiopian immigrants who had scratched together every cent they could to bring their only child to a new and better world and to offer him an opportunity at a favorable future. They had no notion as to what their son would become but knew somehow that he would flourish in this new and free world, where food was plentiful, the rule of law appeared fair, and education was not reserved for only the rich.

Francesca had e-mailed her father often about this special visionary of a teacher, and in each succeeding note it seemed that she was falling deeper to his charisma and charm. Then she started to question her father about his past and his present and whom he really worked for and who were the real good guys in this world of theirs. Each note ended the same, "I love you, Daddy," followed by the words of Eli, "Praise be to the Creator and all true followers."

Brunehoff parked the car in one of the many spaces marked Visitor and headed directly for the main building. He had driven by the entrance way twice and initially had parked the car well off the road and climbed to the adjacent hilltop that afforded him a clear view. With the aid of his Bushnells, he had carefully surveyed most of the grounds. There were no guards or cameras or apparent security of any kind. The oasis appeared to be as open as the learning that was offered up to these young and impressionable minds—minds that would go forth to influence the world.

The receptionist provided him with instructions to Francesca's current class and assured him that parents were always welcome, with or without advance warning. "Just knock and then enter," she had said. "Room 103, the language lab." Francesca would be delighted and surprised.

Delighted and surprised, he hoped, and not disappointed and embarrassed. He approached the room and peered in through the glass in the door. It looked like a mini-United Nations inside with young people of every color and possibly every religion and creed. After a few short moments of study he recognized that the entire class was focused upon the teacher. He was a handsome and dark-skinned young man who gestured with universal signs of peace and insight. *This must be him*, thought Brunehoff.

Just then the teacher stopped and turned directly toward the door. He had seen Brunehoff and motioned for him to enter. Unaccustomed to being the one that was being put on the spot, Brunehoff, nonetheless, pushed down on the lever and entered the room.

"Please come in. You are welcome to join our class, Mr. Brunehoff," warmly invited the glowing and serene Bayanni.

Mr. Brunehoff? How could he possibly know who I am? I have kept even my daughter unaware that I would visit. It would be safer that way, he had reasoned, and if she decided to go with him, they would run and not stop until they were far, far away from all those that brought trouble and anguish to his life.

"Are you a mystic or mind reader as well as a philosopher, Mr. Bayanni?" inquired a clearly surprised Brunehoff.

"You credit me with skills that I do not possess, my dear sir. It is quite simple. We have an intercom system, and Ms. Price has apprised me of your approach."

"Well, I guess the price is right, as you Canadians say," recovered Brunehoff to a room full of giggling girls and laughing lads.

"Good, just like your daughter, quick-witted and humorous as well. Please join us, praise be to the Creator—"

"And all true followers," interjected a quickly recovering Brunehoff to a somewhat-taken-aback Bayanni.

Brunehoff made his way to an empty seat near Francesca and extended his hands palms upward to greet his daughter. She jumped to her father's arms, and the entire class burst into a rousing applause, happy for the reunited pair.

"Daddy, why didn't you tell me that you were coming?"

"Surprise is one of the delights of life, is it not, Mr. Bayanni?"

"Yes, indeed, and it is to be cherished as are all gifts of the Creator. You are welcome here, Mr. Brunehoff. We have but two more one-page assignments to be read by our students, and then there will be a break for lunch. Sit and listen to the words of the young. First, you, Alenia, and then Francesca. Please, let us resume."

Alenia, from Ghana, rose to her feet, bowed respectfully to her fellow students first, then their guest, and finally to their mentor. Then with pride and passion, she proceeded to read her words.

Life Can Be a Many-Troubled Pathway

Life can be a many-troubled pathway. Sadness can rise from almost any place at any time, and pain and emptiness within oneself can override even the most promising of journeys. Hurt, anger, and pain can smear a black cloud over occasions that could bring promise and hope and contentment, thereby darkening all within the reach of despair.

Do we have a choice? Can we see the beauty of the world and those amongst us while shutting out the items that cause us sadness? Can we look only for the good and fullness of life and discard the very problems that drag us down? Can we remain positive and smiling on the surface while wrestling with the demons within?

What is our responsibility as inhabitants of this planet? To sow crops of love and hope that will feed our eternal soul or to find ways and means to satisfy our earthly needs?

Should we choose our stomachs or rather look to provide for our minds and hearts? To what end do we rise each morn, and what do we hope to achieve at the end of our journey? Should we care for others before ourselves, or should we hungrily pursue the things of self and the fleeting satisfaction that comes with such actions? Such questions create a search for a meaning and a hope, for a springtime after long winter storms and a place of quiet solitude to ponder all that present themselves to us each new day.

When one has been gifted with food and opportunity and good fortune, it may be easier to find satisfaction and harmony. However, a hungry soul, one that thirsts for a new reality and a clear understanding, can be starving for internal contentment even with bounty all around. It is the mind and soul of a person that hungers and searches and debates while the stomach is content to feed the cavity and discard all else.

Are we merely stomachs of this world, or do we crave a greater meal? Can we be content with the variety of goods and foodstuffs we consume and ingest, or do we forever have to search for the chef and artist who placed us in this whirling, twirling globe that brings sunlight and rain and good times and sorrow? Why do we care about matters that are not ours to control? Why is contentment such an evasive yet alluring desire?

There is much to consider and choose, but what do we choose and why? Are our choices for our own earthly delight, or are they in search of a new world, a greater feast, and a fuller understanding?

Consume and be content; or allow questions to consume your thoughts, emotions, and actions and stifle happiness and contentment. Enjoy the feast and proclaim the savory tastes, but be prepared to pay the bill, which will surely arrive at each and every table and to each and every soul. Make choices that endure and are not simply waste materials that will be flushed away into oblivion much as our own wastes are discarded without thought or concern. Examine, consider, and contemplate or quickly grab and gobble down all that cross your pathway. This pathway of life is to be navigated, and the stops and starts and hazards and unknowns will surely present themselves to each of us as we continue along at whatever speed and direction we choose—for choice is what we are granted and avoidance of obstacles is what we most carefully seek. Have we chosen the best pathway, or will there be a gaping hole and dark abyss at journey's end? Only time and the summation of one's earthly journey will answer the unknowns of this life of ours. Be careful how you proceed, for there will be a day of reckoning for all.

The class was truly moved by the sonata of the young Alenia, and Brunehoff also was touched. Such words of wisdom from such a youth, not yet a woman. It was stirring and emotional, and her classmates nodded their approval.

Eli Bayanni was clearly impressed. "It was indeed a deep and inspired composition, Alenia. You have done well to examine the right and wrong of our being, to question and to seek answers. I am well pleased with your work. Thank you and praise be to the Creator."

"And all true followers," replied the class.

"Now it is your turn, Francesca, and I'm sure that you also will have inspired and moving words for all of us, including our special guest. Please proceed when you are ready."

Francesca was dressed in a simple white cotton dress and her bright blue eyes shone as her long blond hair glistened in the rays of light streaming through the skylight above. She bowed dutifully to her classmates, then her father, and finally to the one she followed without question or concern.

She began.

Go My Children—Go Now!

And to the first in line, the Master said:

"Go swiftly my son and slow not for the troubles of life or the perils of encroaching danger. Rather, move with great conviction and with full determination to achieve all that you must in this glimpse of time—your very life. Hearken the call of wise men and dispel the lure of earthly delights. Set your mind to the good of man and the improvement of the earth—make a difference, my son, but do so with humility and bowed head, for onto the glory hound will be delivered only the paperthin praise of man that will soon disintegrate as if it never were."

And to the second in line, the Master said:

"My daughter, you will be the mother of many to come, and how they are and who they will become are cast upon your very shoulders. Take care always to show love and kindness and understanding and empathy for those of less fortune. Show your children the things that you value most, and show also how you detest the riches of man greedily attained at the expense of others.

Educate your children in the ways of peace and tolerance and mercy, for it is by those very same values that your offspring and their children and their children's children will know the goodness of life and see through the veiled indifference of others. Bless this world with your presence."

And to the third in line, the Master spoke:

"Blessed are you with an energy and a radiance, my son. Let your light be cast forth so that the whole world may see what you truly hold dear—the gifts of truth, wisdom, and purpose. Caress your energy into a powerful presence that will capture the attention of many, and strive always for the understanding to deliver your good works and encouraging ways to the poor of the earth. Bring to them new purpose and desire and hope for fulfillment, but caution yourself and those you influence to be ever vigilant to honor the very things that you hold dear.

"Go forth, my children, and make this world of ours a much, much better place. Go with haste and compassion for your determination, and smiling ways will bring much-needed peace to this tormented world of yours. Go, my children, go now!"

Silence befell the room. All had been struck by the emphatic voice and carefully crafted words of Francesca. Truly profound. Brunehoff fought back tears, tears that had been held deep within for so very, very long. Tears of pride and joy and all things that were good and noble. Tears of love for his daughter, for the child of Hannah's womb, and a young woman who surely would help lead the earth to a better future than that which the current generation offered. He was so very proud.

Finally, it was Eli that spoke. "Today, we have felt the presence of the Creator in this very room. Each of you, in your own way and with your own words, have delivered up messages of hope and freedom, messages of joy and thanksgiving, questions and challenges. You have enriched the lives of each other and are rewarded with a calming peace that will fill your entire being. As Francesca so beautifully put it, 'Go, my children'—go now, for your class has ended and your teacher is truly pleased. Praise be to the Creator."

"And all true followers," replied an uplifted Brunehoff, much louder than the rest did.

Chapter 32

THE RABBI ARRIVES

"You have some luggage to claim, monsieur?" asked a skinny and aged, old porter as the Rabbi entered the baggage-claim area of Belize's Philip S. W. Goldson International Airport. The old man had noted the Rabbi's elegant apparel and refined walk and knew that this was a man of considerable means.

"Yes, there are two," answered Berhinstein as he carefully scanned the old man dressed in his soiled and official airport uniform and then handed the check stubs to him.

"You are here for a holiday, perhaps, *mon ami*?" inquired the old man, knowing that conversation and inquiry were often the keys to a larger tip. That and the fabricated strain he would show as he struggled to lift usually large and heavy bags onto the cart that he had pushed for so many years.

"Yes, a holiday," replied the Rabbi, "a long-overdue holiday."

"I am sure that you will enjoy our famous cuisine and the splendor of our beaches. Perhaps for a small fee I could arrange for you to enjoy the delight of one of our most beautiful young ladies?" pressed the old man, looking for an opportunity for a still-greater reward.

The Rabbi was becoming annoyed at the persistence of the crinkled old man. When he saw him go through the motions of strain as he removed the two not-so-heavy bags from the conveyer belt and then struggled to place them upon his rickety cart, the Rabbi decided that he had seen enough.

"I am here to rest, and I have taken a vow of celibacy. I would be most pleased if you attend to the bags. Deliver them to one of your splendid taxis that await travelers like me who have just completed a very long journey and arrived in your *belle* and petite country for rest and quiet," firmly stated a tired and aggravated Raheim.

"As you wish, *mon ami*, but if you change your mind—"

"I won't," cut short the Rabbi to the now-somewhat-dejected baggage handler.

"As you wish, monsieur," responded the old man as he pushed his cart through the checkpoint after the Rabbi had cleared customs and immigration.

"Follow me, s'il vous plaît," he spoke again, mixing his French with broken English. It always appeared more interesting to the American and European tourists who came to enjoy the delights of his country. This also usually amounted to a larger tip by unsuspecting tourists who saw a poor old man struggling hard each day to glean a few dollars to bring much-needed bread to his family. Few, if any, saw him snicker and drive away at day's end in a shiny new Porsche and a pocket full of tax-free, mixed currency as he sped down the highway to his very comfortable home on the beach.

He loaded the bags into the trunk of the first cab in line and then brought his right hand to the peak of his cap to salute his client. This was the final straw, thought the Rabbi, as he entered the car and then handed a crisp, new 50-euro bill to a suddenly gleeful old man. The porter tugged at the bill and smelled it and enjoyed his deceptive ways as the taxi left the curb. Inside the cab, the Rabbi also smiled as he knew that the old trickster would have much to answer when the authorities questioned him for passing a counterfeit note.

You get what you deserve, thought the Rabbi, who then opened his briefcase to fetch his cell phone and replace the SIM card with one of the many that he had secured within the lining of the metal case. These he brought to constantly change the source of the many calls that he would make from within Belize and Mexico. Always be prepared and never take anything for granted. There were eyes and ears everywhere, and the careless always fell prey to a proactive and more vigilant foe, he reasoned. He was prepared for today, tomorrow, and soon to be for the Sunday afternoon when the on-field battle would take place, five short days from now.

"Hilton Hilltop and, please, no conversation or suggestions," firmly asserted the Rabbi to a sleepy-eyed driver.

After check-in, the Rabbi called to room 301; and a husky, happy voice answered on the second ring. A "This is me. Is that you?" greeting was followed by a loud laugh.

The Rabbi rolled his eyes and took a deep breath. Then he responded with "Yes, it's me, and if I were you, *mon captain*, I would get my arse up to room 403 as fast as humanly possible."

"Who the frig is this?" demanded the still-husky-but-now-serious voice.

"It is your coach and the one who will lead you to victory in just five days from now *if* you respond to my methods and listen carefully to my teachings," softly but firmly replied the Rabbi and then added, "four oh three in one minute—take the stairs." And then the line went dead.

Within forty-five seconds, a clearly shaken Springbok tapped timidly on the Rabbi's door, which was slightly ajar. He was greeted by "Enter, Sykes, and close the door behind you."

"I am so sorry to have spoken rudely to you, Rabbi. I had no idea that it was you. I thought it was one of the lads," apologized a flushed Darryl Sykes to the stern-faced rabbi.

"Forget it, Darryl, but let's limit our humor until after we destroy the opposition, shall we?" replied a now-smiling Berhinstein. "You know that this match is important to us and it has ramifications beyond the pitch and there will be considerable bragging rights that go to the victors. Not to mention the princely sum that is for all of you to share if you follow my explicit instructions. I have called you here to make known to you our plan of attack and to get you to rally the lads to compete with a deeper-than-normal power and might. Do you think that you are ready to respond to the challenge?"

"Oh yes, I am ready," assured the captain of the rugby giants. "We really want to cream these uppity Brits after the shellacking we endured in the last match. We played without passion or pace and totally let them have their way with us. We have all swore that such a one-sided defeat will never take place again. We have practiced hard and are in great game shape and are only missing one player due to injury. We want revenge and we shall play for keeps."

"Good. Now all you need is instruction and a few new plays, moves that I will introduce to confuse the opposition and have you running free across the goal line and into the folklore of pubs and homes throughout your nation. Do you think that your crew can handle the adoration of a nation of rugby fanatics?" inquired the Rabbi.

"I suspect that we could wash down that adoration you speak of with a few pints of the brewmaster's finest," answered a now-more-relaxed Sykes. "The lads are up for it, to be sure. Each and every one of us look forward to learning all that we can from you, sir. The only man to complete a full season undefeated and make the opponents look like floundering fools. Most of us were still young wantabees when you led the Lions to an undefeated season. Some of us are old enough to remember the now-famous deceptive moves that created havoc for the opposition and victory for the Lions. I know your magic so very well as I have watched the tapes over and over again at my uncle's home. John Sykes, do you remember him, sir?"

"Jumpin' Johnny Sykes, your uncle? Well, it is a small world indeed. Please send my regards to him when you return home to your parade with your pockets full of dollars and your heads awash with praise. But remember one thing and know it well: if you feel that you know my tactics and playbook inside and out, then the Brits will be just as prepared and equally cocky. It is for that reason that I have prepared a few new plays that we must practice over and over again starting at four p.m. this afternoon. Have the team assembled in the lobby and the bus ready to depart for the field at three forty-five sharp. No one should be late, and if they are, they will not play in this match nor any other yet to come. Their days as a Springbok will have come to a grinding halt. Do I make myself clear, Mr. Sykes?"

"Perfectly clear, sir, ah, eh, Coach. Or should we address you as Rabbi?"

"I prefer to be called sir or Rabbi Raheim, but the salutations are not so important as your conduct and discipline on the field. It is there that I will need your focused attention and willingness to do whatever I ask of each of you. Is that also clear, Mr. Sykes?"

"Absolutely and positively clear, sir. The lads will be ready as you have requested."

"Good. Then go now and brief them and tell them to be ready to learn new things and to play with a greater passion than ever before. For I also have watched tapes and your miserable performance or, should I say, lack of performance. The last time you met the Brits was a shock to me. I almost decided to cancel the game for fear of embarrassment and shame, but as I have said, this match carries with it implications that go beyond the sporting world. Don't disappoint me, Darryl. I do not take disappointment well at all. There will surely be heads that roll if any one of you displays anything less than total commitment and willingness to abandon all for the sake of victory. I want to soundly trounce the opponents and give you something to remember and talk about for years to come. Do I make myself clear, Mr. Sykes?"

"Oh yes, most clear, Rabbi Raheim."

Chapter 33

BALDEROUS PREPARES

"Keep trying the hotel and send someone to search the grounds if need be, but get me Berhinstein on my phone and do it now!" shrieked an enraged Enrique Balderous to his chief bodyguard, Eduardo Sabitini. "The rest of you, get out of here and find something useful to do or flush your stupid little heads down the nearest toilet and let them be brought out to sea with the rest of the waste. Imbeciles, I give you one little job to do, one little man to find and you fail. Why am I surrounded by such idiots?" growled an increasingly perturbed Balderous.

"You, Martinez, stay. Fetch me a brandy and call my masseuse. I need relaxation and not the pain of frustration brought on by this pack of useless dolts. Hurry up. Make it fast. I have a meeting with the Chinese ambassador in two hours and I need to be calm and collected."

Outside in the hallway and out of earshot of the furious president, the bodyguards and attendants looked grim and forlorn. Balderous was particularly agitated today, and they knew enough to stay clear of him if that is what he demanded. They were used to being chastised and yelled at and being the recipients of all kinds of verbal abuse. They stayed because they had no choice. If Balderous called you to his personal, staff you would be well paid and your family taken care of, but you would have to endure all manner of insults and degradation. The option was to leave, but then you would be gone forever because no one was excused or permitted to leave without the personal OK of Balderous.

They took their pay, kept their mouths shut and their anger in check. One day, maybe one day, Balderous would be taken down by a sniper or some lunatic farmer who rammed his beat-up old Ford filled with explosives into the president's motorcade. That was wishful thinking, they knew, considering the security that surrounded Balderous; but each of the bodyguards, to the very last one, had vowed that if they saw the glint of a sniper's rifle or a crazed farmer or even a raging bull, they would not be the one to come to the defense of their president that they had come to despise. The masses could be fooled easily enough, but those that saw him every day knew that it was not Mexico that Enrique cared about but himself alone.

Balderous knew that the short notice meeting with the Chinese ambassador was something that he must attend. China had a huge demand for oil, and Enrique knew that he could profit greatly by delivering up this product at an ever-increasing price. That was not his motivation, however, since by the middle of March, he had planned for China to be reduced to a country of a mere eighty million and without any leadership at all. He would meet and greet and smile and say all the right things to the ambassador and his delegation, for he knew that if he did not, the mighty and unpredictable Li Wi Yung could make the next two months most difficult for him. Yung and he were a lot alike, he thought, the primary difference being that Yung controlled the largest fighting force on Earth and had access to all sorts of firepower and nuclear weapons. So for now, it was best to comply with the wishes of the powerful chairman. *After the ides of March, Yung would be no more.* He laughed aloud to himself as he sipped brandy from his crystal snifter, little knowing that Yung and the rest of the NOW were on to him and that the ambassadorial meeting was just another ploy to get closer to the master cleanser.

After a grueling three-hour practice session, the Rabbi and the Springbok B team returned to the Hilton Hilltop to shower and prepare for dinner. The Rabbi was very pleased with their effort but knew that it would take time before he could introduce his new plays to them. First he must have them running like a well-oiled machine and thinking and reacting with instinct and not deliberate thought, all this to accomplish in five short days.

Upon entering his room, he immediately saw the flashing red light on his bedside phone. Someone had called, perhaps Boris, but that was unlikely as Boris always contacted him by cell phone. Land lines had addresses and named subscribers, whereas SIM cards and mobile phones could be bought by anyone anywhere in most countries that didn't have monthly plans or subscription fees or owners. That could be traced.

He lifted the handset and clicked the retrieval code. "You have seven new messages," came the electronic response. "First message." He listened intently to them all, and other than one from the maid asking if everything was satisfactory, they were all from the same source and the same individual: Eduardo Sabitini. With increasing anxiety, each message said basically the same thing, "Please call back to this number. President Balderous is most anxious to speak with you."

Even better than I thought, decided the Rabbi after pondering the messages for a few minutes. Balderous had preempted him and made the first contact. He could use this to his advantage, he was sure.

He used his mobile phone to call directly to Sabitini, who answered on the very first ring.

"*Hola*, who is calling, please?" asked the chief bodyguard to the president of the Republic of Mexico.

"This is Rabbi Raheim Berhinstein and I am responding to your messages."

"Yes, of course, Rabbi, please wait for a moment and I will go immediately to the president to inform him that you are on the line."

Balderous had finished his brandy and was being administered to by the perfect touch of his personal masseuse. He was calm and relaxed but quickly rose from the massage table to take the mobile from Sabitini.

"My dear collegiate friend, it has been a very long time. I had lost track of you after Harvard, and now I understand that you are a full-fledged rabbi and a high-ranking member of the ruling party of the Israeli government. You have done well for yourself indeed."

"Well enough, *el presidente*, but my fortune and fame pale next to your great achievements. I have read the papers and watched the telecasts and have seen how you have brought dignity to your office and food and civil rights to all of the peoples of your large nation. You are to be congratulated and, I'm sure, to be reelected."

"Thank you for those kind words, my dear Raheim, and now that we have applauded each other, let me tell you the reason for my call. You may recall that day so very long ago when you used your skill and deception to defeat Cambridge and win a very grueling and hard-fought rugby match. It was the day that the two large Asians crushed the Indian Singh."

"Yes, I recall that match and how the play turned violent, and I remember also that you alone were there clapping loudly at the end of the game."

"I see that your mind is as acute as ever, my dear friend. I know also that you never returned to South Africa to pick up coaching where you had left off from such a short but sparkling professional season with a perfect winning record. As busy as I am and always have been, I still find time to follow the sports news and especially the team games of brute force and sound thinking, sports like rugby and ice hockey, where referees allow the opponents to play hard and the infractions are punishable with minor penalties. So unlike our national pasttime of football, where diving dancers are awarded with penalty kicks and hard-playing men are sent off for something as slight as an overeager tackle.

"I have watched the papers for any mention of your return to coaching, and now I have learned that you are in Belize and will coach the Springbok B team to a match against their nemesis, England."

"You are indeed very well informed, dear *presidente*, and I am honored that you are still aware of my coaching credentials. The grudge match was confirmed but a few days ago, and I have just arrived in Belize. How is it that you have come to know so very much in such a short span of time, if I may be so forward as to inquire?" carefully asked the Rabbi.

"My dear Raheim, there is little that I do not know if indeed I have a desire to know. And now I will surprise you further by informing you that I shall be at the game this coming Sunday and have been requested by our neighbor, Belize, to line out the first ball. That is the reason for my call, to inform you that I will be there to watch the master magician return from retirement and hopefully to see some good old-fashioned, bone-crunching tackles, perhaps a little blood, and to witness two teams that have a hatred for each other. It promises to be a most enjoyable event and one which I am anxious to witness. Sometimes the affairs of state, while important, are ever so boring and bland. I am greatly looking forward to this contest between two rival squads and most especially to the innovative tactics that I'm sure you will introduce.

"Finally, Raheim, provided that you win the match, I would be most pleased to have you as my dinner guest. I know the finest restaurant in all of Belize and the chef will gladly prepare any food that you desire."

"I have heard that the dining is outstanding here, and I do have a fancy for fresh fish. I suppose that I will have to ensure that my team wins if I am to enjoy both the epicurean delights and the privilege of your company," ever so smoothly responded the Rabbi. "Please come by the dressing room directly after the game to congratulate my players in person. I'm sure that they would appreciate meeting you."

"Your confidence seems remarkable and almost smug considering how badly your team was defeated the last time by the English," snapped back Balderous.

"Confident, yes, smug, no. It's just that I have a weakness for excellent food and will ensure victory to get my fill from what you have indicated is the finest of chefs," politely answered the Rabbi. "Also, I will ensure that you will be pleased with the action on the field and the tenacity with which our team will play. You will not be disappointed at either the result or the flow of the game."

"Sunday it is then, my friend, and bring something new and exciting for me to witness if you can. I grow bored with the administration of my office at times and need a little spontaneity to refresh my interest. Just kindly promise me that there will be great action and all-out war. That and your clever tactics will satisfy me greatly."

"You shall have your war and I shall have my fish," smugly answered Raheim to a laughing Enrique, who bid him adieu, to attend to less-interesting things, in particular, his meeting with the Chinese ambassador and his wearisome entourage.

Chapter 34

Boris Takes Action

All has gone so very well. As usual, Boris had risen to the occasion and now only had the task of disposing of his racist brother-in-law to complete his immediate responsibilities. Then it would be feigned sorrow and outrage at the death of his Russian political comrades and the murder of his "loyal" Markov.

He needed to stay close to Moscow for the next few days to respond to the flock of reporters and TV stations seeking interviews and comment on the terrible loss of the forty-two politicians that Russia would soon suffer. He decided upon two of the Krems that were extremely proficient and could be capable of canceling Cloiters without raising the suspicion of the other Cleansers. He reclined in his swivel chair and put his feet up on his large rosewood desk. He put his hands to his temple, closed his eyes, and ran through a series of scenarios that could possibly work. After ninety minutes or so, he had developed and reviewed what he believed to be the best possible plan to eliminate Cloiters without bringing excess sorrow or suffering to his dear sister Martina or her three young children. Andrek Cloiters may not deserve to be a hero, but if that's what it took to deflect any suspicion from the

Cleansers and to make life a little less painful for Martina, then he would do it.

Sitting upright in his chair, he pressed the tiny black button underneath the top of his desk, and within seconds, a military attendant was at his door.

"My president, how may I be of service to you?" inquired the young man dressed in the royal-blue uniform of the president's private guard.

"Summon Krems 4 and 7 to report here immediately," ordered Boris.

When the two Krems arrived minutes later, Boris asked them to be seated and to listen intently.

"You are to travel to South Africa tomorrow morning via Amsterdam. Your papers and passports will be ready by two p.m. this afternoon. You will pose as newlyweds, escaping the Russian winter and traveling to Johannesburg to embark upon your honeymoon safari. Both of you are to be from wealthy families that have capitalized on the rising price of oil and want only the finest for their only children. This will get you into the country without raising suspicion of the customs and immigration officials," carefully instructed Boris.

"You will rent a car at the airport and drive directly to the Crowne Plaza hotel, where a reservation will await you. Once inside of your room, go to the washroom and extract a sealed waterproof package from the toilet tank. Open the package, which will contain a map, two mobile phones, and two loaded American-made handguns. Memorize the route to the point marked with a large X and then burn the map and flush away the ashes. Dial the local number taped to the backside of the larger mobile. When a man answers, say nothing. Just listen for further instructions. Any questions? None? Good. Dismissed."

After the Krems had left, Boris dialed directly to his main contact within South Africa, advised his old plantation friend of the plan, and asked him to prepare all things for the arrival of the two "honeymooning" Krems. The initial details had been taken care of, and now Boris must await the unfolding of his trap—a trap that would eliminate Cloiters permanently.

When Krems 4 and 7 parked the rental car and checked in as Mr. and Mrs. Mahilov, they took the elevator to the fifth floor and crossed the hall to their room. After tipping the bellboy, they double-locked the door and proceeded to the washroom and found the package inside the tank as Boris had indicated. They opened it up, removed the two mobile phones and guns, and unfolded the map. Locating the *X*, they viewed the indicated route from the Crowne Plaza to their destination and then, as instructed, burned the map and flushed the ashes away.

Next Krem 4 viewed the number on the back of the larger mobile and punched the digits.

On the second ring, a deep voice answered with, "We have been expecting you. Drive directly to the *X* indicated on your map and I will meet you there. It will take you approximately thirty minutes. Pull into the stall marked 137 and wait inside your vehicle. Once I am assured that no one has followed you, I will enter the backseat of your car. Ensure that the doors are unlocked," instructed the male voice. "If there are no questions, proceed promptly as directed."

The drive through the outskirts of the city to the white-owned suburban mall had been uneventful. The Krems arrived a few minutes earlier than expected, found stall 137 near the far end of the complex, and parked. "Well, Mrs. Mahilov," half joked Krem 7 to his partner, "how about a little kiss for your new husband?"

"Kiss you? You will never be so fortunate as to feel the warmth of my embrace nor the sweetness of my lips. Keep your mind on the task at hand, 7, and don't ever believe that you have a chance with me!" snapped back the senior of the two.

Just then the passenger-side rear door opened and closed just as quickly. "Don't turn around," came the husky voice from the rear seat. "Just drive. Take the second exit and immediately turn right. Then continue straight until you reach the first of the cotton fields. You will see two young black men on the right side of the road. Stop only long enough for them to enter the back seat with me."

Within ten minutes the cotton fields appeared, the car had stopped, and two young men had entered the backseat.

"Resume driving until you see a blue bridge crossing a small stream. Pull the car into the dirt road immediately before the bridge. Go approximately 100 meters and you will reach a wide section. Turn the car around and proceed back slowly until we are within ten meters of the main road. There will be a large gum tree there. Park beneath it so that we have a view of the bridge and oncoming vehicles while the car remains concealed from passing traffic," clearly and deliberately stated the unknown and, as of yet, unseen man.

When the car was in position, the mysterious man insisted that they leave the vehicle's engine running and that they proceed on foot to the edge of the bridge and then conceal themselves underneath it. As the Krems left the car, the three other men accompanied them. It was then that they got their first glance at the raggedly dressed tall black man that had been issuing the instructions. Thinking that something must be amiss, Krem 7 stopped, turned to face the middle-aged man, drew his handgun, and pointed it directly at the unknown man's head and said, "Enough! What's this all about? No lies or you will not live to see the sunrise again."

The black man never flinched or even appeared the least bit flustered. After a moment or two, he began, "Careful where you point that weapon, Krem. This is my country and you have no power or authority here and, most of all, no place to hide. I am following the precise instructions of your president and our leader, Sir Boris, and it is he alone that these men and I and indeed all of our people answer to. You would be wise to follow the instructions that I am delivering to you and to do exactly as I say, is that perfectly clear?"

A surprised Krem stared intently at the unknown man, and after what seemed like minutes, he slowly lowered his pistol and tucked it snugly back into his belt along his spine.

"Just do as he says, 7. Like us, he is obviously acting upon the direct orders of President Pretnekof. Don't be an idiot. We must proceed as we have been instructed," berated Krem 4 to her totally off-guard companion.

"OK. OK, OK, it just seems a little strange and out of the ordinary," answered back the male Krem.

"My dear fellow, this is South Africa, and unless you have yet to notice, everything here is strange and out of the ordinary. It is what happens when an indigenous majority is enslaved by an outside and heartless invader who has no regard for human life other than that of those with white skin. This is not Moscow, and if you are to survive to see the sunrise again, you best do exactly as I will continue to instruct. Do I make myself clear?"

"It is perfectly clear," answered Krem 4. "And my somewhat-confused associate will not question you any further. Isn't that correct, 7?"

An obviously outnumbered 7 nodded his head in agreement and said no more.

The unknown man and the two Krems crept into position beneath the bridge. The two young men removed branches, which concealed shovels, coveralls, and a sign from the ditch along the roadway. When they were set at the north end of the bridge and outfitted in the orange garb of a highways crew and the sign, which read, SLOW DOWN BRIDGE UNDER REPAIR was in place, they called out, "Ready."

The unknown man reached inside his pants pocket and withdrew a short-range walkie-talkie, selected channel 2, and inquired, "Team 1, are you ready?" A clear response of "Ready" could be heard. He then turned the dial to Channel 3 and asked, "Team 2, are you ready?" Again a response of "Ready" could be heard.

Finally, he selected channel 4 and inquired, "Team 3, how long before our target reaches the bridge?"

"It will be within three minutes, sir," came back the snappy answer.

"Now, my dear Krems, it is time for action. You must listen carefully and do exactly as I order—no hesitation, no deviation, or you will have Sir Boris to answer to directly. Teams 1 and 2, also outfitted as highways crews, have created temporary detours two kilometers either side of this bridge. Team 3 is high above the road on a platform in a giant acacia tree. They are carefully monitoring the approach of a black Mercedes that is being driven by our target, a certain Andrek Cloiters. When he reaches the bridge, he will have to slow for the rocks that we have placed along the road. It is then that both of you will spring from beneath the bridge and very, very carefully fire one round each into the bodies of our young freedom fighters. You, Krem lady, must aim for the upper arm, and you, Krem 7, must shoot the other young man in the leg. Try to do as little damage as possible as these young men are willingly enduring this pain to carry out the orders of your dear president."

"What the hell—" started Krem 7 but was abruptly halted with a definitive "Shut up!"

"The car will stop, not to help the wounded freedom fighters, but to enjoy the blood letting of the blacks at the hands of two whities. Before Cloiters can congratulate you for being bold enough to shoot these useless peasants, you will both aim your guns at him and each of you will fire one shot directly to his head. Cloiters will fall to the ground dead, you will return your handguns to me, and then as fast as you can, you will run back to your idling car and return to the Crowne Plaza to prepare for your safari. Teams 1 and 2 will remove the detours and disappear from sight.

"When the first vehicle happens along, mere seconds later, it will be that of team 3, who will remove the rocks and sign and shovels and rush the two wounded cotton pickers who had walked to the bridge for a drink of water, to the emergency department of the nearby hospital. Along the way, they will dispose of the orange coveralls and sign. They will tell a story of how an outraged and fearless Andrek Cloiters bolted from his car, called out, and finally fired shots at the two white assailants in an attempt to save the lives of the workers, only to be shot dead by the two white men. They will state that a gray van sped away when they saw a vehicle approaching. Team 3 will collaborate their story, and the wounded men will provide faulty descriptions of the shooters."

"Per Sir Boris's instructions," the unknown man continued, "Cloiters will be viewed as a hero of sorts, and photos of him lying dead with his spent handgun still in his outreached arm will be circulated throughout the media here and elsewhere. All shall be very neat and tidy."

Team 3 reported in, "Target is thirty seconds from the bridge." The Krems readied their weapons; and on the countdown and signal of their unknown commander, they crawled up the embankment, shot the young men as instructed, and then took aim at their helpless prey that had left the car as expected. The rest of the events went down exactly as planned. They saw the two blacks grimacing in pain and a dead Cloiters having his handgun placed into his outstretched right hand after the unknown man had fired it several times into the field.

As they ran toward their car, they heard a loud call, "Enjoy your honeymoon, but keep the mobile phones close at hand in case either Sir Boris or I have further need of your services. Now go!"

The next day, The Johannesburg news was filled with photos of the murder scene and tributes to the brave Andrek Cloiters while the front pages and leading news items of the world media was focused on the demise of the forty-two Russian politicians who were bombed within their own borders.

Boris has some unexpected level of difficulty in explaining what the group was doing so far from Moscow, but with his usual quick-wittedness, he explained the desire to bring food and medical aid to troops along the Georgian border and the surprise visit of their leaders would be a sign of respect and caring for the everyday Russian soldier.

Yet Pretnekof was deeply troubled. He had phoned to console his sister and her children and had promised her that he would find the murders and have them brought to justice. That was the easy part.

The one thing that bothered Boris was that he may have miscalculated that the Cleansers would accept the story of the black cotton pickers considering that they knew that Cloiters was a racist pig. They may eventually accept, however, that it was a cover-up and that there had been no white men at all and that it had been a calculated ploy to get rid of the arrogant Cloiters and deflect the attention elsewhere. The white-controlled media would make the most-favorable presentation of the murdered Cloiters as proof that South Africa was a nation of justice for black and white alike.

The burning irritation that had the great Boris sweating and extremely uneasy was the newspaper images of the prone Cloiters lying dead on the bridge with his pistol clasped tightly in his hand, his right hand. This was noticed by Boris and would surely be observed by others as he and all those that had ever interacted closely with Cloiters knew him to be left-handed. A huge mistake had been made, and the fallout could come raining down from the skies above.

Boris would have to move quickly and use his influence to suppress images of the fallen and bloodied Cloiters. It would be out of respect for the shaken family, who had endured enough suffering already, the media would be told. He would have to move very, very fast and line the pockets of many reporters looking for dramatic pictures to further their own fledging careers.

He was most displeased and would have to call the other NOW members to warn them to be extra careful in conducting their assignments, assignments that may have to be altered or approached differently. Time was precious since most of the NOW members were either personally on their way to their assigned Cleanser or at the very least had dispatched two agents and the two Krems that had been assigned to them. If the Cleansers saw enough photos, surely someone in their group would notice what Boris had observed immediately. This was indeed a matter of serious concern.

Boris pondered the situation and then placed several calls to NOW members and also to the press and station owners of South Africa. It had cost a lot of money and several favors had to be called in, but when he was finished, the next morning's dailies and newscasts made no further mention of Andrek Cloiters. Additionally, he ensured that anybody that placed inquiries or sought pictures from the media or the police force were identified and promptly reported to Boris. After several hours of scheming, he felt that all that could be done had been done. Control was what made Boris tick, but damage control was something as foreign to him as lack of control, and this did not bode well with the usually unflapplable leader of the NOW. It did not bode well at all, and Boris was most perturbed. Usually, an unhappy Boris translated into death of someone somewhere; and this time it would be his old friend, the unknown man, who had overlooked a slight detail but one that could cause the Cleansers to know they were being watched or, worse still, would cause them to react with another strike against the peoples of the earth.

Chapter 35

YUNG IS OUTRAGED

All his clever plans to deal with Garcia, blame the Krems, find the other Cleansers, and create embarrassment for Boris so that he could rise to lead the NOW had come to an abrupt halt. Forty-two Russian politicians on a mercy mission to bring food to their pinned-down troops along the southern border with Georgia had been blown up by guided missiles from unknown aircraft. Chinese missiles, but not launched from Chinese planes or ground personnel. Who could have done this was the question that ate at Yung, tormented him, and angered him greatly. Yet he had other more immediate matters to attend to, and the identity of the mystery attackers would have to wait.

"The international press awaits your information briefing, my chairman. The Russian vice president has called twice and states that his government demands answers. The Americans have been calling all morning, and each time it is a more senior member of the White House staff," voiced a shaking Lung Ho Fat, the secretary to Chairman Yung. "What should I do?"

"What should you do? I'll tell you what you should do. You should find who stole Chinese missiles. We know from where and when. Then you should call the White House and advise them that

China has no knowledge of this attack and that all of our planes and pilots have been accounted for. Then you should call the Russian vice president and express our deep regrets and assure him that your chairman has vowed to uncover the mystery of who launched this attack and will deliver that info directly to him and his president. Finally, if you are not able to accomplish these tasks within the next few hours, you should get into your fancy little German car and drive as far away from here as possible because if I do not have the answers I seek by two p.m. today, you will not live to see another morning. Do I make myself completely clear, Ho?"

"Yes, Most Honorable Chairman. I will continue to work with our agents to determine the thieves of the missing missiles and I will tell the press that you will be with them shortly. Is there anything else?"

"Anything else? Yes, there is something else. Get the fuck out of here and attend to my instructions before I tear you apart with my bare hands, right here and now!" fumed a very upset Chairman Yung.

As was customary when Chairman Yung entered the room, the entire international press rose to their feet and were seated again only when motioned to do so by the chairman himself. They were not accustomed to being overly cordial to anyone, but each and every one of them knew that if they were to be allowed to quiz the mighty Yung, they would have to play by his rules on his playing field. This was Beijing and not *Washingtoon*, as they laughingly referred to the comedy and lack of order that took place at some press conferences in the American capital. Here they were all issued with numbered placards and would have to raise them high and without speaking if they were to get Yung's attention.

Yung viewed the assembled audience and noted personnel from scores of countries and, in particular, important and influential members from America and Russia. He motioned to placard number 18, and the lady from Russia rose to her feet.

"Mr. Chairman, can you now confirm that the missiles that struck our caravan of aid to our troops were indeed made in China and were launched from Chinese warplanes?"

"No, I cannot. In fact, I am not yet convinced that it was a caravan of aid. Perhaps it was Russia itself that did some cleansing of its own. Cleansing seems to be what is on everybody's mind these days, and finding these barbaric creatures should be of much greater importance than determining who destroyed three truck loads of—what was it, food supplies?—being brought to the Russian front by a fleet of trucks bearing Red Cross emblems and carrying forty-two politicians." Yung smoothly turned around the questions to a flushed and quieted young Russian, who slithered back to her seat.

"Next, you, number 34. You may speak."

"Walter Weinreick from the USA, Mr. Chairman, representing CNN. May we please know if you have been made aware of any missing missiles from your inventory? And as a follow-up, how many and from which location?"

"I have not been apprised of any missing Chinese missiles, Mr. Weinreick. Perhaps your news agency is looking to the wrong source? Perhaps you need to ask your own leaders what missiles they have fired in the past forty-eight hours and what four fighter jets were doing along the Russian and Turkey border in the past few days. Perhaps you also are looking to the wrong source of this blatant act of warfare? Next, number 6," indicated the stern-faced Yung.

"Carlos Hernandez, representing the Republic of Mexico, Mr. Chairman. May we know if it is true that you have recently returned from a secret meeting with twenty-four other heads of state and military leaders and that your group were able to determine the identity of the group known as the Earth Cleansers?"

"No, you may not know if there was a secret meeting, for then it wouldn't be a secret anymore, would it? As for the so-called earth cleansers, I can confirm that all of the leading nations of the world continue the hunt for them, but as of yet, we have no definitive proof as to their identity. When we do, you shall surely know about it. Then again, perhaps you could make yourself busy and instead of asking questions not related to this briefing, you could beat a few bushes in your own neck of the woods and see what turns up."

"As a follow-up to my initial question," pressed Hernandez, "are you suggesting that our neck of the woods to be Mexico or the USA or—"

"I am suggesting that your neck of the woods is somewhere other than Asia, perhaps North or Central America, which have jungle forests thick enough to hide almost anyone. If any cleansers were hanging around our forest, we would certainly find them and bring them to a crushing defeat. Also, China has lost many lives to these heartless and ruthless swine. Exactly what was the fatality count in your country, Mr. Hernandez?"

"Well, fortunately we were spared during the initial attack, Mr. Chairman."

"Hhhmmmm, curious, don't you think? Perhaps you would be wise to stay on your own side of the Pacific and see what happens next. It appears to be safer there, and for the record there has only been one attack, so your use of the term *initial* suggests that there will be more. Can you share with us the source of your information regarding an upcoming attack, Mr. Hernandez?"

"I merely meant that—"

"Kindly state what you mean in the future and be careful how you phrase your questions. Next, and this will be the final question, number 44."

"Honorable Chairman, Wang Chi Yan, representing the *Free Press* of the People's Republic of China. There have been reports that you worked through the night and coordinated teams of investigators in an effort to find any trace of missing missiles or aircraft that were unaccounted for. Can you confirm any of this for us?"

"Yes, it's true that I have been up all night coordinating with our staff and ensuring that nothing is out of line with China's security. I'm sure that leaders elsewhere would have been equally diligent if the press of the world was pointing the finger toward them and if they were as innocent as is China. I was merely following my own protocol to lead by example. Now if any of you wish to continue to try to lay the blame for this murderous act upon the People's Republic, I suggest that you do so from outside of our borders. Perhaps the scene of the crime would be a good place to start, or are you not permitted to gain easy access to Russia? We are not amused by this act of violence. We are especially not fond of your belief that because you somehow are convinced that there is evidence that Chinese warheads were involved, that China must be guilty of this unprovoked act. We are not! That is all."

All rose as the tall, broad-shouldered, and growling chairman left the podium and exited the room. They had questioned Yung and learned nothing. In fact, he had deflected their questions back at them, and they were with no more information than when they had entered the room. Strong, cagey, and to be feared, the chairman had eaten them up and spat them out. As he entered the hallway leading back to his office, a wry half smile came to his face but disappeared quickly when he considered that the likelihood was that there were indeed Chinese missiles. He already knew that last year, six had gone missing from a base near Shanghai. He would have a more difficult time explaining that, but the knowledge that no Chinese plane had fired them on Russian turf and that all planes were accounted for meant that he would only have to admit that even the great country of China could be stolen from, if the thieves were truly prepared. It would cause a little stir, but in the end he knew that the blame would have to be placed elsewhere. Where, he was not sure; but as he had intimated, it was likely Russia itself or the USA. Now he would phone Boris and offer condolences while trying to find out if he was privy to or even behind this act of warfare. Then it would be the USA and a demand to know what their planes had been doing flying along the Russian border when they had no right to do so. *Arrogant Americans*, thought Yung, *forever meddling in others affairs and tripping over their own shoelaces in their feeble attempts at deception.*

Inside his office he removed the red phone on his desk from its cradle and punched in a number that he knew so well.

"Agent 4 reporting in," calmly stated Yung.

"Yung, you bastard, what business is it of yours where our politicians travel within our borders. How dare you bomb our people within our own country?" shouted Boris.

"Easy, Boris, you might pop an artery and then the NOW would be left without its fearless leader. Know this and I shall not be repeating it again: we have six missiles unaccounted for, but all of our planes and pilots can be proven to be within the confines of our country during the time of the attack. We didn't fry your damn politicians and we sure as hell are not going to take the blame for it. If I were you, I would be questioning Gilberger and his people. They were the ones with the planes in your airspace, not us."

"I have spoken with Gilberger already, and he assured me that it wasn't them that fired the weapons even though he does admit that they violated a no-fly zone. He blamed the flight pattern foul-up on their reserve pilots and faulty interpretation of instructions. Frankly, I don't think that their reservists are bright enough to have pinpointed our convoy and taken out the trucks carrying our members of government. They would have needed regular forces to accomplish such a task, and that leaves only you, Yung."

"And you also, Boris. Don't you think that I have considered that you were behind this whole scheme? What you hope to gain, I am not sure, but know this: I am not amused."

"What you are and are not is of little interest to me, Yung. What is of interest is learning how your plans are proceeding to deal with Garcia. Your time is running out and we need him located and your team ready to strike when I give the word. From what I have heard from the Krems, they have yet to be contacted by your agents. Do you have an explanation for this, honorable Chairman?" mocked the Russian leader.

"Careful, Boris, you are getting me upset. I called to express my condolences at the loss of your people and you suggest that I am behind the missile fire. Then you chastise me for not being prepared to take down Garcia. It is Garcia I want so very much as I have intimated in Rome. Our agents are in place and Garcia is under constant watch. If your precious Krems have not been contacted yet, it may just be because we are not so convinced that they can be as efficient as our own people. But we will contact them when the time is right. Meanwhile, they can continue to enjoy the night life of Santiago that they seem to fancy so very much, that and the copious amounts of vodka that they consume each day. Judging by the way the Krems screwed up the cancellation of the left-handed Cloiters, those two Krems were probably drunk also. I repeat: don't blame China and don't worry about Garcia—he will be mine before the sun sets on Santiago tomorrow evening, and there will be no mix-ups with whether he was left—or right-handed. He will simply go missing and never be found," answered back an audacious Yung.

"Careful, Yung, you are skating on thin ice and you could quickly find yourself falling through and trapped beneath it. Remember who is the leader of the NOW and remember my orders to you. Have your agents make contact with the Krems, apprise them of the intelligence that you have gained on Garcia to date, and then await my orders regarding the cancellation or capture of Garcia. Remember that we need to take them all at once because if the group starts to see their team disappearing one by one, then they will have advance notice and will surely run."

"I suppose it was OK to amend the plan for your own purposes then, Boris, and preempt the rationale and go for an early takedown of Cloiters. Was that because you feel that the rules do not apply to you, or was it because that racist pig was family . . . and family always comes first?"

Boris was being cornered by Yung, and he did not like the feeling at all. Yung was suspicious of Russia's role in the removal of the political opposition and was now pointing out that Boris had indeed moved ahead of plan to take down Cloiters. Since Yung was aware that Cloiters was left-handed, then others would surely be also.

"Cloiters was about to leave South Africa for Cuba, and we had to move quickly to get to him before it was too late. Letting him fly to Havana and meet up with Varez would mean that we would have to amend our plans or assign someone other than the inept duo of Gilburger and Sarquas to get to the two Cleansers. This all in a matter of a few days on an island country with very few hiding places and no means of easy entry for the unwelcome. In the end, I took decisive action that precluded a Cleanser from eluding us and at the same time removed their ability to continue to assemble at their meeting place in South Africa. That's what leaders do, Yung. They think on their feet and quickly alter plans based upon external matters that unfold. You would be wise to remember that," hissed back Pretnekof.

"And you, my dear leader, would be wise to respect the judgment and methods of the undisputed chairman of a nation of 1.3 billion people, a full 10 percent of whom are at the ready for any method of combat or intrusion."

"Curious, isn't it, don't you think, Yung?" Boris smiled.

"What is curious?" asked an increasingly irritated Yung.

"Well, you say that you have 130 million trained military men and women at the ready, and yet you cannot explain the disappearance of six missiles from your overguarded bases, nor can you explain why three of them have found their way to a Russian convoy, within Russia. It seems to me that you need to return to the classroom and brush up on your defense logic and means of security. You must be terribly embarrassed. Now if there is nothing more, kindly attend to your assignment. I have other calls waiting and have no more time for this game of cat and mouse. And one last reminder: make sure that our two Krems are contacted and involved with the Garcia takedown. Got it?"

"Oh, I've got it, Boris, and as clear as I am about most things, I can assure you that your Krems will be involved."

"Good, then go and attend to your duties and leave the heavy thinking to me," chided Boris as he ended the call.

Sitting back in his reclining chair with his legs crossed upon his large marble table, Yung smiled wider than usual and repeated over and over to himself the words that he had left with Pretnekof, "I can assure you that your Krems will be involved."

Chapter 36

KARAKANNI PLUNGES

Thirty minutes after takeoff from Japan, Masatsu Karakanni sat back in the large swivel chair at the dark mahogany desk within the state plane of Japan. *A little tight*, he thought regarding the chair. *I will have to have a new one made when I take over as prime minister and ruler.* Looking around the cabin, he took note of the interior decor and colors. Too bland and not manly enough, more changes would be needed, perhaps even an entire new plane, something along the lines of the one owned by the Saudi billionaire, Allie bin Sabu, known to the world as Sheikh Cheeks for the copious amount of food that he was forever stuffing in his oversized face.

Yokahana and Isito, his two agents, had settled into the aft quarters and Karakanni rang the bell and the two lovely young attendants from Sasami's personal staff came running.

"How may we be of service to you, General? The prime minister instructed us to attend to all of your needs," answered the older of the two, who was no more than twenty-five years old.

"Well, you could start by changing out of those hideous clothes that resemble a uniform for hotel cleaners and getting into something that would make you more appealing to your general."

"But, General, these are our official work dresses, and we have not brought other clothes with us other than a lighter color of the same uniform. Perhaps you will find something nice for us when we arrive in India. The young ladies of status there really know how to dress to honor their masters." The younger of the two giggled.

"Come here, both of you, and tell Uncle Masatsu what it is that would please you."

As the girls approached, it was obvious that they were not prim and proper when off the job and that they knew how to party late into the night. They made Karakanni's eyes light up, and he motioned to the younger one to fetch a royal-blue suitcase that had been stored next to the door to the imperial bed. Returning with the luggage, the first girl laid it upon the table, and Karakanni instructed her to open it. Inside were the latest and skimpiest of tops and short skirts and silken nightclothes. Both girls ogled over the expensive and very revealing garments and held them up for each other to admire.

"They are all so beautiful, General. Is it your wish that we will select and wear them now?"

"Oh yes, my dears, that is exactly what I desire."

"OK, General, we will choose an outfit each, and we will return shortly to see if you approve of our new look," answered the older and more flirtatious of the two. "We will be just a few minutes."

"No, my dears, Uncle Masatsu desires that you rid yourself of your deplorable clothing right here and now and then slither into something extremely appealing so that my eyes may feast on the pleasure of your sweet young bodies."

The girls looked at each other and then the beautiful and ultrasexy clothing and then again at the general, who was smiling from ear to ear. One whispered into the ear of the other, and slowly they started to disrobe.

"Do you think that we may trouble you for a drink, dear general? It always helps us relax?"

"Surely, my sweets, the bar is fully stocked. Please help yourself to anything that you want."

The girls, who by now were without jackets or blouses, poured two tall gin and tonics and then dimmed the lights and turned on the cabin music. They bumped their perfect young bodies together as they slowly removed each other's skirts and bras. Dressed only in panties and starting to feel the gin take its effect, they approached the general and snuggled up to him, each within one of his massive arms.

"Do you like what you see so far, Uncle Masatsu? Are we pleasing to you?" asked the elder of the two as she unbuttoned the shirt of Masatsu and slowly rubbed his chest.

"Oh, yes, most pleasing indeed, my lovelies, most pleasing indeed."

Then each of them pressed even tighter to Karakanni. They slowly nibbled on his earlobes before teasing his aural cavities and flicking their tongues with the expertise of ladies who knew how to pleasure a man.

Karakanni was moaning with delight and heaving his great frame up and down as the girls kissed their way down his enormous chest and to his bulging belly. When the younger of the two raked her nails even further down, Karakanni panted and cried out. His heavy breathing eased and signaled an end to his planned antics. The girls quietly giggled as they saw the great general reduced to a pile of heaving and spent manhood. A red-faced Karakanni was most embarrassed at his premature climax to what had been shaping up to be an evening of wondrous delights.

"Are you all right, dear general?" the young ladies teasingly asked. "You seem to be in some level of discomfort. Perhaps we could help you release the tension within your loins and bring you to fuller satisfaction?"

"Yes, I mean, no. It has been a grueling day, and perhaps it is best that I retire to my bedchamber to rest for a while before I return to my official duties," answered a most-ashamed General Karakanni.

"OK, Uncle Masatsu, but if you don't mind, Gina and I will remain here for a while and enjoy some more of this fine gin and have fun dancing and trying on all of these beautiful clothes that you have provided for us. Please remember that if you are in need of our services or wish some further attention, we are but a few meters away."

"Sleep tight, my general, and remember to brush your teeth before falling off to sleep," joked Gina.

"Yes, of course," answered the flustered general, who was so very anxious to vacate the room. He never could hold his liquor and apparently not much else either.

As he left the room, the girls smiled courteously; and once he was out of earshot, they laughed aloud at his inability to perform. They returned to their drinks and the fun of trying on the expensive and lovely attire that the overanxious general had procured for them.

The next morning, the captain announced that they would be arriving in Delhi in one hour and that coffee, fresh fruit, and rice congee were available in the dining area of the cabin. Karakanni awoke to find the two girls, Gina and Tina, partially dressed and asleep on the floor with a half-empty bottle of gin on the table and clothes strewn everywhere. Still self-conscious and angry at his lack of ability to control his emotions at the hands of the two young ladies, he decided upon a different approach.

"Get up, get up, we are almost to our destination and I need both of you to be ready," shouted Karakanni. When they didn't move at all, he turned the cabin lights on bright, cranked up the stereo to maximum, and awaited a response. Other than a slight stretch by Gina, they remained oblivious to anything but their dreams. Now the general was really angry and crossed the room and grasped hold of one leg of each of them and dragged them to the edge of the table.

The bumpy ride awoke the sleeping beauties, and they rubbed their eyes and saw the general towering over them. They were still groggy and more than a little confused.

"Please turn town the music and dim the lights, Uncle Masatsu," purred Tina.

"I am not your uncle, and we are here to conduct official business. Now get your asses in gear and get yourselves cleaned up or I will have to throw you from this plane, and although we are over India and approaching Calcutta, it is a long ways to the ground. One more thing, put those uniforms of yours back on and look the part of some dutiful attendants and not the whores that you obviously are. You have shamed yourself with your debauchery, and I will ensure that you do not bring shame to our great country. Hurry up or you will feel not only my anger but also my belt."

As the frightened girls grabbed their clothes and scurried to their cubicles of the Airbus, they were shocked by the general's change of tone and actions. Last night he had wanted to party, but this morning he was a raging bull. "What is it with men anyway?" they asked each other as they hurriedly prepared as ordered.

The general turned off the music and kicked the royal-blue suitcase and its remaining contents against the bulkhead. He had been expecting two innocent young ladies that he could instruct to attend to his every wish. Instead he had received two very savvy women who knew all about how to bring quick satisfaction to a man. He was cheated, he felt, and wanted to punish these girls who would be only too eager to relate the general's premature experience with others in their office. Most of all, he was furious at being fooled and laughed at by anyone, male or female, young or old. No one but no one ever got the upper hand on General Karakanni and lived to tell about it. These two would be no different, he assured himself; and the next time he chose companions, he would be sure to interview them first and not fall prey to the prettiest of the lot. They were usually the first to be taken and also the most vain and experienced in the ways of sexual delights. He should have known better. Now instead of feeling like some strong, vibrant teacher and lover, he felt weak, humiliated, and cheated. This was not a good start to his 20-million-dollar extravaganza.

Once landed, the general, his two agents, and the two young ladies, dressed in their drab working attire, descended the plane. Inside the terminal, he was met by the Japanese ambassador to India, and then he and his entourage were briskly ushered away to a waiting stretch limo. Inside he exchanged pleasantries with the senior official, who was approaching the end of his diplomatic career and looking forward to retirement back in his seaside village in the extreme north of Japan. Karakanni's four companions sat quietly and looked straight ahead. None of them dared to speak without being spoken to or to look toward the general for fear of the glare that would surely be returned to them.

"I have delivered up the package as you have requested, General. I understand the need for secrecy also, but do you think it wise to be staying at the flashiest of hotels in all of India, in the presidential suite, no less? Wouldn't that capture the attention of the press and others? We have very comfortable quarters at the embassy, and all of our lines and means of communication are checked twice daily for any bugs or other forms of monitoring devices. We could make you quite comfortable there," stated the ambassador.

"It is not comfort that I seek, Ambassador. While I'm sure that our embassy could afford me most of the items that I need, kindly remember that I am here for one particular purpose. As soon as I accomplish that, I will be able to provide you and others with all of the details at our debriefing. The hotel is a place of constant comings and goings with minimal security. That is what I wish, as many will come to see me and my people will be dispatched to various locales. This should happen quite casually and without the never-ending gate passes and security checks that slow the process down. I have no time for slowdowns.

"I know you have received the briefing notes from our prime minister's office. I would appreciate it greatly if you attend only to the matters that I request and do not question my methods and reasoning any further. The world has a terrible menace to catch, and I have been appointed to lead the campaign. So kindly do as I say and everything will go smoothly. You have your clerks and trade commissioners to attend to while I have a battle to wage against the forces of evil that threaten our very existence. Be sure that you see the priority differences between you and I, and be ready to provide assistance to our group if and when requested. Is that clear, Mr. Ambassador?"

'Yes, yes, absolutely clear, General," responded the somewhat taken-aback head representative of Japan to the world's second most-populous nation.

Inside the presidential suite, which occupied the entire thirtieth floor of the magnificent and newly opened India Empress, Karakanni sent his four assistants to their adjoining rooms one floor below. He instructed them to be ready to respond to his orders on a moment's notice. There would be no swimming in the luxurious pools or attending the gaming tables or even eating in one of the many fine restaurants that the hotel had to offer. They could order room service since he had ensured for all the delivery boys to be Japanese and to have a security clearance of 3 or higher.

The ambassador had been very cooperative. Although several commercial attachés were initially somewhat put out to be posing as busboys; the large bonus that was promised along with the benefits of being away from the office and having very little to do promised to be ample reward. That and finally being a part of some international intrigue and not stuck at their boring and deep-bowing desk jobs. This had them acting very cool and each behaving like they were James Bond, a Jackie Chan detective, or some other larger-than-life character.

When his assistants had left, Karakanni went directly to the opposite end of the suite. He removed and opened the package, which was inside the cabinet directly above the entranceway to the master bath. Carefully unfolding the wrapping that had been placed with such delicate care, he examined the contents. Inside were four cellular phones, a single American-made Smith & Wesson pistol, and a note from the ambassador, outlining information regarding the other requests of the general.

The general scanned the ambassador's note until he arrived at the part that interested him the most—the current whereabouts of Narinder Singh Singh. It appeared that since returning from South Africa, the ever-cautious Singh had gone into hiding after hearing about the death of Cloiters. He hadn't suspected that it was a planned takedown, but ever conscious of the power and abilities of the NOW, Singh was not going to take any chances. He had informed his personal assistant that he would be going to Bombay on urgent business associated with his manufacturing firm. He had insisted that he was only to be contacted on matters of the utmost urgency and then only via his cell phone. All other details associated with his miniempire of fifteen thousand employees could be dealt with by her or one of his highly paid VPs.

In truth, Singh needed space to think and reason and to plan ahead for the mid-March day that loomed larger with each passing hour. He was the calculating brain, and he needed to be sure that all systems were ready when Balderous called for his weekly update. He wanted to please Enrique. It was not to gain greater prominence within the group but to be left alone with his morphine and business, a business that was set to flourish since his company was the sole Indian manufacturer of protective breathing apparatuses. These were designed to be used in case of chemical or biological attack, and he had patents worldwide. Sales had already skyrocketed since Christmas Day, and now with an extra night shift and increased workforce, he knew that soon he would be the richest man in all India. He could charge inflated prices for a scare commodity that would be in great demand. He, like his Cleanser associate, Garcia, didn't need to be the ruler of men. Why should he if he could buy and own them and have them hooked forever on his lifesaving goods? Ownership was much easier than rule, and Narinder Singh was a master of detail and had carefully plotted his course to riches. After phase 2, he would simply buy anything and everything that tickled his fancy each new day. That was the type of power that Singh sought. Balderous and the rest could duke it out for the right to rule each other. He would silently take care of what was good for him. When the time was right, he would arrange to lose himself to some quiet little Caribbean island or some such place. There he would live a worry-free life of affluence and greed.

Karakanni's initial plans had been thwarted since he couldn't discredit and implicate a man who could not be located. He reasoned that the only way to find Singh was to get close to whoever may know his whereabouts and to convince that person by whatever torturous means to lead him to Singh. Singh had never married, and his parents had long since departed the earth to be born again as other spirits of unknown description. Such was the belief of Hinduism, and although a nonadherent, Singh was very aware of the religion of the majority of his country's people. It was good business to know as much as possible about prospective clients and customers, thought Singh, just another step on the pathway of total preparedness.

Karakanni had decided that Singh's manufacturing complex would be the best place to find a clue to Singh's whereabouts. With that in mind, he set out with his team to find the trail while it was still warm.

Arriving at the company HQ of Singh International Inc., the general had his driver stop at the main gate and inform the security guard that Japanese foreign minister Iticho Nakasuka was here to meet with Singh. He was to inspect the plant before taking delivery of the first shipment of his order of 150,000 protective breathing apparatuses.

When the guard indicated that Dr. Singh was not on the premises and could not be contacted, Karakanni acted outraged and demanded to meet with the direct assistant of Singh.

"That would be, Ms. Pusin," offered the guard. "I'll ring her office and see if she is available to meet with you."

The guard returned to the chair within his tiny post and called to Sarinder Pusin. "We have a very irate client here from Japan. I believe that he is indeed the Japanese foreign minister Nakasuka. He insists that he had a scheduled meeting with Dr. Singh. He is in a stretch limo and has at least four others in the vehicle with him. I don't think that he will go away very easily, and he has demanded to meet with Dr. Singh's direct assistant. He claims to have placed a very large order with Dr. Singh personally and cited the fact that they were classmates and friends together at Oxford."

"Hhhmmmm, OK. Let them proceed to visitor parking, and radio the security there to escort the foreign minister and his party directly to Dr. Singh's boardroom. I will meet with them there," responded the ever-ambitious Pusin, intent upon taking care of business while her boss was away. If she could appease the Japanese FM and secure the finalization of a very large order, then she knew that her boss would be very pleased and reward her for her efforts.

As Karakanni and his group passed through the metal detectors and proceeded up the elevator to the fourth floor of the office building, he thought that Singh had done well for himself very well. He controlled a fairly large company that was poised to make hundreds or millions or even billions once the world came running to his doorstep after the next strike, a strike that the general believed may come sooner than later. He knew that the Cleansers were intelligent and could not easily be dissuaded from their intentions. After the next assault, whenever it would be, it would surely be much larger and much more deadly. Singh would be filthy rich and much of the world would be in agony, hopeful to get access to the protective gear of Singh, at whatever the inflated price.

"Please come in, Minister. We are indeed honored by your visit," warmly greeted Ms. Pusin. "My name is Sarinder Pusin. I wish I could say that we have been expecting you. Dr. Singh left just three days ago on urgent business in Bombay and somehow neglected to inform me of your scheduled visit. May I offer you coffee or tea or perhaps some pastries?"

"No, nothing, thank you, Ms. Pusin. We have come a long way and at much expense, and I am rather shocked that my old college friend, Narinder, is not available as we had arranged. I can't imagine that he would miss this opportunity to reunite and close a major business deal. Perhaps he has amassed enough fortune already and is happy if I take my business to the American competition," slyly suggested Karakanni.

"No no no," hurriedly replied Pusin. "I'm sure that the business in Bombay is urgent but that he must have somehow placed your appointment on the wrong month within his calendar. Perhaps I should send him a text that you have arrived. I will state that you are most surprised that there is an error in the scheduling of your appointment."

"I would much rather that you provide me with his number and I can text or call him myself when I return to the hotel. This whole ordeal has been a huge waste of time, and I am more than a little perturbed and wish to make it known to Narinder directly."

"I can understand your frustration at the mix-up, Mr. Minister, but please understand that I have strict orders from Dr. Singh not to release his number to anyone," Ms. Pusin replied.

"Well, it seems that we have already found what we have come for, Ms. Pusin. Kindly accompany us back to the hotel and we can continue this conversation there," replied Karakanni.

"I really can't imagine why you would prefer to call Dr. Singh from your hotel when I can call directly to him right here and now," inquired the puzzled secretary as she brought the mobile into clear view.

In a flash, Karakanni was upon her, holding her neck in a choke hold as he withdrew the razor-sharp porcelain dagger from his belt.

"Now drop the phone like a good girl, Sarinder, and don't make a sound, or it shall be your last," uttered Karakanni. He held the dagger to her throat and pressed it just far enough so that she knew that he was deadly serious.

"You, Tina or Gina or whoever you are, pick up the mobile and take careful note of the cell number that Ms. Pusin was about to call. Memorize it and be ever so careful not to forget because if you do, the last thing that you will remember is my fist smashing against your head," shouted the general.

Gina done as she was ordered, never stopping to consider the fate of Ms. Pusin or to catch the eye of the general.

Karakanni then told Pusin to stay quiet as he eased his hold on her and that if she made even one squeak, it would be her last. Slowly he released her and motioned for her to get her coat and bag. Once she had them, he indicated to her that they would be leaving. She was instructed to call downstairs to reception to inform them that Dr. Singh was most distraught at missing his important meeting and had asked her to escort the Japanese delegation on a city tour and to make arrangements for dinner. He had also advised her, she would say, to stay with the delegation and await his arrival by the late-evening flight. Finally, she would caution the receptionist not to advise anyone of her plans to meet with Singh and to simply mark her out as sick for the remainder of the day. She would return tomorrow unless Dr. Singh advised her to stay with the delegation and answer to their every need. This was a very important client, but the meeting was to be hush-hush per the request of Dr. Singh.

They took the elevator to the main floor; avoided looking at the receptionist, who was busy with a telephone call; and went directly to the visitor parking section where the limo had been left. Inside the car, Karakanni instructed the very-frightened Ms. Pusin to advise security that they were leaving for lunch and would return in the early afternoon. The guard waved them through. As they left the Singh International Inc. grounds, Karakanni eased his grip on Pusin and told her that she had completed the first part of her requirements very well. He told her that they were going for a long drive and that she should try to relax and enjoy the comfort of the limo. Once they cleared the city perimeter and advanced up the windy road to the hilltop park on the northwest ridge overlooking the city, Karakanni advised Ikiro, the driver, to pull over and stop the car. Next, from his mobile he called directly to the India equivalent of the CIA chief. He said to trace the call that was about to originate from Ms. Pusin's phone and to then identify the location of the mobile to which it was made. Then the chief was to call back immediately with the coordinates of the receiving phone. This was anything but normal procedure, but Karakanni had determined that he had planned well. Threats against the family of the bureau chief and one million dollars in cold, hard cash went a long ways to convincing the chief to provide the information that he needed to find Singh. He laughed.

When he finished his call with the senior spy, Karakanni told Pusin that they should go outside, where the reception was better. He said that she should call Singh and advise him that an old college friend, Prime Minister Anthony Burgess, had just called. He said to tell Singh that Burgess had placed a verbal order for two hundred thousand of Dr. Singh's latest and most-advanced breathing devices.

Pusin placed the call, and upon hearing the name *Burgess*, Singh began to rant and rave that Burgess was no friend of his and had been part of the mob that had ensured that he would not be able to walk upright ever again. He continued on to the listening Pusin about how the death toll in Devon had shocked Great Britain and that Burgess was probably just shopping for the best possible deal. He insisted to her that she should call back to Burgess and quote a price that was list plus 15 percent. That would really get the PM upset, and Singh would be happy enough to lose the business if it meant that Burgess would have to spend more to attain similar goods from the Americans or the Chinese. Either way, Singh would have the last laugh and poor Burgess would be out of pocket more than he had expected to be. When he finally finished, he advised Pusin that she had been wise to call directly to him and that she should keep him informed of any further calls from Anthony Burgess. With that, Singh ended the call that had been three minutes and twenty seconds long. This was more than ample time for the bureau chief to trace and pinpoint the location of the receiving cell.

As Karakanni received the coordinates for Singh, he was shocked to learn that Singh was still within the city. He was lying low at an apartment that he kept rented for occasions such as these, when he wanted to disappear from sight but remain close to the pulse of his business.

He told the chief that his precious family would be safe as long as he maintained his silence and that he should enjoy the second $500,000 that would be delivered in a FedEx Pak to his home tomorrow, a package that Karakanni had no plans to send.

He clutched Pusin by her left arm and walked with her to the wooded area of the cliff overlooking the great city below. "Nice view, don't you think, Sarinder?" said Karakanni without waiting for a reply. With one quick push he ensured that he would be returning to the limo alone.

When the waiting group looked to the general, he simply replied, "She decided to take the more direct route back to the city." He then instructed Ikiro to proceed directly to 116 Skylark Lane, somewhere near the western perimeter of the city and perhaps a twenty—to thirty-minute drive.

Karakanni hadn't expected to receive the call that he did just then on his black mobile. It was Boris, and he was not pleased.

"Just what do you think you are up to, General? Disobeying direct orders, fabricating lies to your own prime minister, and then waltzing directly into the office of the Cleanser you have been assigned to locate. Without the Krems assigned to you, no less. You even have the stupidity to believe that you can fly into Delhi on a presidential jet, clear customs as General Karakanni, pose as your own Japanese foreign minister at Singh's headquarters, leave the compound with his personal assistant, and then what?" angrily exploded Boris.

"The ends justify the means," smirked Karakanni. "I have the coordinates of Singh's hideout, and my agents and I will be there within the hour. I don't need your Krems, and you would be well-advised to let me finish the hunt, for my goal is within reach."

"Your goal, within reach? I think not, Karakanni. Nothing can save you now. I should have known that you would screw up and royally. How did you think you would explain it all? Now I have to once again fix this mess created by an idiotic member of the NOW. I am becoming weary of the fools that surround me, and I also have the collateral damage to deal with. You are truly a half-witted asshole!"

"I found Singh, didn't I, and I think that my methods were quite logical and well planned out," answered a steadfast and defiant Karakanni.

"Logical and well planned out? I think not, Karakanni. Now, where is the girl, Pusin? Put her on the line to me," demanded Boris.

"Well, she is, ah, eh, indisposed at the moment," lied Karakanni.

"Indisposed? Don't you mean *disposed in* the park, laying prone and battered at the bottom of the cliff from whence you pushed her?" demanded Boris.

Karakanni was starting to sweat, and he now knew that he had been under surveillance by Boris all along. He had been too self-assured and caught up in his own scheming to realize or even consider that he was being watched. Now he had been found out, and he was about to scramble for his life as never before.

"Go after me, Boris, and you will never find the location of Singh, not now, not ever," answered Karakanni.

"Oh, I suppose you mean 116 Skylark Lane, General Screw-up?"

"How could you possibly know that?"

"Well, well, well, Karakanni, it seems that you have finally outfoxed yourself, and now you shall have to pay the price for disobedience and failure. Do you think that I would let you or Gilberger or the equally incompetent and arrogant glory hound, Langois, out of my direct contact? You have severely underestimated me, Karakanni, and now you must render up your pound of flesh—or in your case, you fat pig, it would be more correct to ask for three hundred pounds of blubber."

"But, Boris, please let me—"

"Let you what, Karakanni, live to set back even further our plans to take down the Cleansers? Yes, I will reconsider my judgment only if you do exactly as I instruct."

"Yes, yes, anything you say." Karakanni squirmed.

"Take a look to your left and see the blue Toyota. One of my Krems will get out of the car and follow you back to the exact spot where you pushed Pusin to her death. We must recover the body before it is found. Do as I say, Karakanni, or you will never leave your fancy limo ever again. Now hang up the phone and tell your dim-witted agents and play-toy companions that you have need of air and time to clear your head. Tell them to wait inside the car without question until you return in a few minutes. Got it?"

"Yes, yes, I've got it." And with that the line went dead.

As Karakanni made his way back toward the cliff's edge, he was aware of a presence behind him; but when he turned, he saw no one. He continued on; and when he arrived at the spot, he was startled by a man dressed in a black suit, already standing there.

"Is this the spot, General?" inquired the man whom Karakanni had determined must be the Krem agent that Boris said would follow him.

"Yes, I think so. No, wait, it's over here just a few meters more. Here it is. I remember the tree jutting out from the cliff below," answered a fully flustered Karakanni.

"Which tree exactly do you mean?"

"That one down there." Karakanni pointed as he moved closer to the edge to indicate the tree to the Krem. As he did so, the Krem provided a powerful boot to the back of Karakanni, who fell helplessly, screaming through the air to land and tumble somewhere near the broken body of Pusin.

The Krem quickly retreated to the blue sedan that had relocated closer to the point where the two men had entered the forest. He entered the front-passenger seat and withdrew two cellular phones from his jacket as the car accelerated away. As they drove just past the idling limo, he pressed the Send button on the red one. There was a great explosion, but they didn't wait to witness the flying debris or remains of what had been the entourage of Karakanni. Instead they sped down the ridge, and when they were far enough away from the scene of the crime, the Krem that had followed

Karakanni used the other phone to call the master. He had detonated the plastic explosive that he had placed under the chassis of the limo while the oblivious occupants strained to hear who it was that Karakanni had referred to as Boris.

"Number 2 reporting in," he coldly stated. "The sushi has been consumed and the dishes have been washed."

"Well done," replied Boris. "Now get as far away from Delhi as you can and as quickly and as possible. But don't leave India just yet. I will make other arrangements for our good doctor. Got it?"

"Understood," came the reply.

Boris ended the call and quickly dialed again. When a man immediately answered, Boris stated, "The mission has been accomplished. I repeat: the mission has been accomplished. Now enjoy yourself this evening, spend some of that large cash package that has come your way, and be careful not to waver from our plans. Those that do always fall from glory and land on very unfriendly ground.

"You will be called into action by your country's executive in the morning, no doubt, after the pieces of the limo are gathered together and the identities of the occupants are known. After there is evidence of only four bodies, your team will conduct a search of the surroundings, and be sure that you are the first to find the two lovers that leapt to their demise from the cliff above. Your Indian lady friend will be located by the GPS device within her phone. Our large Japanese male can be located by the signal that will be transmitted to the unit that I have provided to you.

"After you find them both, remove and destroy the homing devices, bag the bodies, and take them after nightfall to the place on the river that we have discussed. Once there, set them afloat on the waiting funeral barge and make sure they are doused in petrol and that the flames are adequate to consume all evidence of the two. After that I will advise you how to deal with Singh. Got it?"

"Yes, *el supremeo*, I have got it."

Back at his desk, Boris was still scheming. There was the matter of capturing or monitoring Singh and answering an irate Japanese prime minister who had been duped by Karakanni. He decided that Singh could wait; he was not a threat to flee as he felt secure within the confines of his hideout. He would first ensure that the other NOW members had attended to their assignments before the exposure or cancellations commenced. It would be difficult but not impossible for the great Boris Pretnekof.

Chapter 37

Varez Is Dispatched

As arranged, at 9:00 a.m., Pedro Varez found himself sitting across from USA secretary of state Wilson Gilberger. He had received a visit the afternoon before from the CIA chief himself and had been told to report to Gilberger on a matter of national security. Varez had never met Gilberger but knew enough about him to know that he disliked him immensely. He knew that Gilberger was a lying, finagling, smooth-talking lawyer; and it made Pedro most uncomfortable. He has spent most of the night tossing and turning and wondering why Gilberger had summoned him. Now he was wiping his sweaty palms while trying to show no sign of worry or fear.

"Mr. Varez," began Gilberger, "it has come to my attention that you may be the very man that we have been looking for, a man capable of following instructions explicitly and proving to this great nation your true allegiance to the American people. Are you such a man, Señor Varez?"

Varez was caught off guard by Gilberger's opening statement and after a few seconds was able to respond with a nod and an affirmation that he was indeed loyal to America and that this had become his country also.

"Very good," replied Gilberger, "for what I am about to share with you is of grave importance, and I need an operative that can achieve what is needed by this great nation of ours. I need for you to adopt your Cuban double-agent identity and to return to Cuba and conduct a mission that must not fail. I need you to enter the aircraft-monitoring HQ and determine what stealth planes and drones left California and New Mexico airbases between December 23rd and December 25th. Get me as much tracking info that you can and send it in an encrypted file directly to me."

"But why not just access that information directly from here, Mr. Secretary?"

"Because, Mr. Varez, we suspect a mole, and worse still, we have reason to believe that the deadly virus which hit the Napa Valley was dropped from one of our very own warplanes. If that is the case, the fewer officials that know about our investigation, the better. We cannot risk the Earth Cleansers realizing that we are following this line of investigation. It must be done this way."

"Then, Mr. Secretary, I shall prepare to leave immediately."

Pedro Varez thanked Gilberger for his faith in him, exited the secretary's office and hurriedly walked the long corridor, and then left the White House through the East Wing. Outside the grounds, a smile stretched across his handsome face as he thought of how wrong that Gilberger (and, no doubt, the entire inner cabinet) was about the barrels of deadly destruction. Dropped from the sky by U.S. warplanes. That was a good one. The Americans were as confused as ever, and Pedro was thrilled that they never suspected that he was anything but the ultimate double agent. That part they were right about, but it was Cuba and not the USA that had been benefiting from his cloak-and-dagger deception.

Back at his apartment, he packed quickly and then made two calls on his mobile phone. The first was to his contact within the Cuban military to alert him what had just transpired and that he would be arriving via Montreal the following morning. The second was to Enrique Balderous to inform him of his meeting with Gilberger and what action he was about to begin. Balderous was pleased with the information and felt more assured than ever that the Americans were grasping at straws and on a wild-goose chase. Initially, he was a little curious as to how they had arrived at the belief that USA planes had been involved with the Bh297 virus. Then he reasoned that the splintered remains of the Devon barrel indicated a high-flying and undetectable plane that only the Americans were known to possess. Balderous instructed Varez to do as Gilberger had requested and to report in after he had delivered the information to the White House.

Meanwhile, back in the White House, Gilberger continued to unfold his plan. He had convinced Varez of the need to go to Cuba to glean information that was of totally no benefit at all. He had fabricated the virus lies to deceive the cabinet and Varez and as always to make himself look good and further his own ambitions. Now he must prove to Boris that he could achieve his mission and at the same time ensure that the Cleansers would not have any reason to suspect that Varez had been found out.

Gilberger lifted the receiver of his secure line and punched coded numbers. On the second ring, a familiar voice answered with a guarded hello. Gilberger identified himself with the phrase "the pigeon has taken flight." After a short pause, the husky voice at the other end replied, "We have prepared the coop." Wilson Gilberger smiled and returned the receiver to its cradle. All was proceeding as he had planned the night before, and his real CIA agent within the Cuban government was prepared to ensure that Pedro Varez would not be returning to the United States but would be kept in Cuba indefinitely.

When Varez arrived in Havana, he was greeted by two Cuban military officers and whisked away to a waiting jeep, which proceeded directly to air force headquarters. Once inside, he was escorted to the office of General Felipe Gonzalez, a tall uniformed career man about fifteen years senior to Varez. He was a man known for his dedication to the homeland and as one who tolerated no nonsense from his subordinates. In the quiet of the general's office, the two exchanged greetings, and then the crusty old general pressed Varez for more information regarding his mission.

"It is as I have advised your adjutant last evening, General. The Yanks seem to have reason to believe that the Christmas Day virus that decimated their little wine haven may have been dropped from one of their own high-flying aircraft. They are completely paranoid that there is a mole, maybe even several. Having me come here to discreetly access U.S. flight information is a safe means of not alerting anyone as to the investigation."

"It still seems odd to me. Surely, with the sophistication and secure networks that the Americans have, they should have been able to glean the desired information without the infiltrator or infiltrators knowing. Much of this information is known to dozens of military and civilian personnel and could have been easily accessed," retorted the general.

"Exactly, as I first thought, General! Yet not knowing the clearance level or operational position of the infiltrators meant that any request for such information to other than those who had it already could trigger an alert. The American secretary insisted to me that there was no other way to safely access the details that he requested. Washington is scrambling for answers and clues to the identity of the Cleansers and they are being more cautious than ever."

"So you feel confident, Señor Varez, that all is as it appears to be and that the Americans don't have some secret agenda for sending you here? You are certain that they don't suspect you of supplying highly classified government documents to Cuba or anyone else? After all, the information and spying that you have accomplished for them does not amount to much when compared to what you have provided to us."

"General, the Americans still believe that Cuba thinks that I am spying only for Cuba. That is why they know that I can access your HQ and get the information that they request. They have no idea that their military secrets that I have provided to you have come from me. They trust me totally and would only allow me to come here since that is the case. The elaborate con game that we have played out to them is still working. They think that Cuba has been duped into believing that I am a hero for Cuba while really being an operative for them. They will continue to stumble along."

"Very well, Pedro. You have convinced me that you are loyal to Cuba and that the United States trusts you totally. Wait here while I gather the information that you have requested. I won't be long."

General Gonzales exited the room and left Varez alone. *Strange,* thought Varez, *first he questions my loyalty and then he leaves me alone in an office full of classified information. Maybe the old badger is not as slick as he thinks he is.*

Within ten minutes, the general returned carrying a sealed manila envelope. "Everything that you have requested is here," stated the general. "Flight plans, actual routes, onboard personnel, departure and arrival times, ground crews, etc. I trust that this will please your secretary."

"Don't you mean, *their* secretary, General?"

"Well, you are a spy after all, Pedro, and you do live in Washington, so I am merely stating the obvious," replied the general and then followed up with a burst of loud, cackling laughter.

Varez was not amused and grasped the envelope from the general and quickly placed it into his attaché case. *A sick joke by a less-than-adequate general*, thought Varez. He bid Gonzales adieu and proceeded to walk quickly to the main entrance of the building. *The sooner I get out of here, the better*, he thought. Get the documents back to Gilberger and then enjoy the gratitude that would be given to him. Then he would phone Balderous and receive further praise.

As he approached the security check, he was asked to open his attaché case to have the contents examined. Odd, thought Varez, as he usually was just waved through. Also, there were two inspectors rather than the usual one. Abnormal but not without precedence especially considering the events of Christmas Day, reasoned Varez. In any event, he had nothing to hide and plenty of time to catch the return flight.

When the elder of the two inspectors lifted the sealed manila envelope out of the case, he inquired of Varez as to its contents. Varez responded that it was material provided by General Gonzales and that they could call the general if they thought otherwise.

"First, I will examine the contents," replied the inspector. "And then if we have need of further information, we will contact General Gonzales." When the contents were displayed, Varez was stunned to see what was removed. In addition to the requested material, there were schematics of a new Russian warplane, itineraries of senior members' movements, and even a handwritten note from President Raúl Castro to Gonzales that was marked Urgent and For Your Eyes Only.

A babbling, shocked, and incoherent Varez was handcuffed on the spot and led away to an interrogation room in the basement below. Meanwhile, Gonzales was informing the inspector that he had left Varez unattended for approximately ten minutes and in that time, Varez had no doubt rummaged through his office and grabbed as many valuable documents as possible. He further stated that he had provided Varez with the American flight information that he had requested and that it had been placed in an unsealed envelope. Finally, he confirmed to the inspector that Varez was a double agent that had been providing intelligence to Cuba for many years while releasing not-so-important and declassified material to the Americans. He feigned surprise and outrage at what had transpired and vowed to personally inform the president. He stated that he was disgusted with what Varez had done and that he must have been enticed by the Americans to turn against his homeland.

After hanging up the phone, Gonzales reached into his pocket and removed his cell phone. He dialed quickly to a number that he had memorized but seldom used. When the voice on the other end, answered the general calmly stated, "The pigeon has been penned"; and after receiving a "well done" confirmation, he ended the call.

Back in Washington, Wilson Gilberger lit one of his very expensive Cuban cigars and put his feet upon his desk and reclined slightly in his leather chair. *Burn, you son of a bitch, burn*, he thought to himself, but it was Varez he was referring to and not the stogie that he was puffing on. Gonzales had performed exactly as ordered and would be found guilty of nothing more than leaving a trusted Cuban agent unattended for a mere ten minutes. The U.S. government would be informed by outraged Cuban officials that Varez had been caught red-handed trying to escape with sensitive documents and as a Cuban national would be tried for treason. Gilberger would curse a surprised CIA chief for mixing missions and foiling his plans to get the flight information he sought. Wilson Gilberger would be off the hook with his cabinet and wouldn't have to provide substantiation for his fabricated U.S. barrel-dropping story. Best of all, he could now call Boris and inform him that his mission was accomplished and that the Cleansers would have no suspicion that Varez had been uncloaked as a Cleanser. Rather, he had been caught as a traitor. All of this accomplished within forty-eight hours and without having to leave Washington or dispatch any agents. As he blew smoke rings and stretched wide his arms, he thought that he was indeed the smartest man and brightest light in all the land. After he ascended to the presidency, he would deal with Boris, the Rabbi, and Yung. For the time being, he would relish his latest slick maneuver and prepare to inform the other NOW members of how to accomplish their missions without jeopardizing their secret plans. He was so very pleased with himself.

Chapter 38

BURGESS GOES BRAZILIAN

Prime Minister Anthony Burgess had received some level of relief at the apparition of Anhebo bursting into flames and screaming until death. It made him feel that he could somehow face the task of finding Anhebo and then have her doused in gasoline and burned to death or blown up in her automobile with a carefully placed bomb. Whatever the method employed, he knew that he must get to her quickly and be ready when Boris gave the word. There was much to prepare, and he must attend to the matter personally as Boris had ordered. First he would have to fly halfway around the world to Brazil and do so without drawing attention to himself or his mission. As the PM of a major industrialized nation, he couldn't just cha-cha his way into Rio and seek out Anhebo. He had to arrive undetected as the British PM, locate the princess, and be ready to strike quickly. No loose ends and no mess to clean up.

He summoned the chief of MI5 to his residence to plan the matter and to select the two agents that would accompany him on his journey. After much discussion, it was decided that Burgess would travel under an alias and bearded disguise, posing as a tourist ready to enjoy the beaches and nightlife of South America's hottest vacation destination. The fake passport would be ready in the morning, and by noon he would be on a British Airways flight. His secretary would cite Burgess as resting at home with a terrible flu contracted during his hectic globe-trotting schedule. The two agents would be on the same flight as him but would be seated in economy class and also would be acting as British tourists trying to escape the fog and rain of London's winter. Once inside Brazil, they would meet at the Rio Beach Sheraton and contact the two Krems that were already en route. Then they would use the intelligence network of Boris to quickly locate Anhebo and be ready to strike upon Boris's command. It all seemed simple enough.

The initial plan went like clockwork, and soon, Burgess and the two British agents were out of England and flying high over the Atlantic Ocean. There had been no delays at Heathrow or even suspicious glances. The beard appeared real and together with the tinted hair and glasses and very casual wear had transformed the most widely recognized face in all Great Britain into just another tourist.

Clearing customs in Rio also proved to be very easy. No one had given him a second look, and only one official had commented upon his crisp new passport. Burgess was quick to respond that he was not a seasoned traveler and that since his wife had recently died, he had been advised by his doctor to take a vacation and try to avoid his sorrow and depression. *Easy, so very easy*, thought Burgess to himself. Now if only locating and defeating Anhebo proved so easy, he would be able to cut short his "vacation" and return to England to attend to the needs of his ailing mother, a mother that in reality had passed away many years ago.

By 4:00 p.m. Burgess had settled in at the Sheraton and was enjoying a cold beer and cheese plate when a knock was heard at his door. He peered through the peephole and saw two men standing outside.

"Who is it?" inquired Burgess.

"We are friends of your brother-in-law," replied the shorter of the two in perfect English.

The Krems, thought Burgess, *complete with the answer that Boris had provided to both parties and they were right on time.* He opened the door and ushered them in and just as quickly double-locked the door behind him. Next he called down to room 801 and told the two British agents to come to his suite. Once inside the locked premises, all five men sat around the large circular table in the dining room and began to exchange information.

"We have just spoken to President Pretnekof. He has located our target and has provided us with a plan to apprehend her," advised the gray-haired Krem who had introduced himself by saying "You may call me Joe Smith."

"Excellent!" exclaimed Burgess, feeling that his task had just been made easier and that having Boris directly involved would likely mean that all would proceed with speed and accuracy. "Continue, please!" urged Burgess.

"Well, it seems that our president feels that the best way to draw Anhebo out to the place where we want her is to offer up bait that she cannot resist, to entice her with an opportunity that she cannot pass up, an opportunity that will have her lower her guard to the point where we can easily corner her and capture her without a struggle."

"Capture Anhebo without a struggle?" interjected Burgess. "That would be a great feat for even your illustrious president. And just pray tell, *how* does he propose to do that? With an elephant gun?"

"As I was saying, Mr. Prime Minister, it will be a baited trap, and no, we won't use an elephant gun but rather these extremely effective and very potent tranquilizer darts fired at close range.

They can down a tiger or even an elephant in a matter of seconds, so I'm confident that they can take care of one oversized Brazilian princess."

"You don't know Anhebo," clamored back Burgess.

"But you do," quickly responded Krem Joe Smith, "which is exactly why President Pretnekof determined that you will be the perfect bait."

"What the hell? No way, there is no way that I will agree to be the bait for Anhebo! You may not know, but Boris surely does. I have been a victim of Anhebo's fury long ago and was almost killed by the behemoth. Agree to make myself vulnerable to her again? No no no, it's not going to happen," emphatically insisted an extremely alarmed Burgess.

"It will happen and just the way that our president has outlined to us," clearly spoke up the second Krem, who had introduced himself as John Smith.

"Now I am to take orders from the Smith twins from Russia? What next? Goldilocks and the three bears?" answered back an enraged Burgess.

"Listen carefully, Prime Minister, and hear us out. We all know the penalty for failing to comply with our president's orders. While we have a plan to use you as the bait, be assured that even a beating by Anhebo would be favorable to the price to be paid for not adhering to the president's commands. I'm sure you are acutely aware of that fact," informed Krem Joe to a shaken Burgess.

"So how is this plan of your dear president to unfold and why am I needed as the bait?"

"As you alluded to just now, Prime Minister, you have a history with Anhebo and one which she will feel compelled to finish if given the opportunity. Like all of the Cleansers, she is staying out of the public eye at present since the death of Cloiters and the arrest of Varez. We have located her at one of father's ranches only about two hours from here. We propose to alert one of her staff, who is actually part of our president's network, that you are staying here incognito for the next two days. The staff member will cite information provided by an employee of the hotel who overheard a conversation by your two agents. Once Anhebo learns that you will be gone within forty-eight hours, she will move quickly to find you herself and will be anxious to finish the beating that she administered to you so many years ago. Her strength may have waned slightly over the years, but her rage persists, and it is that very rage that will make her come alone and without careful preparation directly to your room. We will arrange for her to have easy access, and when you return with your agents from your morning jog, she will no doubt already be waiting to confront you alone. What she doesn't know is that there will be three of you and that you and your men will be equipped with the tranquilizer guns. Between the three of you, you will have time to fire before she has time to react. It should be a relatively simple and straightforward procedure," concluded Krem Joe.

"And you will have the delight of seeing the mighty Anhebo reduced to a mound of meat who is unable to move but aware of all that is happening," added John. "The darts will burn into her skin and she will feel like she is on fire."

Fire! Burgess pondered the image of a helpless Anhebo and thought back to the vision he had experienced at the house of Eluija. It was enticing to think that he could stand over the fallen giant and even administer a beating of his own to the princess. Payback. Revenge. It would be so sweet. Then racing through his mind were thoughts of Anhebo with several companions and him and the two agents being overpowered before they could bring down the gigantic princess. That could be a very serious problem.

"Why don't you two Krems wait here for Anhebo's arrival, hidden from sight, and then pop out and bring her down yourselves? It is Boris's plan and you are his faithful agents. You are obviously experienced with the weapons. Why do you need us at all?" inquired a still-somewhat-flustered Burgess.

"The president was emphatic that you should have the pleasure of revenge as a reward for your helping solve the identity of the Cleansers. The weapons are simple and very easy to use. After you have had your fun with Anhebo, you are to summon us via the cell number you have been provided. Then our job will be to reclaim the weapons, load the helpless Anhebo into a laundry trolley, and bring her to our nearby secure location, where she will be shackled and locked inside of a cage, a cage where she will remain until such time as our president gives the order to cancel her or expose her for what she has been doing. Those are our orders and ones which we shall follow explicitly," responded Krem John.

Burgess was torn between the chance for revenge and the possible perils of a plan gone awry. He also knew that this was not so much a reward from Boris as it was a punishment for his own lack of having Scotland Yard predict the recently concluded South African Cleanser summit. Now all four Yard inspectors were dead, and Burgess wondered if a gas explosion *accident* had been the real cause. Boris could have conducted that piece of work also. "Leave no stone unturned and no footsteps in the sand," he was fond of stating to his NOW members.

"When next we meet," stated Krem Joe, "it will be to remove a huge bag of dirty laundry. Once we are out of the hotel and have also removed Anhebo's Hummer, you will be free to return home. I'm sure that the president will contact you upon arrival and apprise you of how the roundup of the Cleansers is proceeding. Soon you shall be back in your own seat of power and your control will be greater than ever when the news breaks of how you and other world leaders have rid the earth of the greatest threat ever known to humanity. You will be a hero, and your place in history will be cemented forever."

The Krems rose to their feet, deposited the weapons and darts on the table, turned toward the doorway, and were gone. Burgess looked squarely into the eyes of his two agents and said, "It seems that we have an elephant to bring down, one which will move as quick as a tiger and be as deadly as a viper. Do not underestimate Anhebo. She is never to be taken lightly. Bring your weapons to your room and practice handling them. We have only one dart each, and unless we all hit Anhebo, I fear that we shall not be able to thwart her until she has inflicted considerable damage to me, your prime minister. That would not bode well for your careers. Now go and meet me in the lobby at seven a.m. tomorrow."

Alone in his room, Burgess practiced the handling and firing of the dart gun over and over again. He would conceal it beneath his towel and would fire as soon as he saw Anhebo and before she had a chance to move. He imagined that she would be sitting on the couch and smiling when she saw him in his disguise. He knew that fire would be burning in her eyes and that she would want to torment him before she broke his neck or cracked his spine. But he and his two agents would strike first and then the mighty Anhebo would be out of his mind forever.

After a fitful sleep, Burgess rose at 6:00 a.m. and headed directly to the washroom. It was there that he came face to face with Anhebo!

"Hello, Anthony," she calmly said before Burgess could utter a sound or make a move. When he bolted for the doorway, Anhebo powered her arm forward, hitting Burgess in the upper chest and crashing him to the floor. Then with fire in her eyes, she placed her massive hands on each side of his head and with one great twist expelled Burgess forever.

When 7:00 a.m. came and then seven fifteen and there was no Prime Minister Burgess to meet the two MI5 agents in the Sheraton lobby, they called to his room. There was no answer. They took the elevator to the ninth floor and raced down the hall to room 901. When repeated knocking yielded no response, they knew that something was amiss. They used the key that Burgess had provided them with and were surprised to find that the door opened easily and had not been chain-locked from the inside. They drew their tranquilizer guns and entered the room. It was quiet with no signs of disturbance and no Burgess in his bed. Upon entering the washroom, they saw him, lying there, in a crumpled heap with his torso pointing one way and his head in an opposing direction. His face displayed a look of terror, and they knew instantly that Burgess was dead.

The Krems were alerted and then their MI5 chief, who instructed them to vacate the building as soon as possible and return to London on the next available flight. The removal of the body was to be left to the Krems who would engage the same laundry trolley that had been intended for Anhebo.

Back in Moscow, Boris cursed the news of Burgess's demise, not because he was to be short the NOW member that had brought knowledge of the Cleansers' identities to him or because he had lost an ally. It was because he had been outfoxed by Anhebo and she was still on the loose and could possibly alert Balderous and the other Cleansers that Burgess had been cancelled. He would have to develop a new plan to capture Anhebo, who would be more elusive than ever. Time was running out, and Boris the Great was witnessing turmoil and lack of execution—items that did not rest well with him.

Meanwhile, after quizzing her staff informant, Anhebo had decided that it was good fortune that had brought Burgess her way and not some trick by NOW members to locate and apprehend her. She called to her loyal friend, Willie Brown, who had just returned to Ottawa and related the happenings to him. Brown said that now was the time for them to move quickly to distance themselves from Balderous and the other Cleansers and that he had the perfect plan to make amends for the ills that they had inflicted to the unsuspecting and helpless masses. He requested her to fly to Canada immediately and meet with him and a likewise-disillusioned NOW member that was also ready to vacate his position of influence.

In London, the returning agents were met at Heathrow and whisked away to a hastily called meeting of the very few that had known that Burgess was not recovering in his sick bed at 10 Downing Street. The MI5 chief informed Willingdon from Scotland Yard and Burgess's secretary that the plan had been botched. He related that the busted body of their beloved PM was somewhere in Brazil and was never to be found or returned to his homeland. Now they must develop a statement for the cabinet, the house, and indeed, the entire nation and world, a statement that their illustrious leader had simply disappeared without a trace and that no one had any knowledge of his whereabouts. There would be outrage and endless questions, but in the end, they reasoned that an investigative team that would be appointed to seek clues would attend to that. An acting PM would be selected, and the nation would be requested to keep hope of Burgess being found and the Cleansers being brought to justice.

Chapter 39

GARCIA IS GONE

Yung has sent his trusted agents Chung Lee and Wah Yip to Santiago, Chile, to corner and then cancel Garcia and to have the world witness that the death had come at the hands of Russian agents. This would really put Boris in a tight spot, he had felt, and the Russian president's plans for a glorious success would be compromised. Boris would have more questions to address, and he would surely be unable to explain this one. The proverbial smoking gun would be Russian, and if Boris disavowed any knowledge, he would appear to be without control of his own secret service. If he stated that he had knowledge of the act, then he would be forced to reveal that Garcia was a Cleanser; and the whole world, including the remaining Cleansers, would know of his plan. This would no doubt prompt an early strike by the Cleansers, and Russia would be the most likely target. Meanwhile, Yung would be at his own battle station two hundred meters below the streets of Beijing and personally impervious to any attack that may be directed toward his country.

The plan was sound and should vault him to the leadership of the NOW. He had only to give the word and Lee and Yip would proceed. He called to Lee for an update and told him to press the speakerphone so that Yip may be included also.

"We have contacted the Krems as you have advised, Chairman Yung. They are still drunk and appear to be worthless as agents. If this is the best that Russia has to offer, then it is difficult to believe that they were once a superpower and are emerging again."

"Save the commentary, Lee," barked back Yung. "Their apparent drunken stupor is no doubt a ploy by Pretnekof to make you feel superior and to get the upper hand. He doesn't trust me and I don't trust him and each of us will go to any means to outwit the other. Just make sure that they are found with the body of Garcia and that there is no linkage to you. Now where is Garcia?"

"Currently, he is enjoying his lunch at the exclusive Santiago Summit. After that he plans to play a round of golf at the summit's course with three business associates from France before returning with them to his city home," answered Yip.

"The Summit Club, good, OK, let me think. The likelihood is that they will all be traveling together in one of Garcia's armored limos. The Frenchmen will send their driver back to his hotel to wait until they are ready to be picked up from Garcia's home. The limo will be easy enough to spot at the golf club since all of his personalized license plates commence with the letters *GAR*. This is what I want for you to do. Place a tracking device under the rear bumper while it is in the parking lot. Then wait just outside the gates of the club but far enough downhill to be out of sight from the view of all. As the limo descends the winding road, it will be forced to stop when they see Lee lying on the road and his car blocking their passage. When Garcia's driver exits the car to determine the problem, you, Yip, will pounce from the roadside bushes and apprehend the driver. Hold your gun to his head and force him to unlock the car if the door has been closed. All of this should take less than ten seconds and will not provide Garcia with enough time to alert anyone of what is happening. Order the driver to take his place back behind the wheel, and you enter the rear with your gun aimed squarely at the head of Garcia."

"Lee, you will get back in your car and be ready to follow them closely. It will be dusk already, but the tracking device will aid you if necessary. Drive directly to the hotel of the Krems and enter through the staff entrance as we have discussed. When you are all inside of the vacant suite that we have arranged and you have gagged and tied the Frenchmen and emptied the contents of their wallets, summon the Krems. Tell them that you have a unique opportunity to capture Garcia and that they must come immediately to suite 411. Tell them that time is critical and that all will be departing within five minutes," continued the chairman.

"When the Krems enter the room, point your pistols at them and order them to attach their silencers. Then have them shoot dead the Frenchmen and the driver. Then quickly you cancel the two Krems. Next, use one of their guns to shoot Garcia, but first tell him that the chairman never forgets and that this bullet is for the time he cheated me at cards so many years ago. Place the gun used to shoot Garcia back in the hand of the Krem and leave the other Krem with his gun also. Wipe clean your pistols and put them in the hands of Garcia and his driver. Finally, fire an additional two rounds from each gun into the furniture. Then get your asses out of there and back to your hotel ASAP and be on the next flight back to Tokyo. Call me when you are at the airport and report that all has been accomplished as I have ordered. If it has not, then forget about the flight to Japan and forget about your families, which you shall never see again. Do I make myself perfectly clear?"

"Yes, Chairman Yung, clear, perfectly clear," they answered in near unison.

"Then get going and don't look suspicious. There are not many Asians in Santiago and probably none at the summit. Make sure that you are not seen, and if someone does see you, then shoot them also. Is that clear?"

"Yes, Chairman Yung," they responded again, and with that the line went dead.

Yung smirked to himself. He was pleased with his plan and pleased that the Frenchmen would be included so as to confuse the police investigators and hopefully also Balderous and the remaining Cleansers. Once he received confirmation from Lee and Yip, he would call Boris and state that the Krems didn't show for their scheduled meeting with his agents and did not answer their cell phone. Yung would state that it was believed that they were in pursuit of Garcia. He would then curse Boris for changing tactics and leaving his agents without knowledge of where Garcia was. Boris would not be able to contact his Krems and would have no explanation for Yung. He would likely tell Yung to have his agents sit tight in their hotel room and await contact from the Krems.

At 9:15 p.m., Chung Lee called to Yung, who answered on the first ring. "Mission accomplished," he proudly announced. "All was completed as you ordered and there were no mistakes. Everything went exactly as you planned, Chairman."

"Good, very good, Lee. You and Yip shall be richly rewarded. Now tell me about the reaction of Garcia when you told him that I was the one responsible and that I never forget. Tell me that he groveled and begged for mercy. Tell me about the look on his face when you pointed your pistol at him," urged the revenge-starved Yung.

Upon hearing the details of Garcia's surprise and plea to be spared, Yung smiled widely. The bastard had sweated and begged and pleaded for mercy. Mercy being a commodity unknown to

Yung, it had not been granted. Now Garcia lay slumped over on a sofa in a Santiago hotel room that the Chinese had never officially visited. The Beijing smog smelled sweet to Yung on this victorious morning as he lifted up his telephone and called to Boris.

"What do you mean they have disappeared?" fumed Boris.

"Just as I have said," coldly stated Yung. "We included your precious Krems as you insisted. It was their shift to follow Garcia as he pranced around Santiago. The last report that my men received was three hours before the shift change and then nothing. They never reported in and never answered their cell phone and they never returned to their hotel room. My men checked. Yet their car is in the parking lot and their clothes and suitcases remain in their room. Either you have had them act independent of me or Garcia knew he was being followed by a couple of drunken half-wits and cancelled them before they could do him any damage. Now I must either find Garcia again, thanks to your bungling fools, or you should admit to me right now that you have dealt with Garcia."

"I have not dealt with Garcia, nor have I had a report from my Krems since last evening. Perhaps it is you, Yung, that have cancelled them and Garcia also? We shall soon find out. I have a device embedded beneath the skin of each Krem, and other contacts in Chile will be able to locate them within the hour. For now have your men stand by and be ready to capture Garcia when I give the word."

"OK, Boris, but make it fast because I don't plan to leave two of my best agents in Santiago seeking a Cleanser that may already be dead, thanks to your incompetent Krems."

"Careful, Yung. This was to be your assignment with the aid of my men, but your men saw fit to enact some kind of on-duty and off-duty careless scheme. This was not authorized by me."

"Nor me," retorted Yung. "I now suspect that your inept Krems wrote their own script and planned to inform you of their heroic capture of Garcia so that Papa Boris would pat them on the back and tell them what good boys they were. Well, it has gone afoul, and now all of our careful work has been in vain. I agreed to accept this mission without full control and with the interference of your men. It was my mistake to trust that your drunken fools were worthy to act in partnership with my highly trained men. Men who, if I find did anything wrong, will be severely dealt with by me personally when they return home. I tolerate nothing less than perfect performance."

"Stand by your phone, Yung, and have your agents ready to act quickly. I will locate the Krems and I will also find Garcia. Then I shall call you and advise you of the updated strategy. Got it?"

"Oh, I've got it, Boris, but make it snappy. I'm losing my patience with this whole mess, and an angry chairman is not something that you need to add to your list of needed repairs. I'll be waiting for your call."

An enraged Boris tried to first contact the Krems but without success. Next he called to the monitoring contact and instructed him to seek out the agents through the embedded devices. Now he must wait, something that he was not accustomed to and, unlike most other things, did not excel at.

When the call came approximately one hour later, Boris was not pleased with the news. The Krems had been tracked to their hotel but were not in their room. Instead, the hotel was flooded with scores of police officers, and it was learned that Garcia, Chile's richest man, was found dead within another suite and that there were several other dead men also. As far as the operative of Boris could determine from the tracking device, it was nearly certain that the two Krems were amongst the reported seven dead. The press has arrived, and once they were permitted inside, the evening papers and newscasts would be filled with headlines and photos. Boris was in trouble, not only with Yung, but with all the other NOW members. Most of all, he feared that the death of Cloiters, the incarceration of Varez, and now the murder of Garcia all within one week would surely alert the remaining Cleansers that they had been found out. Boris knew that they would either meet and regroup, or worse still, the unpredictable Balderous would launch another attack. When it was determined that two of the dead were Russian agents, then it would be his homeland that would surely bear the brunt of the Cleansers' retaliation.

Boris had his plate full. There was the matter of canceling Singh and the explanation needed to the Japanese prime minister regarding Karakanni. He also faced the need to keep control of the NOW and, most of all, to protect his country and himself from any retaliation by the remaining Cleansers. He must act swiftly and decisively. It was too late to cover up the death of Garcia, but maybe he could twist the facts a little, make it seem that the Krems had acted without his authority, that they were not loyal to his administration and had been under surveillance by his secret service for some time. That four days ago they had eluded their trackers and had disappeared from sight. Disappeared but now found dead with Garcia and several other unknown men. Then he thought that that would not be enough. He needed to keep the Russian identities secret and unpublicized.

He called his attendant to his office and instructed him to make telephone contact with the Santiago chief of police. "Tell him," instructed Boris, "that I have information pertinent to his investigation and that he should contact me immediately. Give him your number and alert me as soon as you have contact."

When the tall, gaunt, and graying police chief, Ernesto Mateau, received the urgent call, it perplexed him. What did the Russian president know about the murders, and why did he wish to speak with him directly? On the one hand, he was thrilled to be contacted by the head of such a powerful country; yet on the other hand, he was suspicious as to the president's motives. After tossing the matter around in his mind for a few minutes, he decided to call to Pretnekof. He would see if there were any clues to be gleaned from what appeared as a most bizarre multiple murder and a crime scene without apparent motive.

The police chief identified himself to Boris as Ernesto Mateau and indicated that he was both honored and curious by the president's direct contact to him.

Thanking the chief for his prompt response, Boris continued, "Chief Mateau, I have contacted you because we have reason to belief that two of the men who were found slain with your Mr. Garcia were defectors from our own Russian security forces, possibly working for the Chinese. Our sources followed them to Santiago and to the hotel where the murders took place. We had believed that they were in Chile to pass state secrets to the Chinese embassy. We know also that they had a meeting scheduled with Mr. Garcia, presumably regarding expansion of his business interests into China, although that may have been a decoy. Our operatives lost track of them for only a few hours and, upon returning to their hotel, saw the place swarming with your forces. It is then that they contacted my office and then also that we immediately contacted you. We want to help in any way possible, but I must confide in you that we have a grave concern."

"And what concern would that be, Mr. President?" politely inquired Mateau.

"It is a most delicate matter, Señor Mateau, and one which will no doubt shock you deeply. It has to do with the Earth Cleansers and our knowledge that your Mr. Garcia was indeed a member of this diabolical group."

"Garcia? A member of the Phantom? That sounds preposterous. We have known him to be detached and uncaring, and frankly, he was not endeared to many people here. His demise will not be met with national mourning. Many will even celebrate his death since he cared little for his own country and simply wanted to grow his own wealth. But a member of the Cleansers, well, why would he need or want to participate in such a program?"

"Señor Mateau, the intelligence gathered by our multinational task force is irrefutable. Garcia was indeed a member of the Cleansers. I must ask you to not release this information to anyone since it may well trigger another assault, even worse than the one which we experienced on Christmas Day. This is critical. By keeping this information to yourself, you will be greatly aiding the free world to capture the remaining Cleansers still at large. Also, I will personally ensure that you are cited as an important contributor to the demise of the Cleansers and the return of our planet to its normal means of functioning. Can I have your vow of silence and word of honor, Chief Mateau?" inquired Boris.

"President Pretnekof, I am taken back by this revelation and somewhat mystified as to why you are sharing this information with me. Surely, there is something that you need of me."

"You are most perceptive, Chief, and I feel assured that I have indeed contacted the right man," flattered Boris. "What I need, or rather what the aligned nations of the free world need, is a method to suppress suspicion that we have knowledge of the Cleansers identities and that we are closing in on all of them. If we tip our hand now, all of our hard work will surely be lost and the

Cleansers will flee and regroup. What I need most of all, Chief, is for your investigation to ensure that our two defected agents are not identified as Russian nationals. The Cleansers know that I have been at the forefront of the plans to locate them and having Garcia found dead with two Russians would surely indicate to the others that we were on to them."

"You're asking me to cover up pertinent information in a multiple homicide, Mr. President," responded Mateau. "That would not only be unlawful but also most difficult. I'm not sure it is something that I can do even if I subscribe to your elaborate conspiracy theory involving Garcia."

"It is not *I* that am asking, Chief Mateau, but all of the peoples of the world who wish to rise to see another day. Could you really be at peace with yourself knowing that your actions have jeopardized the lives of possibly millions of others? At what point do you decide in favor of the greater good?"

Mateau was silent for twenty seconds or more, using his analytical mind to ponder the possibilities and their ramifications. He wanted to do the right thing but, by now, was confused as to what that might be. Finally he said, "All right, Mr. President, we will not release photos or details of the two Russians until it appears safe to do so. Meanwhile, we will deflect attention to the three Frenchmen found gagged and tied with bullets in their skulls."

"Three Frenchmen? You found three Frenchmen dead in the suite with Garcia?"

"Yes, and although no identification papers were found on them, their pictures were positively identified by Interpol. They were actual businessmen meeting with Garcia to consider the expansion of his laundry empire into Angola and Sierra Leone. We have confirmation that they were legitimate and that they were sincere in their intentions. The only cleansing intended here was that of soiled linens from hospitals and government offices."

"Hhmm, it seems like small contracts for Garcia and scarcely worth his time," thought aloud Boris.

"Actually, Mr. President, Garcia's quest was not so much to make additional money as it was to establish a foothold in each and every country on earth. Only Bill Gates had succeeded in doing that thus far, and the self-adoring Garcia didn't want to be outdone by anyone. He reasoned that even a small contract would allow him to place a tick mark by two more countries and propel him further down his path of world domination of the industrial laundry business."

"Well, Chief, when you put it that way, it does indeed seem more credible. Now back to the matter at hand. Do you have any leads as to who the assassins were?" probed Boris.

"You will understand, Mr. President, that some items I cannot share even with you. Suffice it to say that the crime scene was such that it appeared conceivable that your Russian defectors shot the Frenchmen, Garcia, and his driver and that Garcia and his driver somehow were able to kill your defectors also. Plausible but highly improbable. I am convinced that there were others involved even though all of the rounds fired have been confirmed as coming from the handguns found at the scene. Someone went to a great deal of trouble to conduct this act and to slip away undetected. It could be the mob or some disgruntled company that Garcia overcharged, but whoever it was, it was done with precision and cunning."

"OK, Chief, thank you for your insight and promise of cooperation. I wish you well with your investigation. Please be sure to remove our defectors photos from Interpol's search, but I feel certain that nothing would be found to identify them in any regard. Great care has been taken to ensure that all Russian operators cannot be identified by any means. Even the fingerprints that you have no doubt already circulated will not produce any connection to these men as Russian nationals. Keep their corpses in the morgue and for the sake of all suggest to the press that they were believed to be Chilean citizens and perhaps even employees of Garcia. Finally, I will leave you with some information that may be of considerable help to you. Check all of the flights that are leaving Santiago today for international destinations. Look for two Chinese men in their late thirties traveling on passports identifying them as Lee and Yip. Find these two men and you will likely be closer to a solution to this baffling case. And, Chief, please do not inquire as to how I know these things, for like you, I have my sources and also have the need to release only minimal pertinent information."

When Boris ended the call, he felt that he had done an adequate job of damage control. The next move would be to either blow up the morgue or break in and remove the corpses of the two Krems. Men that served him well but had been outfoxed by none other than the deceitful and untrustworthy Yung. He was almost certain of that now, as he telephoned to Yung.

"Yung, I have news of Garcia and the Krems. They are all dead. Killed at the Krems' hotel. I'm sure that you have no knowledge of the circumstances."

"None whatsoever, Boris. It is as I have already stated. This is a total surprise to me. Do you have any leads?"

"Only one, Yung, and it comes to me from the Santiago chief of police. Apparently, two Oriental men in their mid to late thirties were seen exiting the hotel through the staff doorway by the on-duty night clerk. He was certain that they were not employees of the hotel and that he had never seen them before. He alerted security, but they were not to be found. Any idea who they could have been, Yung?"

"I know what you are insinuating, Boris, but I can assure you that both Lee and Yip had nothing to do with the murders. It is true that they may have been seen leaving the hotel, but only because they went there to try and locate your missing Krems. This I have already told to you," coolly replied Yung.

"Then since they are still standing by awaiting further orders to find and apprehend Garcia, I suppose that you could have them meet with one of my operatives in Santiago? They can relay all of the details gathered directly to him. I need to find whoever killed my agents and why Garcia was disposed of also. If it wasn't you and it wasn't me, then who could it have been, Yung?"

"I will call them immediately, Boris, and have them meet with your operative," lied Yung, knowing full well that Lee and Yip were already on their way back to Tokyo. "How should they contact your man and where should they meet?"

"How about the airport, Yung? It shouldn't be too far out of their way. That is, of course, if they have not departed from there already."

Yung knew that Boris was on to him and scrambled for a convincing response. "If they have left Chile, they have done so without my authority, and such action is punishable by death. If I cannot reach them, it is because they have fled and are indeed guilty of the killing of Garcia and perhaps even your careless Krems. My orders were explicit: monitor the movements of Garcia, keep the Krems informed, and under no circumstances attempt to apprehend or cancel Garcia until they received word directly from me. While it is hard to believe that such trusted agents could have carried out this act, I am now open to the possibility. I will call you back as soon as I am either able to reach them or am certain that they have fled the country. If the latter is the case, I am truly sorry, Boris. I believed these agents to be two of my most trusted men, and they have conducted many successful missions for me."

"OK, Yung, I will await your call," replied Boris. "And if you are unsuccessful in locating them, then I will have to share the news with the other NOW members. Unfortunately, it will not be favorably received when it is learned that the powerful Chairman Yung, leader of the world's most populated nation and largest army, would engage agents that would turn against their own supreme commander and jeopardize all that we have worked so hard for. Truly, Yung, such incompetence is something that I would have expected from Gilberger or Langois, but not from you. Good-bye!"

A smiling Boris relaxed for a minute at his desk, savoring the moment. He had lost two agents, but their identities would not be known, thanks to a cooperating Mateau and his own plan to destroy the morgue or at least the bodies of the two Krems. Additionally, Yung had been cornered, and he knew that Mateau would determine that Lee and Yip had fled the country already and that Yung would not be able to respond that they would meet with Boris's operative in Santiago. Better still, there would be nothing to tie the NOW to the death of Garcia and the Frenchmen. Then best of all, Yung, who had attempted to discredit and erode the power of Boris, would himself be frowned upon by the NOW members. Garcia was cancelled, Yung sent scampering, and Boris was back firmly in control. *Such is the way of great leaders*, thought Boris, and then he turned his attention to the next tasks at hand—to capture Singh and apprise the Japanese prime minister of the deceit of Karakanni. Then he would deal with the morgue.

Chapter 40

GAME DAY

Back in Belize, it had gone well during the past four days for the Rabbi and part 1 of his mission. The team was vastly improved. This he never fully admitted to the players as he brought them along to his inventive style of play. He was now pleased with two plays he had conjured up that should surely put points on the scoreboard and embarrass the Brits. They would play hard also and would be looking to outscore the South Africans again. The thirst for a starting spot on the national roster and the big cash payoff would ensure that.

Meanwhile, for President Enrique Balderous, much else had taken place. Varez was confined to Cuba, Cloiters and Garcia were shot dead, and Anhebo and Brown could not be contacted. Enrique smelled a rat or rather several of them, but he could not put his finger on the source. His Cleansers had been decimated or lost, and now only he and Singh remained in contact, and even Singh had a story to relate about the circumstances surrounding his missing Ms. Pusin and the surprise call from Burgess. Burgess, who was also missing.

Balderous pondered the situation and weighed his thirst for bloodletting against that of appearing in public, in clear view of thousands of excited fans accustomed to soccer and not rugby. What if there were a sniper? Surely his bodyguards could not protect him in such a circumstance. But he craved to line out the first ball, to hear the fans roar, to see brute force pounding bodies into pulp, and to meet with the sensational Rabbi Raheim. In the end, the decision was easy.

He had the encrypted files containing the location of all the barrels of destruction, he had all the contacts and codes needed to launch another attack even without Brown or any of the others, and he retained his immediate power base. No matter what else was taking place, he, the great Enrique Balderous, would surely survive any personal attack. He would wear his bulletproof vest to the Belize grudge match, and he would ensure that he was always fully surrounded by a bevy of guards. Other than at the ceremonial start of the game, he would remain hidden from public view. Finally, he reasoned, if Brown and Anhebo were truly found out and captured also, they would not release any information to the authorities. So it would be business as usual and then he would unleash phase 2, and it would be mid-February and not mid-March. This would send them all scrambling and deflect any attention to him personally. Millions of Mexicans would die. He, like many world leaders, would be dealing with the tragedy and providing aid and emergency services to their frantic citizens.

Without Anhebo and Brown, he would not be challenged and most of the members of the NOW would also be dead. No Pretnekof, no Yung, and no one to seriously oppose him. Perhaps, thought Balderous, things were not so bad after all.

He finished his tour of the storm-ravished Gulf states and then flew by presidential jet into a tiny airstrip less than fifty kilometers from Belize International. An armored limo awaited his arrival, and he was quickly whisked away to a secure location but a few kilometers from the Marion Jones Sports Complex, where the game would take place. No meeting of dignitaries, no exchange of formal greetings, just him and his entourage and then Berhinstein. Just the way he had insisted to the Belize authorities.

From the sidelines, the Rabbi surveyed the pitch, felt the presence of the crowd as they filed in, and thought back to his coaching days. The thrill of a try, an enormous tackle, and his brainpower fully engaged were truly wonderful feelings. All-encompassing feelings that made the here and now of life stand still and obliterated thoughts of others things. Distraction? No, this was focus and skill and team management. These were the very things that the Rabbi excelled at. His mind was tuned to use its thought to achieve something for himself and for others also. It was now that for the first time in many, many years he realized that he had missed the game so very much. The dirty deeds and conniving tactics that had brought him to control others and ascend to greater prominence all seemed pale next to the fun and enjoyment that he would receive just participating in a game of strength and intelligent thought. For an instant he even reconsidered that he had chosen the wrong path in life, but then quickly dismissed that thought when he saw Balderous enter the stadium. Back to reality. Back to his target. The game was that, simply a game. A ruse conjured up to bring Balderous to where he wanted him and to bring down the leader of the most ruthless and deadliest group to ever walk the earth. It was time to play the game; but it was merely a ploy to achieve his real objective and to restore organizational control to the superior, gifted, and rightful leaders.

"Rabbi Raheim, sir, Rabbi," Daryl Sykes called to his coach, trying to bring him back to the present and the immediate matter at hand. "The lads are ready. Are you ready, sir?"

"Oh yes, Daryl, I am ready, most ready. Today will be a glorious day, and tonight you will celebrate as never before. Victory will be ours, and this nation of Belize will witness a match such as they have never imagined. Just play as I have instructed you and all will proceed as planned."

At that moment, the announcer called the packed bleachers of sporting fans and curious, wealthy citizens to their feet for the singing of the national anthem. This was immediately followed by the assembling of the starting lineups at center field, the coin toss, and finally, the ceremonial line out by President Enrique Balderous. It was at that instant that the Rabbi and Balderous made eye contact for the first time since Oxford days so long ago. Even at thirty yards apart there was a tension, an expectation before the acknowledgment. Then Balderous was gone to his seat inside a sideline enclosure with covered backing to conceal him as much as possible from most while allowing him full vantage of the playing field. Caution and preparedness while maintaining the elements of class befitting his office and himself, thought Balderous.

The whistle sounded and the Springboks opened the match by kicking the ball deep into the British team's zone and then racing downfield at a full gallop to tackle the ball receiver before he had a chance to lateral to a nearby teammate. Crushed to the turf, the receiver gave up the ball to another teammate, who was unable to advance against the furious massing of the South Africans. Time after time, the Brits tried various maneuvers but made little headway toward the opposing goal line. Eventually, after being forced backward by the Rabbi's fleet-footed and fully charged front line, they were forced to kick downfield to relieve pressure and the physical pounding they were taking. The Rabbi looked across the field to Balderous and could see the enjoyment on his face as men were crushed and bloodied by the fury of the match.

Now the Springboks had the ball and they tried to run but, likewise, were stopped and forced to kick with the hope of regaining possession; yet the British held firm. And so it went throughout the first half and deep into the second with little ground being gained by either side and each team limited to two penalty kicks. Then, with the score tied at 6 to 6, the British recovered a fumble deep in the South African zone; and within seconds, they struck by battling their way across the goal line. Now the score was 12-6 for the English with twelve minutes to go, but Rabbi Raheim showed no signs of concern. He called a time-out and informed his team that it was time to test the opponents with one of his trick plays. It was an end around to one flanker and then back to the fly half, who unloaded a huge kick downfield to a mass of speeding Springboks who appeared to have caught the Brits napping. Sykes caught the ball, and a flurry of laterals later, it was Sykes himself diving over the goal line to tie the game at 12 all. The fans roared their approval and Balderous jumped and pumped his fist—finally he was seeing the creativity he had longed for, and it melded nicely with the blood and gore that had taken place up until now.

Less than two minutes to go and the Springboks were pinned deep in their own end, and while continuing to control the ball, they were unable to make much forward progress against the English. Then, one of their men went down and did not move. He appeared lifeless on the pitch. The referee waved for the medics, and the Rabbi sent a substitution into the game for what looked to be the final scrum before full-time. Immediately the British coach realized what was happening. It was the play that he had been expecting, and he knew how to counter it. He had paid dearly for the spy he had stationed at the Springboks field, a spy who had photographed the images from the Rabbi's playbook and had brought them to him. *How careless and arrogant*, thought the British coach when he had received the play that was meant to deceive his team and allow the Springboks to win the match. The Rabbi may be good, he thought, but leaving his playbook unattended while he spoke on his mobile phone and the team showered was less than what he had expected from his opponent. This upcoming play was what he had craved and expected. Now he could thwart the Rabbi's elaborate play and recover the ball near the Springbok's goal line—with just enough time on the clock to work a little magic of his own.

The teams locked down, and the Springbok hooker sent the ball directly back to Sykes as expected. What was not expected was that instead of a lateral to the fresh and fast substitute to the right of Sykes, the ball was thrust far to the left and a wide-open Dwayne Hooper raced unimpeded down the field to the cheer of the standing crowd and the total shock of the British side. As time expired, the scoreboard flashed 18-12 and the Springboks encircled their coach and lifted him high to rest on their shoulders as the crowd cheered loudly. After a minute or two, Raheim was let down and both teams formed lines to shake the hands of their opponents. When the two coaches clasped hands, the Rabbi looked straight at the dejected British coach and said, "Good game, Coach, but next time I would be more careful as to what pictures I am taking and what their true intention is meant to be." With that he was picked up again by his celebrating team and given a ceremonial congratulatory lap around the field for the fans to applaud before he was set down outside of the passageway to his team's locker room. Still undefeated, the Rabbi briefly relished the glory and the adoration bestowed upon him.

Corks popped, and sweat-soaked victors jumped and hollered as they fully savored the precious moment. Taking in that ever-so-sweet feeling of having reached the top. They had destroyed the enemy, the one opposing force, for the moment. Battle scarred and blackened, they enjoyed their stature as they wiped turf and grit from each other's skulls. As seconds quickly became minutes, it was not thoughts of the big payola that would come their way or the "Yeah, we are the champions." It was the common exhilaration that they all felt as athletes and game competitors. It was the torch to be carried forward to the next match and the next opportunity to play again the game. There would be more mountains to climb, more knocks to take, and more beers to down.

For Raheim it was very different. There was no savoring of moments or minutes. No looking ahead to the next match. There was only the enemy, and Balderous would be appearing within the next few minutes. Then the preamble would be over, the dance having been credibly performed and the prey drawn closer to its trap. For the Rabbi, it was now time to perform, directly, within the confines and power of his enemy, and to do so convincingly. The real game had truly begun.

The sound of men marching alerted Raheim as he called out "NOW" to his team. It was time for play 3 as Balderous approached. Entering first were two bodyguards and then Balderous a second later. Jubilance was halted, the players all stood straight and tall, and Enrique Balderous was handed his stage.

"Please, please, as you were. Relax, men. I will keep my comments brief. Congratulations to you all and to your coach," he said as he approached the Rabbi with arms held wide. Clutching the shoulders of Raheim and looking directly into his eyes, he continued, "It is a time for celebration for a job well-done. Your illustrious coach and I will now depart for our own engagement, and I wish you all the pleasures of the city, for you truly proved your worth tonight."

With that they left the room, him, his men, and an alone and unprotected Berhinstein.

Minutes later they arrived at the opulent and exclusive Chez Claude, reported to be the finest of dining establishments in all of Belize. The Rabbi, Balderous, and his security staff were escorted to the rear of the attractively appointed large dining room and then Balderous and Raheim presented with a private table away from the others. It was reserved for very special and influential guests who wanted to dine and converse apart from the other patrons. The table was elaborately set and a vase of fresh flowers served as a centerpiece. As soon as the men took their seats, the wine steward immediately appeared and Balderous requested a bottle of the restaurant's most expensive red from a small vineyard in the Provenance region of France.

"You will enjoy this wine, I am sure, Raheim. It has a wonderful, full bouquet and a deep, rich color, which reminds me of the life\ blood, which flows through our veins."

"I am not familiar with this particular vintage, and I will trust your judgment, which I'm sure remains impeccable to this day. You were always known as a man with fine taste for food and beverage and so much more. I'm certain that you have maintained those standards while finding ways to greatly improve the wealth and welfare of your 110 million citizens, a population that I am told view you as a benevolent and most competent leader."

"Kind words, my friend, and ones which I thank you for. It could be viewed as a blessing or curse that I was the only son of one of Mexico's richest men. It allowed me to sample and appreciate, shall we say, the finer things of life. At the same time, it provided me with an opportunity for an excellent education, which led to my understanding that not all peoples were so fortunate as I have always been. It was education that led me back to my country and into the political arena so that I could make a difference for our people. Not just Mexicans, but all peoples. That is my true quest: to make a concrete difference to the everyday lives of the not-so-fortunate masses," lied Balderous.

"A most honorable ambition indeed, Mr. President. May I say, that judging by the articles I read in newspapers and the summaries that cross my desk, you have made much progress toward achieving your goal," continued to cajole the Rabbi.

"While you, Rabbi Raheim, have succeeded in advancing your position deep into the power pulse of the great nation of Israel. Equally impressive and of considerable additional benefit is that you have donned the cleric's collar. I have cathedrals to make appearances at, but you have the power of the God of the Jews with you as you make laws and further your motives, motives designed to serve your Master above all others."

"Mr. Dear President," commenced the Rabbi, who was then interrupted by Balderous with the surprise statement of "To my friends I am known as Enrique."

"Enrique, such a beautiful name, and I thank you for the privilege of its use. Serving Yahweh, our god, is indeed a pleasure while trying to serve man at the same time is much more difficult. For I know, what was and what will be the reaction of one God, but the aim of man is unclear. *Muddied by numbers*, it has been suggested. Indeed your task is more difficult, without special dispensations, and I salute you for your successes."

"Yes, Raheim, muddied by numbers, we've all heard that phrase since Christmas Day," countered Balderous. "And please, allow me to express my condolences to you on the loss of your family."

"Thank you. Your information regarding my personal life is certainly very up-to-date," replied the Rabbi.

"I must remain up-to-date, Raheim, especially at this time of crisis. Danger and villains may be lurking anywhere."

"Yes, anywhere indeed," replied the Rabbi. "We remain at a loss as to how this *mass cleansing* took place. The international officials I have attended meetings with are truly baffled."

"Baffled," responded Balderous, "yes, that is a reasonable term to define what I and the international leaders I have met with feel. World leaders are puzzled and as of yet have no answers while remaining certain that a second and much-greater cleansing will occur. We view the Christmas Day episode as a successful test for something far greater. Obviously, while masterfully conducted, this initial attack was inconsequential in terms of population control."

"And before we continue, my dear Raheim, since we are uncertain as to the authors of this unexpected act of controlled eradication, may I know how you view it as a God-fearing man? Did your Yahweh forget to inform you? Or were you too busy to listen? Or somehow, while being known to you by what he did do and what he will do in the afterlife he has somehow abandoned the present?" pressed Balderous.

"Actually, Enrique, it remains quite simple. We are all placed on God's earthly highway, and along the way, we make choices since we exercise our free will. And whereas I would have preferred my Lord to advise me and my family of the upcoming cleansing of their town, they made the choice to be there at the time and without knowledge of what would happen. It is the way of life and death and man's earthly process."

Balderous was about to say, "A flawed process," but the steward arrived with the wine, uncorked the bottle, and presented the cork to him. When it was sniffed and a nod of approval given, the steward poured a little into the president's glass for him to sample. When Balderous signified endorsement, the steward poured a glass full for each of them and then exited as quietly as he had appeared.

"Here's to your victory, Raheim, and a thoroughly entertaining match," said Balderous as he held his glass high.

"Thank you, Enrique. I'm pleased to learn that you enjoyed the action."

"Not so much the action as your deception, Raheim. You truly outwitted the British coach on the final play. It was masterful and worthy of a tactician with a flair for the unexpected. The fans were surprised as I must admit was I. I trust our evening will be less deceitful and that we may share many things, things of consequence to the world and to you and I personally."

"I will do my utmost to be clear and transparent, my friend, for the game is over and now the true battle begins. We are challenged as leaders to find solutions for our faltering world, and I am most curious to learn your views on a variety of subjects."

They both took delight in the exquisite wine for a few moments as they eyed each other across the table. It felt suddenly quiet and there was an air of expectation. When

Balderous broke the silence, it was with direct aim.

"Tell me, Raheim, what you truly feel regarding this cleansing that has taken place. Remove for a moment your own personal loss and consider the consequences of the unbridled human population growth that we are experiencing. Is there a way to keep the population fed with rampant growth and increased consumption? Your god of the Old Testament was the greatest cleanser of all and during a time when man's numbers were minimal compared to now. Can we sustain this explosive growth without dire consequences?"

"The deeds of Yahweh were responses to a chosen people that wandered from his teachings and gave in to their own cravings and selfish desires. He used these examples to try and bring man back to a clearer understanding of his wisdom and teachings. Unfortunately, for the greater good, he had to inflict punishment as a means of learning, somewhat like training a child to behave or an administration to adopt guiding principles."

"Yes, guiding principles. But now we are at a time when guiding principles have meant less severe punishment, and by sparing the rod, we have truly spoiled the child. Is there a way out of this mess? Do the unknown renegade Earth Cleansers hold the key, or perhaps you believe that your Yahweh is the one who is intervening?"

"Like you and many others, Enrique, I have pondered these very things. Answers have not come as easily as the questions. Even in our tiny nation with advanced production techniques, we face the danger of an expanding population and its increased needs. All around us it is much worse. China, India, even the United States will face the dire consequences of overpopulation and the continued shrinkage of arable land.

"It is more than global warming and increased incomes and improved health care with people living longer," continued the Rabbi. "There are just not enough food and natural resources for us to sustain this unchecked growth. Something must give. There may be worldwide famine, pestilence, drought, or other natural calamity—or deliberate obliteration by an aligned group of deep thinkers or even warmongers. We will either alter our course or have it altered for us. Life on Earth is not sustainable under the current process. Intervention in whatever form must take place."

Raheim knew that his words were impacting Balderous, who no doubt wished he could jump up and say, "I am the one, the one who has come to cleanse the earth in a humane fashion. To exterminate the unnecessary and to lead nations to controls and a blueprint for sustainability. To act as God. To rule the earth."

Balderous pondered carefully the words of Raheim and then said, "So you are supportive of the mission of the Cleansers? You are in agreement with their plan? Am I to believe that you may be one of them yourself my dear rabbi? Simply carrying out the wisdom of your Lord and Master?"

"No, Enrique, I am not one of them, whoever they may be, but I do believe that they have come forward with an option that has a measure of credibility. Most of the world leaders are busy with the affairs of state and the never-ending meetings and dialogues. All of which, pardon me for saying so, amount to very little as the population continues to speed along like a train with no brakes. The speed must be slowed, and if the brakes are not working, then a bridge needs to be removed or a substantial barrier erected. We cannot continue unchecked."

"Well, Raheim, it appears as we have much more in common than our passion for sporting events. I concur that the earth needs a plan that will lead us to peace and enlightenment and that we need a curbing of the population to achieve this. Unfortunately, not all influential leaders share this vision and are more intent upon personal power and control than in viewing our situation as a global problem, a problem greatly in need of a remedy."

So the dialogue ensued throughout the dinner and into the evening, the Rabbi constantly saluting Balderous and him, in turn, agreeing with Raheim for his views on human curtailment, each seeking to get deeper inside the mind of the other while being careful to avoid displaying the cards that they had yet to play. The Rabbi attempting to get closer and closer to Balderous and Balderous, in turn, seeking to know if the Rabbi was one of the very men that were hunting him.

By the time they had digested the fresh fruit flan and enjoyed their first postrepast brandy, the Rabbi was feeling tipsy but still intent upon depositing the contents of his ring into the snifter of Balderous. When Enrique excused himself to go to the washroom and the brandies were refilled, the Rabbi saw his chance. He quickly unlocked the fastener and turned his hand over so that the powdery white death drug dropped into the brandy glass.

When Balderous returned, he eyed the Rabbi carefully and commented that the steward had refilled their glasses. Then he looked the Rabbi straight in the eye and said, "To show my respect for you and to honor our friendship, I offer my glass to you and I trust you will do likewise for me."

Balderous had anticipated that the Rabbi might be a death angel sent by Boris and Yung and that he would make his move when the opportunity presented itself. He knew that poison could be easily released into a drink and that he had afforded Raheim with the perfect chance.

The Rabbi hesitated for a moment and then Balderous smiled and smugly said, "It would be a huge insult to refuse my request, Raheim."

"Oh, it is not your offer that slows my response, for I am truly taken by your suggestion and I feel greatly honored. The truth of the matter is that I am not a very capable drinker, and the wine and last brandy already have me feeling less in control of myself. I would prefer to save this pleasure for another time, if you please."

"No, Raheim, I will not please, but I will insist. In fact, in true celebratory fashion, it shall be down the hatch and we will exchange glasses now," spoke Balderous in an increasingly hostile voice.

Slowly, the Rabbi pushed his glass across the white linen to within the reach of Balderous, who responded by pushing his glass to the hand of the Rabbi.

"So, my friend, we shall end our splendid evening by drinking with gusto this final glass of brandy, and then I shall be on my way. My men will drive you to your hotel and I will bid you farewell."

Balderous brought the glass to his lips and sloshed the contents quickly down his throat. He glared at the Rabbi who slowly picked up his glass, took one last look at Balderous, and then likewise emptied the brandy as quickly as he could. He immediately felt woozy and set the glass back down on the table.

"I think I'm going to throw up," said the Rabbi.

"No, you won't, Raheim. You will stay there where you are for another few minutes and then my men will attend to you. Meanwhile, I shall head back to my plane and be off to Mexico City. Good-bye, Rabbi, it has been a pleasure."

Within moments of Balderous's departure, the Rabbi eased his head down onto the table. Two of Balderous's men picked him up by the armpits and as inconspicuously as possible removed him from the restaurant. Once outside, they hurriedly drove to the entranceway of the Hilltop Hilton and deposited the Rabbi in the shadows along the roadside where they felt he was sure to be found dead the next morning.

As they sped away to join the waiting plane, the Rabbi raised himself to his feet. He was very drunk, but he had succeeded in fooling Balderous into a rapid drinking of the brandy and an equally quick departure before the effects of the drug could be realized. Now it was time for him to escape as Balderous would be dead by the time that his jet landed in Mexico City and the hunt would be on for the ever-so-clever rabbi.

Enrique Balderous was ruler of all of Mexico and leader of the Cleansers—the most powerful and deadly force ever to inhabit the Earth. He was the heir apparent to a new world order soon to take place while remaining the most cruel and blood loving of men. As he settled back in his private cabin on his private jet, he thought of how he had fooled the Rabbi and the look on Raheim's face as Enrique the Great had insisted that he down the glass of brandy. *I am the wisest, the most cunning, the most gifted, and surely I shall rule the earth*, thought a very pleased Balderous to himself. Then slowly, he closed his eyes, still basking in his sinister abilities as he fell asleep, a sleep from which he was never to awake.

Chapter 41

Brunehoff Must Decide

"So, Daddy, what brings you here unexpectedly? You have always been so very careful to advise me of your travels, and your last few e-mails made no mention of a proposed visit," inquired Francesca of her father.

"I had a meeting to attend in Seattle, and since I was so very close, I thought I would surprise my one and only darling daughter," answered Brunehoff.

"What kind of meeting, Daddy?" pressed a suspicious Francesca.

"Oh, just some government-to-government administration stuff . . . dealing with cooperation on a new set of communication satellites to be launched early next year. Quite boring actually and the meeting was mostly a waste of time. We could have accomplished all that we did through video conferencing, but then I would have missed the opportunity to see you, sweetheart."

"I don't believe you for one second. You may be able to fool others, but remember, I am your daughter and I know when you are not being honest with me. I can see it in your eyes. Something is deeply troubling you, and I wish you would let me into your world so that I can try to help."

"Believe me, Francesca, you don't want to enter into my world," flatly responded Brunehoff.

"And why is that, Father? Is it because I would find computers and technology so very boring, or perhaps it's because you have always lied to me about your role in government and that you don't work for the space agency after all? For a long time I have thought that you are really a spy, an agent for the German government. All of that cloak-and-dagger stuff that pocketbooks are full of. You are a spy, aren't you, and I fear that this assignment that you are currently working on has you troubled deeply," emphatically proclaimed a very assured daughter.

Brunehoff looked at his daughter for several seconds and finally answered, "You are a very perceptive and bright young lady, and after listening to your words of peace and hope just now, I find myself to be so very proud of you. This school has been good for you, and although I was initially concerned that you were relying too heavily on the words of Eli, after meeting the young man, I can truly see the attraction. He appears to be genuine and truly a very enlightened person."

"He is, Daddy, and like you, there is more to Eli than is obvious from one short exchange. He not only speaks with love and calls for peace and justice, but he also takes action, for as you have heard it said, 'Words without good deeds are dead.'"

"Exactly what sort of action do you refer to? Please don't tell me that you are planning to try to influence the powers of the world by some large-scale protest or act of destruction aimed at drawing attention to your noble causes. That would be counterproductive and would put you clearly on the radar screens of the evil forces that truly control and manipulate this world of ours."

"Not my world, Daddy, but yours, a world run by evil forces as you have said and one which is heading toward a collision course with all of the good that remains on this planet. Good that may not have the power and control and might of the governing forces but a good so great and comprised of so many peoples in nations throughout the world that not even the darkness that you fear can curtail its rise."

"You speak of matters that you have no idea about. If only you knew, you would not be so quick to believe that you or anyone could halt the battle that has already begun," coldly advised Brunehoff.

"No idea? Really? If I told you that I know that you are here at the instructions of your masters of the NOW and that you seek one particular member of the group known as the Earth Cleansers, would that be indicative of someone who had no idea? Would it, Daddy? Tell me, would it?"

"You don't know what you are talking about, Francesca, and I would strongly advise that you reconsider what you say and whom you say it to," answered a surprised Brunehoff, intent upon protecting his only child and the true love of his life.

"Then perhaps I should tell you that the one you seek will arrive in Ottawa at five p.m. tomorrow and that I know you are torn between you orders and your conscience. Would that be enough to convince you, Father?"

"How could you possibly know these things?" demanded Brunehoff.

"What did you think, Dieter Brunehoff, that all knowledge was reserved for those who hold power with an iron grip? That the masses of the world could forever be treated as pacifist fools to be used and ruled by those of power and influence? What arrogance."

"Are you telling me that you have people everywhere who have infiltrated the governments of the world and have some warm and cuddly plan of your own to grasp power?"

"Grasp power, no. It is not power that we seek but the righting of wrongs, the introduction of fair play and justice, the freeing of captives unfairly held, and the deliverance of the world to true leaders of concern and caring for all of the Creator's children. That is what we work towards, and our force is mounting, and soon a tide will rise to sweep the unjust away and to set the captives free. We don't play by your rules, but we do engage the technology that the military has brought forth and we use it for good and not evil. That is what I am telling you, my father, and believe me, I would not be sharing any of this with you if I thought for one second that you were really the monster that on the surface you appear to be to others of your group. I believe that you are a good man who has fallen victim to a cruel force and that you have not determined a way to rid yourself of these villains that possess you. That is what I believe and what I am telling you, dearest father."

A tear emerged from the corner of Brunehoff's left eye and then another. Quickly, he wiped them both with his hand. "My dear sweet Francesca, if only there were a way to solve all the ills of the world, but I fear that there is no force great enough. Evil lurks everywhere, and I have encountered and endured much of its dark reach. Someday, when there is time, I will be able to reveal to you many secrets that I have never shared. I even will be able to tell you about your dear, brave mother, who died giving birth to you. Died after escaping from torturous treatment inflicted by villains far more cruel than most of the rich and arrogant lot that control the power of the world today. Villains that have had their final hurrah and should very soon not be able to torture and confine anyone ever again. This your father has set in place."

A sobbing yet able to be composed Francesca looked directly to the father that she had never known but had always hoped really existed. Now she was convinced that her true father was emerging, and it brought great hope to her heart and soul. She had longed for this day, knowing that it may never come. Now across the table from her, in a land of apparent peace, far away from the noise and traffic of the city and set against a deep green forest, she had encountered her "real" father for the first time—and she was overwhelmingly pleased.

"Sweetheart, I have been giving serious thought to my requirements and duties versus my desires and hopes. I can choose to abandon my mission, but then I will never be able to return to Germany or most anywhere. I will be hunted by the evil members of the NOW and I will be disgraced for leaving my country when it was in need of my services. Yet I have found a place where we can be safe and live together away from the treachery and ills of modern society but with access to funds that I have placed in a numbered Swiss account. We can flee together, tomorrow, and then there shall be ample time for each of us to learn so very much about each other."

"Daddy, do you really believe that I can just up and leave and forget the ills of the world and believe that they will vanish as quickly as I will disappear? The evil will be still here, and I will not be able to contribute to its defeat. I could never abandon my allegiance and my desire to make this world as the Creator wishes. That is my mission, and I fully intend to see it through. And you must see your mission through also, for with the virus of the Cleansers comes a global threat such as we have never encountered before, and if you do not attend to your target, then many tens of millions of people may die—all because you wanted to have peace and quiet with your daughter. Don't you find that to be the least bit selfish? Do you really think that we could be happy knowing that we had run, not only from the villains, but also from our responsibilities to create change?"

"Francesca, I understand what you are saying, but you do not know about what I have endured from a very young age and how I fear that I have little time left to live with health and strength. I was injected with harmful drugs from a very young age and even for years after you were born. Soon these drugs will overtake my system and I will be unable to function as you see me now. Is it so wrong to want some time with my daughter and leave the cleanup of the Cleansers for others to attend to?" pleaded a very distraught Brunehoff.

"My dear father, if you have little time remaining, I am truly sorry. I had so hoped that we would be able to spend much more time together and much more often. Little time remaining should strengthen your conviction to accomplish what you know you must do. Neither you nor I could ever be happy knowing that we had run away from the very world that needs fixing and could use our help to do so. We must stay and we must do what we must do. There is no other way."

While Brunehoff considered his daughter's latest answer, two others approached their garden-side table. It was the smiling Eli accompanied by a young lady. Brunehoff instantly recognized her as one of the students from the language lab. She appeared to be of mixed ethnicity, was very tall and slender, and had shoulder-length brown hair that draped down upon her dark T-shirt that bore the large words of POWER TO THE PEOPLE.

A T-shirt in Canada in winter was the first thing that struck Brunehoff as odd, but it was midafternoon, and the mild west coast continued to bask in unseasonably high temperatures that approached twenty-five degrees Celsius. El Niño or global warming or just another unorthodox freak of nature, whatever the cause, it had not rained hard since October and the temperature had remained above freezing throughout the Christmas season.

It was pleasant, and the delighted locals were busy admiring the earlier-than-ever blossoms and planning for their spring gardens.

Rising to greet the two, Brunehoff was motioned to by Eli and asked to please retake his seat. "There is no need for formalities amongst friends, outside the classroom, Mr. Brunehoff. May we join you? I think that I will be able to provide you with some important information in your quest to make the right decision and to adhere to the moral principles that deep down you know to be just," spoke Eli.

"But first, please allow me to introduce you to one of Francesca's closest friends and a young lady who has done much to further the ways of the Creator at great personal risk to herself. This is Anna and she is from Ottawa, the very next stop on your journey, if I am not mistaken. Anna, please say hello to Francesca's father."

A caught-off-guard Brunehoff went through the motions of exchanging greetings with Anna, and then Anna and Eli pulled up two chairs from the adjacent vacant table. Once settled, Eli continued, "Anna has been solely responsible—"

"Pardon me for interrupting, Eli, but what makes you so sure that I am in need of decision making or that I have any plans to travel to Ottawa? Did Ms. Price apprise you of this also?" softly inquired Brunehoff.

"No, not Ms. Price, but Ms. Brown, Ms. Anna Brown, who bugged this table you have been sitting at and who will be leaving for Ottawa tomorrow to greet her father, who has been away for a very long time."

"Don't look so alarmed, Daddy. There is no one here that wishes you harm. In fact, the purpose of this friendly little meeting is to make you aware of the things that we are aware of and to enlist your services to help fight the forces of evil that encapsulate all of us in this not-so-free world of ours. Trust us,

Daddy, and we will prove to you that we are able to accomplish all that is needed to bring down the two camps of enemies and power-hungry freaks that threaten our beautiful world, a world that has fallen to the lure of riches, power, and unjust might. Not all of the masses are meek or self-centered, detached, and apathetic. There is a movement, a groundswell, an alliance of those that desire to reclaim Mother Earth from the rich and powerful and return it to its rightful heirs—the good and caring and noble, those who continue to fight injustice with any and all means at their disposal. Please join this team, Daddy. Your life will be fuller and happier. You shall be rewarded with an inner bounty that can only be delivered up to those that truly put others before their selves."

Dieter Brunehoff had gone from surprise, to disbelief, to bewilderment all in the matter of a few short minutes. He didn't know how to react or what to say. He had been disarmed, found out, and forgiven, all at once. Now his emotions were running wild and his legs started to twitch as he felt nervous rushes of adrenaline charge through his upper torso and to his head. He was dizzy and pale and clearly showed signs of being in need of medical care.

"What is it, Daddy? What's wrong?" frantically asked a worried Francesca as the others looked on.

"It will pass, dearest. It always does. It just occurs much more frequently than before, and the symptoms last longer. If I could just lie on the grass over there in the shade for a while and you were to bring me a cold cloth and a glass of ice water, I will be fine."

"You don't look fine, Mr. Brunehoff, and we do have a staff nurse, and a doctor is not far away. Please allow us to help you," urged Eli.

"No, please, no nurse and definitely no doctor. This infliction of mine is triggered by startles to my nervous system. Just allow me to rest quietly for a while and I will be fine."

The three of them helped him from the chair and across the walkway to the cool dark-green grass of the rolling lawn. Anna removed a sweater from her bag and folded it and placed it under his neck. Eli removed Brunehoff's shoes and loosened his belt and shirt collar while Francesca ran to fetch the items requested.

When Francesca returned, Eli gently raised Brunehoff just enough so that he could sip the cold water through the drinking straw while Anna folded the wet cloth and placed it on his forehead. Then each of the young women took hold of a hand each. They ever so gently stroked and massaged them as Eli applied a soothing touch to his temples at the edges of the damp face cloth. They began to sing softly and sweetly and to attend to him as he had never been cared for before. He closed his eyes and started to relax, feeling the love and affection that was freely offered to *him*, one of the very-evil monsters that they had vowed to fight. Perhaps love was indeed the most powerful of all weapons, briefly thought Dieter, and then he fell deeply asleep.

He was awakened by a cool breeze that blew across the lawn and made him realize that it was still winter. He had a warm blanket draped over him; and the two young ladies were still massaging his hands and arms while the ever-vigilant Eli kneeled directly over him and was praying silently as he held his hands, palms down, just above the forehead of Brunehoff. He had been dreaming, back into the mysterious world of the unsolvable dream that had puzzled him since his flight from Los Angeles to Frankfurt. The dream of masked people who when they had their masks removed by Brunehoff they appeared as his own likeness looking back at him. He turned to see his beautiful daughter, and then instantly he realized that it was her that was beneath the mask. That what he had dreamt was a premonition of sorts. That the unmasking was him realizing that his own flesh and blood had kept things concealed from him in much the same manner that he had kept secrets from her. The masks were off now, and he knew that they were not to be worn ever again.

"Welcome back, Mr. Brunehoff. You look much better now," whispered a smiling and caring Anna to the man who had been selected to kill her father.

"How long have I been out, eh, asleep?" whispered back Brunehoff, not wanting to disturb the praying Eli.

"Perhaps we might offer to tell you how long you have been awake, my friend," softly spoke a still-closed-eyed Eli. "For most of your life has been a labored, troubled sleep and now it appears that you have finally awaken to a new reality and hopefully a new cause. I have felt the rage within your veins and the tempest of your troubled life. It is time that that chapter closes forever and that you awake to a new reality." Then he added while his eyes popped open, "It's been about two hours, and it is time to eat if you feel well enough to stand."

"Two hours, it feels like two days. I am truly rested. The pain and dizziness is gone, and yes, I can stand and surely I can eat. What's for dinner? I am quite hungry," responded a markedly improved and very alert Brunehoff.

"We had hoped that you would offer to take us to dinner, Daddy, with that big government salary of yours. There are many fine dining places within the city and even a couple of excellent ones in the local area near the sea in the quaint little town of Sooke. We don't have much opportunity for such delights, but food is the nourishment of the body, and now that your heart and soul has been administered too, I do believe that we are all ready for the second course." A smiling Francesca laughed.

This was followed by a round of laughter from all four. It seemed to Brunehoff that he had woken to a new reality, a reality that he was very happy with and one that he was intent upon maintaining, for the present at least.

Dinner proved to be excellent, just as they had promised him. The conversation had also been enjoyable, and Brunehoff was able to see that youth was vibrant and sociable and not always following some hidden or secret agenda intended to advance their cause or get one step ahead of the opposition. They took time for enjoyment and laughter, something that Dieter has sorely missed in his own life of discipline, training, and adherence to his masters. Now while waiting for coffee and dessert, he finally turned to the more serious matters at hand.

"Eli, tell me, do you really believe that you have the power to rid this world of tyrants and monsters and return it to the good, oblivious masses that you say exist everywhere? How can you possibly hope to take on Yung in China or Pretnekof in Russia or the roomful of weasels that occupy the government of your neighbor to the south? Pardon me, but don't you feel that you are a little bit overambitious and perhaps even naive?"

Eli clasped his hands together and looked directly to Brunehoff. "If we have given you the impression that we thought ridding the world of evil and injustice would be easy, then I must apologize to you, my friend. As my own father often said, 'Anything worth having is worth working for,'" and indeed we are many and we are prepared to work with vigilance and hope, long into the night. If we do not succeed, this year or next year or in our lifetimes, so be it. But that doesn't mean that the cause is foolish or unattainable, only that the torch will be carried forward by those that come after us. That each new generation will have members who carry our beliefs and will get stronger each day. This has always been the way and it will continue so," calmly stated a confident and self-assured Eli.

Brunehoff was not accustomed to such optimism, and it clearly showed. He didn't want to challenge or offend the very person that had cared for him and had given his daughter hope and a cause much more noble than his own. Yet he needed convincing, and he knew that in the morning he would have to make a decision that would define how he would live the remainder of his earthly life. He knew how his heart was leaning, but his structured and powerful mind told him otherwise. He had been ruled by his mind and had little time for the things of the heart. They had brought him only sorrow at the loss of Hannah and the unfaithfulness of Rebecca.

"Eli, your conviction is impressive and your cause can be considered as just, but how do you take down 100 million trained troops that China boasts or undo the evil of other totalitarian regimes? The world has always been run by the evil overlords. Think back through history to Nebuchadnezzar, Alexander, Khan, Caesar, Napoleon, Hitler, and the lot. Do you see justice and white light throughout the ages? Hasn't this earth of ours always been controlled by the mighty and not the truly worthy?" Brunehoff pried a little deeper.

"It is as you say, my friend, but let's for a moment consider the fact that we no longer live in caves or, in most of the world at least, get punished without a fair trial or are subjected to torture and imprisonment at the whim of a vicious ruler. Our societies have progressed, and while the world is still full of villains and human rights injustices, there has been progress as you can see in this very country where we are assembled. No one here demands that we shoot our neighbor or indiscriminately knife our friend. There is hope, Dieter, and that is what propels us forth."

"Hope? Hope that the tribal warfare that butchers the people in your own country of birth will suddenly cease? Hope that the powerful villains will suddenly have a change of . . . heart? Hearts that they do not possess. Hope that the Middle East and elsewhere will all of a sudden stop lopping off limbs for infractions like theft of a loaf of bread by a hungry man? Hope that man will suddenly lose his will for greed and that the lion shall lay down with the lamb?" countered a still-challenging Brunehoff.

"Yes, Dieter, all of that and more. Our hope is great, and our stratagem is well conceived and has been built upon for a very long time. In the end, the good of the earth shall prevail, the wicked will be abolished, and the proverbial lion shall indeed lay down with the lamb. This is what we believe, and we do so with reason and without pretense."

"Let me explain it to you this way, if I may," continued Eli. "Think of all of the peoples of the earth as plants. Some bear fruit and others wither and die. It is not because of their potentiality that they suffer death, but it comes from poor soil, lack of rain, being overgrown by weeds or choked out by more powerful plants that have suppressed them. Then think of a gardener, a caring, patient, and hardworking gardener that will remove the weeds, till the soil, and provide light and water to the poor, previously overpowered plants. Will they not be enriched by the care and nurture that has been given to them? Will they not respond with growth and open their leaves and flowers in response? We are called to be gardeners, Dieter, and as surely as there are weeds and drought, there is also rain and sunshine."

"If I were with my usual companions, such talk, while being mildly entertaining, would be quickly dismissed as nothing but mindless dribble. Coming from youthful gardeners without knowledge of the immensity of the task or the truly great size of the overgrown garden," answered back Brunehoff as the waiter arrived with the coffees and desserts.

This slight break in the verbal action afforded Francesca a chance to advise her father that Eli was not the enemy. What he said had merit and that her daddy, as a man who had been forced to bite his tongue for all his life, perhaps could continue with that for just another few hours.

"No no no, Francesca, please. Your father is not intent upon waging verbal warfare with me. Rather, I believe that he is truly seeking the white light that we have been blessed with and his powerful mind needs answers to questions. I find our conversation to be noncombatant, and I hope that we can reach this father, who loves you dearly and I truly believe would lay down his life for you. He is not so very different from each of us. Only, he has been without a gardener and surrounded by thorns for a very long time. I find him to be a man of honor who seeks justice and will be won over to our side."

"Hold it right there, Eli. While I thank you for your kind words about how I would do anything for my dear daughter, please don't make me into some sort of saint or even good guy. I have committed many atrocities and even taken lives, all in the name of victory, competition, and my country. I am the thorn amongst the flowers, and you should not send any compliments my way. Also, I am not yet convinced that you have any hope of gaining the upper hand against a villainous force that rules without care or regard for even their own people. How can you possibly hope to clean up this fallen world of ours?"

"By reaching the misguided people who truly do have power and influence and convincing them to join the allegiance of the good and caring. Our force is blossoming, and with each day, new growth is taking place. If we can reach powerful men such as you, then the task of convincing the masses will be much more easily accomplished. Don't discredit yourself, please, Dieter, for we know that you have suffered greatly for a very long time and have been forced to behave differently from what your hidden heart tells you that is right."

"OK, then what am I supposed to do to amend my ways? Get on the plane to Ottawa tomorrow with Anna and sit next to her and talk about gardening while scheming to kill her father? Is that your idea of white light? It sounds more like white rule to me. Don't forget where I have come from and the nature of those that I have represented. How can you possibly condone the taking of a life while trying to save others? I really don't get it," tersely replied Brunehoff.

"You will, Dieter, you surely will. Yes, we want you to get on the plane with Anna tomorrow and yes, we want you to seek her father, but no, we don't want you to kill him or convince him of the fact that our way is right. During the past six months and especially since Christmas Day, Mr. Willie Brown has lived a very troubled life. When Anna made him aware that she knew of his evil club and the virus that he had masterminded and the destruction that he alone had conjured up. Finally, when she said she had forgiven him, well, then he saw the light and he is now one of us.

"He will always be deeply bothered by what he has done, and he will never find peace in this life of ours. However, we believe that he will find ways to halt the destruction and thwart the ways of his evil associates. Deep down he is not so very different from you: a good man who has fallen victim to the evil of the world. Now he is eager to strike back against those that have harmed him since so very long ago. He just wants the opportunity to make amends and is quite prepared to offer up his life if that is what it will take," spoke Eli.

"Well, I am relieved to learn that you are not on some equally distasteful mission as those that I have kept company with. I am certainly pleased that Willie Brown, the one and only Cleanser that I have maintained any respect and admiration for, in fact, the one who I have envied for being able to live in a land of freedom, is, as you say, onside. If Willie is in, then I guess that you can count me in also!"

"Thank you, Daddy. You can't imagine how wonderful this makes me feel. You have truly made my day and strengthened my convictions. There is a difficult road ahead and we may not see the fruit of our labors in our lifetime, but we will have done our duty and prepared the garden for others to continue to improve. You make me very proud."

"Yes, proud indeed, Dieter, very proud. Praise be to the Creator."

"And all true followers," responded all to Eli's words.

Chapter 42

JANUARY 15

So very, very much had transpired in the past week. The Cleansers had been decimated or defected with only a lonely Singh remaining with his warehouses of potentially unneeded breathing apparatuses. Anhebo had fled to Canada to meet with Brown, to remove them from any further cleansing activity, and to listen to the vision brought forth by the daughters of Brown and Brunehoff. Remorse and guilt had been forged together with hope and enlightenment.

The Rabbi had succeeded in returning to Israel, and no amount of Mexican suspicion would result in having him fingered as responsible for the death of Balderous. There were no witnesses, no proof, and apparently no motive. He had worked his magic on the field and carefully crafted the end to the kingpin of the Cleansers. He was pleased with his tactics and the ease at which he had escaped. His partner in crime and master of the NOW, Boris Pretnekof, was also pleased and knew that the Rabbi would always find a way to deliver exactly what had been asked of him. This gave Raheim much comfort and reason to feel very secure in his position of rising power. He felt assured that Boris would not act without him and that together they could outfox Yung.

Boris had provided insight to the Japanese prime minister. The missing and never-to-be-found General Karakanni had been exposed as the self-loving and imperialist pig that he truly was. While he was pleased with the final outcome of the Rabbi's game, he was alarmed that the trusted Brunehoff had seemingly vanished. He had allowed him to go after Brown without the aid of any assigned Krems. There were no tracks to follow. Something was wrong, exceedingly wrong, and Boris knew it. Neither Brunehoff nor Brown could be located, and Anhebo also was not to be found. What could this mean? Was there a connection? He had trusted Brunehoff to take down Brown, a mistake that would not be repeated. He would dispatch Krems 1 and 2 to Canada and, with his mafia net, find Brown and dispose of the mastermind chemist. That would leave only Anhebo and Singh. Singh he could cancel at will, and Anhebo alone posed no threat to him. Then it would be back to the matter of discrediting the slimy Gilberger, and finally he would go after his ultimate prey—Yung.

Meanwhile, Chairman Yung had uncovered a startling surprise of his own. Something that he had not contemplated but was most pleased to learn. The "Smiths" had returned to China and brought with them the documents of the three French businessmen. Amongst the papers and hidden within the passport folder of one of the Frenchmen, his investigators had found a computer microchip. It contained encrypted code that his team of experts was able to crack within forty-eight hours. The contents were startling. It was not about laundry expansion into French Africa but details of all the locations and dispersal plans for Bh297 virus strikes against India and China! The Frenchmen were more than businessmen; they were part of the Phantom's team, Garcia's concealment network, and they were preparing to initiate phase 2 by decimating entire cities in the earth's two most populated nations. Beijing, Shanghai,

Tianjin, Qingdao, Shenyang, and 100 more Chinese cities with populations over one million were all targeted to be destroyed! Only the money magnet of Hong Kong was to be spared.

The more Yung read, the more he knew what he must do. Keep the information to himself—for now at least. His decipherers had not been allowed outside the confines of their lab or permitted to communicate with anyone since their decryption had commenced. He had wisely loaded the lab with enough food and supplies for a full week and had cut off all communication to the outside. No phones, no e-mails, no anything. No one but the translators with knowledge of the contents of the code.

Yung pressed the small red button on his intercom; and his secretary, Lung Ho Fat, entered his office and closed the door behind him.

"Yes, Honorable Chairman, how may I be of service to you?"

"The five decipher experts have completed their work, and I am now in receipt of all of the pertinent information. The information they have provided is extremely sensitive and must be closely guarded. I wish to reward them for their efforts and propose an immediate vacation for them and their families. Go directly to the lab and escort them here to meet with me."

As the secretary scurried to the lab to fetch the translators, Yung called to the motor pool and instructed the duty sergeant to have a passenger van and driver wait outside the main entrance of his city palace. When Ho Fat returned with the five decipherers, the chairman welcomed them in and, with a slight wave of his right hand, dismissed his loyal secretary. He invited the team of three men and two women to be seated, and personally poured each of them a crystal glass of very special sherry and raised his own as a signal for all of them to celebrate their work.

"You are all to be commended for your diligence and hard work," the chairman began. "Without your efforts, we would not have warning of the horrific genocide planned against our great nation. We would be helpless to counter these reprehensible plans and China would be in ruin and unable to recover. You and I and all of your families and all of my government officials would be dead. The Cleansers would ascend to power and the earth would be changed forever. The People's Republic is indebted to you, and I personally thank you."

Neither the military nor civilian staff of Chairman Yung was accustomed to the softness of his voice or the compliments that were being bestowed upon them. They all feared Yung greatly, and only the warmth of the sherry allowed them to keep from trembling in his presence.

"As you can imagine," Yung continued, "this knowledge you have unraveled must be kept a secret until we are able to fully dismantle the threat and arrest all of the villains responsible for these monstrous acts against humanity. I need each of you to make no mention of what you have learned to anyone. In exchange for your silence, I have prepared a very special gift for each of you and for your families also."

Yung reached below his desk and lifted up a black leather briefcase and placed it upon his desktop. He unlatched the case, lifted the top, and twirled it around to face the five loyal decryption experts. All were stunned to see the packed contents of renminbi notes of various large denominations.

"This money is to be shared equally amongst you, for you have all contributed to the unscrambling of the code. My desire is that you spend it all at the great shopping centers that surround our Olympic stadium. Buy wondrous gifts for your spouses and children and your parents and, of course, yourselves. Surprise your loved ones as I have surprised you! Also, you are to be excused from duty for two full weeks and with your families flown to my winter palace in Guangdong province to enjoy the fruits of your success. A car and driver awaits you now at the entrance below. Go now and enjoy your shopping and surprise your families."

All five bowed deeply to their generous chairman and uttered meek words of thanks as the chairman spun the attaché case around and snapped shut its clasps. He handed it to the senior of the five, a man who had served his country for some thirty years.

As they departed the room, Yung pressed again the red button on his intercom and Ho Fat reappeared.

"Pour yourself a sherry, Lung, and savor its sweetness, for your next task will be less savory."

"And what might that be, may I ask, Honorable Chairman?"

"Patience, Lung, wait for it. If I know the desires of all peoples, and believe me when I say that I do, you shall soon know that your next task will be to act with disbelief and outrage—something that you do most adequately, having been schooled by me so very well. Patience, Lung. It is what separates the confident from the uncertain," instructed Yung to his ever-faithful and fearful assistant.

A loud explosion rattled the glasses on the table and shook the pictures on the wall. Yung glared at a surprised Ho Fat and suggested that he should rush outside to see what had happened. He couldn't resist adding, "Make sure that the motor pool checks all of the remaining vehicles for bombs." He returned the tiny detonating device from his left hand to the confines of his center-desk drawer, knowing full well that it may be needed again to trigger another case of bonus funds.

With Garcia and the Frenchmen dead, his own translators blown up, not even his secretary knowing the contents of the encrypted files, Chairman Yung felt secure and empowered. Now he could initiate the raids on the Bright White laundries throughout all of China and claim the virus barrels for himself. Then China would be rid of any possible virus attack from the remaining Cleansers. He could frame his full focus to his most ardent goal—the downfall and destruction of Boris and with it his own rise to control of the NOW. As he continued to sip his sherry, he felt it somehow tasted sweeter than before. *Success and well-conducted plans had a way of enriching all*, thought Yung, as he smiled at the large framed portrait of himself that dominated the room.

Back in Canada, at an undisclosed location near the nation's capital, the realigned beginnings of a third powerful camp were quickly emerging. Brown and Brunehoff had fully awakened to the persistence of their daughters, Francesca and Anna, and to the warming words of Eli—that and their own disgust at how they had lived their lives.

Also, Anhebo had arrived and, after much discussion, had vowed that she would abandon the plans of the remaining Cleansers and adhere to the principles of the Creator as they had been outlined to her by an increasingly exuberant Eli. She offered up the full force of her considerable fortune and influence to help steer mankind to a cleaner path and a more righteous future. In doing so, she received the benefit of a peace and calm that she had not known but had always searched for. *Finally*, she thought, *I am with the ones I wish to associate with, and we are on a road that will indeed improve the world.* However, eating at her mind deep in the recesses of her brain was the one undeniable fact that there were far too many humans on this planet. Regardless of the elaborate plans for redistribution and parity as so eloquently put forth by Eli, she knew that there would be turmoil and much death still to come. It would be at the hands of the NOW, the Cleansers, Mother Nature, or God Almighty himself. There was no future for an overpopulated planet that continued to grow with reckless abandon.

Eli was firmly convinced that Brown, Brunehoff, and Anhebo were all onside. In spite of the seemingly never-ending litany of questions and negative responses, he made a decision to bring them deeper into the fold. He excused himself from the gathering to make a very important cell phone call. Returning after a few minutes, the group became quiet as they all looked to him for some news or information regarding his call.

"I must tell you that I have just spoken with our leader, and while delighted that the three of you have joined our ranks, she remains skeptical that each of you have truly reformed and can be totally trusted," slowly announced Eli.

"She?" perked up Anhebo. "Who is this leader of whom you speak?"

"As of now, the Leader has cautioned me to not share any insightful details with you, not until such time as we are certain that each of you are fully committed to our cause and have proven yourselves to be totally in line with our common beliefs."

"So we are to follow a new leader who will remain nameless and faceless to us? We are to abide by the principles of the 'collective' as you refer to yourselves, but when it comes time to inform us of your strengths and depth of infiltration throughout the world, we are to be left out? What kind of recruitment and trust is that?" flared Anhebo. "How can we possibly be effective if we are blind to our own causes and plans?"

"My friend, Anhebo, I hear what you are saying and I understand your obvious frustration. Each of you is accustomed to being extremely well-informed and leading missions and being entrusted with great responsibilities. Yet kindly consider our situation.

Barely three weeks ago, two of you were at the forefront of an horrific attack on the peoples of this earth, and the other one was a man who would conduct the will of his master without question, a master whose intentions are diametrically opposite to our own. Our cause has been centuries in the making, and many have died for adhering to what we believe to be the most righteous of beliefs. Our leader, our entire circle of prominent and caring members throughout the world are now aware of your defections to the Collective. But they wish to be prudent and assured of your true purposes and motivations. Trust like this does not come easily and cannot be taken lightly for the dark forces of death and destruction are all around us. We truly believe that much must come to pass before we are able to ascend to the new earth that we hope and pray for," stated Eli.

"I have indicated," he continued, "that I am fully won over by your change of heart, but others in our inner circle, more influential than I, still have doubt. For these reasons I am unable to share much more with you. Just believe as we do, just align your hearts to love and justice as we have . . . and please be patient. I have much else to share with you about the depth and breadth of our united cooperative and how we have members in high-ranking positions in most of the governments of the world. There are also millions of adherents from the middle classes and a huge groundswell of poor peoples throughout the earth in nearly all countries and of most religious persuasions. When the time is right, all of these diverse peoples will unite for the common good of the planet and its inhabitants. These commonalities have been made known to us by the Creator, and we follow this thread without fear or selfishness. We consider it to be noble and right and the way in which our world is to unfold and finally come of age. So please allow a little time and be prepared for a mission that will illuminate your true colors."

"What mission, Eli?" inquired Brunehoff.

"That also cannot be discussed as of yet, Dieter, but suffice it to say that each of you will be greatly challenged. When you have completed what is asked of you, there will be no doubt whatsoever of your allegiance, and provided you succeed, all will be made known to you," replied Eli.

"Considering what we have been a part of, I consider that to be good enough for me," calmly but emphatically announced Willie Brown. "I can never undo the wrongs and deaths that I have caused, and I do not expect any consideration from anyone that comes from a righteous stance. I have committed a great sin against humanity and I am fully prepared to sacrifice my miserable life if in some way it can help further the cause of goodness and hope. I have been on the wrong path and I chose to stay there. I could have disappeared long ago, and while I can find reasons for my actions and conduct, none of them are any longer acceptable to me. I will be prepared to carry out any and all instructions. I have learned a great deal from my daughter and I will follow her passion and wisdom until the end of my days. I am so very sorry for my past."

"I also bear much remorse," stated Brunehoff. "All of my life I have had to answer to others while knowing that their actions and characters were greatly flawed. I also could have disappeared before now or had a change of heart. Saving the lives of my parents was an excuse and not a reason. Following the lead of a brilliant madman is something that I should have terminated years ago. Giving in to my anger and love of success in combative bouts cannot be blamed on others but me alone. Like my new friend, Willie, I am also prepared to give my life for the future of humanity. I only hope that my challenge will be successful and that in some small way, I am able to restore a level of respectability that my dear Francesca can continue. My time is fading fast, and I wish more than anything to make a contribution to all that is right before my earthly plight ends."

All eyes turned to Anhebo, and she slowly viewed each of them in turn. She saw the forever-changed Brown and Brunehoff being embraced by their loving and forgiving daughters. Their words had impacted her greatly. She also saw the bright and cheerful young Ethiopian. Risen from poverty and through devotion and hard work, occupying a position of prominence and influence. A position that he would gladly forsake if it could further the cause of his beliefs and the ways of his creator. She thought of the many masses she had attended and confessions she had made to her Lord and her god. All paled next to the passion and good works of Eli. She pondered her position of power and might and how she had ascended through brute force, intellect, and the considerable resources of her father. She had been gifted with opportunity and rewarded with riches, riches of man that seemed worthless next to the riches promised by a loving and forgiving god and creator.

Then something happened that overwhelmed the gigantic and powerful princess and caused her to shed tears that flowed freely down her cheeks and to the floor below. She looked up and spoke in a broken but coherent and emphatic voice, "My friends, *friends* is a term that I have not had the privilege of using for such a very long time. In my thirst for power and control, I have turned my back on all that is holy and worthy. I have become a crazed and unhappy woman who rises to each miserable day seeking reconciliation while continuing with my actions against humanity. Like Dieter and Willie, I cannot undo my actions and cruelties, but like them I can contribute with all of my might now that I have truly seen the light. I also am now prepared to sacrifice all, including my earthly life, for the greater good of humanity. For the first time since I was a very little girl, I truly feel blessed. Not by the forgiveness that I hope to receive nor by the challenge to make amends for my many acts of cruelty, but by the privilege of being amongst true friends—trustworthy soul mates that have unshackled my heart and set my spirit free. My life has changed forever, and I will abide by all of the teachings and actions of my new friends and loved ones. Thank you, Eli, Francesca, and Anna, for what you have bestowed upon us. Thank you for the opportunity to contribute to truth and love and to forsake our egocentric selves. Truly my life begins today." Anhebo sobbed uncontrollably.

Eli rose to his feet. Tears trickled from his eyes also and from those of Willie, Dieter, and their delighted daughters. Tears of forgiveness and freedom. Tears of joy.

"Praise be to the Creator," managed a visually moved Eli.

"And all true followers," answered the determined voices of the five others.

Chapter 43

GILBERGER GETS HIS REWARD

Wilson Gilberger could scarcely contain himself. With Balderous dead, the threat of the Cleansers had all but disappeared. His president and the U.S. cabinet were left squabbling with China and Russia regarding who had bombed the Russian convey. He had received congratulations from Boris for his nifty disposal of Varez. The cursed Brunehoff, who had knocked him out cold, was missing and not likely to resurface alive. Burgess and Karakanni were presumed dead or in hiding.

All this left Gilberger considering how he and Sarquas could succeed. Maybe use Langois somehow to discredit Yung or Boris and the Rabbi? Then assume control of the remnants of the NOW and bring greater notoriety to himself. The presidential election would be his opportunity to grasp power, and he knew that there were few obstacles to that. He must, however, remove, displace, cancel, or discredit the two most powerful NOW members or the USA would at best remain on equal footing with the great powers of Russia and China.

He picked up his desk phone, clicked the small black plastic electronic device provided by Boris, and called to the office of Rebecca. Her assistant stated that she was in a meeting with the president but that he would advise Ms. Sarquas as soon as she was available that the secretary of state wished to speak with her.

Barely five minutes later, his phone rang and Rebecca spoke first, "Gil, where are you? Why didn't you pick up?"

"I've been very busy, Rebecca," shot back Gilberger.

"I've been stuck in a meeting all morning with Rush, Roth, and Walker. Why weren't you there? The Chinese and Russians are turning up the heat regarding the missile firings. It looks like we may be fingered yet since our planes were in a no-fly zone, but Roth and Rush both swear that no American pilot fired the Chinese missiles. The fact that it was LC-291 fighter jets in a no-fly zone makes the matter worse since Rush and Roth are refusing to allow our latest LCs to be examined by others."

"It's a standoff at present," continued Sarquas, "but the media is demanding information. Sooner or later we will have to allow inspection. That or locate the real perpetrators. It's a hell of a mess and not one that we will easily dispense with. Another huge pain in the ass and more work for me."

"Hhhmmm, I have to figure out a way to use these scattered pieces and assemble them into something whole for us. Remember, we have to be totally prepared and totally in control if we are to be swept to power in the next election . . . and we are to discredit and displace Boris and Yung."

"And the Rabbi," added Sarquas.

"The Rabbi? He's a joke. Without Boris he will be easy to overcome. Mere child's play."

"Tell that to Balderous," quipped Sarquas.

"Shut up, Rebecca."

Rebecca Sarquas had been through a torturous time these past few days. Endless meetings. Her longed-for lover, Brunehoff, had disappeared. Having had to dismiss passes and innuendos from White House staffers while trying to maintain an attitude of professionalism befitting her stature. She was tired and wanted no more crap from Gilberger. The man who promised her everything but as of yet had delivered nothing for her benefit. She considered telling Gilberger to F off but wisely reconsidered. There would be no advantage in such a move. She needed allies and not enemies, and Gilberger had promised her the vice presidency—if she could wait long enough.

"OK, Gil, we'll play it your way. You decide what to do about Yung and Boris and I will tell Rush and the others that our brilliant secretary is devising a plan for their approval. That should keep them quiet for a while."

"That's better, lover. I'll find a solution and you keep the others out of my hair. Now come over here and give your champion a big, fat kiss," smirked Gilberger.

"Sorry, Gil. Duty calls. I have to get back immediately. Let's save it for when you have something solid to celebrate. Then you will get what you deserve and there will be no holding back."

Gilberger's thoughts flashed back to their time on the Air Force One together and was about to make some snide remark, but Rebecca had already hung up. The slippery, sleazy, and self-adorning secretary of state stared blankly at the ceiling. He knew that if he wanted Rebecca, he would have to deal with Boris and Yung. What troubled him was that there didn't seem to be an easy way. The Cleansers had been decimated, and with Burgess and Karakanni gone missing, his influence within the NOW had diminished. He needed a plan, and he would develop one. He just needed to focus and concentrate, he decided, focus and concentrate and engage his devious mind to find a solution that would allow him to grasp the power he needed, the power he was prepared to sacrifice anything and anybody to achieve.

Meanwhile, Yung had pondered his own solutions. He had commenced the roundup of the Chinese Bright White barrels, and he had tested the virus. Remarkable! More powerful than anything his people had ever cooked up. It was soon to be all his. All of it. Then there were the Indian barrels. He could get them also. He could torture Singh into full cooperation to learn the proper dispersal methodology. Then he could either gather up the barrels and bring them across the border to him or he could have Singh release the barrels throughout India as planned, another nuclear nation and a giant population out of his way. Yung, the victor. Yung, the magnificent!

In scheming of ways to get to Boris, Yung became enraged when he thought of how he still had to answer for the Chinese missiles that had annihilated Pretnekof's elected opposition, how Boris had planned and executed the entire ruse, a brilliant piece of work. Now he must, together with the USA, explain actions that he had not participated in. The little Russian prick had gotten away with murder again, and no one but he was sure of it and he had no proof. This really angered Yung. Then it came to him, and his scowl turned into a grin and then a huge smile, a smile that showed his teeth and gave him a huge surge of delight.

He picked up his red phone and entered a code he had memorized when Boris had first assembled them. One ring, two rings. Still no answer. By the third ring, Yung was ready to curse, but then a voice on the other end was saying, "Hello, who is this?"

"If you need me to ID myself, then you are not the person I am looking for," answered Yung.

"Chairman, what an unexpected pleasure. How may I be of service to you?" excitedly came the response.

"I will outline the process soon enough. First I must know that you are still committed to a NOW without Boris and that you will cooperate with me fully to achieve that goal."

"Yes, fully, totally, with my life."

"Good, ensure that it doesn't have to come to that. Do as you are instructed and Boris will be canceled. But first I need a favor, a sign of sincerity that only you can make happen."

"Yeeessss, Chairman. What is it that you wish of me?" came a tentative voice.

"You have to convince your government to acknowledge that it conducted the missile attack on the Russian convey."

"What? Are you crazy? Admit to that? Especially when we didn't do it. No way, it can't be done!"

Oh, it can be done and it will be done, or you will be done—forever. And don't you ever again address me as you just have, for if you do, you will beg for death as I slowly remove your miserable life from you. Is that clear?" demanded Yung.

"Yes, perfectly clear, Chairman," came the quick-fired response.

"Get busy. I want to hear news of this before I wake tomorrow."

Yung hung up the receiver and felt that he had chosen the right course of action while Gilberger cursed aloud at his situation. Yung had pounced before Gilberger could react. He was pinned by his own big mouth that had pledged his allegiance to Yung. It wasn't a real allegiance, just a decoy until he could ascend to the presidency and then he could deal with Yung. But that would be the future. This was the here and now. He had to oblige the chairman by convincing his own government to plead guilty to an act of aggression they had not conducted. He had to get the USA to inform China and Russia and the entire world that it was America that had fired the Chinese missiles. If he could do this, then Yung would be off the hook and free to advance his agenda. Gilberger would be the immediate beneficiary of Yung's appreciation. That would buy him the time he needed to prepare to get the advantage on the unsuspecting Yung after they had canceled Boris.

But how to get the White House brass to admit to the firing of the missiles? After a long pause, he called again to the office of Rebecca. This time she answered herself.

"Ms. Sarquas, I have a mission for you, one which will greatly advance your worth and lead to a resolution to this Russian missile fiasco that has been so tedious for you."

"Gil, this had better be good. I am racking my brain looking for any way out. We can't openly accuse Yung, not with China holding our national debt. You know how strongly that madman can react. We can't point the finger at Boris given that it was his people that perished. It would be an international insult to one of the earth's current great leaders. We would be raked over the coals even if we had suspicions that Boris was behind the whole damn thing. Worse of all, our planes were there, and even if we deny responsibility, we will be called on to produce the planes in question. Then the secret of our new weapons and guidance systems would be practically on public display and we will have lost our weapons advantage. So what do you suggest, O gifted one," flatly inquired Sarquas.

"I suggest that you listen very carefully to the one person who can make this mess go away—me. Now, here is what you need to do. Use that charm and attraction of yours to convince Rush, Roth, and Walker and whoever else that the only way out is for us to admit that we were the guilty party. That it was our own pilots that fired the missiles on the Russian convoy. That they were following the orders of their terrorist captors who held their commander and members of their families hostage. That they even suggested that the capture of our dear president was eminent. They had no choice but to comply—it was either fly or die! Tell the world that our pilots safely returned to an airfield controlled by the terrorists and that they were blown up on the spot before they could exit their cockpits. Tell them that we couldn't come forward earlier because we were tracking the terrorists and didn't want to tip our hand. Tell them that the terrorists have all been captured and will be tried, found guilty, and swiftly brought to justice."

"Just how do you expect—" started Sarquas, but Gilberger quickly cut her off.

"Listen, bitch, and listen well. I don't have time for your interjections!" fumed Gilberger.

"You can use the Nevada file footage from the controlled destructions of the early LCs in the desert. You can grab a few helpless hostages from Guantánamo Bay and pin the rap on their leaders. Put that brain of yours to use and hop to it. Do I have to solve every fuckin' problem that pops up? Can any of you or your collection of fools do anything without my intervention?

"Believe me, the press will eat it up. Especially when you mention that all three pilots were married and had young families but can't be given a proper funeral until their hostage families are found and freed. Bring out the crying towels and this whole mess will blow over and no one will have knowledge of the LC-291s. The world's focus will remain with the threat of the Earth Cleansers and we shall be free to proceed with our own agenda."

It was a second or two before Rebecca realized that Gilberger had ended the call. She was dumbstruck. He had called her a bitch, had chastised her, sworn at her, and insulted her. Things would never be the same. Never. She had stayed close to Gilberger because of the promise of the vice presidency, but he could have that. She didn't want to play second fiddle to a crazed egomaniac who put himself above all else.

Minutes later, when she felt her composure returning, she reasoned that Gilberger's plan had some merit. It was a bit far-fetched but could possibly work. Everyone should believe them because no one would consider that the USA would admit to something that they had not done. Not only would it be embarrassing but it also opposed this administration's style of denying everything unless you were caught red-handed. Even then, it was like pulling teeth.

She would bring *her* plan to the president and the others. She would argue the logic and suggest that if anyone had a better idea, then they should bring it forward. When no better plan was expounded, then it would be up to Rush to make the final decision. She knew that he would support her. Then she could be free to concentrate on her new agenda: how to sneak out of the USA and find her Dieter wherever he may be. He had disappeared, but she recalled with great clarity what he had told her during their last meeting. She knew how to contact him, and she would do it. Then she would follow him wherever he wished to go and do whatever he wished to do. It was time to return to her heart and her lover and to get as far away from Gilberger as she possibly could. Forget about power. Forget about control. Just get out of Washington and disappear . . . with Dieter.

"Gentlemen, thank you for returning," began Rebecca. "It appears that we are at a stalemate. Our planes were sighted in a no-fly zone, and neither the Chinese nor Russians are admitting to the attack on the convoy. Also, we concur that no one else could have carried out this act of aggression. That leaves us as looking like the guilty party and about to have our secret fighter jets exposed to the entire world. What could be worse than losing our military advantage?"

"No much, if anything. We may as well say that we done it to get everyone off our backs and out of our hangers," half joked Roth.

"Exactly!" proclaimed Rebecca. "But we can make it work to our advantage and have the world feeling sorry for us poor Americans."

Twenty minutes later, when she had finished stating and debating the only way out, the others had to admit that it was a better plan than any that they had mustered up. More so, they believed that it could and even would work. All present congratulated her for her brilliant thinking and suggested that she could someday become the country's first female president if she continued to solve complex problems with ingenious answers. It was then that the cobra struck with her venom.

"Now that you are all agreed, I have some further information to share with you, information that you will find extremely disturbing. First, let me say that our secretary of state has not been completely honest with you. He has been conniving for months to get the advantage on all of you and to pave his way to being the next president. I witnessed his trickery and lies at the summit meeting and have seen how he has kept things from you and deceived us all.

"The capture of Varez was meant to show his true master, Boris Pretnekof, that he had accomplished his assigned task. Think about it. The only way that he was able to convince you to allow Varez to go to Cuba was by suggesting that the barrels of destruction had been dropped from one of our own military bases and only Cuba could have the flight information that we needed. Varez, our spy, was apparently caught with sensitive and secret Cuban intelligence that he was trying to bring back to America. I am telling you that Varez was our spy, but he was set up by Gilberger and his insiders in Cuba. It was an elaborate ploy to make you believe him while he ensured that we would be discredited once again. For further proof to ensure that he would be blameless, he accused the CIA of having poorly screened spies and spoiling his master plan to get the flight info that we needed, info that does not exist since no American plane dropped any death barrels.

"Earlier today, I asked Gilberger why he was not attending our meetings regarding the Chinese missiles, and he just laughed and said, 'Those bozos will just make a mess of it. It is a waste of my time. I will concentrate on the eradication of the remaining Earth Cleansers and thereby raise my profile and rise above the buffoons that surround me.'

"Finally, I told him that I had a plan and that I thought it would work. I made the mistake of sharing some of the details with him and he called me a stupid bitch. He said that it was interesting but not likely to work. Then after a pause and that ugly smirk of his, he said that if I were successful in convincing you that my plan would work, that he would claim that it was his idea. He is such a slimeball, not truthful to any of us, and while his sights are set on the presidency, his loyalties are firmly entrenched with his old college buddy and mentor, Pretnekof.

"It is time to dispose of this traitor once and for all, and I'm sure there are no shortage of volunteers amongst you. You all hate him, and he has been manipulating all of us for a long time. Who will be the one to rid our nation of this diabolical little swine?"

First Walker, then Rush, and then Roth, rising to his feet, all emphatically growled that they would be the one. Roth was particularly outraged and said that this was a job for a military man. He said that he could make it look like Gilberger just disappeared and would make sure that he would never be found. The others backed off and told Roth to make 100 percent sure that Wilson Gilberger would never be heard from again.

"No problem," assured General H. T. Roth. "The slimeball will get what he deserves. All I need from you, my president, is to insist that Gilberger comes to my office thirty minutes from now. My secretary will have left already. Tell him that Sarquas offered a creative solution to the missile firings and that you want for him to have all of the details before I release our story to the world. He will come running right to my waiting arms. Then our only problem will be to continue to wipe up the unknown Cleansers and of course to select a new secretary of state who is totally loyal to this administration."

"Yes, yes, H. T., very good, well done. Spare me the particulars, but inform me when Gilberger is no more," mumbled the president.

"One more item," interjected Rebecca. "I can aid in the ID'ing of the remaining cleansers. I would have done so before but for the threats that Gilberger directed to me and my family."

"Remain, Ms. Sarquas, and share all with us. General, you may leave," spoke a newly infused president.

Twenty-five minutes later, Roth sat back at his desk, awaiting the arrival of Gilberger. He had hatched a hasty plan. He surprised himself that he could do it so quickly. He had unlocked and emptied the large foot locker that he so proudly displayed with all his other military memorabilia. He had loaded his pistol and screwed tight the silencer.

When the door opened, a fuming Gilberger stormed in.

"I understand that that little tart Sarquas is claiming credit for my plan," began Gilberger. "Stupid wench. Always looking for credit at the expense of others. You make sure, H. T., that the real developer of this plan, *me*, receives the reward that is deserved. You make fuckin' well sure of that!"

"Oh, you will receive the reward that you deserve, Wilson." Roth smiled.

Then ever so quickly, he raised his pistol that was resting on his right thigh and pointed it directly at the forehead of a surprised Gilberger. He pulled the trigger, and Gilberger buckled backward and fell partially into the foot locker that Roth had so carefully placed. Roth lifted the lifeless legs of the dead secretary and squeezed his slight frame into the locker and bolted it shut. He checked to make sure that no blood had stained the marble floor. Then he gathered more of his military possessions into two wooden boxes, and when he was satisfied that all was well, he picked up his phone and called to the motor pool.

"This is General Roth. Send two men to my office to load personal effects into my jeep, and make it snappy. I have an urgent meeting to attend and must be out of here in fifteen minutes."

As Roth was waved through the White House gates, he accelerated down Pennsylvania Avenue and weaved his way to a quiet, secluded place on the Potomac River. It was dark as he removed Gilberger from the locker and loaded rocks into all his pockets. He then tied a twenty-pound WWI cannon ball around his neck. He dragged Gilberger into the icy water until he was neck deep himself—then he let him sink and hurriedly rushed out of the river and loaded the foot locker back into the jeep and sped away. On the way back to his city apartment, he stopped briefly to dispose of the unmarked handgun in a dumpster, and then it was home to a warm shower and laundry of all his clothes. Gilberger may eventually be found, but there would be no tying the murder to him. He had given the slimy liar what he had deserved, and he felt no remorse whatsoever. He would wait until the next morning to greet the president and apprise him that the traitor had received his just reward. Then he would remind Rush that a vacancy existed for which he would be the perfect candidate.

Chapter 44

SARQUAS TAKES FLIGHT

The next morning as they were discussing where they could hide and be free from the long-armed reach of Boris, Brunehoff's cell phone rang, not the one he normally used, but one that not even Boris or the Rabbi had knowledge of. He knew that it must be Rebecca. What could be so important that she was calling to this number? He answered the phone with a subdued hello.

"Dieter, where are you? Can you speak?" inquired Rebecca.

"Yes, I can speak, but my location must remain unknown for now. What is the urgency? Why have you called on this number, Rebecca?"

"So much has happened. Some things you are surely aware of, but there is news also. We are about to admit to the attack on the Russian convoy, but we didn't do it. Gilberger is dead and I have had my fill of Washington and the NOW. Soon I will be on the run just like you, and I want to escape with you to that very special place that you have always told me exists. Tell me what to do, Dieter, and where to meet you and how we can be free."

Brunehoff was silent for a few moments while the others listened attentively to a one-sided conversation. "Rebecca, so much has happened to me also. I abandoned the order to cancel

Brown after I had received a revelation and change of heart and, well, a conscience. I have come to accept that our NOW leaders are ruthless villains, no better than the Cleansers, which they hunt. Boris, the Rabbi, and Yung are all tyrants, and I have now joined with others that know these things also. We are firmly committed to ridding the Earth of their control and helping create a world of hope, perhaps even peace and harmony. Something good that will last. There will be no warm beaches or moonlight swims or carefree days. At least not until all that needs to transpire has taken place. We must wait, Rebecca, and you must make a decision to follow what is right and honorable and to rid yourself of your selfish and power-hungry past," insisted Brunehoff.

"It sounds more like you have had a religious experience rather than the birth of a conscience, Dieter. How could you possibly change all that you have been a part of and join these 'others' that you speak of? Are you sure you are OK? You seem lucid enough, but maybe you are just confused and tired of all of this cloak-and-dagger stuff?"

"Yes, Rebecca, I am tired of my past life and the demons that haunt me. I want to make retribution for many of my past wrongs. I have aligned myself with a force of truth and honor that will cause the mighty and powerful unjust masters of the world to relinquish power and to return the earth to its rightful heirs. I am totally convicted to this new cause and will use my last breath if necessary to bring down Boris, Yung, the Rabbi, and anyone else that stands in the way of the realigned world."

"Wow! You have caught me off guard, Dieter. You truly sound convincing. How is it that you have arrived at this *raw* decision? Surely someone has greatly influenced you. Could it be another woman?"

"Don't worry, Rebecca, there is no other woman. I remain as I was when you last saw me at the summit. It seems like so long ago. So much has happened. I have made my decision and I am content with it. Now you must make yours. Join with us and help rid the world of tyranny and deceit or run away from the NOW and hide out in obscurity for the rest of your days. It is entirely up to you."

"You have really caught me by surprise, Dieter. I want to be with you so very much, but I had envisaged tropical sands and warm waters and fun-filled nights, not waging war with the very villains I am trying to escape from. Are you sure this is what you want to do?"

"Oh yes, Rebecca, I am very sure. I have never been as sure of anything before in my life, and no matter what you say, you cannot dissuade me from the mission I have embarked upon," affirmed Brunehoff.

"OK, my love, I choose you and your noble cause over the life that I have lived up until now. Just promise me one thing, Dieter, and I will abandon my treacherous ways and come running to you."

"What is it, Rebecca?"

"Promise me, Dieter Brunehoff, that you will love me and that you will marry me."

"Rebecca, you know that I have always loved you, even after you broke my heart very long ago. I have never forgotten you and I have lived a life alone. That is changing now, and if you truly wish as you have stated, then you must embrace not only me but the cause that I have now committed my life to. Only then can we speak of bells and flowers and a life as partners. Do this, Rebecca, or forever regret your decisions."

"OK, Dieter, I promise to listen to your story of revolutionary change and hear the wisdom that seems to have been bestowed upon you. Then if I am fully convinced, I will adhere to the principles of your beliefs and make you the happiest man on this planet."

"Rebecca, stay close to your phone and consider what you have said and what we have discussed. I will call you back in precisely four hours. That should give you ample time to be assured that you really want what I am offering. Make sure, Rebecca. There will be no turning back."

"I will be waiting for your call, my handsome prince, waiting for you to rescue me from this unfulfilled life of mine. I will come running to you and I will leave all else behind."

"In four hours, Rebecca, be ready."

When Brunehoff looked up, he saw the eyes of Eli, Brown, Anhebo, Anna, and Francesca firmly fixed upon him. He knew that they were waiting for an explanation.

It was Eli that spoke first. "Dieter, you have wisely chosen not to disclose any of our plans or secrets to Ms. Sarquas. To be sure, the Collective is very aware of her position of prominence within the NOW and the special hold she has over the American president. We are also acutely aware of the relationship you have maintained with her for a very long time. What I personally am not sure about is how a woman such as this could abandon her evil ways and embrace truth and justice and the ways of the Creator. Before you invite her to meet with us, I must contact the Leader and have her permission for us to allow this to happen."

Next it was Anhebo who spoke. "She is a loose cannon, Dieter. Have you forgotten how she forged her alliances and vaulted her way into the White House? Can a woman such as this ever totally be trusted? Maybe she is even now acting upon the orders of Pretnekof and your time on the phone with her has allowed the evil master time to get a fix on our coordinates."

"She may be right, Dieter," responded Brown. "We have to get out of here ASAP. We already know that Pretnekof is searching for both you and I and that there are few if any safe havens away from the reach of his mafia mob and the Krems, which he commands. And all of Canada will be searching for me. Everyone, gather your things and let's get out of here!"

The six of them vacated their suburban Ottawa hideout and drove the minivan south toward the USA border. They debated whether or not they could trust Rebecca Sarquas and the ways in which she could aid or interfere with their plans.

Eli then contacted the Leader, and to his surprise, she was elated at the promise of Sarquas joining them. It seems that they had met on several occasions and that the Leader had silently hoped that someday she could convince this gifted woman to ascend to more-noble causes. She told Eli to have Brunehoff fetch Sarquas at terminal 1 in Toronto and to then drive directly to a safe house in nearby Mississauga. There they would receive further instructions.

It was approximately a six-hour drive to Toronto, and along the way they discussed many things, including how each of them could contribute to their common cause. They were becoming a tight-knit group of family and friends, and with each passing hour, they drew closer to understanding each other and their common destiny. Anhebo and Brown joked about how they would no longer have to drink with Balderous. Anna silently looked to Anhebo and admired her determination and fearless attitude and preparedness, all qualities that her mother had possessed—before she died in that terrible accident four years ago. Francesca quietly reran what her father had said about her mother being brave and escaping the madmen and . . . dying giving birth to her. Brunehoff listened intently to everything that Eli related to him while periodically glancing behind at his lovely daughter.

After four hours, Brunehoff called to Rebecca's mobile; and when she confirmed that she was ready to join them, he told her to take the 1:15 p.m. United Airlines flight from Washington (WAS) to Toronto (YYZ). He instructed her to use her NOW-issued alias and that if asked, she should state that she would be visiting a sick uncle and would be staying only four days. He told her he would be waiting for her as she cleared customs and entered the arrivals area. When he ended the call with "I love you too," he was quickly teased by Anhebo and Francesca and could see the contained smiles of the others.

Once Sarquas arrived and was met by Brunehoff, they hurriedly exited the airport and boarded the curbside minivan. As Eli pulled away, introductions were made and Rebecca seemed relieved to be with a group of people that she immediately felt at ease with. Everyone, that is, except Anhebo. They were having initial difficulty reconciling their great differences and backgrounds and suspicions of each other.

Within the hour, they were all inside the sprawling safe house; and before they could unpack and settle in, the phone rang. Eli picked up the receiver and, after receiving a brief instruction, pressed the speakerphone button.

"The Leader has chosen to speak with all of us collectively. Her voice will sound muffled and will remain so until such time as she is assured of your loyalty and devotion to our cause. Please listen carefully and answer any questions directed to you as briefly as possible. Thank you."

"Good afternoon to you all. Welcome to the Collective, Anhebo, Rebecca, Dieter, and Willie. We are extremely pleased that our talented Eli and Anna and Francesca have succeeded in bringing you all together. Together with many others to aid in advancing the curtailment of the evil domination of our blessed earth. Much has taken place during the past three weeks, and much more will surely unfold in the weeks to come. We are aware of your pasts and your individual skills and abilities. With selected individuals from within our fold, we are proposing to have you expose, defame, and even terminate, if necessary, the remaining member of the Earth Cleansers and those of the NOW. We know much about Yung and Boris and the Rabbi and even Gilberger and Karakanni. Burgess is missing and not likely to resurface. As for the Cleansers, it is our belief that only Singh remains from the inner circle. Does that sound correct to you?"

"This is Anhebo speaking, and I can confirm that Burgess is dead and that I have no regrets for what I have done."

"This is Brown, and I can confirm that only Singh remains at large and that we *must* get to him before Boris or Yung does. With Singh's knowledge of the virus and where all the barrels are stored and how to initiate attacks, he is most dangerous."

"This is Rebecca Sarquas, and I can confirm that Karakanni has been dead for more than a week and that yesterday, Gilberger was also eliminated."

"This is Brunehoff, and I can confirm that Boris, Yung, and the Rabbi are indeed terribly powerful adversaries. Within the NOW, there is also the French vice president, Langois, who is a mere chauvinist puppet, and I have the ability to get close to him. He is not as serious of a concern."

"Langois—I should have known. Hhhhmmmm. My friends, thank you for your updated information and concerns. I will be meeting with senior members of the Collective in the morning and will be able to report back to you within twenty-four hours. In the meantime, please try to mentally prepare yourselves for the fight of your lifetimes. We do not expect it to be an easy task to dismantle the NOW, and we are fearful that the virus barrels could fall into their hands. That is why I must ask you, Willie Brown, to provide Eli with a complete listing of the stockpiles of virus barrels and how we may destroy or neutralize them. Also, I need to know how they have been dropped and who controls the aircraft. I can't imagine that Balderous or any of your Cleanser group have the aircraft required to carry out the strikes that we all witnessed on Christmas Day."

"Madam Leader, if that is how I am to address you for now, I have to tell you that you are misinformed regarding the aircraft. There were none, and none are required for phase 2, which has been scheduled for March 15th. All of the barrels were delivered by truck, and more than twelve thousand still exist. They are scattered throughout the world in densely populated areas and within the confines of the Bright White laundry empire owned by Garcia, from Chile. We used cellular phones to trigger the acid-covered barrels, which then burst apart and splintered as if they had been dropped from above. I can provide a complete listing to Eli," responded Willie Brown.

"Very clever, Mr. Brown, very clever indeed. However, I suspect that matters are now worse than I feared. Garcia was found dead with three Frenchmen who were apparent businessmen, but we believe that they were actually confederates of Garcia and the Cleansers. Are you aware of this?"

"If their names were Savard, Burgeron, and Picard, I can confirm that they were the coordinators for intended strikes on China and India. One of them, Savard, I suspect, would have been carrying a microchip sewn into his passport folder. Were you or are you able to gain access to their identification papers?"

"Confirming the identification of the three Frenchmen took longer than usual as all were found without wallets or identification of any kind. But they were indeed Savard, Burgeron, and Picard."

"Then this can only mean that Boris or Yung got to them first and now have knowledge of the exact locations of at least two thousand barrels!" exclaimed Brown.

"Pardon me," interjected Brunehoff, "but both Rebecca and I know that Garcia was the assignment of Yung."

"And two Krems," added Rebecca.

"But I recall the final words of Boris to me," said Brunehoff. "He lamented that he had lost two of his best Krems in Chile and that he was almost certain that Yung's men had murdered them."

A silence befell the gathering as they each came to the realization that the crazed and power-hungry Chairman Yung now had knowledge of all the barrels in China and India. Also, he would surely seek to capture Narinder Singh Singh and have him under his direct control to administer a cleansing of his own.

When the silence was broken, it was the Leader that spoke. "We must hasten our actions and alter our program. If Yung gets to Singh first, he will surely unleash death such as the world has never known. If Pretnekof gets Singh, then Yung will still be in control of hundreds of barrels of death virus, but the Russian president will gain knowledge of all else. Either way, the earth will be in great peril and it will be difficult for us to advance our agenda or maybe even survive. It has now become imperative to locate and apprehend Singh and to bring him to a safe haven where he can be sheltered and kept from Yung and Pretnekof. I will formulate a plan, and it will involve you, Dieter, flying to Delhi and capturing Singh. Our people will meet you there. You must ready yourself now and be prepared to leave as soon as possible. There is no time to spare. Let us hope and pray that we can get to Singh first. I will call again within the hour. Praise be to the Creator."

As the line went dead, a less-than-enthusiastic response of "And all true followers" was brought forth by most of the others.

Chapter 45

THE RACE IS ON

The next day, President Boris Pretnekof was deeply troubled. Brunehoff had not been located. Brown had not reported for work as scheduled and, like Anhebo, also could not be found. Gilberger and Sarquas were also missing. He was no closer to ending the death threat of the Cleansers, and his bastion of faithful followers had dissipated like flies. He and the Rabbi were left with only the allegiance of Langois, and they were up against an angry Yung, who claimed that his Chilean assigned agents were also AWOL.

Then there was the fact that the Americans had claimed responsibility for the attack that he had orchestrated to rid himself of his Russian opposition. Why would they fabricate such a story? Without Gilberger and Sarquas, he had no way of knowing, but he suspected that it was somehow tied to the death barrels and American plans to keep their latest fighter plane technology to themselves.

His carefully laid plans were crumbling, and he was scrambling for answers and what action to take next. With Brown, Anhebo, and Singh still at large, the threat of the virus being released still loomed as large as ever—especially if they had access to associates within the U.S. military capable of dropping the deadly payload.

The master was scrambling—totally without his usual control and solutions.

He called to the Rabbi and they discussed what could be and what should be done. Eventually, they decided that in addition to continuing to scour the vast Canadian landscape for Brunehoff and Brown, they should attempt to monitor the movements of Yung and to get to Singh and cancel or capture him as soon as possible. Without Singh, the threat of attack may not be lessened, but they could at least torture him for answers and find out where the suspected stockpiles of barrels were being kept. Boris was not accustomed to being outsmarted, and this made him exceedingly angry. His non-Mafia power base had crumbled outside of Russia; and now he and his talented friend, the Rabbi, must move quickly to get to Singh. He called to his ever-faithful Indian contact but was advised that he had left for the weekend with his family, no doubt to enjoy some of the money he had received for dealing with Karakanni. It would be twelve hours before he was able to make contact and order that Singh should be apprehended from 116 Skylark Lane. Singh was to be brought to a place where he could be questioned away from the police and any nosy media.

He needed to locate the death barrels and he needed to protect his power and his control. With control of the barrels, he would have control over Yung. Then with the virus death threat removed and Yung fearful of retribution for his elimination of the Chilean Krems, Boris would be once again in control of the unfolding of the future, a future that had become more murky by the moment and more uncertain than ever before.

He assigned the Rabbi to have their network determine any airline tickets purchased under the names of Wilson Gilberger or Rebecca Sarquas or their NOW aliases of Edward Walters and

Elizabeth Matthews. Find out if they have fled the USA and where they may have gone. Something was awry.

In Beijing, several hours earlier, Chairman Yung was pleased that his instructions to Gilberger had been followed and that the USA had admitted to the launch of the Chinese missiles against the Russian convoy. He laughed aloud when he heard the explanation conjured up by Gilberger, but when he called to congratulate his lying associate, he was alarmed to learn that he had been missing for more than twenty-four hours. What could possibly have happened to him? He called to the NOW mobile phone of Sarquas, but there was no answer, and the GPS had been deactivated. Posing as a Chinese trade commissioner who had expected a call from her yesterday, he contacted her office and was informed by her apologetic secretary that she had not reported for work today. He offered to deliver a message to Sarquas when she arrived, but Yung hung up.

Something didn't add up, and the chairman was very suspicious. He pondered his options for a moment and then decided that he must immediately move to locate Singh, something that he should have already dealt with! He cursed to himself and buzzed to Ho Fat. When his assistant appeared, Yung told him that he had learned of an imminent and large second strike by the Earth Cleansers and that it would be launched upon India and possibly even China. He told Ho Fat to summon "the Smiths" and "the Does" (as the operative teams had been code-named) and for them to go to his office immediately. He would deploy them to India to capture and bring Singh to him. Then he would have the control and knowledge that he needed to launch an attack on Mother Russia and Israel. He would do so with such a horrific force that Boris and the Rabbi would never recover and the remnants of the NOW could be rebuilt with no one to challenge his supreme authority. Best of all, he would have the carefully calculating Singh at his disposal and, as such, knowledge of all the other barrels. He would be supreme!

Now there were three teams racing against each other to get to Dr. Narinder Singh, each desperate to get to Singh first and each prepared to sacrifice anything and anybody to do so.

When the Leader called back, Brunehoff was ready to leave for the airport and a cab was waiting outside. He was booked on an overnight flight to Paris with a good morning connection to Delhi. He would be there within twelve hours. She instructed him that he should take a cab to the Delhi Royale, where a reservation awaited him. He would be met there. When Brunehoff protested that he worked best alone and that he could find Singh, the Leader reminded him that the rules were different now and that he played on a different team and fought for a different purpose and, most of all, that time was running out. They may already be too late.

She informed the group that the list of storage sites identified by Brown and transmitted to her by Eli would be promptly passed on to national authorities in every country. It had already commenced in Europe. She said that she would make sure that the media and police would be informed also so that no upstart dictator or rising star politician could claim the death virus for themselves. She felt that they should be able to secure most of the barrels before Yung or Boris did but admitted that there were some countries where almost all was corrupt or suppressed. Some crazed African warlord or Arab oil sheikh might still cause initial localized damage if they were able to learn to trigger the acid-laced surface. That would take a degree of sophistication beyond many. The greater likelihood is that such a person would put the barrels in hiding until a skilled accomplice, willing or otherwise, could be found or captured.

The two thousand barrels within India and China would be more difficult to secure as both Boris and especially Yung had a head start, a short but deadly head start. Then she added, "We have a possibility to salvage India, but we are mostly nonrepresented and virtually powerless within China. More than 1,100 barrels will be in the hands of Yung, and he will have no reservations about releasing their contents into Russia first and then who knows where next."

"Then I should change my plans and fly to Yung," answered Brunehoff. "Try to convince him that since I am on the run from Boris. I have fled to him. Then at the first opportunity, I will bring down the chairman."

"No, Dieter, this is not a job for the world's greatest warrior. Even if you could get to Yung, he would be suspicious since you had disobeyed Boris and fled to him. He must know that you find him more repulsive than Pretnekof. He would want you dead and would never allow you to get close enough to kill him. It's better that you proceed as planned and go after Singh. Only one person I am aware of is capable of getting to Yung."

"It's me and I'll do it," spoke up Sarquas. "Gilberger is gone and I have fled the U.S. Yung knows that I have no time for Boris since he has had no time for me. I can paint a believable picture to Yung and I can get very close. Get me the right poison and I will eliminate the great Li Wi."

"If you were to succeed, Rebecca, you must realize that there will be no way back. We will not be able to get you out. The suppressed cabinet of Yung will not spare you. You will likely die a terrible death," answered the Leader.

"Then you shall have your proof of my commitment to the beliefs of the Collective and especially my promise to my Dieter."

"If you do this, Rebecca, then this is good-bye," said Brunehoff as he lowered his hand-carry luggage and thrust his powerful arms tenderly around her. Francesca began to sob, and then Rebecca did also.

"Yes, good-bye to this world and this life, my children, but with hope of a reunion in the great beyond. Go now, Dieter, and go with great conviction. Eli, kindly prepare for Rebecca's flight to Beijing," instructed the Leader.

Releasing his hold of Rebecca and kissing her softly on the lips, he picked up his bag, kissed the forehead of his darling Francesca, and then looking painfully to all the others, he opened the door and walked to the waiting cab. There would be no looking back. His focus would be Singh, and then if there were time, well, maybe . . .

Yung had met with the "Smiths" and the "Does" and had dispatched them—via Air China to Hong Kong and on to Delhi. They were scheduled to arrive at terminal 2 of Indira Gandhi International Airport a mere twenty-five minutes before Brunehoff did. Collaborators and firearms would await them at the airport, and already Yung had begun the search for Singh. The factory had yielded no clues, and after the mess that Karakanni had made, it was unlikely that Singh would show himself.

The next morning, Brunehoff was leaving the Delhi terminal when he caught a glimpse and then a full look at two Chinese men that he instantly knew to be Yung's. They boarded a waiting sedan, and Brunehoff immediately hailed a cab and ordered the driver to stay close but not too close to the car in front. When the cabbie squawked with resistance, Brunehoff quickly produced a crisp U.S. $100 bill and the tail was on, over one bridge and then another, through the heart of the city, and up the ridge to an area of prominent homes. Finally, thirty minutes later, the black sedan came to a halt in the driveway of a gated residence.

"Keep driving," insisted Brunehoff.

When they were a few blocks away, he halted the cab, threw another $100 bill to the driver, and left the cab. He instructed the cabbie to keep going and to forget all that he had seen. He made his way back down the main street and then slowly to the house where the sedan was parked. He walked past the house, rounded the corner, and traversed the road at the rear of the sprawl of rich estates. The property was fully walled to the sides; and rear and several surveillance cameras were present, monitored but not fortified, a deterrent to thieves but a nonobstacle for the trained warrior.

One more pass and Brunehoff had found a way in. Partway along, the east-side wall was obscured from the home by a large jacaranda tree; and with the speed of a racer and the poise of a dancer, the warrior was up the tree, down a long limb, and onto the property. He ran for the cover of a garden shed and then used his bare hands to tear three nailed boards from the rear of the shed. Once inside, he slowly eased open the door just far enough to get a view of the house. The east side had only three windows, and two of them had the curtains closed, and the third appeared to be a washroom. There was no sign of movement, and Brunehoff knew that at fifty meters away he could make it to the house in much less than ten seconds while avoiding the scrutiny of the cameras. He closed the door, left again through the hole he has created, and sped toward the residence. He eased his way toward the plastered wall and ran to one of the curtained rooms. He listened, tried the window and found it locked, and then moved swiftly to the next room. Here the window was slightly ajar and he could hear voices in the distance—Chinese voices.

Brunehoff slide open the window and raised himself silently into the empty bedroom. He saw the closet and made his way to it and closed it behind him. The voices were clearer now but still indiscernible. There were five of them, and he heard one mention Singh and Skylark Lane. He reasoned that they would be leaving soon to locate Singh. He slithered back out the window and around the east side of the building, keeping low to the ground. When he reached the corner, he glanced once, then twice, and saw that the sedan was within fifteen meters. He wound the dial on his wristwatch and a small pointed metal object protruded—a key of sorts. One last look and Brunehoff darted to the rear of the car and deftly unlocked the trunk. He slid inside and closed the hatch behind him, and there he waited.

Five minutes went by and then ten while Brunehoff waited. Then he heard the front door open and footsteps approaching the car. All the car doors opened and shut, and the car raced away. Four or five elite Chinese agents with the latest in assault weaponry and one unarmed and repentant, aging warrior racing to Skylark Lane to capture Singh. It seemed fair, thought Brunehoff. *They have the weapons, but I have the element of surprise, and after I dispose of the first one or two, I will have fire power also. Then I will take down the rest and escape with Singh.*

Within a few minutes, the car came to a slow stop, and barely audible voices could be heard just before the car doors opened and the occupants departed. A few seconds later, Brunehoff crawled out of the trunk and fled behind a string of parked cars along the sidewalk. Up ahead, across the street, no more than twenty meters away, he could see Yung's men; and they were approaching 116 Skylark Lane. He had to move quickly. As he edged along the sidewalk tight to the parked cars, he ducked down as he heard another vehicle quickly approach and pull into the driveway. This one bore official Indian government plates, and three men carrying handguns emerged. This surprised the Chinese, who kept walking while Brunehoff hung back across the street near a utility pole. The two uniformed officers and their black-suited companion approached the front door, forced it open, and entered. The Chinese spoke briefly and then turned around and also entered the house.

Brunehoff knew that Boris had mafia connections throughout India and these were likely his men. Now there were eight armed men in one little house, seeking one small man, and an unarmed Brunehoff was left outside all alone. He crossed the roadway and slipped into the building through the same front door as the others. He could hear shuffling of feet and glass breaking toward the rear of the interior. And then the familiar pa-thump, pa-thump, pa-thump of handguns with silencers. Then crashing sounds. Then a brief silence before Mandarin voices were heard with one shouting in English, "Get up, Singh! Never mind your arm. The bullet can be removed. Get up!"

Brunehoff was near the foot of the stairs now and tucked himself into the alcove as Yung's men and Singh approached. It was then that he struck. Faster than any hired killer or trained assassin, the great German martial arts master struck bodies in rapid succession, breaking limbs, crushing skulls, and pulling ribs from their torsos. No more than fifteen seconds had elapsed and four Chinese were either dead or rendered helpless. Without a whisper, he grabbed Singh and swiftly scanned the kitchen, where he saw the three dead Indian officials and the lifeless body of the remaining Chinese agent.

He looked to a fear-stricken and totally shaken Singh, who could barely manage to say "Brunehoff, is that you?" before he passed out.

Brunehoff let Singh slide to the floor, and he searched the pockets of the Indian driver until a set of keys was found. Then he slung Singh over his shoulder and fled to the government car. Racing his way out of the neighborhood, he drove directly for the Delhi Royale and along the way used his mobile phone to call the number given to him by Eli.

When the receiver answered with a "Yeeesss," Brunehoff simply said, "In the parking lot of the hotel in three, maybe four, minutes. I will be in a black official government car, plate number AVD 7779. I have Singh. Be there!"

"We were getting worried when you didn't show up on time, Mr. Brunehoff. We expected you to contact us before you went after Singh. What about the agents of Yung and Pretnekof, any sign of them? And just how did you locate him so quickly?"

"Later," said Brunehoff, "just get Singh to a safe house and contact the Leader and update her. Tell her that the agents of Yung and Pretnekof have been eliminated. Be ready to switch cars with me. I will have to get out of here immediately."

Leaving Singh and the others behind, Brunehoff sped away and headed for the airport. From there it would be onto Dhaka, Bangladesh, and from there he would fly three thousand kilometers directly to Beijing and into the realm of the monstrous Yung. He would make an attempt to save his dear Rebecca and to destroy the evil Yung, an apparent impossible task but one that he would undertake nonetheless. If Rebecca was prepared to die for him, then he would be prepared to die for her or with her. Either way, he was intent upon bringing down the powerful chairman in the deep heartland of his own turf. It would be his gift to his new alliance and a sign of true reform to his Francesca. After what Rebecca had done to show her love for him, he would risk all for her.

Chapter 46

BORIS AND YUNG REACT

When the elderly lady directly across from 116 Skylark Lane saw an official government car pull into the driveway and the occupants enter the home with firearms visible, she became alarmed. Seconds later, witnessing five Oriental men in dark suits silently enter, she knew that something awful was about to happen. She called to the local police and frantically told what she had observed. The desk officer that answered had her state her name and address and to then return to the window and get the license plate of the official vehicle. She peered between the drapes and was surprised to see that the car was no longer there. She returned to the phone and reported her finding to the now-dubious officer who paused and asked her if she had been drinking or had taken excess medication. She insisted that she had seen exactly what she had reported then added that they had better hurry before she called the local newspapers that would be sure to come. She said that she would tell them that she had called the police first but they dismissed her as a drunken or overmedicated fool. He asked her to please hold the line.

The desk officer conferred with his superior and said that he felt the woman might possibly be telling the truth and that there was a squad car in the general area. They agreed that it would be prudent to check out her story and thanked her for the information and asked her to please stay inside her home as they may need to meet with her later.

When the squad car arrived and the two officers entered Singh's rented residence, they were shocked at the human carnage that they saw. Strewn throughout the hall and entranceway were four bloodied and broken bodies. All appeared dead as displayed by contorted torsos and protruding bones and ribs. Farther along in the kitchen, they found the three Indian officials shot dead along with one more Oriental man. The senior officer radioed to their station and reported what they had found. The younger of the two went outside to throw up.

Within minutes, more police arrived and then the media, who were refused passage beyond the yellow-taped crime-scene area. They waited outside as more vans and TV crew arrived. Eventually, the Delhi chief of police agreed to speak to the media and said that he could confirm that 116 Skylark Lane contained the bodies of eight men. Three were Indian and the other five were Oriental, possibly Chinese. No motive was known nor were the identities of any of the victims as of yet. He stated that more information would be forthcoming after the forensic team had ample time to examine the bodies and the premises.

The evening papers carried front-page headlines of the mass murder, and the TV news commenced with reporters standing outside of 116 Skylark Lane and indicating that eight dead bodies lay inside. The Krems, who had been holed up in the south of Delhi, saw the news and immediately recognized the address. They called directly to Boris.

"Speak," answered Boris.

"This is K1 and I have news to report. It concerns 116 Skylark Lane. Eight bodies were found there today. Five Chinese and three nationals. I am not sure if Singh was one of them."

Boris was taken aback. His official men would have been there. Two or three. Someone could have Singh! Or he was dead. Either way, the result was not good.

"Get back there now and get positive ID—I must know if Singh is dead. Find out everything that you can and report to me as soon as you arrive."

"Yes, master," answered K1 as he signaled to his partner to get ready to leave immediately.

Boris cursed himself. He had not taken Singh earlier, and now his chief was dead and possibly Singh too. He had left it all too late. Now he must think.

His mobile rang again. This time it was the Rabbi.

"I have investigated our two Americans. Gilberger has not left the U.S. by air at least and the American government search for him and Sarquas continues. Sarquas has used her NOW alias to fly to Toronto, where she stayed one night before departing yesterday for Beijing."

"Toronto and Beijing?" echoed Boris. "What is going on?"

"There is more," added the Rabbi. "We have screened video surveillance tapes of the arrival area at Pearson International, and there is clear evidence that she was met by none other than Brunehoff. Furthermore, the departure tapes show Brunehoff leaving for Paris, and the ticketing records reveal that two of the passengers on that flight connected to Delhi. One was a young woman—"

"And the other was a forty-year-old man!" exclaimed Boris.

"Yes, and I have further tracked Brunehoff, under his Swiss alias of Luc Berdon, as having just departed Dhaka—on a direct flight to Beijing."

"Good work, Raheim. It can only mean that both Brunehoff and Sarquas have really defected and have gone after Yung. Our team in Delhi has been killed. No doubt Brunehoff was responsible for their deaths and that he has either eliminated or deposited Singh to some unknown third party. They must be planning to cancel Yung and not flee to him. Otherwise, Brunehoff would not have also eliminated the five Chinese agents of Yung at Singh's hideout. They have embarked on a mission of their own and are no longer under our control. But we have something that they don't know we have and we will use it against them. We know where they are going and what they propose to do. Now we have to use our sources within Beijing to pinpoint Yung, and once we do, we will find Brunehoff and Sarquas also."

"Is it wise to go after Yung at this juncture?" carefully inquired the Rabbi. "Why not let Brunehoff and Sarquas first attempt to accomplish the task for us?" If they succeed, then we will be rid of the chairman once and for all. If they fail, then Brunehoff and Sarquas will not live to be a threat to us and there will be nothing to suggest that we sent them after Yung."

"Maybe, Raheim, maybe not. Just think, if Brunehoff can enter Beijing and eliminate Yung at his home base, where he is so carefully guarded, then he will become a greater threat to us. Time and time again we have witnessed that there is no one that can take down the great warrior. We must prepare. Yes, we can allow Brunehoff to make his attempt, but we must be very close by, and if he succeeds, then that will be the time for us to eliminate him also—even if it takes one of Yung's missiles or tanks to do so. Brunehoff served us well for a very long time and he has always done as I have asked.

It is only now that he has turned away from our team and either set out on his own or joined forces with others."

A pensive Berhinstein replied, "I don't think he is acting alone this time. Sarquis is not enough to take down Yung, and Brunehoff is not about to sacrifice his lifelong girlfriend. There must be a network of others, but it can't be the remnant Cleansers. Brunehoff would never support their goals. He is either acting independently or there is a *new* team to which he has become aligned. Maybe with the death of Balderous and Garcia he has joined with Brown, Anhebo, Sarquas, and others to form a new force? It certainly couldn't be one of the terrorist groups, and I doubt that the Americans would be so exacting and able to control Brunehoff."

"There is no one else with enough substance. A few madmen, perhaps, and the odd dictator or two, but none would be acceptable to Dieter," continued the Rabbi. "I suppose it could even be the group currently known as the Collective or RAW and calling for a realigned world. As you know, they have been on the world's radar forever, but we have never taken them serious or believed that they could sway anyone with power to follow them. Their name is always changing and they seem totally harmless and yet people of great notoriety have joined their ranks. They do have a secret leadership, and they supposedly boast great numbers. It is time that we investigate them further, but I can't believe that they are capable of these tactics. Also, much has changed since Christmas Day, and they could possibly be a force to contend with—especially if they have Brown and Brunehoff and Anhebo. Still I doubt that they have risen in power enough to plan such maneuvers. Evidently, they are committed to their Creator and world peace and fairness for all, the regular stuff. They would not be on such a murderous trail as this, would they?"

"When does Brunehoff arrive?" asked Boris.

"In approximately three hours from now," replied the Rabbi.
"And Sarquas?"

"She should already have arrived at eight a.m. this morning, Beijing time, so about four hours ago," replied the Rabbi.

"Good. You will have ample time to alert the Krems and our Chinese cohorts. Have them watch the airport for Brunehoff and tell them to keep a safe distance. We don't want him to know that we are tailing him. He should lead us to Sarquas and from there to Yung himself. I'm unsure as to how Brunehoff plans to cancel Yung, but I'm certain it will be creative. The inclusion of Sarquas is curious, and she may be the one who is to get close to Yung. The chairman has always been at odds with our Brunehoff, but Sarquas has had encounters of her own with Yung, and I know he is enamored with her. She is likely the key to getting close to Yung. Phone me when you have any update. I will stand by here and deal with the matters of state. Things that seem very ordinary and inconsequential at this time but nonetheless necessary to maintain our position," ended Boris.

Three hours later, back in Beijing, Yung had just received the Delhi news and was, as usual, furious. Five of his best men were dead and likely Singh too. His efforts to capture Singh and unleash the virus upon India had been thwarted. His evolving plan to use Singh to pinpoint the barrels throughout the world was not to be. Someone was one step ahead, and he naturally suspected Boris. Who else could it be? What could he do next?

Gilberger and Sarquas were missing and Brunehoff could not be trusted. He had to defend himself against Boris. He felt that the best plan would be to launch an assault with the virus on Russia. It would take time and planning, and he would have to ensure that he was not suspected as being behind the attack. He knew that time was becoming critical as he now feared that Boris was closer to reaching him than he had previously thought.

If Boris could eliminate Gilberger and Sarquas and Singh, then maybe he could get to him also. Likely he was still being aided by Brunehoff and the Rabbi even though Boris had announced that Brunehoff was unaccounted for, surely another decoy by the masterful tactician. But Gilberger and Sarquas were not aligned with Boris. They had successfully convinced their president to accept responsibility for the attack on the Russian convoy. They would not have done this if they were loyal to Boris. It was more likely that they were in hiding from Boris and would make contact when the opportunity presented itself. Yes, and he would tolerate Gilberger to be close to Rebecca—Rebecca, who still made his heart beat fast and his passion flare no matter what she would say or do.

Chapter 47

REBECCA AND YUNG

Ms. Rebecca Sarquas had taken a cab to the Ritz-Carlton on Financial Street just a few blocks from the infamous Tiananmen Square and the winter palace of Chairman Li Wi Yung, supreme commander of all China. She was already close to her target, but she needed to get much, much closer. She had had many hours to sleep in the luxurious first class of Singapore Airlines and with it ample time to contemplate how she would approach Yung.

As a precaution, she used the cell phone given her by Eli to call direct to the NOW cell of Yung. She knew that an unreceptive Yung would have difficulty in tracing her call. On the first ring, Yung saw the name displayed as Elizabeth Matthews and his eyes lit up. He knew that it would be Rebecca. His heart beat faster.

"Trugol, my darling, where are you? I have been so worried about you."

"I had to get out of the States after Gilberger was disposed of by the henchmen of Boris and his little sidekick. Apparently, Boris was not amused by Gilberger's missile story and had him cancelled. I knew I would be next. I barely escaped to Toronto and from there to Paris and then onto the one place where I felt I could be safe."

"You should have come to me, sweetheart. I can protect you from Boris and everyone else. Where are you?" repeated Yung.

"Would you really protect me, Li Wi? I have trusted others before and they have either abandoned me or tried to kill me. Brunehoff disappeared when I needed him, and Boris was about to cancel me when I managed to flee Washington. Gilberger promised gold but delivered nothing. But you, I want to believe that you would really be there for me. Would you, my handsome prince, would you really be there for me?"

Yung's blood was racing and his heart was rushing at a much-accelerated rate. She had called him her handsome prince. He must have her!

"Rebecca, I will protect you and honor you and together we can rule this world. Come to me, my sweetness, and your days of fear and drudgery will end forever. I will make you my queen and you shall want for nothing."

"Nothing, big boy, nothing at all?"

"Nothing at all ever, my sweet. You will bask in sunshine and jewels and bathe in fragrances and oils so sweet that your lovely body will become even more silken and glowing. You will be my true goddess of love and I shall treasure and cherish and . . . ravish you.

"Easy, big boy, you are getting yourself all worked up."

"I *am* all worked up, Rebecca. You know how I long for you. Come to me now or allow me to fetch you. Tell me, where are you, Rebecca? I must have you with me."

"OK, my chairman, you have put forth a compelling desire, which I believe to be authentic. I have few options. I feel that I can trust you and only you to protect me."

"Then where are you?" insisted Yung.

"I am here, in Beijing, very near to your palace. I told you that I had escaped to the one place I felt safe. I will be with you my king . . . and I shall ravish you also," declared Rebecca.

The chairman was caught off guard. This seemed too good to be true. In Beijing. No Gilberger. Ravish him!

"I will send a car for you now! I must have you with me."

"Patience, my anxious lover. Prepare yourself as I will likewise prepare. I need time to shower and dress and make myself ready for you. Put on one of your silk robes. You know how handsome and strong you look in those. I will call back in one hour and I will expect that your duty slate will be cleared and that the bedchamber of the *Yung king* will be prepared. Then you may fetch me and . . . well, much else."

The line went dead and Yung was breathing heavily. She had come to him. This was no trickery, no deception. This was the real thing. She had examined her options like the smart woman that she was. She had decided that she could be safe and cared for with opulence nowhere else but with him, lord of Asia and soon-to-be king of the world. He was to have the prize that he had so long coveted. He was to have Trugol and he was not about to share her with anyone. Not now, not ever!

Rebecca smiled as she lathered her beautiful body. Knowing that she had thoroughly excited, titillated, and most importantly, convinced Yung had aroused her. She would have one last sexual splash during which Yung would be pricked with a pin containing the deadly Amazonian venom of Anhebo. He would be paralyzed almost immediately and dead within a few minutes. He would not be able to call out for help or to strike back. Her job would be done.

Then there was no best-case scenario. She would not have time to flee Beijing before the lockdown. Even if she wasn't detained by the palace staff, they would soon know that Yung was no more. She would quickly be at the end of her road also. Her life sacrificed for a Creator that she did not know and a lover whom she would never see again.

When Dieter Brunehoff arrived as Luc Berdon at Beijing Capital International Airport, he immediately called to the RAW-issued cell of Rebecca. It rang five times, but there was no answer. He carried on through customs and Immigration processing and called again. This time she answered on the first ring.

"Dieter, my darling, where are you? Are you OK? What about Singh?"

"I'm fine. Mission accomplished. Singh delivered. And I'm here."

"Here? You mean Beijing?"

"Yes, Rebecca. I have come to help you. We can still be together . . . provided we eliminate your target and escape from here."

"Your timing is unbelievable. I am just drying off and about to dress for my date. I am to call him in fifteen minutes. He's preparing his palace for me. It's only ten minutes away. I'm sorry. I had to lead him on. It was the only way. He thinks that I want to rule with him."

"Be careful, Rebecca. He's not easily fooled. He will have his guard up after losing five agents in Delhi."

"You are still the man of steel, precious. Now that you have arrived, I believe that I can actually get out of here. I have a cancellation plan but no secure method of escape. I thought I would just observe what and whom I could on the way in, and then as soon as Anhebo's poison was inserted, I would wiggle my way out of there. It's just now that I finally realized that I have no possible way out of China."

"Your entrance would be much easier than your exit. And there is little chance that I would be able to get inside. We will have to do it differently. When you call him, tell him to follow your erotic desires with you and to fetch his princess in a wondrous limo. Tell him that it has always been your fantasy to drive along the Great Wall and pass the Forbidden City while making forbidden love with him. Tell him that it will be your biggest turn-on ever and that he will not be disappointed. From what you have told me, it sounds like he trusts you completely, and I know he has always been ravenous for you. He will have a driver and a guard but likely no others. He won't be expecting you to attempt anything . . . nonsexual."

"And then what? You follow behind in a cab and kill the three of them when I stop for a pee break?"

"Something like that. I haven't figured it all out yet."

"OK, I'll try, but if he suspects anything, then I'm sure it's back to the palace and into the royal sack. You will have to wait for me outside the perimeter and hope that I can get out. Then it will be just you and me and 100 million soldiers and police hunting us."

"What hotel are you at?"

"The Ritz-Carlton on Financial Street, suite 1202."

"I just have time to get there if you can stall him for ten minutes. Tell him you fell asleep in the tub and just need a few more minutes. Tell him, well, you know how to do it, Rebecca."

"I'll have him here in a limo and you be ready to follow us. Be careful, my love."

"You too . . . Rebecca. I'll be watching for you."

As Brunehoff entered the cab and told the smiling driver that he would be needed for most of the day, the cabbie was delighted. When a wad of USA $100 bills was passed forward, the cabbie knew that this was no ordinary fare. He also knew that this was more money that he had ever held at one time and that his passenger would want some very special treatment.

Minutes after Brunehoff's cab arrived at the Ritz-Carlton, a long black limo pulled up to the entrance in front of him. No official plates—it could be Yung not wanting to advertise his presence. Then he saw the front-seat passenger get out and open the rear door as a radiant Rebecca slowly descended the few steps to the car. She looked stunning, ultrasexy, and Brunehoff wished that it was he and not the unseen Yung waiting in the limo. Their night in suburban Toronto had been brief but wonderful and he wanted to be with her so very much. Instead, he had to watch as she slithered into the domain of Yung, a creature no better than the evil captors that had ruled his youth.

Yung's limo eased its way onto Financial Street, and Brunehoff's cab slipped in behind him. Slowly through the traffic, they proceeded north away from Yung's palace. The plan was working, and Yung was becoming more vulnerable the farther they traveled. Rebecca would use her charm to keep Yung preoccupied, and he would jump at his opportunity when it presented itself.

Five minutes later, Brunehoff the spy became acutely aware that he too was being followed. It was a black BMW, and the driver and passenger appeared to be Caucasian and not Oriental. This could only mean that these were Krems and not Yung's men. Boris and the Rabbi had probably traced him via his Swiss alias. He had gone from being the hunter to being the prey. He couldn't be sure if the Krems were aware that he was following the limo, and he didn't want to jeopardize Rebecca's plan and probably get her killed in the process. He had to break off his tail of Yung's limo and lead the Krems away. Then he would have to dispose of the Krems quickly and try to relocate Rebecca and Yung.

"Turn right here, Chen, and get onto the freeway and continue north out of town. Be ready to exit at a moment's notice. Keep within the speed limit and don't look back," instructed Brunehoff.

The BMW followed Brunehoff's cab without hesitation. It either meant that they were unaware of Yung and Rebecca's limo or that they would advise Boris and within minutes there would be another car in hot pursuit of the limo. Unlikely, reasoned Brunehoff. Yung was a greater threat than he was to Boris, and Yung's elimination would bring Boris back to undisputed control of the remnants of the NOW. He believed that Rebecca would succeed with her plan to eliminate Yung, but unless he could get free of the Krems, he wouldn't be there to rescue her. He couldn't call her, not with Yung present. She was alone, for now.

He would have to act quickly, or he wouldn't be able to locate the limo before it was too late for Rebecca. There must be a way to shake loose of the Krems or to eliminate them. His cab couldn't outrun the beemer, so he would have to confront them.

"Listen very carefully, Chen. Do exactly as I say and there will be another fistful of Yankee greenbacks for you. Take the next off-ramp just ahead, at the last possible moment, without any warning. As you do so, accelerate quickly, and when you get to the intersection below, come to a full stop and stay stopped."

"OK, boss, but—"

"But what?"

"Can I have those dollars now? I don't know who is following us or why, but I'm sure it's not me that they want."

Brunehoff thrust another bundle of bills to Chen as he sharply turned off the freeway. Dieter then lunged through the open window and rolled onto the roadway and down the embankment. Quickly uprighting himself, he ran toward the intersection. He could see the Krems' car approaching the now-stopped cab barely forty meters ahead. The BMW came to a halt behind the cab, and two men exited with pistols at the ready as Brunehoff moved toward them from behind. Just as he was about to dispatch them, one suddenly turned and fired a shot, which hit Brunehoff in the left shoulder. He continued forward and within an instant had downed his assailant and moved to break the neck of the second Krem. Bleeding and in pain, he snatched the pistol of the second Krem, turned back to the BMW, and sped around the cab of the bewildered Chen and back onto the freeway. He must find and rescue Rebecca.

Meanwhile, a scant two kilometers away, cruising past the Great Wall, Yung was undressing Rebecca as she responded to his lustful advances. He was like a man possessed, wanting her, needing her, and thrusting himself upon her. She kissed him deeply, and while Yung fumbled with his trousers, the spider struck with the poison of the Amazonian. The look of shocked disbelief was frozen onto Yung's face as she managed to free herself from beneath his hulking frame. She reached into her bag and called to Dieter.

"It's done and I will be too unless you get me out of here. The driver and the bodyguard are unaware that our playtime is over. I need for you to rescue me. Are you still behind us?"

"No. Where are you exactly?"

"Hell, I don't know. I'll turn on my beacon and you should be able to track me. There, it's done. Do you have me?"

"No, not yet, wait. Yes, I have you now. Listen carefully, Rebecca, we are almost done. Wait until I signal you and then use the intercom to inform the driver that the Chairman appears to have had a seizure and that you're not sure if he's breathing. Act hysterical. They will hurriedly come to a stop on the roadside and open the rear doors to see what has happened. Then I will be upon them and you will be free. Get ready, Rebecca. We will only have one chance at this."

"OK, OK, I'm ready, but hurry up. Seeing Yung barely alive and helpless is freaking me out. Hurry, Dieter, hurry!"

"I see you now. I'm approaching from your left side. I'll be there in a few seconds. Wait for it . . . now! Now, Rebecca, scream to the driver!"

The Chinese reacted as Brunehoff had predicted and never saw him approach the limo as they were both halfway into the backseat. He fired once, then twice, and the protectors of Yung were no more. He thrust them into the rear with the half-dressed Rebecca and the now-dead Yung. Then swiftly he closed the rear doors, jumped into the driver's seat, and sped away.

"Dieter, are you crazy? Let's get rid of these bodies and head for the hills!"

"No, Rebecca. We *can't* leave the limo here. When Yung's body is discovered, Beijing will be in a state of shutdown and we will never get out by plane. Our best option is to drive directly to the airport, leave the limo in the parking lot, and get on the first flight to anywhere."

"You're wounded and will need a doctor. You'll never get past security."

"We have to. You'll help me bandage it when we get there. Remove his jacket and rip off the driver's shirt and be ready to use it to bind me tight. Our only hope is the airport . . . and one more thing, Rebecca."

"What?"

"I disposed of two Krems that were following me. They were tailing me in the car that I ditched. Boris will be expecting them to check in. When they don't, he will order airport surveillance. We have to make a very fast getaway, or China will be our final resting place."

Chapter 48

THE LEADER

One more short drive and Brown had gone totally underground. No one could find him. His daughter was also missing, and all that Canada's government relished with Willie's fame had quickly evaporated. Something strange had happened, and it was a cause for alarm within much of Canada's administration. You couldn't just have a Nobel Prize-winning professor return from a sabbatical and then immediately and mysteriously go missing. Not one of the greatest scientific minds on the planet—a man who had mastered his masters at MIT and in the scientific community forever thereafter. Brown was the native son who was an unconquerable spirit of intellect, drive, persistence, and national pride.

Willie Brown was not a quitter, ever. Yet he had reformed and now answered to a different cause. His purpose and intensity were greater than ever now that he had embraced his lost self. He would be part of the cure and no longer the pestilent expression of the arrogant. Who was he to play God? A chemist turned exterminator? Those people in England, USA, Israel, China, and so on and on—never to live again. He alone had created the virus to annihilate them. He alone was to bear responsibility, not Balderous or Anhebo or Garcia, but he alone was the instrument of death.

Willie was thus a most receptive personage to be brought into the fold of the Collective and the reasoning of the Leader. He had sinned gravely and knew that he could not undo his past and that he would sacrifice his future if it meant saving the present. He was now deeply committed to the Creator's teachings, and he was so proud of his daughter, who had uncovered his crime and brought him to this point. He was repentant to the point of self-sacrifice and he knew it. His life would be freely given if it helped the Collective. He would work tirelessly to round up and secure the barrels of virus poison that he had created.

Something easier said than done! There were massive connector codes and protocols to ensure that the right people in the right place got the right delivery notice for the right barrels to be moved and unloaded. He felt that the Leader would be somewhat surprised at the magnitude of the task. It wasn't as simple as phoning the Bright White depots and saying, "Oh, those three thousand series barrel that you have, we'll be by on Wednesday to fetch them." No, it was much more complex than that. There were safeguard procedures. If a Cleanser "implant" suspected anything, he was to report directly to Singh—Singh, whom he had just now learned was on a flight from Delhi to Paris and was soon to be within the protective fold of the Collective. He would be the key to ensuring that the roundup was completely accomplished—whether he chose to cooperate or was forced to do so. Either way, Singh would do what was required and would be a tremendous aid to the gathering of the barrels of death.

Holed up in an apartment complex in the Canadian tourist town of Niagara-on-the-Lake, neither Willie Brown nor his daughter, Anna, dared go outside. The Krems of Boris could be anywhere, and they were actively hunting for him—they and half of the Canadian CSIS spy agency and the RCMP. They remained indoors with Eli

373

and Francesca and the easily identifiable Anhebo and listened to the teachings of the Creator as put forth by Eli.

Anhebo and Brown had become closer and closer during the two days that Rebecca and Brunehoff had been away. They had so much in common, and they spoke continuously as they awaited their opportunity to work with Singh and to do whatever else the Leader would ask of them. It was different now without Balderous and his violent temper and flawed plans. They were glad to be free of him and the diabolical scheme that they had been a part of.

Early on the third morning, Eli and Francesca went shopping for groceries and Anna was still sleeping. It was then that Brown poured out his heart to Anhebo. He told her that he had been alone for a very long time and that he missed the affection of a female companion. He ended with telling her that he thought that they could make a great team and that he was attracted to her.

The princess blushed and was initially speechless. Eventually, she responded, "Willie, I have been alone much, much longer than you. I have not been with a man since my youth. I put all of my energy into wrestling, education, business, and our cleansing development. Ever since the incident with Burgess at Oxford, I determined that the men I had met were wolves and scum and I have since lived my life in celibacy. Perhaps I have never met the right man under the right circumstances . . . until now. I only know that I still have my anger and that I have a longing for something that I have not been able to identify. Maybe it is a friend, a male companion, or a lover. I am not sure. My life has been so lonely, disciplined, and focused. I have had no affection or close friends and have long ago become estranged from most of my family. I have a need, but until now I was not able to identify it. Do you really think that we could become closer?"

Willie Brown looked at the stunningly beautiful and powerful bronze-skinned woman as she sat cross-legged on the coach. Her shoulders were bare and she was dressed in a slight tank top and matching green silk skirt. She exuded femininity and had a beautiful glow about her that prompted Brown to give in to his urge and approach her. He sat next to her and slowly embraced her. Her body was trembling, but she offered no resistance.

"Please, Willie, teach me to relax and to love."

Brown lightly placed a hand on her right cheek and stroked it gently. Then he moved his hands to her shoulders and exposed neck and massaged her tension away. As he readied himself to kiss her fully on the lips, they were both panting with rising passion. His lips were now only inches away from hers, and he continued his advance.

Suddenly, they heard the key turn in the door and the sounds of Eli and Francesca entering the apartment. Quickly they broke apart and Brown moved to the chair near the fireplace. Eli and Francesca entered and announced that they would be preparing a hearty breakfast and hoped that they were both hungry.

Willie responded that they were starving, and then they both laughed. It seems odd to Eli and suspicious to Francesca, who smilingly asked, "What's so funny, you two?"

"Oh nothing," replied Anhebo, "it's just that we have been wondering whether you would be bringing a box of cornflakes and some yogurt or that we would be able to enjoy a full old-fashioned Canadian breakfast. I guess Willie won this one, and we are both happy for that."

As Eli and Francesca returned to the kitchen to prepare the meal, Willie and Anhebo pursed their lips and then blew a kiss to each other. Soon they would be together; it was something that they both wanted and knew would happen.

Down the hall and behind the open linen closet door, Anna Brown had peered through the crack and seen and heard all. Her father had come back to her and was now also finally able to allow himself to seek female companionship. The Creator had blessed and chosen him for a special purpose. She had a new friend in Anhebo and approved of her and her father being together. She hoped that they would grow close and that in some small way her own suffering at the loss of her dear mother would be lessened. Willie Brown was a stepfather to her, but from age five, he had raised her as his own and she had always called him Daddy. He had had the first love of his life raped and murdered by the fledgling NOW and had lost Anna's mom to cancer. If anyone deserved another chance, it was him, and the newly reformed Anhebo seemed perfect to her.

At her desk and staring the rattled Singh directly in the eye, the Leader put forth her best argument as to why Singh should provide his unconditional cooperation. She made a compelling case and cited the defection of Brown and Anhebo and the death or incarceration of the rest. She appealed to his roots and family's sense of decency. Then she suggested that amnesty was an option rather than torture. It was then that Narinder Singh Singh began to truly sing. He told all and promised all. If he was to be spared, then he would ensure that all would unfold perfectly.

The leader demanded a list of all Bright White implants and particulars as how to proceed without causing suspicion. Singh complied by accessing the coded database on his mobile and downloading to her secure site. From here, with Brown and Singh's help, she could have her people and local authorities navigate to the barrels in over 100 countries and complete the roundup, provided that nobody screwed up or tipped off an implant. If there would be a problem, it could be dealt with.

Previously, while her power base increased and she made more decisions that would affect the lives of many, she had always paused and reflected. As of late, those pauses had become almost nonexistent; and now, as Singh was escorted away and she was briefly alone, out of the blue, like a bolt of lightning, she abruptly realized it. She wondered if she had become more and more like the dirt and filth of the earth that she had continued to have exposed. All in the name of the Creator and the Collective, but perhaps deep down to follow her own selfish human agenda. She felt dirty, soiled by life itself and her part in it.

She had "parked" the Creator in her own ascension to power, and she was now clearly aware of it. She had become caught up in the hunt and the chase, and she wondered to herself just how much of it was from her earthly self and what portion truly was the wisdom of the Creator.

There had been challenges always, but her faith had remained strong. Her belief in the Creator was paramount in her life since her experiences and apparitions as a young child. But that was long ago, and now the Creator no longer visited her as before. Or were those visits real or imagined? Was she fooling herself all these years, or did the Creator really still care for this earthly creation? There had been signs over the years that had been interpreted by "the enlightened" as coming from the Creator. As of late, in these troubled times, she had found her own power; and along with it came doubt. She was fighting the demons within herself, and since Christmas Day, the demons had been winning.

Her head ached; her body lacked sleep. She needed a reprieve but knew that it would not be coming. Things had accelerated, and with Yung still on the loose and Boris yet to be dealt with, there was much to do . . . and she would have to continue to use schemes as terrible as theirs if she was to lead the *forces of right* to its victory—she, who had not wanted or pursued this leader position but had been both chosen to compete and elected to secretively lead. As if her public prominence and position were not enough, now this additional and greater responsibility had been bestowed upon her.

For an instant, she wished she could be that innocent little girl again, but that was not to be either. Instead, she would have to be stronger than ever and finish what had begun and prepare for what would happen if Sarquas was unsuccessful and Boris eluded her emerging plan. When all major matters were resolved, she would have time for the Creator and the peaceful and harmonious path. For now, it was not to be. This lack of time for contemplation and reflection had upset her personal control and tranquility, and her doubts now repulsed her. Smiling to herself finally, she realized that since she was repulsed by who she had become, then there was still hope for her.

The Leader attempted to call Eli, but the safe house phone was busy. That shouldn't be. Something must be wrong. She dialed to the handset that had been issued to Brown, who saw his mobile illuminate with the letters *MD*. He knew that MD was not a doctor but was really the code letters for the Leader. His number had been called, and he somehow knew that it was time for him to prove himself.

"Willie, what's going on? The house phone is busy."

"It's Eli. He's talking to someone," answered Brown to the crystal-clear voice.

"Who?"

"One moment please, I will check," answered Brown.

He returned within a few moments to say that it had been Rebecca and that she and Brunehoff had eliminated Yung. Dieter was wounded, and they were about to attempt to flee the country.

"Brunehoff with her! Fleeing to where?" urgently inquired MD.

"Eli said that she couldn't say yet. They were just about to enter the terminal and look for the earliest flight to anywhere safe," answered Brown.

"Very well, please assemble the others. I will call the house phone in two minutes," responded the Leader.

Brown returned to the living room and called to everyone to assemble at the table for the incoming call. He had heard that voice before. It was familiar. He couldn't place it, but he would. It was perfect English, but he didn't think that she was British or American. No, she was not—so who was she?

The phone rang, and they were greeted by the customary muffled voice of the Leader. She indicated that it was good news that Yung had been eliminated and that now there would be hope for the people of China to wisely choose a new president, one who would be open to the Collective as they grew in power.

She expressed concern for Rebecca and surprise at the movements of Brunehoff. She reminded them that they both knew that their chances of a successful mission *and* an escape were slight. She asked Eli to inform her of any further communication from either of the two.

She paused for a moment and then said that the time had come for Anhebo and Willie to prepare for their mission. They were to be picked up at 3:00 p.m. and smuggled across the busiest of all Canada-USA borders at Niagara Falls. Outside of Canada, Brown would not be looked for. They would be provided with fake passports and IDs along with airline tickets, euros, dollars, and credit cards. Once inside the USA, they would be dropped off at Buffalo Niagara International Airport to board a Delta Air Lines flight to JFK. From there it would be overnight to Rome.

"Rome?" inquired Brown.

"Yes, Willie, Rome."

"So we are going after Boris and the Rabbi?" jumped in Anhebo.

"No, not exactly. Within Rome, Pretnekof and Berhinstein are very well protected. It will be a most difficult place to dispense with them, but at least it is away from their countries, where there would be political and military upheaval and there would have to be two hits—not just one."

"When you said 'not exactly,' just what did you mean?" pried Anhebo.

"I meant that you are not to go after them. As big and as strong and as determined as you both are, you have to accept that you are a corporate tycoon and a brilliant chemist. Your mission will be to be spotted by the enemy and pursued. They will be more anxious than ever to seize you now that Singh has been lost to them. You will be captured, and it is then that you will be brought to them at their secure enclave. We have many, many others assembled and prepared to rid our planet of those two, and we have key insiders within their Mafia ranks. The tiny devices that Eli will give you to swallow when you touch down will ensure that we can track you. I'm sorry but you are to be the bait and I am to set the trap. The rats will not come after me but you. There may be no escape. For that I am truly sorry."

"Rat bait," spoke Brown. "I never did like rats. I guess if we can rid the earth or two of the biggest ones, then it will be worth it."

"Daddy, I don't want you to go . . . but I know you must," sobbed Anna. "And you must return, both you and Anhebo. I know you will find a way to escape. Please, Daddy, come back to me."

"My child," spoke the Leader, "your father knows the seriousness of the situation and also had come to know of the many illicit activities that their targets control from their Rome headquarters. We all know that an out-of-control Pretnekof could create worldwide havoc. These rats are not easy to get to, and only the promise of getting the two missing Cleanser heavyweights, and their knowledge of the virus will be enough to have Pretnekof want to see them face-to-face. When he learns of the demise of Yung, he will be bolder than ever. This may be our only chance for a very long time to dismantle the empire of Boris the Great as he will move quickly to align his forces and supporters. I fear that if we fail in this attempt, that the world will be in for a very rocky ride. We have little choice, and again I am deeply sorry. It is unlikely that your father and Anhebo will have much of an opportunity for escape, but we will do all that we possibly can to get them out alive."

"With Yung gone, the White House without leadership, and the Russian government devoid of challengers to Pretnekof's authority, he will be able to advance his agenda to rise to new heights. The Rabbi will ensure that Israel will be his ally, and together they will be able to exert great influence throughout the world. Their combined militaries and mafia network will outweigh that of any other truly united forces. If they seize control of the Arab oil as we suspect, most of the world will have to buy its black gold from him. As he increases his personal and his countries fortune and power, other will march to his beat and for us he will be unstoppable. With the dismantling of the NOW and the Cleansers, it is only you, Willie and Anhebo, and of course, Singh and Brunehoff who present serious obstacles to him. He will want to ensure that none are left to foil his plans," stated the Leader.

"We do know for certain that both are to be in Rome within two days to meet with their Mafia core. That's why Willie and Anhebo must get there *tout suite*. Officially, Boris the great nonbeliever has chosen to visit the Vatican and apprise the Roman Catholic pope of the successful curtailment of the Cleansers. The two are to make a live, televised statement together. For Pretnekof it is just a cover for him to attend to his Mafia meeting. The meeting has been set, and our informants, or rather insiders, have reported that there is disquiet and squabbling from within the ranks. The president and the Rabbi will want to squelch this unrest before it gets out of control," added the Leader.

"So how are we to take down the rats?" inquired Brown.

"And get out alive?" added Anhebo.

"As I have said, you are to be the bait. Once we have a firm fix on your position and with the aid of our Mafia infiltrators, we will be able to quickly muster a strike force to where you are being held—likely the secure estate of Pretnekof. We will also have the element of surprise. The infiltrators will open doorways and mislead video-monitoring personnel, allowing our strike force to enter unnoticed. Once they penetrate the inner sanctum, we will greatly outnumber your captors and should be able to effectively capture all these thugs and put an end to the reign of Boris once and for all."

"If I may please inquire," it was Eli that spoke. "What will become of them? What will happen if gunfire starts up? How will we be able to defend an assault on the very-popular president of Russia? How will we explain all of this to our legions and faithful masses throughout the world? How can we justify this in the name of the Creator?"

"My dear, faithful, and loving Eli, it would be better that you not concern yourself with these matters. For whereas two wrongs do not make a right, we also know that there are times when we must fight fire with fire. This is surely one of those times. *The* time! Our prime objective will be to rid the earth of Pretnekof and Berhinstein and to usher in a new democracy that we have all hoped and longed for. Does the end justify the means? In this case, I am sad to say that it does. The rats and their accompanists will be 'removed' and will not be heard from again. Only a very few will have knowledge of what has happened to them, and to the world they will seem to have vanished," replied the Leader.

"Dear leader, first Brunehoff kills a gang of bad guys in India to capture Singh, and then he and Sarquis eliminate who knows how many more to kill Yung. Now we, the so-called good guys, are to make the president of Russia and a very prominent member of the Israeli government disappear for all time. Forgive me for asking, but are we certain that we are truly following the way of the Creator?" pleaded a shaken Eli.

"Eli, your questions and statements are heard. Unfortunately, we have little time and apparently no other choice. If there were some peaceful way to bring forth a righteous rebirth, I would certainly follow it. As of now, there is no other way."

"Then it must be done as you have indicated," answered Brown. "We will be ready to depart for Rome and the sewer rats, and we will prevail. I truly believe that."

When she had ended the call, the Leader considered her plan. It could work but, as Eli had indicated, at a great cost. Yet there was no other way. Even the reformed Brown now seemed closer to and more in step with the Creator than she did. Her decisions and directives were all about more death and less concern for collateral damage. She had become hardened and unrelenting and for the first time in a very long time, had not ended her call without the words "Praise be to the Creator." Saddened and overcome with emotion and all alone, she wept.

Curled up and confused, she finally had fallen asleep. Exhaustion and her torrid pace along with her confusion had overcome her.

One hour later, she awoke refreshed and with a new realization. She had been attempting to stamp out the last of the bad guys, but where did it end? With Boris and the Rabbi? Or would there be more? Walker would surely succeed with Gilberger gone and his wife was on her team, but there was still China and some Arab nations and parts of tribal Africa and the military might of North Korea. This was not going to be a quick fix. It would take time and they would be met with resistance and she would have to respond again and again, perhaps.

Another thing that she had somehow also realized was that she had been chosen because she could get the job done. With remorse, perhaps, but the job would get done. Was this the message of the Creator all along to her? To be strong? To make the tough decisions necessary to bring rebirth to creation? To refresh the earth?

Optimism returned to her, and she even smiled. She would play her role; and then the truly good of the earth, people like Eli and Anna and Francesca and many others, would work hard to ensure that goodness and fair play and equality and food for all would exist. There was a way with redistribution to support the population and to educate and feed them. So much change would take place; she felt sure of it.

But for now, there was Boris and the Rabbi to dispose of. Nothing else mattered.

Chapter 49

BORIS AND THE RABBI

When the Krems of Beijing did not report in, Boris considered the possibilities. They could have been canceled or apprehended by the forces of Yung. Unlikely, Li Wi would have phoned already to gloat. They could be so close to their prey that they couldn't respond. Maybe, but also unlikely. Then there was the third possibility: that Brunehoff has detected them and had made short work of his trained assassins. That seemed the most likely. That would mean that he and Sarquas were still after Yung, and given the seemingly invincibility of Brunehoff, they might just succeed.

He called to the Rabbi to alert him. "Raheim, we have a situation. I have just returned from a cabinet meeting, and there are no messages from the Krems. They should have checked in by now. Their mobiles ring but do not answer. I have received no confirmation from my texts. I suspect that Brunehoff has canceled them and that he is about to try to get Yung."

"If this were true, this would be very good fortune for us, Boris. If Brunehoff survives the henchmen of Yung, then we can be ready for him at the airport."

"We don't have people in Beijing capable of taking Brunehoff at the airport, Raheim. There is no time to send more Krems."

"Boris, we do have the alias under which Brunehoff is traveling, and right now your office could advise airport security and Beijing police to be on the full alert for one Luc Berdon. Tell them that if he shows up there, it's because he has killed their great chairman Yung. Tell them to shoot to kill. Let the Chinese finish the task."

"Yes, Raheim, Yes! Brilliant. I'll also alert them to the alias of Sarquas. She is no threat to us, but our Dieter may use another alias and even a disguise. He could sneak through alone, but not with Sarquas. She would be noticed even with a second alias, and I don't believe she has one."

"Then we will only need to deal with Brown and Anhebo, but I don't believe they are real threats with the others gone."

"Don't be too sure, Raheim. Singh is still unaccounted for. Someone has him and could use him, someone connected to Brunehoff."

"Then, Boris, it couldn't be Brown and Anhebo. Dieter would never use the virus to indiscriminately wipe out any opposition. He would be more likely to use his bare hands to deal with his assignments. I strongly doubt that he would be aligned with the Cleansers under any circumstance. It's just not possible after what he has been through."

"Yes, I agree, but something or someone has control of Brunehoff. I just can't figure why he and Sarquas would go after Yung right after Brunehoff captured Singh. Something just doesn't add up."

"Agreed. We'll have to discuss it in Rome. There are other matters to consider. You have to appear as the shining savior when you meet with the pope of the Catholics and make your announcements to the world, and I have to determine the extent of unrest and power struggle within our own ranks and to investigate this *collective* further.

"Trying times indeed, Raheim, but I feel confident regarding my address to the peoples of the earth, and I'm sure that you will be able to pinpoint any problems and disquiet within our organization," answered Boris. "Enlist as much help as you need for the investigation of this *collective*. I'll alert Beijing authorities and you check with Anatelli for updates. Call me back in one hour—sooner, if you have pertinent information."

"Yes, Boris."

As they disconnected, each pondered the extraordinary turn of events. Some things were favorable, while others were unexpected and of immediate concern. Much was needed to take place, and there were unknowns. Unknowns were not the usual fare of either Boris or the Rabbi, and each knew that they must proceed very carefully but with a high degree of trepidation.

When the mob's Roman bureau chief and faithful servant to Boris, Antonio Anatelli, answered the call of the Rabbi, he sounded most anxious. This was unusual for such a hardened criminal, so it was somewhat of a surprise to the Rabbi.

"Settle down, Antonio, and tell me what you have to report," calmly chided the Rabbi.

"OK, OK, first I believe that Baggio is indeed the mole and that he has alerted others outside of our ranks to the business of our enterprises. This could blow up in our faces, and I am not even certain if he has others within our fold. This is not good, Rabbi, and I think that action must be taken . . . immediately."

A calm and explicit Berhinstein answered with "Take care of Baggio, Antonio, and do it today. Make sure that his body is discovered by the other lieutenants, and then tell them that this will be the fate of all who challenge the leadership or direction of Boris and I. Make sure that he tells all first. Do I make myself clear?"

"Yes, very clear, Rabbi, very clear."

"Good."

"There is more!"

"What, Antonio?"

"It has to do with the Earth Cleansers. I have just received a report that our people have witnessed the arrival of Brown and Anhebo. They are traveling under fake IDs, but there is no doubt that it is them."

"Where, Antonio?" urged the Rabbi.

"At Fiumicino Airport."

"Anhebo and Brown in Rome? It can only mean that they are there to attempt a hit on Boris and I. You are having them tailed?"

"Yes, they are proceeding into the city center as we speak. Donatelli's team is following them. They will not elude us."

"Good, Antonio, very good. It seems that the missing duo have entered into our domain, a domain from which there shall be no escape. Have Donatelli follow them at a safe distance, and when you are certain that we can capture them, strike and do so quickly. Don't kill them. We will want to interrogate them. There is much that they can tell us. Get busy and provide me with any and all updates."

"Yes, Rabbi, I will keep you posted."

The Rabbi pondered the new developments and knew that he should update Boris immediately. Boris would be pleased that Baggio had been unearthed and that Brown and Anhebo had been located. The ill-prepared pair had chosen to go after him and Boris, in their own center of operations no less. Foolish people. Soon they would be tortured to spill all, and he and Boris would have all except Singh and Brunehoff. Boris would surely take care of Brunehoff and Sarquas. Singh alone was no threat to anyone. The numbers of the opponents were rapidly decreasing and the opposition to him and Boris was becoming less. Soon they would rule as they had always planned and there would be no force on earth to challenge them. He would exact his revenge on Brown for the death of his family, and he would ensure that the suffering would be painful and long lasting. Vengeance would be his!

He called to Boris to update him, and Pretnekof was very pleased. Locating the overambitious Anhebo and Brown plus ID'ing Baggio was better than expected. The president advised the Rabbi that he had initiated the process of alerting the Chinese authorities to be on the lookout for Brunehoff and Sarquas. They would not escape Beijing by air.

Then, Boris asked the Rabbi to hold while he took a call originating from Beijing. It was airport security. It seems that Elizabeth Matthews and her wheelchair companion had already left Beijing International by American Airlines and that they were en route to Kuala Lumpur.

"What the hell is going on, Raheim?" he exclaimed, after telling the Chinese to search the airport parking lot for Yung. He told them that he was sure that the loose cannon Brunehoff was on a one-man mission of destruction and that Yung, like Singh and others before him, had surely been eliminated by the wacko warrior.

Boris and the Rabbi were aware that nothing seemed to be able to stop Brunehoff, but they knew that they must first attend to the matters at hand, Baggio bludgeoned to death as a show of power and Anhebo and Brown captured and tortured and forced to tell all. They would have more than their pound of flesh, and it would be chocolate coated. The days of the enemy, the unknown, and the infiltrators were numbered.

Fearing only Brunehoff now, they discussed arrangements to have operatives waiting at Kuala Lumpur International, where Dieter and Sarquas would arrive. They would get him this time, and he would never trouble them again. Pleased with the developments and their management of the situations, they thanked each other and ended their call.

Meanwhile, back in Rome, Antonio Anatelli made one more call.

"The trap has been set. The rats have taken the bait, and soon we shall be able to bring forth the exterminators. All is proceeding as you have instructed."

"Good, well done, Antonio. Keep me posted," and with that the Leader ended her call. Two years previously, Anatelli had been in a car crash and had been nurtured back to health by a doctor and nurse who convinced him that the way of the Collective was the true way of light and hope. He had informed them of his many sins and transgressions and offered to help bring down the truly evil men that had forced him to shoot his brother. This information was kept carefully guarded within the Collective and saved for the very occasion that was soon to be.

Chapter 50

ROME

As Boris and the Rabbi readied themselves for Rome, they were acutely aware that huge surprises were still capable of happening. There had been so many already. Their creed of "Vigilance in all matters, to the death!" echoed in the minds of the surviving two.

Anatelli had succeeded in disposing of Baggio in a most graphic of ways. The dismembered Baggio had sent a clearly visible sign to the inner circle that deceit and personal agendas were not to be tolerated by the leadership. Not now, not ever. They would reinforce that fact by the canceling of three lieutenants that Anatelli had identified, and they would do it so that the others would all bear witness. Then these rumblings, this would-be uprising, would be squashed and put to rest forever. None other would dare challenge them from within their Mafia ranks.

Brown and Anhebo had been apprehended at gunpoint as they were disembarking their taxi outside the hotel. The duo had offered no resistance and were now securely locked away in the Roman home of Boris.

After his speech to the world and the formalities surrounding his interaction with the pope, Boris would personally extract the information he needed from Brown. Then the great chemist and his

Brazilian accomplice would be of no further use to him. He would reward his most loyal companion, Raheim, with the opportunity for vengeance for those that killed his entire family.

Brunehoff was still on the loose, and this troubled Boris more than anything. Their Chinese intelligence had correctly reported that he and Sarquas had escaped Beijing for Kuala Lumpur, and he had moved swiftly to have ten men awaiting their arrival at the Malaysian airport. What he didn't expect was that although they had been ticketed to Kuala Lumpur, they had vacated the plane at a scheduled stopover in Seoul. With several hours' head start and knowledge that he would be hunting for them, they could be almost anywhere. No wonder Yung was so frustrated at times. But now Yung was no more. This had been confirmed. He and his attendants were found dead in the rear of the limo. Even the Krems had been found busted and dead. Again the work of Brunehoff, no doubt. China was in a state of lockdown, and as the news eked out through the world media, people everywhere would wonder what unexpected malady would be next.

He should have had Raheim investigate fully the ticket purchases, a huge oversight; he had acted carelessly. It was not about to happen again. Raheim was back at the helm, but it may be too late. Brunehoff would surely not have Rebecca use her Elizabeth alias again. He was too smart for that. He would set down Sarquas, and then the warrior would hunt for his final prey, him, President Boris Pretnekof. Dieter was capable of going after him anywhere. Even at the audience with the pope or back home in Mother Russia under constant guard. He must find Brunehoff.

The Rabbi, with his usual cunning and efficiency, was keeping his people busy trying to electronically track Brunehoff and Rebecca. His dominant thoughts, however, were not of Boris, their Mafia madness, the Collective, or even finding Brunehoff. Since the news of the capture of Brown arrived, he could only think of his departed family and the opportunity to exact an eye for an eye and a tooth for a tooth. He had had more than eyes and teeth taken from him. Brown would have to endure the pain he still felt. The Cleanser had a daughter, and he would have to watch her suffer and die, Raheim had decided. Brown's pain would be great, and he would beg. Raheim had not been afforded that opportunity.

The Leader's people had witnessed the apprehension of Brown and Anhebo. They had been at the airport all along the way and stationed at the hotel. They had followed them at a very safe distance and with several different cars, and now they knew the location of the rats' nest, the very place that Anatelli had suggested that they would be taken. The stomach contents of the bait would get them much closer.

She knew that Pretnekof and Berhinstein would be at their nest tomorrow and she would be ready to attack. Anatelli had set the sequence in motion, and she had assembled a large strike force. Some may be lost, and she could not guarantee the safe removal of the human bait. But then, finally then, it would be all over. No more madmen. No more murderous, conniving thugs. No more immense wrongs to be righted. Just the pathway to freedom and righteousness to follow. Then she would have time to interact with her Creator and to follow peaceful ways. Of this she had convinced herself.

The pope at eighty-five years was much, much older than the Russian president. He had lived long and had experienced much. Like Boris he was also well informed of all that he chose to know. He knew, for instance, that Boris Pretnekof was not the good guy that the Western media continued to portray him as. He was aware that Pretnekof's thirst for power was great and that he would do anything to grab control of the world. This and much else he learned via his network within the world's largest organization that represented one-sixth of the earth's population, a "worldwide web" that had something that Boris would never command—the confessional. Although most individual priests and bishops never broke their seal of the confession, juicy tidbits from reliable but protected sources did find their way to his personal attention.

The pope had known of the Collective for a very long time. As their underground alliances increased, it gnawed away at the number of Catholic followers that had been under the realm of the Roman church. This was a continued cause for concern for some within the College of Cardinals, but for this pope, it was not. He was actually delighted by it. If God the Creator unfolded a way for peoples of different race and color and creed to amalgamate, it paralleled what his church had succeeded in doing. But this time, it was not force-fed or the outcome of religious wars. It was the free movement of everyday people to connect in the best way that they knew how—peacefully and with compassion, inclusiveness, and love. This would firmly point back to his church as the keeper of the faith for the past two thousand years. The Collective was not viewed by him as a threat but rather the culmination of all that he had worked and prayed for.

He would sit quietly by as Boris grabbed the initial limelight and then the Leader executed her plan to put an end to the Russian tyrant. If he so wanted, he could amass great numbers of law-enforcement officers at the nest of Boris and the Rabbi and even expose the murderous conduct of the Leader, but to what end? No, he had decided that his role was to witness the unfolding and not to interfere. This he believed his god had so directed. He would remain pious and prayerful, and others would deal with the downfall of Boris and the Rabbi. Then as the Collective flocked to their leader and the earth experienced a rebirth, his church would be there, in step with the realigned world and ever faithful to his true Lord and Master.

At his arrival in Rome, President Boris Pretnekof was met by officials from the Vatican and whisked away in a cavalcade of limos and police vehicles to the sanctuary of the Holy See. As he entered within the inner sanctum of the seat of the Roman Catholic Church, he thought of how he and not the pope should be the one to be adorned and bowed down to. Like so very along ago in South Africa, he thought of how he could truly be the leader of all the earth's people. This announcement that he was about to make to all nations regarding the capture and demise of the Earth Cleansers had been carefully crafted for maximum impact. He would be applauded and cheered and saluted and broadcast around the globe while the pious pope would appear as a mere onlooker, another fan of Boris the Great. Choosing to "share" his spotlight with the pope was not to be. It would be his name that would be prominent on this afternoon and not that of the tired old pontiff.

When the formalities had been concluded and the microphones and television cameras fully in place, Boris felt a surge of power and self-adoration. He had brought down the Cleansers, and now he was to get his just reward.

In perfect English, he commenced, "People of the earth, families and children and soldiers and workers throughout the world, I bring you great news. The evil perpetrators of our planet have been uncovered and will be brought to justice. Those that have survived our well-planned onslaught have been incarcerated and will never again be free to rain down death and destruction upon the peoples of Mother Earth. We shall continue to work together as free nations, aligned as never before, to bring forth truth and justice and to continue with our peaceful reform.

"I speak for many others of like-mindedness who have suffered great losses in their home nations. And I vow to you, my dear people, that such a collection of evildoers shall never again be able to assemble in order to send fear and death to you . . . not while I remain president of Russia and leader of the forces of freedom. You have my solemn word that we shall have a greater world to look forward to and a brighter future for all. Stand by me as we enact policies and procedures to ensure that your world and my world will never again be held hostage or subjected to the rule of the ruthless and selfish. Be strong and optimistic and peaceful. The dawn of a new era is upon us, and you shall be free to avail of its bounty and caring for all. Stand by me, dear people, and we shall surely have much to celebrate. May you all remember this day of deliverance."

When he finished, there was a flurry of activity as media officials jockeyed to get close to the great Russian president. But it was not to be. He left immediately through the passageway directly behind him and was ushered into a waiting sedan that exited the walled city state and sped away to his lair, his hideout, where he would be reunited with the Rabbi and they would extract the information they desired from Brown and Anhebo.

The Rabbi had arrived later than expected but in time to catch Boris's speech. It made him chuckle at the audacity of his partner. Flamboyant boss to the end. A boss that would join him within minutes. Anatelli had advised the Rabbi of where they were keeping Brown and Anhebo, but he would have to wait for Boris to arrive.

As it left the city and sped into the fading light of the January night, Boris's sedan moved closer toward its destination. It carried a very smug president who felt that he had once again accomplished what only he could. What he alone could mastermind and accomplish. Upstaging the pope on his own turf—that was a first for even him. There would be more firsts as he advanced. He was convinced of that, and it would help propel him forward until he ruled all.

Anatelli's men were all in position. Their communicators were connected, and they had jammed any eavesdropping that the rats' attendants could have in place. As a prominent member of the mob and head of security, Anatelli had it easy to gain access and displace the on-duty personnel, ever so easy. When euros were flashed, things happened; and if they didn't, the problem was eliminated through other means. Now with hardware monitors replaying earlier tapes and security protocols breached, the doors were wide open for the forces of the Leader to enter undetected.

When Boris arrived, he was met by the Rabbi, who politely insisted that they should attend to Brown and Anhebo at the master's earliest convenience. Boris saw the anger and hatred in his friends' eyes and said, "Yes, Raheim, we shall go now. Where are they being kept?"

"In the storage room in the basement. Anatelli and four others are with them. They are cuffed and bound," replied the Rabbi.

"Anatelli and four others with weapons. Do you think that is enough to contain two helpless cleanser fools?" joked Boris. "They are awfully big."

"Yes, big and soon to be broken," flatly responded Raheim.

Making their way down the main-floor hallway, Boris and the Rabbi were moving at a faster-than-usual pace, both intent upon confronting the Cleansers and extracting knowledge that would lead them to the recipe for the barrels of death. They hurried down the stairway and into the lower floor. Two doors along was the storage room, and two guards were posted at the doorway. As they saw the approaching two, they smartly stood to attention and saluted.

Then the smaller of the two tapped lightly on the door three times, pressed down on the handle, and swung it open inwardly.

Inside, with the door now closed, both Boris and the Rabbi approached their two bound captives and looked deeply into the eyes of Brown first and then Anhebo. The fear and terror that they hoped to see was not present, and they each silently thought that these were warriors in their own right and were prepared to die before they would give up any secrets.

"So, Willie Brown, we meet again after all of these years. Unfortunately, this will not be a sporting match, and you have arrived in Rome to never return to your Canadian freedom. We can make this very painful for you and Anhebo and even your darling daughter, Anna, or you can cooperate and I promise to spare your child and make your deaths painless. Are you prepared to cooperate, Mr. Brown, or shall I have Anatelli and his thugs administer Roman-style punishment first?" boasted Boris.

Brown looked up from his chair and directly into the depths of both of them and said, "First, you will never reach my daughter. Of that I am now certain. Killing me will send her deeper underground, away from your control."

"Careful, Brown, my reach has greatly increased of late, and I can find anyone I so choose . . . anywhere and anytime," spat back Boris.

"Second, we are determined to die before we give up knowledge of the concoction. Especially to you two. We are reformed and have to live with the death and fear that we unleashed. It will not happen again through us. But before you get started with what you feel you must do, consider this: we propose a trade for our lives and then we all walk away from here. No follow-up, no comebacks."

"A trade? A trade? You make me laugh. And you irritate me greatly at the same time! You have nothing to offer me! You are two fools that thought you could enter my realm and succeed in what . . . getting captured?" shrieked Boris.

"Actually we do have something to trade, Your Majesty, a certain wayward warrior of yours."

"What are you talking about?" shouted Boris.

"Dieter Brunehoff," answered Brown.

"Brunehoff, you can deliver up Brunehoff?"

"Oh yes. We can do that. I know where he has been and what he has done in India and then China. And oh yes, I know where he is now. He trusts me. Otherwise, he would have canceled me when he found me arriving in Ottawa. We were friends long ago and our daughters are friends, and he was looking for reform. I just helped him along. But if it's my skin or his, then it's time for the warrior to pay the piper."

"You piece of trash. You disgusting excuse for a man. You murdered my family and now you want to trade your life for that of your friend? You don't deserve to live. Or to die painlessly. I will cut you myself!"

"Raheim, Raheim, my friend, settle down," comforted Boris as he patted the Rabbi's shoulder. "Let's hear what Mr. Brown has to say. Brunehoff is our last remaining threat. Let us not lose sight of that."

"Brown, you have a chance, but I must have exact coordinates for Brunehoff, and we must have him under surveillance before I will agree to release you. But we can make you a little more comfortable in the meantime. Now tell me, Willie, where is he?"

"Then it's a deal?" asked Brown.

"No, Boris, please, I beg you, no deal. I must honor my family."

"Enough, Raheim, enough! Your family is gone. Brunehoff is still here and I want him. There will be no further discussion."

"Willie Brown of Canada, I will make the deal: the coordinates for your freedom. You have my word."

"And you, Rabbi?" inquired Brown.

Boris looked to Raheim and then nudged him lightly. Finally, the Rabbi answered, "Yes, and my word also."

"OK, then it's a deal. You'll find him right here at your nasty little den. He's here to free us and to take you down. We were the bait and you have entered the trap. Give me my mobile there and I'll show you *exactly* where he is."

A look of fear overcame Boris as his face went from angry red to ashen gray. He looked at the cuffed and bound Brown and then did as he asked.

Within a few seconds, Brown had a schematic of the estate house on the screen. "Check it out. He's upstairs at the far end of the house, in the laundry."

Boris saw the red glow on the screen and told Anatelli to take two others and the two door guards with him and to storm the room. Then he added, "I'll wait here."

Five minutes seemed like an eternity, and there was much gunfire before Anatelli returned and looked to Boris and said, "It is done. Brunehoff is dead."

"Excellent, excellent, excellent!" shouted a most excited Boris. "I must see!"

"Wait," yelled Brown, "we had a deal. You gave your word. Free us first!"

"My word? Free you, Brown? No no no, we will not free you. We will learn all that we need to know from you as you and your Brazilian friend die a most painful death that I'm sure Raheim will insist upon. I have no word for you," gloated Boris.

"You worthless swine," shouted Anhebo to a snickering Boris.

Brown looked at the two of them as they hovered apparently victorious over him. "I had hoped it would be different, Boris. I really did. I agreed to this mission and I wanted to see if there was any part of either of you that was worth saving. There is not. It's lucky for you that Anhebo is not permitted to deal with you as she did Burgess. It's lucky for you, Rabbi, that I have learned to march to a different drummer. You will not have to endure the suffering that you would have given us."

Immediately, Boris and the Rabbi both felt the muzzle of a weapon in their backs.

"There is no Brunehoff here, Comrade Pretnekof. He is far away in a very safe and warm place. Where you and the Rabbi are going is hot, extremely hot," slowly spoke a very composed Anatelli.

Witnessing Brown and Anhebo being unlocked and untied, both Boris and the Rabbi were truly speechless. Then each of them felt a syringe being jabbed into their backs as Brown and Anhebo left the room with Anatelli. They felt their bodies becoming numb, and now they were unable to speak as their captors released them into a gnarled pile on the storeroom's cement floor. From here they would be unceremoniously dragged from the premises and buried deep in the monumental trash heap that Rome added to each day. Finally, they would be home, and the earth would not be troubled by them ever again. The rats would be returned to the garbage, where they belonged, and the world would rise to a new dawn of hope and cooperation.

Chapter 51

EPILOGUE: THE IDES OF MARCH

They did come, as she beckoned them forth, from the very reaches of the earth itself. Pilgrims: chosen, mandated, and commissioned. Brought forth to commence a new beginning, a reset, a start again—of all that had been man up until NOW.

In the six weeks that had passed since Boris and the Rabbi had been disposed of, much had transpired. Tens of millions of children and women and men from all walks of life, from all races and creeds and religions and nonreligions had answered the challenge of the Leader. They had assembled in their public squares, the community halls, and in the streets surrounding their seats of government. They had come dancing and singing, bearing banners of hope and carrying flowers of sweet fragrances. Life had changed, and the impact was felt globally as never before.

The media had played their part. They had exposed the leaked documents tying Boris the Great and his once-powerful NOW membership to the immoral characters of the underworld. The popular leader had been exposed as ruthless, heartless, and detestable. When the Russian people learned the truth about the missiles and how the opposition was eliminated, they vowed that never again would Russia allow a dictator. They moved by millions to the new hope. A huge shift was taking place.

China had also been freed from a tyrant, a man consumed by his own self-love above all else. In the end he had given into his lust and exposed his vulnerability. The China that had emerged like a locomotive at the turn of the new millennium was now hardwired to the new world, and finally its citizens knew what was happening everywhere. When they assembled in great numbers spilling out from Tiananmen Square and into the streets, there was no military or police to restrain or stop them. No man needed to confront a tank. Enough had been enough, and there was much hope and anticipation. A new way would emerge, and everywhere there was emancipation for all the peasants and working class.

America's Walker would surely be the next leader of the USA, and he was on her team. The mass outpouring of people throughout the country had seen to that. America would have a new helmsman, and he would steer a course that followed the natural flow of the birth of all things new. It would be steady as she goes, but no weapons would be aboard his vessel.

Israel and Jewish people everywhere were ashamed of what Raheim had done and were moved to express remorse publicly, feeling somehow that the actions of one had tarnished them all. They had lived through great struggles and now saw a new pathway was opening up to them, a channel that could let them reach across cultural and religious lines and embrace their neighbors. In Jerusalem, the military bulldozed down razor-wired separators; and Christians, Muslims, and Jews embraced each other as they chanted words of freedom throughout the streets. As the cities swarmed with people, a convoy formed and headed to the Palestinian-occupied enclosures. More and more vehicles joined along the way, and when it eventually reached the Gaza, the TV stations were reporting tens of thousands of singing occupants. All barriers were torn down and checkpoints destroyed by a mass movement of mixed peoples. Freedom reigned, and previous opponents shared food and drink. Everyone rejoiced!

Even the most downtrodden and tyrant-run of African peoples overran the palaces of their warlord rulers, who had fled to wherever they could hide—for a short while. The celebrators danced their way to great gathering sites. Here the drums played nonstop and merriment continued throughout the nights. When great food drops were made, the people sang louder and accepted their portions in an orderly manner. Hope had landed and with it a promise of a new beginning for all.

The tyrants, oppressors, dictators, persecutors, and autocrats of the entire world had dissipated into oblivion. They would forever be in fear and without supporters would never rise to power again. Their time was over and a great flowering was taking place.

Brunehoff and Sarquas were officially still unaccounted for. The Leader knew that they had fled by car from Canada deep into the mountainous ancestral home of Rebecca's people. Dieter's bullet wound would heal, but the poison his body had endured could not. The warrior would rest, his duty having been performed. Rebecca would administer to him, and they would treasure each day as a gift.

Anhebo and Brown had resurfaced in Canada, and their pending wedding was made public as was their membership and prominence in the Collective. Their secret past was intended to remain buried forever. They had embraced the teachings of the Creator as a means to atone for their sins and to give new meaning to their lives. Brown had gone from pruning and conflict to rebirth and peacefulness; Anhebo, from loneliness and anger to love and serenity. They knew they were meant to be together. They would be an integral part of the great redistribution.

Francesca and Anna would be there also, and their young lives were about to flourish with clarity and vitality. Eli, ever faithful and ever conscious of the Creator's teachings, would serve as a guiding light and play an unmistakable role in the realigned earth. His heart was pure, and the Leader needed him as a living symbol of truth and determination.

At her desk, she had at first sighed at the task before her to reorganize the world. The Cleansers and the NOW had been defeated or had reformed. Yet there was so much more to still do. Then almost magically, the pieces had quickly come together. The barrels had all been secured, and there were no madmen running completely loose. The human population was demanding a franchise for all, and true liberties were taking place throughout the earth. Her challenge had gone from impossible, to not easy, to under serious reconstruction. She had fulfilled the mission that she had been selected to lead, and if it did not succeed this time, then there was truly no hope for the human condition.

She had found her true self again and was no longer troubled by the methods she had employed. She was free again to be with her creator, her companion, and friend. Was it the Creator who had led her to deal as she had with the arrogant and racist Pierre Langois? The very day after the termination of Boris and the Rabbi, she had called him to her office and said, "Monsieur Langois, for your actions and attitudes, you shall be sent to the desert sun of Africa and you will live alongside poor tribal peoples and will administer to their needs. You will be their servant, and you shall know how it feels to be without your power and control. Am I still too easy, Pierre?"